LOVE AT FIRST FIGHT

My back slammed against the wall and my eyes locked onto the fierce gaze of my opponent. "What *are* you?" asked the wolf with the smoldering brown eyes.

Oh, my God.

The wolf pressed the weight of his powerful form against mine, his forearm glued to my chest. But the pure intensity of his presence was what held me in place. I didn't dare *shift*, move, breathe. My mind froze, unable to concentrate on anything but him.

The fierceness of his eyes softened as a phenomenal heat surged across the length of his arm and into my body, electrifying my already racing pulse. I shuddered.

And so did he.

The wolf abruptly released me. I stumbled, off balance and undeniably freaked out. He reached to catch me, but I staggered away.

Blood and ash saturated his long-sleeved shirt, and a chunk of fabric hung loose over his bloody right thigh. I swallowed hard, awestruck as the damaged muscle knitted together and re-formed into new pink flesh.

I staggered back two more steps. He followed, palms out. "Don't be afraid. I'm not going to hurt you," he whispered.

Sealed with a Curse

A WEIRD GIRLS NOVEL

CECY ROBSON

A SIGNET ECLIPSE BOOK

SIGNET ECLIPSE
Published by New American Library, a division of
Penguin Group (USA) Inc., 375 Hudson Street,
New York, New York 10014, USA
Penguin Group (Canada), 90 Eglinton Avenue East, Suite 700, Toronto,
Ontario M4P 2Y3, Canada (a division of Pearson Penguin Canada Inc.)
Penguin Books Ltd., 80 Strand, London WC2R 0RL, England
Penguin Ireland, 25 St. Stephen's Green, Dublin 2,
Ireland (a division of Penguin Books Ltd.)
Penguin Group (Australia), 250 Camberwell Road, Camberwell, Victoria 3124,
Australia (a division of Pearson Australia Group Pty. Ltd.)
Penguin Books India Pvt. Ltd., 11 Community Centre, Panchsheel Park,
New Delhi - 110 017, India
Penguin Group (NZ), 67 Apollo Drive, Rosedale, Auckland 0632,
New Zealand (a division of Pearson New Zealand Ltd.)
Penguin Books (South Africa) (Pty.) Ltd., 24 Sturdee Avenue,
Rosebank, Johannesburg 2196, South Africa

Penguin Books Ltd., Registered Offices:
80 Strand, London WC2R 0RL, England

First published by Signet Eclipse, an imprint of New American Library,
a division of Penguin Group (USA) Inc.

First Printing, January 2013
10   9   8   7   6   5   4   3   2   1

PUBLISHER'S NOTE
This is a work of fiction. Names, characters, places, and incidents either are the
product of the author's imagination or are used fictitiously, and any resemblance
to actual persons, living or dead, business establishments, events, or locales is
entirely coincidental.
   The publisher does not have any control over and does not assume any responsibility for author or third-party Web sites or their content.

ALWAYS LEARNING   **PEARSON**

To Jamie and our children,
for being my light in the darkness.

ACKNOWLEDGMENTS

I'm fortunate to have many people in my life to thank, particularly my editor at NAL, Jhanteigh Kupihea, and all the members of the Penguin team. Thank you for bringing my baby to life.

To my super agent and dear friend, Nicole Resciniti: you believed in me when no one else would. I am blessed God brought you into my life and into my heart.

To my husband and best friend, Jamie, I love you beyond words and my gratitude for your patience, support, and kindness knows no boundaries. Where would I be without you and our babies? You are my greatest gifts.

To Mr. James Harte, who was more family than friend. I miss you.

To Susan Griner, a wonderful author, mentor, and friend.

To the original WEIRD GIRLS fans: Amy Carnell, Maria Hanley, Crissy (McMullen) Roth, and Elizabeth Stuart. Thank you for cheering, laughing, and gasping in all the right places. You gals rock! Special thanks to Valerie (McMullen) Secker. Val, your encouragement, enthusiasm, and edits helped me get noticed by my super agent. Thank you. Thank you. Thank you!

To my agency sisters and pals, Amanda Carlson, Marisa Cleveland, Jen Danna, Amanda Flower, Marianne Harden, Melissa Landers, and Lea Nolan, your support and friendship mean the world to me. So glad we get to go to "prom" together.

To my brother, Douglas Galdamez, for always thinking I'm smarter than I actually am. And to my parents, Armando and Carmen Galdamez, for all their sacrifices. Papí, you were right; in this country anything is possible.

CHAPTER 1

Sacramento, California

The courthouse doors crashed open as I led my three sisters into the large foyer. I didn't mean to push so hard, but hell, I was mad and worried about being eaten. The cool spring breeze slapped at my back as I stepped inside, yet it did little to cool my temper or my nerves.

My nose scented the vampires before my eyes caught them emerging from the shadows. There were six of them, wearing dark suits, Ray-Bans, and obnoxious little grins. Two bolted the doors tight behind us, while the others frisked us for weapons.

I can't believe we're in vampire court. So much for avoiding the perilous world of the supernatural.

Emme trembled beside me. She had every right to be scared. We were strong, but our combined abilities couldn't trump a roomful of bloodsucking beasts. "Celia," she whispered, her voice shaking. "Maybe we shouldn't have come."

Like we had a choice. "Just stay close to me, Emme."

My muscles tensed as the vampire's hands swept the length of my body and through my long curls. I didn't like him touching me, and neither did my inner tigress. My fingers itched with the need to protrude my claws.

When he finally released me, I stepped closer to Emme while I scanned the foyer for a possible escape route. Next to me, the vampire searching Taran got a little daring with his pat-down. But he was messing with the wrong sister.

"If you touch my ass one more time, fang boy, I swear to God I'll light you on fire." The vampire quickly removed his hands when a spark of blue flame ignited from Taran's fingertips.

Shayna, conversely, flashed a lively smile when the vampire searching her found her toothpicks. Her grin widened when he returned her seemingly harmless little sticks, unaware of how deadly they were in her hands. "Thanks, dude." She shoved the box back into the pocket of her slacks.

"They're clear." The guard grinned at Emme and licked his lips. "This way." He motioned her to follow. Emme cowered. Taran showed no fear and plowed ahead. She tossed her dark, wavy hair and strutted into the courtroom like the diva she was, wearing a tiny white minidress that contrasted with her deep olive skin. I didn't fail to notice the guards' gazes glued to Taran's shapely figure. Nor did I miss when their incisors lengthened, ready to bite.

I urged Emme and Shayna forward. "Go. I'll watch your backs." I whipped around to snarl at the guards. The vampires' smiles faltered when they saw *my* fangs protrude. Like most beings, they probably didn't know what I was, but they seemed to recognize I was potentially lethal, despite my petite frame.

I followed my sisters into the large courtroom. The place reminded me of a picture I'd seen of the Salem witch trials. Rows of dark wood pews lined the center aisle, and wide rustic planks comprised the floor. Unlike the photo I recalled, every window was boarded shut, and paintings of vampires hung on every inch of available wall space. One particular image epitomized the vampire stereotype perfectly. It showed a male vampire entwined with two naked women on a bed of roses and jewels. The women appeared completely enamored of the vampire, even while blood dripped from their necks.

The vampire spectators scrutinized us as we approached along the center aisle. Many had accessorized their expensive attire with diamond jewelry and watches that probably cost more than my car. Their glares told me they didn't appreciate my cotton T-shirt, peasant skirt, and flip-flops. I was twenty-five years old; it's not like I didn't know how to dress. But, hell, other fabrics and shoes were way more expensive to replace when I *changed* into my other form.

I spotted our accuser as we stalked our way to the front of the assembly. Even in a courtroom crammed with young and sexy vampires, Misha Aleksandr stood out. His tall, muscular frame filled his fitted suit, and his long blond hair brushed against his shoulders. Death, it seemed, looked damn good. Yet it wasn't his height or his wealth or even his striking features that captivated me. He possessed a fierce presence that commanded the room. Misha Aleksandr was a force to be reckoned with, but, strangely enough, so was I.

Misha had "requested" our presence in Sacramento after charging us with the murder of one of his family members. We had two choices: appear in court or be hunted for the rest of our lives. The whole situation sucked. We'd stayed hidden from the supernatural world for so long. Now not only had we been forced into the limelight, but we also faced the possibility of dying some twisted, Rob Zombie–inspired death.

Of course, God forbid that would make Taran shut her trap. She leaned in close to me. "Celia, how about I gather some magic-borne sunlight and fry these assholes?" she whispered in Spanish.

A few of the vampires behind us muttered and hissed, causing uproar among the rest. If they didn't like us before, they sure as hell hated us then.

Shayna laughed nervously, but maintained her perky demeanor. "I think some of them understand the lingo, dude."

I recognized Taran's desire to burn the vamps to blood and ash, but I didn't agree with it. Conjuring such power would leave her drained and vulnerable, easy prey for the master vampires, who would be immune to her sunlight. Besides, we were already in trouble with one master for killing his keep. We didn't need to be hunted by the entire leeching species.

The procession halted in a strangely wide-open area before a raised dais. There were no chairs or tables, nothing we could use as weapons against the judges or the angry mob amassed behind us.

My eyes focused on one of the boarded windows. The light honey-colored wood frame didn't match the darker boards. I guessed the last defendant had tried to escape. Judging from the claw marks running from beneath the frame to where I stood, he, she, or *it* hadn't made it.

I looked up from the deeply scratched floor to find Misha's intense gaze on me. We locked eyes, predator to predator, neither of us the type to back down. *You're trying to intimidate the wrong gal, pretty boy. I don't scare easily.*

Shayna slapped her hand over her face and shook her head, her long black ponytail waving behind her. "For Pete's sake, Celia, can't you be a little friendlier?" She flashed Misha a grin that made her blue eyes sparkle. "How's it going, dude?"

Shayna said "dude" a lot, ever since dating some idiot claiming to be a professional surfer. The term fit her sunny personality and eventually grew on us.

Misha didn't appear taken by her charm. He eyed her as if she'd asked him to make her a garlic pizza in the shape of a cross. I laughed; I couldn't help it. *Leave it to Shayna to try to befriend the guy who'll probably suck us dry by sundown.*

At the sound of my chuckle, Misha regarded me slowly. His head tilted slightly as his full lips curved into a sensual smile. I would have preferred a vicious stare— I knew how to deal with those. For a moment, I thought he'd somehow made my clothes disappear and I was standing there like the bleeding hoochies in that awful painting.

The judges' sudden arrival gave me an excuse to glance away. There were four, each wearing a formal robe of red velvet with an elaborate powdered wig. They were probably several centuries old, but like all vampires, they didn't appear a day over thirty. Their splendor easily surpassed the beauty of any mere mortal. I guessed the whole "sucky, sucky, me love you all night" lifestyle paid off for them.

The judges regally assumed their places on the raised dais. Behind them hung a giant plasma screen, which appeared out of place in this century-old building. Did they plan to watch a movie while they decided how best to disembowel us?

A female judge motioned Misha forward with a Queen Elizabeth hand wave. A long, thick scar angled from the corner of her left jaw across her throat. Someone had tried to behead her. To scar a vampire like that, the culprit had likely used a gold blade reinforced with lethal magic. Apparently, even that blade hadn't been enough. I gathered she commanded the fang-fest Parliament, since her marble nameplate read, CHIEF JUSTICE ANTOINETTE MALIKA. Judge Malika didn't strike me as the warm and cuddly sort. Her lips pursed into a tight line and her elongating fangs locked over her lower lip. I only hoped she'd snacked before her arrival.

At a nod from Judge Malika, Misha began. "Members of the High Court, I thank you for your audience." A Russian accent underscored his deep voice. "I hereby charge Celia, Taran, Shayna, and Emme Wird with the murder of my family member, David Geller."

"Wird? More like *Weird*," a vamp in the audience mumbled. The smaller vamp next to him adjusted his bow tie nervously when I snarled.

Oh, yeah, like we've never heard that before, jerk.

The sole male judge slapped a heavy leather-bound book on the long table and whipped out a feather quill. "Celia Wird. State your position."

Position?

I exchanged glances with my sisters; they didn't seem to know what Captain Pointy Teeth meant either. Taran shrugged. "Who gives a shit? Just say something."

I waved a hand. "Um. Registered Nurse?"

Judging by his "please don't make me eat you before

the proceedings" scowl, and the snickering behind us, I hadn't provided him with the appropriate response.

He enunciated every word carefully and slowly so as to not further confuse my obviously feeble and inferior mind. "Position in the supernatural world."

"We've tried to avoid your world." I gave Taran the evil eye. "For the most part. But if you must know, I'm a tigress."

"Weretigress," he said as he wrote.

"I'm not a *were*," I interjected defensively.

He huffed. "Can you *change* into a tigress or not?"

"Well, yes. But that doesn't make me a *were*."

The vamps behind us buzzed with feverish whispers while the judges' eyes narrowed suspiciously. Not knowing what we were made them nervous. A nervous vamp was a dangerous vamp. And the room burst with them.

"What I mean is, unlike a *were*, I can *change* parts of my body without turning into my beast completely." And unlike anything else on earth, I could also *shift*— disappear under and across solid ground and resurface unscathed. But they didn't need to know that little tidbit. Nor did they need to know I couldn't heal my injuries. If it weren't for Emme's unique ability to heal herself and others, my sisters and I would have died long ago.

"Fascinating," he said in a way that clearly meant I wasn't. The feather quill didn't come with an eraser. And the judge obviously didn't appreciate my making him mess up his book. He dipped his pen into his little ink-well and scribbled out what he'd just written before addressing Taran. "Taran Wird, position?"

"I can release magic into the forms of fire and lightning—"

"Very well, witch." The vamp scrawled.

"I'm not a witch, asshole."

The judge threw his plume on the table, agitated. Judge Malika fixed her frown on Taran. "What did you say?"

Nobody flashed a vixen grin better than Taran. "I said, 'I'm not a witch. Ass. Hole.'"

Emme whimpered, ready to hurl from the stress. Shayna giggled and threw an arm around Taran. "She's just kidding, dude!"

No. Taran didn't kid. Hell, she didn't even know any knock-knock jokes. She shrugged off Shayna, unwilling to back down. She wouldn't listen to Shayna. But she would listen to me.

"Just answer the question, Taran."

The muscles on Taran's jaw tightened, but she did as I asked. "I make fire, light—"

"Fire-breather." Captain Personality wrote quickly.

"I'm not a—"

He cut her off. "Shayna Wird?"

"Well, dude, I throw knives—"

"Knife thrower," he said, ready to get this little meet-and-greet over and done with.

Shayna did throw knives. That was true. She could also transform pieces of wood into razor-sharp weapons and manipulate alloys. All she needed was metal somewhere on her body and a little focus. For her safety, though, "knife thrower" seemed less threatening.

"And you, Emme Wird?"

"Um. Ah. I can move things with my mind—"

"Gypsy," the half-wit interpreted.

I supposed "telekinetic" was too big a word for this idiot. Then again, unlike typical telekinetics, Emme could do more than bend a few forks. I sighed. *Tigress, fire-breather, knife thrower, and Gypsy.* We sounded like the headliners for a freak show. All we needed was a bearded lady. *That's what happens when you're the bizarre products of a backfired curse.*

Misha glanced at us quickly before stepping forward once more. "I will present Mr. Hank Miller and Mr. Timothy Brown as witnesses—" Taran exhaled dramatically and twirled her hair like she was bored. Misha glared at her before finishing. "I do not doubt justice will be served."

Judge Zhahara Nadim, who resembled more of an Egyptian queen than someone who should be stuffed into a powdered wig, surprised me by leering at Misha like she wanted his head for a lawn ornament. I didn't know what he'd done to piss her off; yet knowing we weren't the only ones hated brought me a strange sense of comfort. She narrowed her eyes at Misha, like all predators do before they strike, and called forward someone named "Destiny." I didn't know Destiny, but I knew she was no vampire the moment she strutted onto the dais.

I tried to remain impassive. However, I really wanted to run away screaming. Short of sporting a few tails and some extra digits, Destiny was the freakiest thing I'd ever seen. Not only did she lack the allure all vampires possessed, but her fashion sense bordered on disastrous. She wore black patterned tights, white strappy sandals, and a hideous black-and-white polka-dot turtleneck. I guessed she sought to draw attention from her lime green zebra-print miniskirt. And, my God, her makeup was abominable. Black kohl outlined her bright fuchsia lips, and mint green shadow ringed her eyes.

"This is a perfect example of why I don't wear makeup," I told Taran.

Taran stepped forward with her hands on her hips. "How the hell is *she* a witness? I didn't see her at the club that night! And Lord knows she would've stuck out."

Emme trembled beside me. "Taran, please don't get us killed!"

I gave my youngest sister's hand a squeeze. "Steady, Emme."

Judge Malika called Misha's two witnesses forward. "Mr. Miller and Mr. Brown, which of you gentlemen would like to go first?"

Both "gentlemen" took one gander at Destiny and scrambled away from her. It was never a good sign when something scared a vampire. Hank, the bigger of the two vamps, shoved Tim forward.

"You may begin," Judge Malika commanded. "Just concentrate on what you saw that night. Destiny?"

The four judges swiftly donned protective ear wear, like construction workers used, just as a guard flipped a switch next to the flat-screen. At first I thought the judges toyed with us. Even with heightened senses, how could they hear the testimony through those ridiculous ear guards? Before I could protest, Destiny enthusiastically approached Tim and grabbed his head. Tim's immediate bloodcurdling screams caused the rest of us to cover our ears. Every hair on my body stood at attention. What freaked me out was he wasn't the one on trial.

Emme's fair freckled skin blanched so severely, I feared she'd pass out. Shayna stood frozen with her jaw open while Taran and I exchanged "oh, shit" glances. I was about to start the "let's get the hell out of here" ball rolling when images from Tim's mind appeared on the screen. I couldn't believe my eyes. Complete with sound effects, we relived the night of David's murder. Misha straightened when he saw David soar out of Taran's window in flames, but otherwise he did not react. Nor did Misha blink when what remained of David burst into ashes on our lawn. Still, I sensed his fury. The image moved to a close-up of Hank's shocked face and finished with the four of us scowling down at the blood and ash.

Destiny abruptly released the sobbing Tim, who collapsed on the floor. Mucus oozed from his nose and mouth. I didn't even know vamps were capable of such body fluids.

At last, Taran finally seemed to understand the deep shittiness of our situation. "Son of a bitch," she whispered.

Hank gawked at Tim before addressing the judges. "If it pleases the court, I swear on my honor I witnessed exactly what Tim Brown did about David Geller's murder. My version would be of no further benefit."

Malika shrugged indifferently. "Very well, you're excused." She turned toward us while Hank hurried back to his seat. "As you just saw, we have ways to expose the truth. Destiny is able to extract memories, but she cannot alter them. Likewise, during Destiny's time with you, you will be unable to change what you saw. You'll only review what has already come to pass."

I frowned. "How do we know you're telling us the truth?"

Malika peered down her nose at me. "What choice do you have? Now, which of you is first?"

CHAPTER 2

I gathered my sisters around me. "I'm going first. I can handle Destiny better than the rest of you."

Taran wasn't having any of it. "Screw that, Celia. I'll go. It's my fault we're here. Besides, my badass shields will protect me from that fashion emergency."

I wasn't so sure, but I reluctantly nodded. Taran hugged us briefly before confronting Destiny. Emme grabbed my hand again for comfort. I gave her another little squeeze. Shayna didn't need comforting. So long as I stayed strong, she wouldn't panic.

I took a deep breath to calm my nerves. *If Taran doesn't do well, we'll get the hell out of here or die trying.*

Taran stepped forward, and once again the enthusiastic Destiny did, too. I stiffened when she touched Taran's head. To my surprise, other than a little shudder, Taran didn't react. A moment later, her memories of the night in question flashed on the screen.

We found our sister had an extremely graphic memory. The first image was innocent enough; it showed Taran and David dancing together at a club. When they entered David's limo, things took an unexpected turn. Moaning, groaning, and grunting aside, there were some talents people shouldn't know their sisters possessed. Emme buried her face in her hands. Shayna cringed. She glanced back and forth from the screen to me.

"Make it stop," she pleaded.

Oh, honey, I wish I could. I was torn between gouging out my eyes and ripping the flat-screen off the wall to beat Taran with it. *What* was she thinking? This totally went against our "must not date anything that consumes blood" rule we made last year—the *first* time I caught her flirting with a vampire. I rubbed my face. Good heavens. It was bad enough to invite a vampire into our home, but to end up having her escapades broadcast like the finale of *American Idol* was so wrong.

The vampires seemed to enjoy the show. A few fanned their faces and shifted closer to their neighbors for a little cuddle time.

"Tell me when it's over," Emme whispered.

An uncomfortable length of time passed before we actually segued to the assault in Taran's bedroom. I watched David roughly bind Taran's hands with his tie and expose his fangs, which struck me as strange. This wasn't foreplay. This was a predator immobilizing prey.

I raised an eyebrow at Shayna, who shook her head, equally confused. Vamps were never hostile to their victims. They didn't have to be. Humans found them irresistible, and the experience supposedly proved orgasmic for both. Everyone in the courtroom remained mesmerized by the scene. I wasn't. I tensed, knowing the moment that would seal our fate quickly approached.

On the screen, Taran yelled, "You bastard! Don't you dare bite me!" The rows of vampires behind me hissed like a nest of angry serpents. Taran's core flared blue and white before it catapulted a fireball into the aforementioned bastard. The next image showed me breaking down Taran's door. My green eyes were wild and my long curly hair a mess from sleep. Yet it was the skimpy tank top and lace panties I'd worn that made me blush. I glanced at Misha, who gave me yet another appraising look-see.

My eyes narrowed. *Is he flirting? No, of course not. He's probably just hungry. Men don't flirt with me. They race away screaming.*

I returned my focus to the screen in time to watch myself wrench David up and heave him through the window. The onlookers gasped when they watched me touch his flaming form with my bare hands. Vampires *hated* fire. Fortunately, they also witnessed Emme and Shayna freeing Taran from her binds, proving they were uninvolved.

When the final image showed the four of us staring down at the pile of blood and ash scattered on our front lawn, Destiny released Taran's head. Taran slumped to the floor and promptly vomited. We ran to her.

"Son of a bitch," she muttered between coughs.

While some obviously repulsed vampires mopped up Taran's mess, another female judge fixed her eyes on Emme. I wasn't surprised. Emme had our father's fair skin and blond hair, distinguishing her from the rest of us who inherited our Latin mother's darker tones. I thought Emme resembled an angel in her soft pink dress. The judges probably thought she resembled dessert.

The judge played with the edges of her robe in teasing strokes. It was hard to appear slutty in an outfit that resembled a muumuu with a zipper, but this vamp managed. She leaned forward, crooning to Emme in an alarmingly alluring voice, "Come to me, little one. There's something I wish to share with you alone."

Emme stepped closer to me. "I'd rather not," she responded.

Judge Malika turned to her colleagues. She whispered, unaware my hearing was as sharp as hers. "Sofia just tried to call their weakest one and you saw she failed to react. Clearly, these Wird sisters are immune to our magic, and yet young David attempted to feed from one."

The others nodded, but otherwise said nothing. I bit back a smirk. Since vampires were strict about keeping their existence a secret, it was illegal to drink from someone who couldn't be hypnotized into forgetting the experience. They were also required to erase fang marks by licking the wound. I thought we'd gained some leverage until I caught Judge Malika's sinister glee.

"Young David attempted an illegal feed," she said. "Your response, however, was exceedingly violent. I sense your collective power. You could have easily contained David and contacted his master. Sir Aleksandr would have dealt with him."

"Excuse me." Shayna cautiously addressed the judges. "We didn't know your rules. We were just trying to protect our sister."

Judge Malika pursed her lips. "Then perhaps you shouldn't associate with those whose ways are unfamiliar to you."

Her condescending tone infuriated me, but I thought better of lashing out. Instead, I tried to clarify her words. "According to you, David committed a serious crime. What would've happened to him if we had contacted Misha?"

The four judges raised their eyebrows in unison, and a wave of muttering rippled through the courtroom. I realized I had insulted Misha by failing to use his proper title. My scowl deepened. Considering we might die at his hands, I didn't give a crap about formalities.

I glanced over, expecting him to take offense. Instead, he gave me a small nod and a wide, wicked grin. Either I'd impressed him with my backbone or my backside. Regardless, no way would I allow him to take a chunk out of me.

The male judge answered me instead of Judge Malika. He wasn't any peachier. "*Sir* Aleksandr would have turned young David over to us to discipline. As per our laws, we would have sentenced him to three months of daily torture sessions, but not death." The judge trained his focus on Taran. "You set him on fire. Had you been alone, we may have excused your actions by reason of self-defense. But you weren't." He pointed an accusing finger at us. "You were all present; therefore the fight was unjust." He sat back and crossed his arms, inordinately pleased with his reasoning.

I shook my head, refusing to accept his judgment. Something wasn't right; vampires didn't attack without provocation.

"Now, if there is nothing further, we will adjourn and return with our verdict." Judge Malika nodded to dismiss Destiny.

My sisters gasped, likely shocked at how quickly Her Honor had wrapped up our case. Well, not if I could help it . . .

"Wait. Take my testimony." Perhaps there was something I'd seen to explain David's aggression. I took a breath and stepped forward, ready to meet Destiny, and knowing I was probably in for a lot of pain. Unlike Taran, I didn't have protective shields to keep me safe from harm.

Destiny shrugged and cracked her knuckles right before she grabbed my head. Instantly, it felt like she'd replaced the blood to my brain with battery acid. My cries were horrid as every nerve in my body rioted from the scalding torture. Despite all that, and my full-body convulsions, my version of that night's events popped into my mind and onto the plasma screen.

I watched David crash into Taran's dresser when she launched her fireball into his chest. He glared at me when I cut off his screams by crushing his throat. Precisely then, I heard Judge Malika's voice echo in my head. "Stop!" It was as if she'd hit the pause button on a remote. In the frozen image, David's eyes flashed green—the bright peridot green from a bloodlust infection.

Urgent whispers filled the courtroom as Destiny released me. I crashed to the floor, vomiting. Unlike Taran, I purposely aimed for Destiny's hideous white platform sandals. All sympathy for that pitiful ensemble was gone, considering the torment she'd subjected me to. To my credit, I didn't cry, whereas Tim continued to sniffle somewhere behind me.

The room spun. I staggered to my feet. To my right, vampire guards restrained my struggling sisters. Shayna's breath came fast, and tears streamed down Emme's face. Taran was all fury. "I'm okay," I choked. It was a lie. My entire body hurt like I'd taken on a wererhino. But I knew I'd recover.

The guards released my family after a firm nod from Judge Malika. They rushed to me. Emme grabbed me in a tight embrace. Her soft yellow light quickly encased me, instantly extinguishing my remaining pain and nausea. She obstructed part of my view, but I caught Shayna reaching for her toothpicks and converting the minute pieces of wood into long, sharp needles.

Taran clenched her teeth and gathered her fire around her. "I'm sorry, Celia. But don't worry; we're getting the hell out of here."

Except for the judges and Misha, all the courtroom attendants surrounded us. As they closed in, I exposed my fangs and claws and matched the vamps' hisses with a low, threatening growl.

"The Wird girls are not to be harmed. Return to your pews." Judge Malika spoke softly, but the authority in her voice silenced the house. Within seconds, the audience resumed their seats as if there had never been a disturbance.

I maintained my defensive posture. "Taran, turn down the power. Shayna, hold your position." My sisters nodded.

Judge Malika tapped her long nails against the dais. "It appears chronic bloodlust played a hand in the events. Since young David's fate would have been the same had he stood trial, the charges against the defendants are dismissed."

Taran glared at her. "Wait just a goddamned minute. You're letting us go, just like that?"

I glared, too—at Taran. "Zip. It. *Now*."

Taran narrowed her eyes. "This is bullshit, Celia. Something's up."

"Would you rather stay?" Judge Malika asked in a way that clearly said she'd like us to.

Shayna slipped in front of Taran with her palms up.

"It's cool of you dudes not to eat us and stuff. We just want to know why so *we*"—she motioned her head back at Taran—"don't ever end up here again."

Emme tugged frantically on Shayna's sleeve. Not me. I was ready to knock them both out and throw them over my shoulders. "Seriously? Can we just get the hell out of here?"

The male judge explained slowly, like nothing as stupid as us could possibly exist. "David was in the beginning phase of chronic bloodlust."

I frowned, confused. I knew bloodlust occurred when a vamp went too long without a feed, and the freaky green eyes had been a giveaway. It was easily remedied, though, by providing the vamp with a supervised feeding so he or she didn't completely drain the donor. "What do you mean, chronic? I thought bloodlust resolved itself after the infected vampire is fed."

Judge Malika responded. "Chronic bloodlust results from a powerful magic wielder's curse. It makes a vampire's appetite insatiable. The more he feeds, the more he desires, and the deeper he falls into insanity. He'll lose his beauty and grow in size and strength from overindulgence. His only focus is to continue to eat at any cost."

"Dude, that sounds sick. How do you cure it?" Shayna asked.

"There is no cure. The vampire must be destroyed," Malika answered stiffly.

"But how did you know David had *chronic* bloodlust?" Shayna pressed.

Malika smacked her lips like she could still taste her breakfast. "The first sign was the aggression David demonstrated toward your sister. Violence toward our food is unnecessary. We have no need to kill our prey to feast well. The second was that there was no reason for deprivation. You live in *Tahoe*. Millions visit there each year; David could have easily fed anytime he wished. Now, if there are no further questions, *leave*."

Judge Zhahara scowled with majestic beauty, likely bummed we wouldn't be sentenced to some miserable death. But when she turned her sights on Misha she smiled with all the warmth of a cobra. "Sir Aleksandr, step forward. Explain to the court why you allowed chronic bloodlust to go unnoticed and undisciplined in your family."

We tried to exit the courtroom. Misha blocked our path. At first I thought he'd poised himself to attack. I leaped in front of my sisters to protect them. He ignored us, addressing the judges instead. "I assure the court I hold the strictest control over my family." His voice belied his rage. "On my honor, I will not only discover how this infestation occurred, but I will also hunt and kill all those responsible." He then turned to us and bowed. "Ladies, you have my deepest apology for this unfortunate incident."

Incident? Between my date with Destiny and the legions of orthodontically challenged waiting to munch on us, "incident" didn't quite sum it up. "Take your apology and shove it up your—"

Shayna covered my mouth. "Dude! Are you nuts?"

"Oh, Celia, *please*. Let's just leave," Emme begged in a frantic whisper. "It's almost their lunchtime, for goodness' sake."

I allowed them to escort me out of the courtroom while keeping my eyes on Taran. She runway-strutted the entire length of the aisle. Before making her grand exit, she threw one last comment. "By the way, *Sir* Aleksandr, your vamp sucked in bed."

I continued to watch Taran until she safely returned to my side. But unlike most males who met Taran, Misha wasn't captivated by her. No. His hungry gaze fixed on me.

CHAPTER 3

I thought of Misha as I jogged my tenth and final mile alongside Lake Tahoe's shore. Fangs and master vampire status aside, he was a beautiful man. A beautiful man who should have tempted me as easily as a fish to a line. And yet there was no temptation. Strange, though, to have someone so attractive see me with desire. Most men ignored me to gawk at my pretty sisters. On the rare occasion a potential suitor did glance my way, my predator side unleashed and intimidated the crap out of him. But what did I expect? My inner beast remained my powerful and loyal guardian, sharing my heart and spirit. She made us tough, strong, and a little scary . . . she also made us lonely.

I was only nine when our parents died. As mere humans, they hadn't stood a chance against the gun-wielding burglars who broke into our home. I took on the parental role, willingly if not fiercely. Someone had to step up. Someone had to keep us safe. But as much as I tried, as hard as I fought, sometimes it wasn't enough. Even a tigress could become prey, especially in a foster system full of predators.

Years of fear and betrayal made it difficult for us to trust anyone. We didn't really have friends, except for Bren, the only *were* we knew and our Wiki into the supernatural world, and Danny, my buddy from college. It was hard to let others in. Especially for me. In many ways, I remained that young girl determined to keep herself and her little sisters safe.

I increased my speed, gliding along the cold, moist sand and trying not to let the pain from my past and the solitude of my present consume me. It was better for men to fear me, I reminded myself. If they feared me, they couldn't hurt me. Again.

Go to your happy place, Celia. Go to your happy place.

That was easy, considering where I ran. A cool April breeze swept along the lake, rippling light waves to splash along the large boulders and bringing a fresh whiff of Tahoe's magic to my nose. My inner tigress purred. God, I loved it here. It was strange to think of a lake as a friend, but it was. Tahoe made me feel happy and welcomed—a rare feat, considering the crap we'd been dealt....

I scented the werewolves before they appeared around the bend. They ran with the natural grace of their wilder sides and jumped easily over the small chunks of snow that remained along the beach. The breeze blew against me, so they couldn't track my scent, but they would notice me soon enough.

The leader ran in front and six pairs followed closely, all in human form. When we first moved to Tahoe, I didn't think there were but a handful of *weres* in the whole area. Now I scented them in the woods where I frequently hiked and along the walkways of the quaint shops near our house.

I guessed they needed to keep up with the rising vamp population.

Without thinking, I focused on the leader. He smelled like all wolves: of earth and a touch of fire. But like all beings, he had an extra something special to mark his scent unique. His aroma was that of water crashing over stones, clean, hard, strong. And while his redolence sent a wave of goose bumps cascading up my arms, it was his physique that stole my breath. He wore a black, long-sleeved University of Colorado T-shirt and black running shorts that inched up his powerful legs as he effortlessly raced along the sand. My gaze traveled from those rugged legs to his muscular body. He was well over six feet tall and, boy, was he *cute.* His chiseled cheekbones set off his strong jaw, darkened by a five-o'clock shadow. His nose was sharp, yet not so big that it didn't fit his face. Thick, straight dark hair hung slightly over his eyes. And damn, those eyes, they were light brown and absolutely mesmerizing. I caught myself staring and our gazes locked.

Bren once warned me never to look a *were* in the eyes. "We're temperamental assholes, Celia," he'd said. "It doesn't take much to challenge my kind."

It was stupid, but I refused to avert my gaze, and so did he. To make matters worse, I gave him a small, shy smile, completely out of character for me. His dark eyebrows furrowed; he was probably trying to figure out what I was doing. I was, too, for that matter.

We stared at each other as we drew closer. It wasn't until I knew he got a hint of my scent that his expression changed. He stopped and turned as I passed by. The others ceased to run as well.

"Did I tell you to stop running?" he half growled, half shouted at them. His voice echoed in a deep timbre behind me, above another splash of waves. I liked the way it resonated and, for some strange reason, wanted to remember it. I doubted I would, but that face . . . I wouldn't forget that face.

The other wolves quickly resumed their pace. I peeked over my shoulder as I continued to run, the wind sweeping my long hair like a dark sail behind me. The leader stood rooted to the same spot while the others sped away. He tilted his head and continued to gaze at me, his expression a mixture of confusion and intensity. He jerked toward me suddenly, only to abruptly stop. My smile widened. I stared at him a second longer before finally continuing around the bend.

The wolf's steamy presence gave me a new burst of energy. I ran a little faster, with a quick bounce to my steps, leaping over the large boulders that cascaded along the small incline to the road. I spotted the shortcut through the woods that led into my neighborhood. I paused briefly, allowing the ears of my beast to search for any subtle sounds of animals scurrying. The last thing I needed was to accidentally brush against some woodland creature. Another Celia-ism I failed to share in court was my ability to *change* into other creatures—although never on purpose. If an animal came in contact with me, and I couldn't block its spirit, a bit of its essence transferred into me. One violent seizure and some drooling later, I'd emerge as that critter. The problem was, I couldn't immediately *change* back—especially if stressed. I accidently stepped on a skunk once. The same week I was awaiting the results of my nursing boards. Needless to say, my sisters spent a week shoving lettuce down my throat and praying I wouldn't lift my tail.

My hearing picked up a flock of quails and a few chipmunks. They scampered away when they felt the presence of my beast. I relaxed slightly and hurried along. The tall, thick pines darkened the path, no matter the time of day. Only small snippets of sunlight trickled through, dancing along the trunks and forest floor, highlighting the fallen needles and mounds of frozen snow. It was always a few degrees colder than the beach. I didn't mind. My inner furry beast kept my metabolism high and my body warm, and this forest satisfied my animal side's desire to roam.

I inhaled deeply to absorb the freshness, only to stop when I locked on a foreign scent.

Something lurked in the trees. And it didn't belong.

I hummed to quiet the growl that threatened to escape, and casually ambled along until my nose fixed upon my prey's location. The moment I caught it, I swept up a stone and launched it into the large white fir to my left.

"Ow!"

I charged the *were*. He crash-landed with a hard thump into a dormant rhododendron bush. He surprised me by not poising to attack. Instead, he sat up and rubbed his head . . . rather pathetically.

He glanced at the blood on his hand, then back at me. "What the fuck? I was only trying to get a look at you."

"What?"

He stood, wincing and wobbling as his crushed skull snapped back into place. Judging by his feline scent, he was either a werebobcat or a werecougar. Since he wasn't more challenging, I went with werebobcat. "You're one of those chicks from vamp court, aren't ya?"

"Excuse me?"

He frowned. "I said—"

"I know what you said, moron! What I want to know is why you're here?"

"To look at you," he repeated once more. "You know. 'Cause I heard you're kind of freaky and—"

Werebob's catlike screeches persisted as I resumed my pace toward our neighborhood. Perhaps my knee to his nuts would teach him to watch who he called a freak.

Loser.

The trees parted just a few yards away, revealing the house closest to the path. Unlike some of the huge developments here in Dollar Point, our division was basically a wide cul-de-sac with eight beautifully crafted and large custom Colonials. We didn't have access to a pool or tennis courts like other communities, but we were set away from the main road and had a great view of the lake. Our yard was small, but skillfully landscaped and backed into a greenbelt. If it weren't for our grouchy neighbor, Mrs. Mancuso, it would have been our own little piece of heaven.

Jesus had the Virgin Mary. If the devil had a mommy, it would have been Mrs. Mancuso.

I jogged to the end of the path and onto the sidewalk, stopping when I reached our mailbox. As I stretched my muscles, a sleek ivory limo rolled to a halt in front of our house. The driver stepped out and opened the back door. The vampire with the bow tie I recognized from court emerged. Most vampires paraded around like the rock stars of the supernatural world they believed themselves to be. Not this little guy. His crew-cut blond hair suggested military. His neat brown suit and red bow tie suggested 1950s college professor. He glanced around anxiously, his dark eyes widening when he saw me approach.

He adjusted his jacket before smiling politely. "Hello, Celia. Forgive me for arriving unannounced—"

"Who are you and what are you doing here?"

My bluntness made his jaw slack, but his polite smile quickly returned. "I am Petro."

His Russian accent was subtle, and his voice not nearly as strong as Misha's. He also lacked the typical vampire swagger. If it weren't for the alluring scent of sex and chocolate vamps carried, I wouldn't have been sure he was vampire. I blinked, waiting for more.

"Petro Makisma," he repeated, as if I should know him.

Petro glanced at his driver in the awkward silence. The driver kept his poker face, yet left me with the impression Petro's lack of notoriety was nothing new. Petro shifted his feet. "Ah. I'm here to extend my apologies and those of my entire family."

Again, I waited.

His shoulders slumped. "Sir Misha Aleksandr and I are of the same family."

The hardening of my face made him step behind his driver. In all fairness, it wasn't my prettiest look. "Oh. Him."

Petro's jaw nearly unhinged. He glanced at his driver again, who gave the palms-up "go figure" response. I supposed Petro expected the mere mention of Misha's name to excite me. *Think again, Petie.*

The front door to my house opened and my sisters hurried outside. Taran must have sensed the vampire mojo. "Who the hell are you?" Taran asked when Petro greeted them warmly.

Petro's smile faded once more. I was starting to feel bad for the guy. "He's Petro Makisma," I answered for him. Their blank stares told me they'd never heard of him either. Taran eyed Petro's bow tie like it could bite. I walked to her side. "He's here to apologize on behalf of his family." More blank stares. "He's with Misha."

"Oh," they all responded.

Petro urged his driver forward with a gentle nudge of his small, neat hands. "The gifts, please, Antonio."

I stepped back, giving the driver ample space in case he chose to attack. Unlike Petro's five-foot-five frame, this guy was behemoth. A Goliath to Petro's David.

The driver returned with a stack of wide crimson velvet cases. He handed one to each of my sisters, saving the last one for me. I quirked a brow at the lush case. A small silver plaque, engraved with my initials, lay fixed at the center. When I wouldn't take it, the driver opened the case. Dime-size diamond earrings glimmered with enough brilliance to blind. Between the earrings rested a small, handwritten note on thick, expensive stationary. The little card read:

> *My Dearest Celia,*
> *   Looking forward to dinner.*
> *   Your humble admirer,*
>
> > *Misha Aleksandr*

This time, it was my jaw's turn to fall open. First of all, there was nothing humble about Misha. Second, damn. Just, *damn.* I glared at Petro. "You can't be serious."

Petro frowned. "I assure you they are the highest caliber of diamonds. However, if you prefer a more classic emerald to match your eyes—"

"We don't want the jewelry. And we especially don't want to go out to dinner with some idiot who tried to kill us!"

"Speak for yourself, Celia," Taran said, admiring the sapphire-and-diamond bracelet she'd already snapped onto her wrist. She frowned at my scowl. "What? It's the least that rich bastard could do."

Emme dropped her gaze, blushing as pink as the diamond at the center of her platinum necklace. "Everyone deserves a chance at forgiveness," she said quietly.

"He tried to have us killed." I repeated my words slowly. Apparently, though, all it took was something shiny to distract them. Surely Shayna would be reasonable.

Nope.

Shayna juggled her sapphire-encrusted daggers. "Oooh—*look*. They sparkle in the sunlight."

Petro cleared his throat. "Forgive me, Celia, but I believe he intended the dinner invitation to be a private rendezvous."

Petro jumped at my scowl. "I'm *not* having dinner with him."

It was then I heard what sounded like a bottle being dropped behind our house. *Now what?* I jogged around back, slowing to a stop when I caught a wereraccoon rifling through our garbage. A *naked* wereraccoon in human form. His aroma of bark and dry leaves was unmistakable. I couldn't believe it. It should have been comical. But I wasn't laughing.

His hairy legs stiffened. Slowly he raised his head from the large plastic barrel to see me standing there, gawking at him.

"Um. Hi," he mumbled through a mouthful of food.

He paused before bolting toward the lake like his life depended on it. Because it did. Of course our evil neighbor had to come home from grocery shopping just then.

After all, when else would Mrs. Mancuso have had the opportunity to see me chasing a naked man across my front lawn? She crossed herself as I ground to a halt in front of her.

I watched the wereraccoon disappear into the patch of woods as he ran faster than any naked guy with flapping male parts should. Taran's WTF expression said it all.

Petro's driver gave a one-shoulder shrug. "Welcome to the supernatural world," he muttered.

CHAPTER 4

Finding a wereraccoon rifling through your trash sucked.
Having a can of Lysol thrown at you while being called
a tramp by a woman with enough neck skin to make a
purse sucked more. But getting stalked by the supernatural paparazzi just about threw me over the edge. In ad-
dition to the wereraccoon and werebobcat, every mystical
freak imaginable had made an appearance. I scented
them *everywhere*. They hid in our bushes, peeked in our
windows. I even found a werepossum sleeping under our
porch.

My knuckles ached from pummeling the two wererats
that rang our doorbell in the middle of the night, reeking
of witch's brew and begging for autographs. *And* I was
coming off my sixth twelve-hour work shift in a row.

So when a master vampire showed up on my doorstep, let's just say I didn't welcome him with open arms.

"What do you want, Misha?"

Misha frowned, giving him a totally unfair sexy brood.
"You're not wearing my earrings."

The earrings marked the beginning of the parade of

expensive gifts Misha had sent in an effort to apologize for vampire court. "Giving us jewelry and paying off our mortgage doesn't change the fact you almost had us killed. You can't buy us, Misha. We're paying you back for the house."

"The master sent flowers and candy, too," one of his idiot bodyguards said from the walkway.

"Oh, yeah, 'cause nothing says, 'I'm sorry I wanted to torture you,' like chocolate truffles." I narrowed my eyes at Misha. "Just tell me what you want." The corner of Misha's mouth curved slightly while the two goons behind him exchanged "I have dibs on her liver" glances.

"I came to see you."

I stood in the doorway in the tank top I'd slept in and a pair of yoga pants that had been begging to go to the big laundry basket in the sky. My wild curls and I had fought. They'd won. I hadn't showered, and I resembled something the wereraccoon was chewing on before he ran like the dickens. Yet Misha's hungry gaze swept along my body, despite my hell-on-a-cracker appearance.

I leaned one arm along the doorway and rested my other on my hip, annoyed. "Why? Did you run out of virgins or something?"

Misha's gray eyes flickered with stirring mischief. "If I had, should I expect to find one here?"

"Nope. We're all out, too."

"Hmm." Although it sounded more like *yum*.

Misha lived in Tahoe City, a ridiculously wealthy area packed with multigazillion-dollar properties. I doubted he'd driven the six short miles to our home in Dollar Point just to borrow a cup of virgin. A few moments passed, enough time for that cocky expression to slowly dissolve and shadow with foreboding torment. "I need your help, Celia. I fear it is rather urgent."

My human side warned me to run far and fast. Whatever scared Misha would surely scare me. My tigress held us in place. She thought we should hear out the reigning Prince of Darkness. I refused to invite him in, though. Inviting one vampire meant only he or she could enter. Inviting a *master* allowed him and everyone in his keep access to our home, so we agreed to meet at a nearby café. I reasoned that he wouldn't have sent flowers and gifts just to kill me later. And while he didn't make my insides flutter like that wolf I'd met, Misha wasn't exactly hard on the eyes.

After making my waves as presentable as the laws of big hair would allow, I traded my pathetic ensemble for workout clothes. My plan was to go for a run after our chat. I was running more—a lot more—hoping for another glimpse of that sexy wolf.

I drove to the Kings Beach Cafe and slipped into the booth where Misha waited. Two waitresses rushed to our table. I thought they were going to fistfight to see who would wait on us—or should I say, wait on Misha. The waitress with the most robust figure won.

"Good afternoon. I'm Tiffany. Would you like to hear the specials?" That's what she said. Judging by the way Tiffany's breast casually brushed against Misha's arm when she handed him a menu, she really meant, "I'm not wearing any panties."

Misha gestured to me with a subtle wave of his hand. "Perhaps you should start with my lovely companion."

Perhaps she shouldn't have. Tiffany did a double take and huffed. In her preoccupation with Misha, she'd failed to notice me. I smiled and gave her a pinky wave. "Just a chai tea latte, please."

Misha kept his eyes on me. "The same for me as well."

Tiffany returned in record time . . . and braless.

Hello. I'm still here, Tiff.

Misha smiled at my scowl. "Would you like anything else, my darling?"

"No."

I'd meant to sound annoyed. I blamed Misha for taking away our anonymity. And yet, as Tiffany flounced away, I found it increasingly difficult to feel anything but curiosity. Misha sported yet another designer suit. This time he'd tied his long blond hair back from his shoulders. He may have dressed for the corporate world, but there was nothing nine-to-five about him. Misha was model perfect. And Misha knew it.

So then what was he doing with me? Hell, I didn't even wear makeup.

He'd selected a corner booth where the sun peeked through the shades. I couldn't help but smile. Bram Stoker had it all wrong. Sunlight had no effect on preternatural beings. Only sunshine created through magic could do them harm. Crucifixes didn't work either: Many vampires were devout Catholics, although they usually snacked on the priest following confession. Vampires did, however, drink human blood. That much was true. Blood preserved their youth, enhanced their beauty, and kept their organs functioning. And while vamps took their fair share, it was less than humans donated to blood banks. Unbeknownst to humans, though, vampires ran most blood drives. Guess that explained all the shortages.

"So what do you want?" I finally asked.

Misha's face turned grim as he quietly explained. "The morning following vampire court, I killed my second in command. He had been a member of my keep for the past hundred years."

Suddenly, tea with Misha sounded like a very bad idea. My claws crept out, digging into the underside of the wooden table. "Why did you do that?" I asked, hoping he had a damn good reason.

"My family and I woke to the screams of my maid. It took us mere moments to reach her, yet we were too late. Andres had drained her completely."

Oh, God. "Bloodlust?"

He nodded.

"Misha, how is this possible?"

Misha shook his head. He reached for his tea, but changed his mind. "It shouldn't be. I manage my family carefully. They feed well."

If it wasn't a lack of feeding, then it had to be magic. "Then some whack-job witch obviously cursed him."

"I believe you mean cursed *them*."

My eyes widened. His menacing tone told me he meant more than Andres and Taran's hell date. "How many are we talking about, Misha?" He gave me a hard stare. "Misha! How many?"

"Twelve."

Vamp court had been just a week ago. My mouth went dry. "Twelve vampires in seven days." I blew out a shaky breath. "All yours?"

"Yes."

"Have you discovered the witch who cast the curse?"

"No. I am not certain a curse was cast."

I took a drink from my cup, trying not to think about an army of vampires stalking through the streets and thick forests of Tahoe. Ski season was over, but summer was quickly approaching. That meant thousands of tourists shopping, golfing, swimming, rock climbing, camping, and hiking. Not to mention the year-round residents.

I paused, realizing what Misha said made no sense. "What do you mean, you don't think a curse was cast? Isn't that how the bloodlust pendulum swings?"

"The blood of my vampires is linked to mine. Had a curse been cast, I would have felt it here."

Misha placed my palm over his heart. Hard muscle tensed beneath the smoothness of his silk shirt. His steady heart beat rhythmically. *Bump, bump. Bump, bump.* Mine was more of a *pitter, patter, thump, crash, thunk.*

It had been a long time since I'd *touched* anyone. And touching Misha made me uncomfortable.

Misha must have felt my trepidation, because he released my hand before I could snatch it away. His head tilted with amused interest, but he spared me further humiliation by continuing. "Witch magic is playing a part, yes, but how remains obscure. I suspect a rival master is the key behind the attack against my family."

"Why a master and not just a witch?"

Misha motioned to one of his goons, who handed him a large manila folder. "Celia, there is tremendous upheaval in the vampire world. Masters are seeking any excuse to challenge one another to the death."

I leaned on my palm. "Okay . . . but why?"

"A master's death at the hand of another master transfers all power to the victor." He flashed a cheerless grin. "My kind seeks power and wealth obsessively, sometimes at any cost."

I nodded. "You *are* a bunch of greedy bastards."

Misha paused at my brutal honesty before chuckling.

"The victors in Europe, Asia, Africa, and Australia have emerged. Through a mutual agreement, they have decided to stay in their respective regions, unwilling to go to war. Yet the leaders of the Americas have yet to be determined." He placed six photos in front of me and pointed to the first four. "Antoinette Malika, Zhahara Nadim, Sofia Rocio, and Roberto Suarez."

The judges from court. I nibbled on my bottom lip, a sense of unease building deep within me. "All masters in the area?"

Misha nodded. "All the masters on the West Coast have settled near Tahoe. They are energized by the magic of the lake."

I rubbed at my arms, knowing what he meant. Tahoe both enlivened and settled my beast. My eyes focused on each photo, only to widen at the picture of a fair-skinned vampire with crew-cut blond hair and dark brown eyes. "Petro. Petro . . . is a *master*?" I picked up the photo and examined it carefully. Petro remained vampire pretty, yes, but something about him seemed so nerdy. It was probably due to his awkwardness. And the damn bow tie didn't help either. I placed the picture back on the table, shaking my head. "He didn't feel strong to me."

Misha stroked his chin. "You are correct. My brother is not as strong as he should be."

That got my attention. "You're *brothers*?" When Petro had said they were of the same family, I presumed he meant Misha had sired him.

"We share the same master." Misha focused on his picture, hints of sadness and shame finding their way into his strong voice. "Petro is not like the others of our station. The only power he appears to possess is the ability to create the undead." He flicked the edges irritably with his fingers. "The grand master considered ending his existence decades ago, embarrassed by his . . . inelegance. Petro's keen intelligence is the only thing that spared him."

Feelings of not belonging poked irritably in my gut. I could relate. So could my sisters. But that didn't mean I'd make Misha aware. "Which grand master?"

Misha pointed to the last picture. "Uri Heinrich. He *turned* me and Petro vampire."

Uri smiled pleasantly in the photo. His short dark hair and well-trimmed beard made him appear dashing, despite the honest-to-God olive green opera cape he wore. Yet a sense of power danced around his photo. If a mere picture did this, his presence would likely knock me out of my sneakers. "Why would your own master try to kill you now? He could have easily stolen your power upon your creation."

Misha leaned back, hurt reflecting from his ominous gray eyes. "It is possible I have lost the grand master's favor." His gaze traveled to each of the pictures, falling lastly upon Uri's. "In the last century, I have gained the potency it took my rivals several centuries to achieve. The wealth I acquired for the grand master and his fondness for me may not spare me from his desire to attain a greater power." He tapped the photo. "And yet if he chooses to strike, I do not believe it would be now. The grand master is patient. He would likely wait until the others and I finish ourselves off so that he may take the champion's collective power."

I went through the pictures again. "Can a vampire cast a bloodlust curse?"

Misha shook his head. "No vampire can work such magic. And as I mentioned, I would have felt it."

My brain searched for a possible solution. Bren had educated us on the supernatural world based on his personal experiences as a werewolf. Prior to meeting Bren, Danny advised us by studying old magic chronicles. Still, there was so much we didn't know. I played with the edges of my hair. "Can a vampire influence another preternatural?"

"Our control works only on humans. And magic from different mystical races cannot be combined. It clashes, with the dominant power ultimately extinguishing the other." He drummed the table impatiently. "I sought an audience with the leader of the local witch clan, but she denied any involvement. Had she lied, I would have sensed it."

I slowly sipped my tea. No matter how I sliced it, Misha was screwed. As a master, he was responsible for the actions of his family. He had no choice; he had to kill his infected vampires.

But he also needed to figure out the cause of the infestation.

I waited to see if he would say more. He didn't. "Why are you telling me this?" I finally asked.

"The first stone has been cast. It is my belief it was done by Zhahara Nadim. She is my closest adversary in both power and business, and maintains the company of a former head witch. Zhahara despises the earth I stand on and has sworn to ruin me any way she can."

I remembered how eager she seemed to dig her vindictive fangs into Misha. Yet, I couldn't hide my grin. "Did you dump her or something?"

Misha didn't answer, but his one-sided smile spoke volumes.

"You *did*, didn't you?" I shuddered. I'd heard of Zhahara, even before being graced with her wicked bitch presence in vamp court. She was considered the Doris Duke of Lake Tahoe—very rich, very elusive, very much someone you stayed away from. "I guess hell hath no fury like a preternatural female scorned."

Misha chuckled. "Is this a warning, my dear?"

"Unless you plan to date me, too, no."

Misha didn't deny it. *Uh. Oh.*

I cleared my throat. I wanted to date a master vampire as much as I wanted to get declawed. "You said you needed my help. What can I do?"

"You can help me invade her home and kill her."

CHAPTER 5

"Why do you regard me in such a manner?"

The "such a manner" Misha referred to included my jaw scraping the floor and my eyes bulging out of my skull. I blinked back at him. "Oh. I'm sorry. I just didn't realize you were nuts."

Misha leaned toward me. "Celia, if Zhahara is behind this, it is now within my rights to destroy her." His body seethed with rage. *"I will not submit to anyone."*

My entire body straightened. Inside me my tigress came to her feet, ready to emerge. The scent of my tension must have reached Misha. He closed his eyes and took a breath. "Forgive me. My anger has nothing to do with you." He focused hard on the photos. "I am certain Zhahara threatens my family. Yet I do not have enough vampires left to fight her. You and your family have no ties to the supernatural world. You're the only ones I can trust. Help me destroy Zhahara, Celia. Help me end the bloodlust."

I leaned away from him and crossed my arms. "What makes you think we could be of any help?"

He paused. His gaze bore into mine with uncomfortable intensity. "Celia, I can feel the power dripping down your body."

I suddenly felt naked again and had to cross my arms over my breasts before speaking. "Why should we help you? You're nothing to us and you almost got us executed."

"The bloodlust infestation forced me to wrongfully seek vengeance. For that I am truly sorry."

"Oh, yeah, I'm sure it's kept you up at night."

I could almost see Misha's anger dissipate. A slow smile spread across his handsome face. He placed his lips close to my ear. "I only did as you would have done in my place, my darling," he murmured.

His breath tickled and gave me chills. I dismissed it as part of his vampire charm. "You don't have to get so close. I can hear you from where you're seated."

Misha's mouth parted; he was apparently confused as to why I didn't immediately straddle him and shove my tongue down his throat. *Geez, hasn't anyone ever told this guy no before?* I stole another glimpse at him. A lock of hair rested against his perfect skin, while his gray eyes sizzled enough to fry my thick lashes. *Okay. Maybe not.*

Misha resumed his more serious demeanor. "Consider this, Celia: Do you think Zhahara will stop after the fall of my family? How many others will she infect, and how many of those will go on to kill innocents? Hundreds, perhaps thousands of lives may be lost—not just vampire, but human, as well. When David attacked Taran, he had just trace beginnings of chronic bloodlust. Were your family merely human, he would have killed you all."

I stood to leave. "This isn't our problem, Misha. Give Destiny a call. Maybe she's free."

Misha motioned for me to sit again. I did so only because his gesture seemed more of a request than an order. "My maid's death and the escalating level of bloodlust within my family obliges the court to prosecute me, despite their conceivable involvement. I have until the next full moon to unearth and eliminate the perpetrator."

I froze. "And if you don't?"

"I will be left with two choices: Kill all my family—infected or not—to eliminate the plague or be condemned to death."

Good God. "So it's either your life or those of your family?"

"Yes."

Whoever cursed Misha's family was hell-bent on destroying him. I glanced back at the photos, understanding why it could easily be one of the judges. Misha's death sentence would be at their hands, therefore granting them his power. If Misha killed his family, he'd also be vulnerable for attack. I didn't know how to respond. If roles were reversed and there was no other choice, I would sacrifice my life to spare my sisters without hesitation. And while masters didn't regard their servants with the same love, there was no mistaking Misha's remorse and fear. It would destroy him to kill his own. Still, all sympathy aside, Misha had no right to drag us into his mess. "What about Petro? You think of him as your brother. Can't he be of help?"

Misha stilled like I suggested something asinine. "Vampires are only as strong as their masters. He and his keep would be devoured like lambs."

He didn't think Petro would be of any help. And he didn't want to jeopardize his existence. Yet he would chance ours. "I'm sorry for what you're going through. But I won't risk my sisters' safety."

Misha's gray eyes darkened. "They are already at risk, Celia. You just fail to see it. My downfall alone will not end the bloodlust."

Hank, the vampire witness from court, came to stand by us. At first, I thought he was attempting to strong-arm me into helping Misha, but he didn't even glance in my direction. "Forgive me for disturbing you, Master."

Misha kept his eyes on me. "What is it?"

"Aric Connor is on the phone. He wishes a word with you."

"The mongrel can wait. Do not interrupt me again."

The "mongrel" apparently heard him. Cursing and growling in a strangely familiar timbre erupted from the cell phone. My inner beast jerked and I rubbed my chest, expecting it to hurt. I didn't know this Aric guy, but he obviously didn't fear Misha.

Hank disconnected the call and stalked away. Misha leaned back in his seat, unaffected. He tapped a finger against the table, apparently considering what to say. Several awkward seconds passed before he spoke again. "Celia, you are so young. You cannot fathom what it is to watch your family die."

I swallowed hard. "Actually, I can." He frowned, but his eyes softened upon taking in my appearance. My back was rigid, my fists clenched, and I readied to pounce. Everything about me screamed, *Fight, attack, maul—everything—*except my eyes. Recalling my parents' deaths betrayed the sadness I always kept hidden, an emotion I refused to allow Misha to witness. "You put us through hell, Misha. You can't expect flowers and gifts and flirting to erase such a threat. Just as you can't expect us to drop everything to help your cause."

I stood to leave, but not before Misha clasped my hand and kissed it. "Make certain the decision you reach is a just one," he whispered. It wasn't a threat—at least, I didn't take it that way. They were more the words of a desperate man, or, as I reminded myself firmly, a desperate vampire.

CHAPTER 6

My sisters arrived home from the hospital shortly after my run. I failed to find the wolf again. Any other gal would have moved on. But I wasn't any other gal. And those dreamy brown eyes belonged to no mere man.

Taran yanked off her scrubs in the middle of our family room, anxious to get out of her work clothes. I'd once overheard a coworker making fun of us for being nurses. "God, they are so codependent," she'd complained. "They can't even have separate careers."

Screw her. She didn't know becoming nurses at a young age helped Taran and me gain custody of our sisters following the death of our foster mother.

Emme moved slower than usual, appearing lost in her thoughts. "You okay, Emme?" I asked.

She nodded. "Mr. Luther died today."

Emme cared for the terminally ill. She used her gift to grant her patients a peaceful good-bye. And with her honey blond hair, fair skin, and soft green eyes, perhaps her patients envisioned her as their own personal angel welcoming them into heaven.

"I'm sorry, sweetie."

"It's okay. He's been telling me he was ready to go and see his wife." She lay on the couch with me and leaned her head against my shoulder as I hugged her. "Shayna had a delivery today. It's a reminder, you know. Life does go on."

Shayna grinned my way. "The family said you delivered their first child and wanted me to tell you hi."

Shayna's positive and cheerful personality made her the ideal person to help women through the stress and pain of labor. My favorite part was the delivery. I loved babies. The best part of my job was handing a mother her child for the first time. But it also made me a little sad. Children in my future didn't seem possible without a father.

Taran swore as she undid her hair. "If I ever consider working an extra shift, just shoot me. Some idiot overbooked the cardiac lab by three patients. And I was the only one who could start an IV. Seriously, what are they teaching these bitches in nursing school these days?" Out of all of us, Taran seemed an unlikely Florence Nightingale. But she knew her stuff. And after taking care of our foster mother, she had a soft spot for the elderly.

Taran took the last pin out of her hair and fluffed her dark waves against her shoulders. "What did you do today, Ceel?"

"I went out with Misha. Bloodlust has plagued his home. He's had to kill twelve of his vampires, but not before one drained his poor human maid. He has until the next full moon to discover the cause or be sentenced to death. Oh, and get this: He wants me to help him kill the master vampire he thinks is responsible."

Nothing like a little supernatural drama to shut up a bunch of chatty girls.

"Well, *shit*," Taran finally said. "I think we could all use a drink."

Between the tripped-out supernatural paparazzi, the severely deranged infected vampires, and my fixation on a steamy werewolf, the last thing I wanted to do was party. But seeing as I was actually considering helping one master vamp kill another, then yeah, a few beers might not be a bad idea.

I preferred to dress for comfort rather than fashion. Yet I'd allowed Taran to shove me into her Rodeo Drive–meets-Vegas clothing and adorn me with cosmetics—just to get her off my case about possibly helping Misha. It worked.

She and Shayna happily glided ahead of us through the sea of gyrating bodies at the Watering Hole. I wrapped my arm around Emme and led her through the rough crowd. Humans naturally avoided the path of a tigress, despite my five-foot-three-inch frame, but these selfish drunks would trample anyone as tiny and passive as Emme.

Dance music pounded harder than the feet hitting the floor to Gaga's latest. We ambled to the rear bar, where Bren was talking to two women. He winked one of his blue eyes when his werewolf nose picked up our scent. "Hey, babes. Take a seat!" He motioned to a booth a buxom brunette and her male escort had just abandoned.

"My goodness. That girl is so popular. Every time I see her, she has a different date."

I supposed Emme missed the dance party in the guy's pants. "She's a prostitute, Emme."

Emme did a double take. "She can't be. She dresses nicely and lives in Tahoe."

Taran laughed. We'd caught up and were close enough to be heard. "That's because the skank charges more than we make in a week, Emme. Her biggest problems are sore knees and her growing immunity to penicillin."

"Why would her knees—"

Emme's deep blush told me she figured it out. Thank God. I wasn't a "you can ask me anything" type of gal.

We were about to sit when two girls jumped into the booth. I wouldn't have cared as much if they hadn't knocked Emme aside in the process. The closest one paled as she caught sight of me. She yanked her friend's arm and quickly found someplace else to be. Bren joined us, drinks in hand. He handed me a Corona with a lime before taking one for himself and having a seat next to me. "Nice scowl, Ceel. I think you actually made the brunette mess her pants."

I watched them until they disappeared. "I barely looked at them."

Bren rubbed at his dark scruffy beard as he laughed. "Trust me, babe. Even your subtle glances are scary as hell."

He took a long pull on his beer and draped his arm around me. I leaned against him. "Is Danny coming?"

"No. He's in Santa Barbara at some stick-up-your-ass science convention, trying to get laid."

I quirked a brow. "You can get laid at a science convention?"

Bren chuckled. "I could. I don't think Dan can. He's trying to bang some biochemist working in the research lab next to his. For his sake, I hope she's as hot as he claims. His last lay could scare Christ off the cross."

I almost choked on my beer. Bren and Danny were the ultimate odd couple. Danny was human, neat, book smart, and hardworking. Bren was a *lone* werewolf, a slob, liked porn, and never woke before noon. And yet they remained the best of friends. Bren would take a bullet for Danny.

Bren grinned as he watched me take another a sip of my Corona. "It's good to see you out, babe. It's been too long."

I shrugged. "I needed to get my mind off things." *Too much laundry, stress at work, crazy vampires hiding in bushes waiting to eat us . . .*

"No kidding," Taran muttered.

Bren narrowed his eyes at me. "Celia, you're not seriously thinking about getting involved with all that vampire shit, are you?"

"How did you . . ." Shayna suddenly felt the need to concentrate on her martini. "Shayna! You told him?"

Bren chuckled. "I called while you were in the shower. All I did was ask her what was new and she sang like a canary." He shook his head. "The master vamp assholes are trying to off each other. Let them. But keep your skinny ass out of it. Nothing good ever comes from playing with leeches."

I straightened. "I'm not playing. I'm totally serious."

Bren's typically jovial spirit vanished. "So is this blood-lust shit. If some vamp is fucked-up enough to release that poison, she's not going to care who gets in the way."

"But isn't that more of a reason to stop her?" I argued.

"The hell it is. Leave that to pack *weres*. It's their goddamn duty to guard the world from all the mystical evil shit."

I didn't agree with Bren, but I also didn't want us to fight. And neither did Emme. She tugged on Bren's "I heart Tahoe babes" T-shirt. "Guess what, Bren. Celia has a boyfriend."

I sighed. "Misha is *not* my boyfriend."

Emme's jaw dropped. "I meant that wolf you met on the beach."

"Oh . . . him. He's not . . . I mean, I don't even know him." I squirmed a little, wondering why my body suddenly felt so hot.

Taran's all-knowing smirk inched its way across her face. God, I hated that smirk. "No. But you want to. *Really* want to." She danced her eyebrows. "Don't you, Ceel?"

I stiffened. "I'm not sure I know what you mean." Bren laughed out loud. I couldn't blame him. I was a horrible liar. Discussing a male I'd only been able to fantasize about bordered on pathetic—considering my sisters frequently enjoyed the company of real-life suitors.

Shayna shifted her weight excitedly in her seat. Her face beamed, her butt bounced, and her finger pointed directly in my face. "You've been running every day, twice a day, since seeing that wolf. Don't think we've been falling for that, 'Ooh, I have to go shopping again. Does anyone need anything from the store?'" She nibbled on her lip. "So . . . have you seen him?"

"No." Despite my marathon-length runs, I hadn't caught one whiff of that wolf's addicting aroma. Even if I had, I wouldn't have known what to do. Mostly I just wanted to see him again. And hoped maybe he would approach me.

My faced burned hotter, especially when my sisters grinned my way. It seemed strange how the mere thought of the wolf brought an easy smile to my face.

Taran winked at me. "Ceel, we *have* to find that big, bad wolf."

"Bren! What the hell are you doing?" Bren's boss screamed at him from the bar.

"I'm on break, Paul!" Bren shouted back.

"Break's over, dipshit. Get back to work!"

Bren rolled his eyes and returned to his station at the bar. Immediately a cluster of women with horrendous boob jobs swarmed him. If Bren weren't so popular with the ladies, Paul would have fired him years ago.

I'd barely finished my third beer when a small pack of wolves in their human forms entered the club. Every vertebra in my spine stiffened, hoping *he* walked among them. My shoulders slumped with disappointment when my wolf failed to appear. Still, I couldn't relax. The powerhouse pack tingled my senses like a shock wave.

The wolves stalked across the crush of dancers toward the bar, shoulder-to-shoulder, moving smoothly as one. The human patrons perceptibly sensed the wolves' dominance at a primal level. Some gawked; others cuddled closer to their partners. Most scrambled out of their way. A few of the brave straightened, growing wary of the sudden danger.

Bloodlust, supernatural stalkers, and werewolves. What was next? Locusts and four horsemen? Taran's irises briefly turned white. "Celia, three *weres* are coming toward us."

"I know. I picked up their scent." My tigress instinctively growled. The wolves' collective power had been strong enough to change Taran's eye color and send my tigress's territorial instincts into overdrive.

"Good grief, they're huge. Are they the same ones from the beach?" Emme asked, sounding hopeful.

I shook my head. "No, they don't look familiar."

The *weres* didn't need to do more than glance at the guys sitting across from us, and the six guys crowding the booth vacated fast. The *weres* claimed the space and watched us closely once they picked up *our* scent, ignoring Bren's watchful gaze from the bar.

Weres didn't typically attack, but that didn't mean I'd turn my back on them. They were tall, over six feet, with the large chests and lean muscles typical of wolves. One was Native American, with long, loose black hair that hung past his shoulder blades. He was good-looking in an "I'll rip your throat out in one bite" kind of way. But his most prominent feature was his eyes. They reminded me of the start of a dangerous storm, a turbulent brown that bordered on black. The *were* sitting next to him was Asian, possibly Japanese. He had short black hair and a thin, well-trimmed goatee. And unlike his friends, who wore jeans and T-shirts, he'd dressed in slacks and a button-down shirt with the sleeves rolled up. He was handsome in a stoic way. His presence held a sense of calm, but his dark almond eyes remained vigilant.

The third wolf reminded me of a rock star. If he were on a stage, girls would've thrown their panties at him. His messy blond, spiky hair must have required a lot of hair gel to perfect. He carried a definite edge, but his face possessed a boyish charm. I glanced around to see what had made him smile. I knew we were in trouble when I caught Emme blushing and smiling back.

Oh, crap.

Part of me wanted to grab her and run when he approached our table. Instead, I remained still, despite the rise in my hackles and the growl rumbling in my throat.

To add to my unease, the other two *weres* exchanged glances and followed.

"Hi," he said to Emme. "I'm Liam, Liam Smith." He nodded toward the Asian. "This is Gem, and that ray of sunshine over there is Miakoda."

"I go by Koda," the Native American said. He shot Liam a snarl that caused my claws to protrude, but Liam ignored him.

Emme smiled so sweetly at Liam, I feared the poor sap might need insulin. "I'm Emme Wird. These are my sisters, Celia, Taran, and Shayna."

No one said anything at first. Koda, Gem, and I were too busy sizing each other up. If it came down to it, I thought Bren and I could take them in a fight.

Liam remained oblivious to the tension. "Would you like to dance with me, Emme?" he asked, extending his hand.

"Sure." She strolled off before I could stop her.

Shayna, who could sense the growing strain between Koda and me, intervened. "How about a dance, big guy?" she asked.

This broke Koda's eye contact with me, and he seemed genuinely surprised. "Are you talking to me?"

Shayna's grin lit up her face. "Well, duh. I'm looking right at you, dude."

It wouldn't have shocked me if no one had ever asked Koda to dance before. He was a scary mo-fo of epic proportions. Shayna wriggled to the edge of the seat to leave, but not before I shoved the toothpick from her martini into her hand. She giggled and kissed my cheek. "Don't worry, Ceel," she whispered, glancing at Koda from the corner of her eyes. "I've got this one."

Koda moved aside to let her out of the booth. Shayna

grabbed his hand and led him out to the floor like a well-trained poodle rather than a two-hundred-and-fifty-pound werewolf. I couldn't believe it. Taming someone like that was impressive even for her.

I turned to Taran, who had been unusually quiet. Gem slid into the booth next to her. They stared into each other's eyes, but not in a challenging way. Most guys gawked at Taran. I was used to that. Yet the way Gem stared at her wasn't sexual; it was tender, and it put me on edge. I couldn't understand what the hell was going on, but thought it best to run interference.

"So, what kind of name is Gem, anyway?" I asked, trying to rip his eyes off my sister.

"My nickname is Gemini. My real name is Tomo Hamamatsu."

"Is that your astrological sign or something?"

He returned his gaze to Taran. "Something like that," he muttered.

Taran said nothing. Hell, she barely breathed.

I pinched the bridge of my nose. *Another fun night out with the girls.*

I enjoyed a good paranormal romance as much as the next gal, but there was only so much lovey-dovey crap I could take. After fifteen minutes of watching Taran and Gemini reenact the last few seconds of *Ghost*, I left to take a seat at the bar.

The brunette flirting with Bren scowled at me the moment I slumped onto the stool. I slammed my purse onto the bar, tired of dealing with petty bitches. "Do you have a problem?"

Bren groaned when the tramp ran like I'd set her sequined miniskirt on fire. He shoved a lime into another

Corona and handed it to me. "Are you trying to ruin my chances of getting laid?"

I played with the bottle. "Sorry. It just sucks to always be the one without a date."

My stomach clenched with the immediate sadness my words brought me. I hated admitting how lonely I was.

Or how badly I wanted to fall in love.

Bren leaned forward. "Ceel, you have a killer body and are smarter than hell." He grinned. "You're also beautiful. And you don't even fucking know it." He reclaimed the beer, took a swig, then handed it back. "But you know what your problem is?"

"I scare people?"

"Yes. Shitless. But that's not what I meant." He sighed. "You haven't found anyone who can compete with the strength of your beast." His smile faded. "You need to find your equal, babe."

I glanced back at Taran and the wolf she'd so easily enthralled. "What if I can't?"

Bren didn't answer me. He may not have known how much I longed to be in the strong arms of a man who wanted to share his life and passion with me. But he did know better than to give me false hope. I downed my beer and went to the bathroom. When I came out, Bren's floozies were once again throwing themselves at him. I didn't want to continue to bug him, so I left the bar area to check on my remaining sisters.

Shayna ripped it up on the dance floor. She laughed as she moved, totally showing off. Koda surprisingly kept up with her. He appeared to be having fun, but I still wouldn't have jumped for joy at the sight of him in a dark alley. When a couple of guys stopped to watch Shayna, one glimpse from Koda sent them scurrying toward the exit.

Emme and Liam faced each other along the far wall. They weren't dancing, but they stood pretty damn close. Liam stroked the side of her cheek and spoke softly while she smiled shyly at him.

Liam didn't appear threatening, but I didn't want Emme to forget he was a *were*. I slunk around a few guys dancing until I reached Emme. She jumped when I tapped her shoulder. I barely blinked before Liam took a protective stance in front of her. He laughed, and patted my head when he saw it was just little ol' me.

I would have drop-kicked him had it not been for his next comment. "Sorry, kid. By the way Emme jumped, I thought someone was trying to hurt her."

I couldn't believe it. Liam had only just met Emme, and he was already prepared to stomp ass in her defense.

Emme peeked around Liam's big body. "Hi, Celia." She frowned when she caught my surprised expression. "Is everything all right, sweetie?"

She was obviously in safe hands with this wolf. "Um. Yeah. Listen, I'm hot. I'll be out by the lake if you need me."

Emme nodded, but appeared concerned. Liam patted my head. Again. "Don't worry, kid. I'll watch out for her."

"You'd better," I said in a low growl that clearly meant business.

Liam laughed and turned back to Emme, whose eyes widened with alarm at my "I may have to pummel your date's ass" scowl. I didn't gut Liam only out of respect for Emme, but that didn't mean I'd wait around for another pat on the head.

And what did he mean by "kid"? I stormed away. *Patronizing asshole.*

The music switched from the floor-shaking "In the

Ayer" to the soft, aching melody of "Lightning Crashes." From where I stood, Shayna beamed expectantly at the mountainous Koda. Surprisingly, the smooth wolf dancing so effortlessly moments before glanced down awkwardly at my beautiful sister with the dazzling grin. He froze, his eyes searching hers, but failed to act.

Shayna carefully slipped his mammoth arms around her slender waist. Koda hesitated briefly before smiling softly and bending forward. Shayna encircled his neck. And just like that, they became one. It was a perfect choreographed moment in time. One that shouldn't have been so difficult to watch.

But it was. Regardless of how much I didn't want it to be.

I could have come to the club in one of my many slip dresses or in a nice pair of jeans and a sweater. Instead I'd allowed Taran to dress and accessorize me like a ridiculous Barbie doll.

And it hadn't made a difference.

I walked out of the club and into the night.

And I kept on walking.

CHAPTER 7

Damn it.

The almost full moon gleamed against the dark blue night. Time was running out for Misha . . . and for Tahoe if the impending bloodlust crisis wasn't contained. My steps turned slow and cautious at the thought.

I'd told Emme I'd be out by the water if she needed me. But she didn't need me. She had a guardian of the earth on her arm. I sent her a quick text letting her know I was going home. I needed to mull over Misha's proposition.

My focus remained ahead, away from the noisy street where the upscale clubs along the lake battled it out for the rush of new tourists . . . in time to see Petro exit one of the five-star restaurants. Two high-priced call girls led him toward his white limo. His eyes widened upon seeing me, and, despite the illumination of the fluorescent streetlights, I could see his face redden.

I pretended I hadn't noticed him or his dates. Women likely washed Misha's feet with their own hair. And there was Petro, master vampire, forced to pay for sex.

A throng of twenty-somethings, chatting and laughing with excitement, hurried across to where the velvet ropes awaited. Valets turned away perturbed drivers attempting to pull in, claiming the lots had reached maximum capacity. I alone moved against the restless crowd and crossed the street, seeking solace from the increasing madness.

I shoved my way through a mob of pedestrians, their large numbers spilling out of the crosswalk.

And that's when it hit me: the familiar scent of fire, earth, and water crashing over stones. My knees buckled and I almost fell. The wolf from my run stalked toward me, a blond bombshell, with a Victoria Beckham bob, fastened to his arm. She spoke to him, but he didn't appear to listen. His head snapped up and his eyes widened the moment he saw me. A few anxious tourists circled around him as his pace slowed. The blonde tugged on his arm, her voice garbled as if she were speaking underwater. Yet he failed to acknowledge her, keeping his gaze firmly fixed on mine.

The blonde's tugging became more urgent as our steps converged, her muffled voice becoming louder. "Are you listening? What the hell's wrong with you?"

Ten more steps. The wolf's piercing gaze intensified.

Five more steps. The sounds of the street disappeared.

One step . . .

His brown eyes blazed with fire.

My neck craned and my body whipped around as we passed, refusing to leave the forceful grip of those eyes.

I stopped.

And so did he.

A couple of drunks bumped into me as I remained cemented in the middle of the street. The wolf stood only a few feet away, but it felt like miles. More people brushed past us, their steps quickening until everyone had cleared the street.

Everyone but the three of us.

The blond she-wolf with him glanced openmouthed back and forth between us, her shock swiftly turning to fury. She growled, deep, hard, and deadly. *"Mine."*

My jaw slackened. *Yours?* Her words pierced me like the sharp edge of a knife. *He's . . . yours?*

A deafening car horn made me jolt. I was blocking traffic and didn't even know it. More cars joined in, their angry horns making my sensitive ears burn. In a painful rush, the full cadence of the city overloaded my senses. I stumbled and kept moving. This time I didn't look back.

I hustled for five blocks in the torture devices Taran called shoes, shaken by what had just happened.

Did he do something to me? That didn't make sense. The wolf appeared just as freaked as I was. *Aw, hell.* Could I have done something to him?

I shook my head to clear it and forced the experience from my mind. *It doesn't matter, Celia. He's not yours to take.*

The thought alone made me slow down. But what had I expected? Someone that striking would never know a lonely night.

I slipped off Taran's deadly interpretation of footwear and called a cab. The cold sidewalk alleviated the aching of my swollen feet, but it was no match for the sense of longing the wolf had caused. I paused and lifted my hair, willing myself to calm, and hoping the brisk night air would whisk away the evening's frustrations.

It didn't work. As much as I dreamed of seeing him again, I never imagined it would be on the arm of another female. Disappointment beat shock into submission.

When the cab arrived almost forty minutes later, I crept into it, disturbed by the unusual ache gnawing at my chest.

"Where to, lady?" the cabbie asked.

"Dollar Point."

The portly cabbie adjusted his baseball cap, but didn't bother to turn around. Most of the hair he had left hung from his ears. "Sixty bucks," Prince Charming muttered. He jumped when he caught my scowl in the rearview mirror. "I have to charge more when I cross the state line!"

"It's less than twelve miles away."

"I don't make the rules, lady. I'm just trying to put bread on the table."

I slumped in my seat. "Fine."

Sixty bucks for a sixteen-minute ride in a car that reeked of stale cigarettes and armpit. I rolled down the window for some fresh air and debated whether to return to The Hole—not for my sisters, they were fine— but to get another glimpse of those steamy baby browns. I abandoned the idea. His girlfriend wouldn't be happy. Not that I blamed her. If he were mine, and some girl tried to—

The metallic scent of blood burned through my nose.

"Stop the car!"

"What?"

I shoved my feet back into Taran's death traps. "Stop the car *now*!"

The cabbie pulled to the side. I bolted out before he finished parking. "Hey, wait. You have to pay!"

I raced toward the scent of death and spilled blood

saturating an alleyway between a hair salon and a bookstore. Taran's shoes dug into my tender feet like white-hot needles, but I didn't stop, propelled by the need to investigate the dread plaguing the starlit night.

But when I stumbled into the alley, my pace slowed to a crawl.

There wasn't a body there.

There were two.

Both women. Both young. Both with clothes splattered with their own blood. Their broken bodies lay near a Dumpster, amid a scattered field of discarded newspaper and tabloid magazines.

I wished fang marks had pierced their necks. Fang marks would have been welcome. Instead chunks of serrated flesh hollowed through to the vertebra, like a hungry dog had chewed down to the bone.

Except it hadn't been a dog.

Their bodies were nothing more than sunken shells of gray shriveled skin over bone and withered muscle, drained of the blood that once nourished their organs and allowed them to breathe, laugh . . . live.

One of the women, a dark brunette, rested with hips twisted in the opposite direction from her torso, her eyes wide with blatant terror and pain. She probably would have screamed. But you needed a throat and vocal cords to scream. She had neither, just portions of mutilated flesh.

My heart stopped when I caught sight of the petite honey blonde with long wavy hair. *Jesus.* She could have been my Emme.

Heavy footsteps echoed behind me. I whipped around, growling.

The cabbie stumbled to a halt, falling to his knees and

panting heavily. His stark white face traveled from my protruding fangs to the dead women at my feet. He staggered backward. "Don't hurt me. . . . I didn't see anything. I-I-I didn't see anything."

I retracted my claws and scary teeth. "I'm not going to hurt—"

The cabbie shook his head feverishly. "I didn't see anything!" He stumbled to his feet, slamming into a garbage can in his haste to get away. Large empty bottles of hair product bounced and rolled onto the concrete behind the terrified cabbie. His heavy legs pumped until he skidded around the dark corner and disappeared.

I reached for my phone and just stared at it, unsure who to call. An infected vampire was on the loose. More people would die. Bren would race down here to be with me, but then what would we do? Calling the police seemed appropriate . . . if I were dealing with any run-of-the-mill psycho serial killer.

Shit.

My fingers swept across my touch screen, searching for Misha's phone number. In my haste, I continued to hit the wrong contact. Twice I dialed my manager at work. *Yeah, like Maureen would charge to the rescue.* I took a breath to steady my thundering heart and finally pushed the right button.

The phone rang once, twice.

"Hello?" a sleepy female's voice purred.

I hung up.

Shit. Shit. Shit. And that's when it hit me. Pack *weres*, like the ones with my sisters, guarded the earth from mystical evil. My eyes skimmed over the women and their mummified physiques. *Oh, yeah. I think this qualifies.*

I hit the speed dial. *Come on, come—*

A rush of fury, sweat, and fresh blood swept in from the entranceway.

And that's when I knew I was no longer alone.

"Don't. Move." The deep voice sounded more animal than human. But screw him—I moved anyway, crouching with arms and claws out.

Two *weres* the size of my refrigerator lurked at the mouth of the alley, their stances wide, blocking my escape. Tears and gashes covered their T-shirts and jeans. Blood and drool caked their chests. They marched toward me, fists clenched, growls low and deep.

I glanced down at the bodies, no longer certain an infected vamp had feasted.

I tried to swallow back a growl. It didn't work. "I don't want any trouble."

"Too late for that, sweetheart. Chris, she's yours. We'll cover you."

We'll?

A wolf leaped over the far brick wall with the fluid ease of an eel in water. Except I'd rather have taken on an eel. Four hundred pounds of pissed-off lupine with midnight black fur stalked toward me baring his razor-sharp fangs.

He charged. Goddamn it, he was fast.

But tigers are faster than wolves.

I pivoted, digging my claws into the nape of his neck and his back. With a grunt, I used the wolf's momentum to propel him headfirst into the wall. The entire building rumbled, chunks of brick fell like hail, and a crack the size of my wrist split the mortar above his head. He shuddered once and slumped, his head firmly fixed to the building.

I'd expected more of a fight. And so had his buddies.

They exchanged shocked expressions and paused, trying to calculate their next move. I used their momentary confusion to race toward the wall. In a single bound, my hands grasped the ledge of the wall. Before I could throw my legs over, one of the wolves grabbed my ankle. I kicked with my free leg. Agonized howls blasted through the night. I made contact, yet he wouldn't release his grip. He fell back and took me with him. We landed hard with me on top. My one-hundred-and-ten-pound frame wasn't enough to knock the wind out of him, but my jabs to his gut were.

His friend, a redhead, hauled me off, yanking my arm painfully behind my back and dislocating it from my shoulder. I roared and raked my remaining stiletto down his shin, stomping it into his instep. My dominant right arm hung uselessly at my side, but my left connected straight up to his jaw, silencing his pained howls. The second he loosened his hold I *shifted*.

My body, clothing, and anyone I took along for the ride dissolved into minute particles, sliding through soil or concrete as easily as sand through a colander. The downside? I couldn't breathe or see.

By luck I sprang up as the wolf twisted his back to me, his fists up, his head scanning the alley. I kicked him squarely across the knee. Bone crunched on impact and he fell with a sickening splat. My instep connected with the back of his skull before his buddy with the Mohawk tackled me to the ground. Taran's shoe remained firmly nailed to his face, perhaps a disturbingly comical sight to some. Not to me. I roared when his weight sent jolts of agony into my shoulder like the rapid bullets from a gun. I *shifted* down and across the cement floor, my lungs out of breath, screaming for air.

Thank God I'd moved far enough. I resurfaced on my back and scrambled to my feet. Mohawk growled and swore, furious. My *shifting* had left him fused to the concrete from the elbows down. He kicked his legs uselessly.

"Stupid bitch!"

I kicked him in the face, snapping his jaw. *"Watch your mouth."*

The redhead rebounded unexpectedly and swung at my face. I dropped my head to avoid him, but he managed to graze me. The force from his powerful blow sent me spinning. He came at me again and again, legs and arms swinging like a blizzard of windmills. I dodged and scooted, off balance from the shoe still attached to my foot, my ineffective arm, and the horrid ringing in my ears.

The redhead's speed remained quick, but hasty. The moment I saw an opening, I spun and grated my back claws against his stomach. His bowels spilled like overdone spaghetti. I'd barely gasped at the sight when a more dangerous predator blindsided me at full velocity.

My back slammed against the wall and my eyes locked onto the fierce gaze of my opponent. "What *are* you?" asked the wolf with the smoldering brown eyes.

CHAPTER 8

Oh, my God.

The wolf pressed the weight of his powerful form against mine, his forearm glued to my chest. But the pure intensity of his presence was what held me in place. I didn't dare *shift*, move, breathe. My mind froze, unable to concentrate on anything but him.

The fierceness of his eyes softened as a phenomenal heat surged across the length of his arm and into my body, electrifying my already racing pulse. I shuddered.

And so did he.

The wolf abruptly released me. I stumbled, off balance and undeniably freaked out. He reached to catch me, but I staggered away.

Blood and ash saturated his long-sleeved shirt, and a chunk of fabric hung loose over his bloody right thigh. I swallowed hard, awestruck as the damaged muscle knitted together and re-formed into new pink flesh.

I staggered back two more steps. He followed, palms out. "Don't be afraid. I'm not going to hurt you," he whispered.

His deep voice hummed with soft reassurance. I wanted to believe him, but his soaked shirt and the attack by his pack cautioned me against it. And yet despite all the danger and my growing trepidation, my tigress settled into a strange sense of calm.

"What are you doing?" Mohawk screamed. *"Kill her!"*

The wolf's spine straightened as rigid as a steel pole. "Does she smell like a vampire?"

Mohawk stopped his snarls, but exhaled in short, angry spurts. *"No."*

The wolf continued to watch me. "Then I will not harm her—and neither will you."

I didn't know why he felt obliged to defend me. He didn't know me. Didn't he see I could defend myself?

The wolf let out a breath and extended his hand. "I'm Aric Connor."

I gasped softly. Aric was the same wolf who had called Misha. When I stared at his palm like an idiot he slowly dropped it to his side. He eyed me a moment longer before withdrawing. The wolf I'd embedded into the wall stirred and whimpered. The Mohawk guy still anchored to the concrete spat with rage, "Watch your back, Aric!"

Aric ignored him and the black wolf, and focused on the redhead. The wolf sat with his legs sprawled, frantically trying to stuff his bowels back into his abdomen. "Tommy. *Stop*. You need to quiet and focus."

Tommy immediately ceased his desperate efforts. His hands shook as moist intestines continued to spill over his arms and through his fingers.

"Good. Now breathe. Slowly. Become one with your wolf and allow him to heal you."

Tommy trembled, but nodded and closed his eyes.

Like a reverse tug-of-war, Tommy's body pulled in his battered insides like a child sucking in long strands of pasta. It was hard to watch and hear. The bile in my stomach rose brutally, but I wouldn't pry my eyes off my attackers.

When the last of Tommy's parts found their way home, a thin transparent film formed over the deep gashes. But unlike Aric's, the skin would not seal shut. Tommy buckled onto his side, panting and sweating, onto a heap of bloodied newspapers. Aric removed his navy shirt and tied it firmly around the wolf's lesions, leaving a small gray tee to keep him covered against the brisk night air. He clasped Tommy's shoulder. "Don't worry. This will keep your wound closed until you've had time to mend."

Tommy nodded, curling into a protective ball. Aric left him and took in the scene. He sniffed the air, tracking the small droplets of splattered blood until they morphed into angular streaks along the corpses. He motioned to the honey blonde. "The vamp bit her first. And broke the other's spine when she tried to flee."

"How . . . how do you know he killed the blonde f-first?" Tommy stammered.

Aric inhaled deeply. "The blood on her clothes is a full minute drier."

Mohawk gasped. "That vamp drained her in under a minute?"

Aric nodded. "The bloodlust in his system had advanced, making his appetite more voracious." He leaned over the brunette's face. "Did you see her teeth? They're pushed in. He covered her mouth to keep her from screaming while he finished his first meal."

Aric circled the women, frowning. He bent and examined their remains. "The bodies are already in rigor." His scowl deepened as he inhaled. "The bastard didn't leave them one ounce of blood." He reached for the cell phone in his back pocket and made a brief call. "It's Aric. I've got two more in an alley near Northwood Boulevard and McCourry. Tommy's hurt. I'll need him transported."

"We're on our way," someone said on the other end.

The midnight black wolf yanked his head free in a crash of falling rubble. With a roar he bolted toward me, teeth bared.

"*Don't touch her*," Aric warned.

The wolf stopped his onslaught as quick as a flick of a switch. Good for him. I was done taking shit.

The kid with the Mohawk whose eye I had, well, gouged out, flipped. "Why are you defending her? For all you know she's in league with the bloodluster!"

"I am not!" I snarled.

Tommy, the redhead, scowled despite the worsening color of his skin. "We saw you standing over them. We know you're not human." His upper lip curled. "And you're sure as hell not one of us."

Aric narrowed his eyes, his voice bordering on rage. "*Use your goddamn noses.*"

Mohawk shook his head violently. Taran's shoe flew off his face, leaving a big, gaping, bloody hole. None of the wolves reacted. I was ready to hurl. "Aric, she can do things," Mohawk insisted. "Maybe she can cover her lies, too. For shit's sake, look at what she did to my freaking arms!"

Aric must have thought Mohawk merely lay on his elbows. His eyes widened when he saw the idiot's limbs fixed to the concrete. He frowned. "What are you?" he asked again.

My growls would not be silenced. "It's none of your business what or who I am. I've done nothing wrong!"

Police sirens screeched in the far distance. Aric leaned back on his heels. "Maybe not. But I would ask that you fix my student."

Aric's words slapped the PMS right out of me. "*Students? These are students?*"

"They're supposed to graduate this spring." Aric's gaze swept over my petite frame before frowning back at his boys. "Now I'm not so sure they're ready."

Fantastic. I seriously thought I'd whooped ass. Here all I'd done was beat up a bunch of high schoolers. My eyes took in their tall, burly forms . . . and baby faces. I groaned, humiliated. *Maybe I could take on Justin Bieber for an encore.* Their movements during our rumble had been more choreographed than reflexive—like they'd spent a lot of time sparring and very little time in actual brawls. That should have been my first stupid clue. I limped toward my *shifting* victim.

Mohawk growled hideously, but Aric's glower immediately silenced his audible protests.

My head shot toward Aric; I was confused as to why he continued to defend me. He didn't know me. *I* was the protector. *I* didn't need protecting. Still, if I abandoned his pack mate, it would take nothing short of a jackhammer to free him.

My good hand reached cautiously toward one of Mohawk's long spikes. "Don't move. It will only take a moment." I concentrated briefly and *shifted* him out of the concrete as easily as if he'd lain in a puddle of water. Mohawk jerked, staring at his arms in terror, as if he'd expected to be amputated.

Aric tilted his head, examining me closely. I grasped

my injured arm defensively, convinced he'd already labeled me a freak. So when he gave me an approving nod, it caught me by surprise. And so did the kindness in his voice. "Thank you for releasing him."

Mohawk's outrage masked the drying scent of blood and garbage from the Dumpster. "Why are you thanking her? She could have killed us!"

Aric faced him. Immediately the Taylor Lautner poser dropped his gaze and moved back. "If she wanted to kill you, she would have ripped off your heads or torn out your hearts," Aric hissed. "But she didn't—even after you attacked without cause. Don't blame her because she tried to defend herself!"

Aric's protectiveness heated my face with humility. I wasn't used to anyone watching out for me, and I knew it was wrong to want it—*especially* from a male. I growled, furious and overwhelmed with the need to explain. "I wouldn't have touched any of you if you hadn't jumped me. Never once did you ask me what happened!"

Aric moved away from his wolves and faced me again. "What did happen?"

I tightened my hold around my arm. "I was taking a cab home." I glanced at the poor women who would never again watch the sun rise. "I smelled . . . *death* and leaped out of the cab to investigate. They were already like this when I found them."

Aric pointed to the cabbie's baseball cap on the littered ground. "Who does that belong to?"

My tigress made us notoriously vigilant and yet I hadn't noticed the cap. Probably since I'd been preoccupied fighting for my life. "It's the cabbie's. He chased me, but then ran away when he saw their bodies."

Aric turned to the black wolf. "Find him."

The black wolf sniffed the cap and disappeared, becoming one with the night. The blasts of sirens inched closer, adding to my distress. My head jerked back to Aric. "Where is he going?"

"To find your driver. Otherwise, you may get blamed for the murders." He frowned. "What's wrong with your arm?"

"It's dislocated."

"I suspected as much. It's hung limp since I saw you. Why haven't you healed?"

I backed away, averting my gaze. "I mend at a human's pace."

Aric's eyes widened slightly before he stalked toward the wolves. "Tell me what you smelled when you caught her scent."

Tommy wrinkled his nose. "I don't know. She smelled weird."

Aric's tone lowered an octave. "Did you scent any of the victims' blood on her?"

The wolves exchanged glances, understanding softening their deep-set scowls. "No," Mohawk replied. "But she stood right next to them—and she's not human."

Aric loomed over them. "You attacked an innocent bystander! Just because her scent is unfamiliar does not make her your enemy." He motioned toward my arm. "Look at her. Her body has not healed. Had you cast a fatal blow you would have ended her life." Aric shook his head and scoffed. "There is no excuse for your actions."

The young wolves dropped their heads. "Sorry, Aric," they mumbled.

"It's not me you owe an apology to!"

The young wolves sought to kill me, and continued to

disrespect me. While I didn't like it, their actions didn't surprise me. What I couldn't comprehend was why Aric cared.

I shuffled toward him. "It's fine, Aric."

Aric faced me at the sound of his name. "No. It's not."

The sirens boomed louder. Several SUVs and a few police cars screeched to a halt across the street. Blue and red lights flooded the alley like an old seventies disco, sliding over the corpses and coloring their gray skin a sickly lavender. The scene reminded me of the many crime dramas on TV. Yet it was too much to hope that the credits would roll, the show would end, and the crew would remove the synthetic bodies for future episodes. These women had no future. Their lives had been viciously robbed in their prime.

My eyes skimmed over their ruined outfits. Their style of dress and trendy shoes told me they'd taken pride in their appearance. Now, their sunken faces would haunt me forever.

It's not fair.

"Are you all right?" Aric asked quietly.

I nodded, more so he wouldn't sniff my lie.

The soft hammering of feet awakened my tigress. *Weres* of all species rushed the alley. They skidded to a stop upon seeing me. "She's with me," Aric warned when they attempted to circle me.

I didn't know what position Aric held, but everyone there did. They moved away, careful to give me space. Two escorted Tommy out while the others gathered around the bodies.

Time to go.

I limped backward, jumping when I accidently stepped on a sharp piece of cracked mortar. Aric retrieved Taran's shoe and handed it to me. It would have been an awesome Cinderella moment if my back claws hadn't shredded through the leather and the heel didn't have the wolf's eye still attached.

My stomach rolled. "Um. You keep it."

Aric glanced at the pierced eyeball. "Ah. Right." He sighed. "My students will pay for your things—"

"Don't worry about it." I removed Taran's other shoe and tossed it into the Dumpster. It hit the lid with a loud clang. I then padded toward the exit, stopping only to grab my battered phone and purse.

"Where are you going, miss?"

Aric's question surprised me. It also sounded odd being addressed as "miss," especially by him. "My name is Celia." I pushed my hair out of my eyes to get one last look at him. "I'm going home."

Aric approached slowly. I guess he worried about frightening me. But I wasn't scared, just freaked out by his presence and all the remaining adrenaline from the fight.

He stopped when he stood two arm lengths away, the same distance most men ever dared to approach. But then he surprised me by taking another step closer, followed by another. *Oh, yeah. I don't scare this wolf one bit.*

"Let me take you home, Celia. There could be more infected vampires. You're covered in blood; you'll be easy prey."

I liked the way he said my name, like he'd known me forever. My legs moved without permission and my words formed without thought. "Okay. Thank you."

I trudged alongside Aric, careful to avoid any debris that would slice my feet. The strength of my beast toughened my skin, but it had its limits. My soles waved figurative white flags and begged for a good soak. I sighed the moment my toes touched the walkway, relishing the small amount of relief the cool concrete provided.

Aric scratched his head. "Do you, uh, want me to carry you?"

He's offering to carry me.... I blushed like an idiot. "Um, no. Thanks. I'll manage."

"I'm parked three blocks away. You can wait here while I get my car."

The last thing I wanted was to remain in the company of *weres*. Aric had kept them from attacking, but his absence might make them reconsider. "I'm fine to walk."

We hiked up the small hill, past a local bakery with a wide door. The lingering scent of fresh-baked croissants was a welcome aroma compared to the sour stench of blood and death. "How many humans died tonight?"

I hadn't noticed Aric watching me until I glanced in his direction. He paused for a few beats, likely debating whether to tell me. "Nine," he finally said. "All women. All inside the city limits."

I nibbled on my lip, but didn't like the taste. Something had splattered on me. I just hoped it wasn't Tommy's insides. "All from bloodlust?"

Aric nodded slowly. "You seem to know a lot about what's going on."

"A friend—" I stopped. Misha was hardly a friend. "Someone I know mentioned what was happening." I skipped away from Misha territory, careful to avoid Aric's questioning glance. "How many infected vamps were involved?"

"Three. All in varying degrees. The one who attacked the women in the alley drained seven of the victims."

Good Lord. "Are you sure?"

Darkness shadowed Aric's face. "Yes. Their throats had been devoured in the exact same way. The other two weren't as sick, but they sure as hell were on their way."

I froze suddenly. My tigress eyes replaced my own, searching the street for signs of movement.

"He's not out there, Celia." Aric's gaze locked with deep fascination onto my face. "I killed him."

I blinked my beast side away. Aric cocked his head. He didn't comment on my unique ability to manage my inner animal. He also didn't appear disturbed by it. I focused on his chest. The blood from his other shirt had soaked through to his tee. I wasn't sure what changes a bloodlust vamp underwent during the different stages of the infection. But the women in the alley had been ravaged. Whatever Aric fought must have been chilling as all hell. "Did you kill him on your own?"

Aric nodded. "My students tried to help, but the thrill of the hunt made them careless. I ordered them to stand back." He pushed his long hair from his eyes. "I finished him. But not before the prick took a chunk out of my thigh. While I healed, I sent them to search for more victims." He stopped to face me. "Had I known my wolves would attack you, I never would have allowed them from my sight."

The fire to Aric's irises returned and the scent of his anger hit my nose like a tangible force. The urge to calm him consumed me. Instinctively I reached to touch his face. Aric watched my hand slowly inch toward the increasing warmth of his skin. But then common sense bitch-slapped me upside the head and I jerked my hand away. *What's wrong with me?*

I took off, humiliated by my reaction.

Aric, of course, easily caught up. "Celia—"

"Why are you so pissed at your wolves for attacking me?"

"You're innocent," he answered simply.

My steps slowed as if the walkway had transformed into sand. I focused ahead and tried to ignore the sins from my past that rushed to the forefront of my mind. "You don't know me, Aric. You're wrong to think I'm innocent."

"No. I'm not."

I tilted my head to gauge Aric's face. His tone sounded severe. Yet his strong masculine features held nothing but kindness. It seemed surreal for such a powerful being to be so compassionate. Except there was no doubt he meant what he said.

"Any other being would've killed those boys, Celia. You spared them at a great expense to yourself."

Perhaps. But I'd refrained more for myself than for them, and namely because I didn't relish killing anything.

Aric inched closer, sending his body heat to flicker across my skin in a playful caress. A small, sexy grin spread smoothly across his face, stealing my breath.

Whoa.

My mouth parted and I smiled back. It was easy. I liked how it made me feel. No. I liked how *he* made me feel.

But then Aric stopped smiling and cleared his throat. "My car's just ahead."

What?

It took me a moment to follow, unsure what I'd done to ruin the moment. Then again, I'd probably imagined the whole moment. God, I was pathetic. The small beep from his key fob finally made me move. I crossed the street to where his shiny black Escalade hugged the corner near a bridal boutique.

Aric kept his back to me and his breath came out slow and controlled, as if working to calm down. I thought he'd changed his mind about taking me home until he wrenched open the car door. "I'll help you inside."

"No. I'll manage." His rebuff hurt me, although I wasn't sure why. I'd only just met the wolf. His actions shouldn't have bothered me.

But they did.

I held on to my injured arm and used just my legs to climb into the monstrous hybrid. My flexibility and strength made it easy. Yet my injury caused my usual grace to falter. My backside fell into the seat, but it was the bounce off the tight leather cushion that sent a rush of pain up my arm and into my shoulder.

Damn it. I grimaced, but managed to swallow back a grunt.

My eyes remained shut when Aric's warmth enveloped me. Slowly I opened my lids. I stared, mesmerized as his gaze locked onto mine and he held out his hand. "Don't move," he whispered. "Let me take care of you."

Aric reached for my injured arm, careful to touch the sleeve of my dress and avoid my bare skin. His movements were measured and cautious, as if he held a delicate piece of crystal rather than the powerful arm of a tigress. I wanted to protrude my claws—just to prove I wasn't weak. But the effort would have left me howling in pain, defeating the purpose and making me appear more stupid than strong.

So I kept still, and for once allowed someone to take care of me.

Aric gently slid my arm through the seat belt. His steady, gentle movements anchored time. He continued to manipulate my arm in a graceful dance until he finished working the seat belt around me and clicked it into place. Without a word, he shut the door and walked around to the driver's side.

Aric paused before opening his door, once more taking in slow, deliberate breaths.

Several long seconds passed before he climbed in and cranked the engine. "Where do you live?" he asked, his tone low and gruff.

I gave him my address, though my voice shook as I spoke. Aric punched the coordinates into his GPS and took off. It was only when we crossed the Nevada border and were into California that he finally spoke again.

"I saw you earlier tonight, and at the beach."

"I know." I glanced down at my hands, which were filthy and caked with dried blood. My body tensed as I waited for him to explain this unusual draw between us. When he didn't, I questioned him about the night. "Are you a cop?" Aric seemed to oversee the investigation, but that didn't clarify why he had students.

"No. I'm a teacher and Chancellor of Students at The Den."

"Den?"

Aric smiled, allowing his tight grip on the steering wheel to loosen. "It's a private school for wolves. We just opened one in Squaw Valley. It's where my kind learns the normal school curriculum and the skills they'll need to protect the earth."

I nodded, but it didn't explain his presence in the alley. "So why were you the one in charge tonight?"

Aric stopped smiling and focused on the road. "My duty as a *were* obliges me to fight evil. Those in law enforcement will care for the victims and notify their families, but I'll continue to manage the situation as a Leader of our kind."

Leader? My throat went dry. "So you're like … *royalty*?"

Aric's face reddened. "I'm a pureblood werewolf, Celia. I come from generations of *were*-only family members." He shrugged. "Purebloods are just held in higher regard, that's all."

Oh. Is that all? And I was a mutt by supernatural standards. *No wonder he's so guarded.*

"Is this your street?"

"Yes." I pointed toward our house. "It's the light blue custom Colonial with the white door."

Aric pulled into our driveway. The moment he put the car in park, I released my seat belt, careful not to let it swing back and hit my right side.

"Celia, wait." Aric unfastened his seat belt and twisted his body to face me. "Tahoe's head witch has the power to heal. I'll call her so she can tend to your injuries."

We'd had a smackdown with the local witches when we first moved to Tahoe. I didn't trust them. I didn't like them. And I sure as hell didn't want them touching me. I shook my head. "No. That's okay. I can wait."

Aric frowned. "I can't leave you like this. It's either magic or I take you to the emergency room."

I nibbled on my bottom lip again, but it still tasted nasty. I so needed a shower. "I'll be fine, Aric. I know another healer. She'll take care of me."

Aric tapped his palm against the steering wheel, his face shadowed with concern. "The head witch is the only healing witch within two states. I don't think you should trust just anyone to touch you."

"She's not a witch. She's my sister." I smiled softly. "And I trust her with my life."

Aric's brows softened with understanding. "Okay, but don't get out of the car without my help."

Aric opened my door in the time it took me to adjust my hips. I thought he would just hold my arm and assist me with my balance. I didn't expect him to sweep me into his arms, carry me up the drive, and place me on the ground. It happened so fast I barely blinked, yet his divine heat lingered even after my feet touched the cold, soft lawn.

My toes squirmed against the grass. "Uh, thanks for the ride and everything."

"You're welcome." Aric crossed his arms and circled me to examine my shoulder. "I can pop your arm back into place. It will hurt, but at least it will help your sister in healing you."

Emme could realign bones, but I wasn't sure she was strong enough to shove my upper arm back into the socket. And I sure didn't want Taran experimenting. "Have you done this before?"

Aric nodded. "Fairly frequently. Our young wolves like to roughhouse. Learning to realign bones prevents them from mending incorrectly, since our healing ability is so fast." He shrugged. "Otherwise we'd have to rebreak their bones every time they got hurt."

I didn't know Aric. Not really. But for some odd reason, I trusted him. "Okay. Whenever you're ready."

And that's when Aric took off his shirt.

The soft fabric skimmed over perfectly golden skin and rock-hard abdominals tight enough to launch a brick into orbit. A whisper of hair traveled the length of his belly button to where his jeans hung low on his hips.

Holy . . .

Aric stopped removing his shirt when he pulled it just above his small, erect nipples. This wasn't real. This was some kind of Hollywood hottie video shoot on TV and all I wanted to do was hit pause.

"What's wrong, Celia?" he asked.

I whipped around to face Mrs. Mancuso's house, mortified to be actually *gawking* and possibly *drooling*.

I focused hard on Mancuso's lawn jockey. It was forty freaking degrees and the breeze from the lake had picked up. I should have been cold, but Aric and his eight-pack warmed my core just fine and dandy. "Wha-what are you doing?" I managed to stammer, whereas my tigress insisted I should shut the hell up, turn back around, and enjoy the show.

Aric edged his way around to face me, removing and twisting his shirt around his neck with each step before fully slipping it on backwards to the clean side. "I have to hold you against me in order to adjust your shoulder. There's blood all over the front of my shirt. I didn't want to get any on you," he explained.

"Thanks," I said a little too high-pitched for my normally husky voice. "I appreciate that."

Aric quirked a brow, but when he inhaled my scent his eyes widened with surprise. He was silent for several seconds before gesturing to my arm. "Are you sure you want me to do this?"

There were many, many things I wanted Aric to do, and none of them pertained to my busted shoulder. *Yowza.* I needed to take a cold shower, and possibly invest in electronic devices.

"Celia?"

Right. I focused on the pain and hoped I wouldn't go

down like a wimp. I nodded and closed my eyes. "Go ahead."

Aric's strong arms wrapped me in a bear hug, his contact hard and gentle all at once. For the second time that night, his body heat encased me. My face fell against his muscular chest. My God, the aromatic blend of his scent mixed with musk from battle drove my tigress insane. *Don't purr. Don't purr. Oh, Jesus, please don't let me purr.*

Aric's voice tightened. "Your heart's racing. . . ."

"S'okay."

"Brace yourself. This is going to hurt like a mother."

Aric didn't lie. There was a brief crunching sound when he rammed my limb back in place. I thought he'd snapped my spine. A thousand blades stabbed at every nerve in my neck, arm, and shoulder. My head flew back and my back arched. I didn't cry or whimper, but damn, did I want to. Aric held me tight.

"I'm sorry," he whispered. "That was a bad idea."

I pumped the fingers of my right hand. It remained sore, but I could manipulate it. "No. This is better," I said between breaths.

Aric released me and stepped back, his jaw clenched tight enough to shatter Mrs. Mancuso's lawn gnome.

"I'm fine," I insisted. "I'm tougher than I look."

Aric shook his head. "No. You're not. You shouldn't have been out there tonight, Celia."

My head snapped up.

Aric stared hard at the ground. "Look, something is coming. Something severe enough to threaten every life in the area. I'd like you to leave town for a while."

I couldn't believe what I was hearing. "I can't just leave, Aric. This is my home; my life is here."

Anger flared in Aric's eyes. "I can't explain what's happening. But if you stay, you might get hurt."

I motioned to my shoulder. "It's too late for that, wolf."

"Celia—"

"You don't know me, Aric. But there's something about me you should." I straightened to my full height. "I don't just run because someone tells me to."

I stormed up my front steps and unlocked the door, not bothering to turn around.

Every part of me sensed Aric watching me. In the reflection of the glass pane on the door, I looked upon the almost full moon. Aric was wrong. I knew what was coming. I'd seen the aftermath in the alley and I could feel the darkness as it dug its way through my skin. Tahoe was in jeopardy.

Decision time had arrived.

CHAPTER 9

I finger-combed my wet curls as I walked into my kitchen to prepare some tea, lamenting how I ended things with Aric. *Good Lord, what a night.* I'd been waiting to see him. Dreaming of speaking to him. Wanting to spend time with him. Dead bodies and alley brawls aside, my wishes had come true. Only to leave me back where I started, wondering if I'd ever see him again.

While I hadn't liked him ordering me around, he'd helped me and kept me safe. And yet my temper prevented me from wishing him so much as a good night. *Nice, Celia.*

A sound like a half knock drew me toward the door. I growled in anticipation of another paparazzo. My heart just about stopped when I opened the door and saw Aric leaving my porch. He froze at the bottom of the steps before sighing and glancing in my direction. "Hi."

"Hi." I looked toward the driveway, where his Escalade remained parked. "Have you been here this whole time?"

"No. I left and came back." He motioned toward my shoulder. "I wanted to make sure you were all right."

I adjusted the belt around my thick cotton robe. I was all about dressing to impress. "W-would you like to join me?" I pointed behind me. "Inside, I mean. I'm making tea. Hot tea." I grimaced. *Behold my magnificent sentence structure and charm. Envy me!*

Aric's smirk set my already pink cheeks on fire. He spared me by not laughing as he jogged up the steps and wiped his feet on the mat. He paused. "Maybe we should drink your tea outside. I don't want to mess up your house."

Most of Aric's clothes remained splattered with blood. But I wanted him to feel welcome, especially after leaving on such a sour note. "Don't worry about it. It's probably dry by now."

Aric smiled. "You sure?"

I swallowed hard. God, I loved that grin. "Yes. Please have a seat."

Aric crossed the dark wood floors into our large open family room. Aside from my bedroom, it was my favorite room in the house. The walls were a light sage and the trim was white. Black-and-white nature photographs that Shayna had snapped hung in silver frames on one wall. The opposite wall had a brick fireplace at its center flanked by built-in cabinets that held books and our small TV.

Aric carefully lowered himself onto our cream-colored sofa as I started the gas fireplace. "This is nice."

"Thank you." I paused to watch him lean forward and rest his powerful arms against his legs. His long hair fell over his brows, but did nothing to shadow the intensity of his eyes. I opened my mouth, then shut it, slightly stupefied that the male who'd occupied my every waking thought sat in my home, on my couch, because he wanted to ensure I remained safe. I wanted to say something witty, smart, charming—

"Is something wrong?"

I jumped. "Nope. I'll be right back with your . . . stuff." If I thought he wouldn't have heard me, I would have beaten my head against the nearest wall. I returned to the kitchen and tried to relax.

"Do you live here on your own?"

"Um. No. My three sisters and I bought the house together." I placed wheat rolls Emme had made on the tray along with pieces of butter I quickly cut into flower shapes.

"There're four of you?"

I paused in the middle of filling the second mug with tea. The way Aric emphasized the word "four" I knew he meant something more. I returned to the family room with the tray and placed it on our large wooden coffee table. I sat on the love seat angled next to the sofa. "There's only one of me." I lifted my mug to my lips, trying to keep my tone light. "My sisters don't share my powers."

Aric watched me closely, waiting, I suspected, for me to elaborate. When I didn't, he didn't push me. I smiled. He was kind. But I owed it to my sisters not to disclose too much. He sniffed at the mug. "What is this?"

"Chai." I chuckled when he blinked back at me. "It's a tea made with spices, honey, and milk."

He sipped it carefully. "Mmm. It's good. Real good." He took several long sips before his tongue swept over his top lip. "I like it."

I stared at his mouth, wondering how soft his lips were and how good they would taste. A slow, sexy grin inched its way along his strong, stubbled jaw. His eyes sparkled as they met mine. I couldn't remember how to breathe. "I really like it," he murmured once more.

Say something. Anything. Tell him you love him and want to have his puppies. "Haven't you ever had tea before?"

Shit.

Aric gave me a hard stare. "Real werewolves don't drink tea."

I threw back my head and laughed, only to wince when pain rumbled into my shoulder.

Aric came to my side, taking my mug and placing it on the table. He straightened my arm. "Maybe I can help." His fingers massaged me through the thick cotton of my robe, edging their way slowly up my arm to my shoulder. My breath caught. Aric's touch electrified me. His voice lowered in pitch. "Tell me if I'm being too rough."

My heart pounded in my ears as his fingers pressed and swept over my sore muscles. But then I became aware of an added heartbeat.

His.

I watched his hands move along my arm, a deep heat building between us. My chest ached from lack of breath.

"Shhh, it's okay. Try to relax, Celia. I promise not to hurt you."

Visions of hearing his words whispered in the dark spun in my mind. I inhaled deeply, forcing myself to breathe. Slowly, oh, so slowly, my body began to accept his touch. My head fell back; I was hypnotized by the tremendous comfort he brought me. A purr mixed with a soft moan escaped my lips. Aric froze.

And that's when I realized the side of my robe had fallen open.

Aric bolted upright as I jumped and yanked it closed.

"Sorry—sorry." He backed away, his breath hard and fast. "I should . . . go." He rushed out, pausing at the door, but failing to look back at me. "Don't forget what I said. You and your family will be safer if you leave Tahoe tonight."

I watched the door shut behind him, slumping onto the couch when he started his Escalade seconds later. I opened my robe and stared at the girls, mortified and convinced the universe hated me. If he had to see my breasts, why couldn't it have been the perkier of the two?

I groaned as the phone rang, covering up when I saw who called.

"Hi, Misha," I said before he spoke.

My sisters ambled in less than ten minutes later. I disconnected my call, surprised they were alone and lacking the smiles I would have expected after spending time with a sultry pack of wolves.

Taran tossed her purse aside and flopped onto the couch next to me. "Shit, Ceel. Where the hell have you been? Misha's staff has been calling us nonstop."

Emme and Shayna knelt in front of me. Emme placed her hand on my knee. "We've been looking everywhere for you since you walked out of The Hole. Why didn't you answer your phone?"

"It sort of got damaged." I frowned. "I sent you a text, Emme. Didn't you get it?"

Emme shook her head. "I'm sorry, Celia. My battery was low. I left my phone charging upstairs."

"Okay. But never mind me; what happened with your wolves?"

Shayna grinned, but her smile lacked its typical glee.

"Dude, Koda and his friends rushed out of the club shortly after you did."

My eyes widened although I probably knew the reason. "They did?"

Shayna nodded. "Koda got a call while we were slow dancing. It was strange; a moon appeared on the screen, but he didn't answer it. He just grabbed Liam and Gemini and they took off." She shrugged. "I thought maybe he liked me, but he didn't even bother to say good-bye."

At least he didn't run off at the sight of your boobs.

Emme crinkled her nose. "Did you call Bren? He's been worried. Especially once he realized Misha's vampires were trying to find you."

"Ah. No."

Taran wiped the mascara beneath her eyes with her fingertips, then gestured to the cordless phone in my hand. "Then who were you on the phone with?"

"Misha. I'm going to help him kill Zhahara."

My comment hit Taran like a physical slap. Her blue eyes fired with anger as her head whipped toward me. "Like hell you are!"

I let out a breath. "Taran, I just got off the phone with Misha. Bloodlust is spreading like fire. He's been forced to kill again."

"Well, sucks to be him."

I shook my head. "You don't get it."

Taran jumped to her feet. "I don't have to get it. This is bullshit!"

I rose and slipped off my cozy bathrobe, revealing the bruises to my shoulder, arms, and back. My entire right side resembled the continent of South America, each contusion highlighting a different country. My sisters screamed. Loudly. Emme stumbled to her feet in her rush to heal me.

"Oh, my goodness. What happened to you?"

"I found the big, bad wolf."

Emme screamed again. "Your boyfriend did this to you?"

I sighed. "No, Emme. His students did." *And he's not my boyfriend . . . but I wish he could be.*

I explained everything after Emme healed me, leaving the flashing-the-werewolf part out.

Taran paced back and forth across our wood floor. "Look. I'm sorry about those women and all. That seriously has to be the worst way to die. But your wolf has a point. This is *so* not our problem."

"He's not my wolf." I stared at my fingertips. I had to scrub them to get all the blood off. "And that blonde . . . God, she looked so much like you, Emme." My heart clenched as I remembered. "She could have been you."

Shayna clasped her hands over her mouth. Taran swallowed hard. And Emme—poor Emme—didn't move.

"I'm going to Misha's house tonight. I was just waiting for you to get home."

Taran's leopard stilettos tapped the wood floor until she met me face-to-face. "Not without us you're not."

I suspected Misha was rich, like all master vampires, but when we pulled onto his property, I didn't expect to drive almost a mile just to reach the front gates.

"Damn," Taran muttered when I finally stopped our Subaru.

The exterior of the massive compound appeared to be surrounded by a tall stone wall. Gargoyle heads protruded randomly from the barricade. Their snouts spewed water, but in the darkness they appeared to drip blood. I could barely see the house from where we waited; the trees lining the driveway blocked my view. Maybe it was the gargoyles or the thickening clouds overhead, but I suddenly had second thoughts.

I cracked my window, hoping for an intercom so I wouldn't have to leave the safety of the car. I scented two vampires. One of them eyed us suspiciously through my window. The other assumed a stance directly behind our SUV. If he thought I wouldn't run him over, he was wrong.

"State your business," the vampire to my left spat.

"Hey, dude," Shayna greeted him from the backseat. "We're here to see Misha. He invited us over."

This made the vampire smile. "For dinner?"

This was not the night to piss me off. I rolled my window completely down and yanked the idiot closer—by his throat. "No, we're here to help save your master's life," I snapped. "So either you open the gate or you explain to Misha why you're missing your arms and your buddy has my tire marks running up his chest."

"Let them through," a disembodied voice commanded. I realized the gargoyles were more than decorative features. Someone watched us from strategically placed surveillance cameras in each.

I released my grip on the vampire's neck. He hissed threateningly, but stepped back to let us pass. "Pansy-ass bastard!" Taran yelled as we drove through the gate.

Anger extinguished my fear, and now my inner beast prowled, restless to prove herself, but as I entered the property, my trepidation returned once more. Blue slate lined the double-wide driveway. We crossed over a stone bridge before finally circling an enormous fountain. Water cascaded over the beautiful stone waterfall and into the fountain's pool. I drove most of the way around the circle and parked facing the exit in case we needed a quick escape. We stepped out to the monstrosity Misha called home.

The exterior of Misha's compound resembled a well-manicured park, and the house was a three-story, Mountain Craftsman–style masterpiece. The soaring wood trusses at the entry and art glass doors drew me to the rustic elegance. The rooflines were layered with deep eaves and ornately carved gables. The foundation of the house appeared to be stacked stone, and the facade was either cedar shake or timber. I shook my head as I gawked at the porch supports built with stone bases and massive hewn-wood columns. *Crap, did he take down a forest to build it?*

"Dude," Shayna whispered. "This has to be a lodge. He can't possibly live here."

I couldn't blame Shayna for thinking that. There must've been a lot of money to be made among the bloodsucking elite.

Petro rushed down the front stairs as I stepped out of the car. A few of his family trailed behind him. My God, he looked awful. Dark circles shadowed his eyes, and perspiration drizzled down the sides of his face. He hurried to my side and gripped my hands. "My brother seeks to destroy Zhahara."

"I know, Petro. That's why I'm here."

His jaw slackened before a glimmer of hope flashed across his terrified face. "Will you help him, Celia?" He glanced back at my sisters. "Will all of you?" Tears welled in his eyes. "Misha cannot defeat such an opponent alone, but he considers me weak and refuses my help."

I took in Petro's crumbling state. It was a wonder he

could stand with how badly his anxiety battered his small form.

Petro's voice cracked. "Please help him, Celia. I don't want to be alone."

Emme gasped softly behind him. Yeah. Petro seemed to share our same fears. "I'll see what I can do. But I'm not making any promises." The hope he carried slowly faded from his features, but he nodded and released me. I watched as his family helped him into the limo, wondering whether Misha had played a role in keeping him alive all these years.

My sisters followed my lead up the stone steps to a set of massive carved doors. Two more vampires appeared. They pushed open the doors and we stepped into an elegant foyer with a cathedral-style timbered ceiling and floored with huge blocks of bluestone.

I continued forward with Taran to my right. Shayna and Emme followed no more than two steps behind us.

Misha approached with five vampires behind him, wiping his bloodied hands on a thick white towel. Deep-set lines shadowed his beautiful face, and the scent of a fresh kill lingered on his clothes. A female vampire meekly approached and took the soiled towel from his hands. She kept her head low and quickly scurried away, careful to avoid Misha's increasing rage.

I let out a breath. "How many did you kill tonight, Misha?"

"Five. Not including the three killed by wolves this evening . . . And the one who just revealed herself to me."

"You're down twenty-one vampires." It wasn't a question. I could do the math.

Misha answered with a stiff, furious nod. "Again, forgive me for not taking your call when you first sought me. My priority at the time was to hunt those who attempted to escape." He motioned to a large entryway on our left. "Ladies, if you will join me in the next room."

Misha escorted us to a dining room roughly the size of Delaware. Four vampires dressed like naughty Catholic schoolgirls offered us food and beverages. We declined. And not just because of their creepy outfits.

The air carried a thick layer of dread interwoven with Misha's rising anger. Ten vampires convened at the enormous dining room table. We perched at the end. Misha sat to my left, and although five empty seats remained, Hank and Tim, from court, stood behind him.

Misha leaned back on a chair that resembled a throne. He slowly motioned around the room. "With the exception of my men at the gates, these vampires represent the last of my family. I have until tomorrow night to decide our fate."

I placed my hand over the smooth stone table. "Misha. How certain are you that Zhahara is the one behind the bloodlust?"

A faint sparkle of hate flickered in Misha's hard gray eyes. "After I killed the fifth of my keep, I sent three of my best spies to investigate Zhahara's compound. I destroyed two of them days later. The third went absent and I have been informed he drained seven women tonight." He stared at me for several seconds. "My time is up, my darling Celia. I must account for these murders or prove them to be the work of another master."

Shayna glanced back at me before addressing Misha. "I don't mean to ask a stupid question, but . . . have you spoken with Zhahara directly about it?"

Misha's eyes never left mine. "Zhahara has not been heard from since our time in court. Yet my remaining spies insist she returned to her compound and has not emerged. My plan is to storm her home tomorrow and find the evidence I need to exonerate me."

Taran crossed her arms. "What if it's not her?"

Misha leaned back. He likely wasn't accustomed to anyone challenging him. His lush mouth tightened into a firm line before curving into a small smile. "Zhahara remains my only lead to saving my family. I have no choice but to act."

Taran said nothing more, but I knew she saw his point. Otherwise she would have argued until Misha died or she needed to wear Depends.

"Have you reached your decision?"

I didn't acknowledge my sisters when I answered. "I think I have. I'll give you my decision by morning."

Misha nodded slowly, but said nothing more. No witty comment, no flirtatious demeanor. Nothing. Just a vampire desperate enough to seek help from strangers.

I stood. So did Emme and Taran. Shayna pointed to the two antique swords mounted over the mantel of the dining room fireplace. "Can I borrow those, dude?"

A vamp scrambled to retrieve them following a small gesture from Misha. Shayna grinned upon feeling the weight of the ancient swords in her hands. "Cool."

"I fear they are not as sharp as they once were," Misha said slowly.

Shayna's blue eyes sparkled. "Don't worry. I'll make them work."

We headed into the foyer when an oh-too-familiar voice boomed from behind the thick doors.

"I'm not asking for an audience," Aric growled. "I'm telling you, he *will* see me!"

The wide wooden doors crashed open, and my big,

badass wolf stormed through, flanked by the wolves from the club, a few unfamiliar *weres*, and oh, yeah, the blond she-wolf with the Victoria Beckham bob. I don't know who was more shocked, them or us.

Oh, crap.

"Son of a *bitch*," Taran muttered when she noticed Gemini.

I'd forgotten about Blondie, but she remembered me. Her eyes glared almost as fiercely as Aric's when she saw me.

Almost.

Aric stalked toward me. "What are you doing here?" He didn't wait for me to answer and fixed his scowl on Misha. "What is *she* doing here?"

For the first time since our arrival, Misha actually smiled. Although I wished I could say it lacked any malice. He snaked his arm around my shoulders and pulled me close. "Celia is a friend. She is considering helping me in my quest to prove my innocence."

I'd never seen a wolf implode. But I almost did then.

Aric grabbed my arm and yanked me from Misha's grasp.

And that's when all hell broke loose. . . .

CHAPTER 10

Everything happened at once. Emme screamed as were-beasts and vampires collided like a herd of angry buffalo. Growls and hisses erupted in a furious staccato, rattling the windows, framed paintings, and crystal chandelier. The she-wolf's fist jetted toward my face. I ducked. She would have nailed Aric in the chest had Misha not tackled him *through* the wall and into the library. I shot after them, but the she-wolf seized my waist and launched me across the foyer. The bones of my back cracked when I bounced off the opposite wall. My ears rang, but not loudly enough to muffle a high-pitched squeal, the crunching of plaster, and the demolition of furniture.

I landed hard on my knees, more pissed than hurt, ready to rumble. I pushed off the floor and stomped toward the she-bitch, momentarily stunned by her appearance.

She lay near the massive hole Misha had made with Aric's body. Her short blond bob stood on its ends, tips smoking. Taran must have jolted her with lightning in retaliation for taking me for a ride.

Sadly, she didn't seem happy with her new look. "Ugly *freak*," she spat. "This is all your fault!" She clambered to her feet and heaved a Victorian hall stand at me.

She misjudged my speed.

She also misjudged my sword-wielding sister.

Shayna leaped into the air and spun with ballerina elegance befitting her thin frame. Light reflected off her swords as she used her gift to transform the dull blades into deadly sharp weapons. With a piercing *whoosh* she sliced through the giant stand like a sheet of paper. Two perfectly even pieces crashed to the floor as she landed on one knee, arms outstretched. She twirled the swords as she rose, her tense muscles screeching for action. "*Don't touch my sister!*" she hissed.

A small smirk found its way to my lips. Luke Skywalker could suck it. He had nothing on Shayna.

Frustration and rage pervaded the blond wolf's bellow as she bounded toward Shayna. I leaped in front of my sister, believing one good toss deserved another. My fingers grasped the wolf's crispy hair and pant leg as she pounced. Her screams wafted throughout the foyer as I pitched her through the large oak doors and into the great outdoors. Blondie's butt dug a straight line across Misha's meticulous lawn. Good thing that tall aspen was there to deflect her skid; otherwise the little cutie might have kept going.

My feet barely made a sound as I barreled toward her. She charged, her features contorted with fury, her hot breath visible in the cold night air. She snarled. I roared. The moment we connected we hammered blow after blow.

My strength surprised her; so did my ruthless strikes to her face and stomach. She'd learned to fight. Raised on tough inner-city streets, I'd learned to survive. Her aggressive offense quickly changed to defensive blocks and retreats. I wanted to knock her out, furious she'd put her hands on me. Despite my anger, I allowed her to draw back. The fight riled my beast, yet that didn't mean I'd allow her to kill.

This time.

I slammed into the crushing embrace of a werebear, his grip fracturing at least one of my ribs. This time I couldn't silence my shrieks.

"Do you want to take her?" the bear growled.

The she-wolf's eager grin widened. She stopped smiling when I broke the bear's nose and cheekbones with my rapid head butts. The bear dropped me with a spew of curses and a crapload of negative comments about my mother.

The moment my feet touched the cold ground I *shifted* down and behind him. He pivoted around as I surfaced, his lids peeling back when my fist met his groin. Other than a little gurgle, no sound escaped.

I finished breaking to the surface. My hands held my broken rib as I fractured his left knee with my foot. He collapsed, gripping his man parts, and threw up.

Children obviously weren't in his foreseeable future.

I lunged at the wolf, angry as all hell that she would have attacked me had I not broken out of the bear's vise-like grip. I may have fought dirty, but she was a dirty fighter. We fell onto a wrought-iron table set. I punched her a few times in the face before another wolf hauled me off by the hair. I rammed my elbows wildly and broke *her* ribs before picking up a chair and knocking her into Misha's wooded property.

I tossed the chair aside and returned to face Blondie.

She backed away, hands up in surrender and blood dripping down to her skimpy designer blouse. I kept her in my sights, debating whether to knock her out, but Emme's screams had me bolting back to the house.

God, I was furious. Bloodlust plagued Tahoe. How the hell had *we* become the enemy? I needed to help my sisters and find Aric.

Something hard whipped me across the legs as I leaped toward the entrance. I crash-landed on the stone steps. The sharp edges sliced me across the breasts and shins and knocked the air from my lungs in a painful rush. My fractured rib slid torturously beneath my skin, but if I wanted to live, I needed to move. Fast.

I flipped onto my back, holding tight to my side. Pieces of wood lay by my feet. It seemed Blondie had found a nice thick branch to hurl against my legs. My eyes trailed from her soiled black dress pants to the sharp, pointy shard of wood she aimed at my heart. I rolled out of the way and kicked her in the skull. She shook her head and struck again, but my next blow to her noggin made a snapping sound and ass-planted her onto the walkway. I yanked her up by her skimpy shirt and rammed my finger into her chest with each word I growled. "You're. Pissing. Me. Off!"

Granted, I was beyond pissed from the moment I saw her touching Aric. But she didn't need to know that. Besides, my tigress preferred to intimidate at every given opportunity. Especially when someone tried to kill us.

I *shifted* her underground and jetted into the house. My ribs hollered in protest as I dove onto the floor to avoid the sizzling *were* Taran shot overhead with her lightning. "Eat shit, Snoopy!" she yelled from down the hall.

Emme stood in the center of the demolished foyer, next to what remained of the chandelier. She fought to separate Liam and a vampire using the full potency of her *force*. Liam's growls cut amid the escalating chaos, rattling the chandelier's crystals and Emme's fragile nerves. His muscles tightened beneath his torn shirt, geared to *change* and release his beast.

The vampire snapped her vicious fangs, impatient to bite. "I can already taste your blood, mutt," she sneered. From her knife-length nails hung the shredded pieces of Liam's shirt.

Their shared hatred thickened the air, making it hard for me to catch my breath. One of them was going to die. I knew it. And apparently so did Emme. Sweat glistened on her brow, and her fair skin deepened to red. The opposing forces circled each other, but neither could get through Emme's power. They thrashed and beat against her hold, ready to draw blood.

Emme's strength wouldn't last much longer, but she wasn't in immediate danger. Shayna was. She balanced on an oval table in the great room, splattered with blood, her swords at the ready. Three enormous werewolves in their powerful beast forms circled her with fangs bared. She shifted her weight from side to side, her long, sleek ponytail whirling behind her. Determination strengthened her pixie face. She wouldn't allow them to take her down.

And neither would I. *Time to come out and play, baby.*

Like a ripple of water flowing across my skin, my tigress emerged, tripling my petite stature into an awesome body of dense muscle, fur, and razor-sharp claws.

My T-shirt, jeans, and sneakers fell in tattered threads at my colossal paws. The *change* didn't typically hurt, but my injuries caused the already sore areas to stretch painfully and my broken rib to separate further. I collapsed, struggling to push past the relentless stabbing at my side.

I forced myself onto all fours, but not before a five-hundred-pound red wolf lunged past me and jetted toward Shayna.

Fear for Shayna turned to shock as he struck the other wolves like a mighty sledgehammer to a set of bowling pins. The wolves rolled away, their claws scratching against the stone floors as they quickly scurried to their feet and attacked once more. But the red wolf's deep rumble forced them back. The others exchanged glances and snarled, yet none appeared willing to take on the herculean wolf.

The red wolf communicated to his pack through thunderous growls in alternating pitches and subtle twitches of his body. I didn't speak wolf, but I understood him to mean, "Back the *fuck* up. *Now!*"

The wolves slowly abandoned their target. They paused to glower at me before hustling to the back of the house, where Aric and Misha continued their supernatural smack-down.

The red wolf turned his back to face Shayna. His body *changed*. Fur retracted and bones and tendons contorted, transforming the limber figure of a beast into the formidable body of a man. A sea of black satin hair spilled over rock-hard muscle and rust-colored skin. The wolf disappeared. In his place stood the gargantuan Koda.

Shayna slowly lowered her swords, her jaw falling open with an audible pop. Koda gripped her waist and gently lowered her to the floor with as much effort as it took to hold a pen. He kept his hands at her hips and twirled her caringly, sniffing at the bloodstains and examining her for injuries. Shayna appraised him, too.

Just not in the same way.

Her already wide eyes narrowly missed falling out of their sockets once they headed south of Koda's waist. Koda's thick brows set with concern. "Did they hurt you?"

Shayna shook her head, but didn't say anything. I couldn't blame her. Koda's butt cheeks were tight enough to crush wood with a single clench. I couldn't imagine the frontal view was any less impressive.

"Son of a bitch!"

My paws tore down the hall toward the sounds of Taran's not-so-ladylike insults. I skidded into the immense kitchen, where she stood on the countertop, gripping a cabinet door to keep her balance in her damned platform pumps. More wolves had arrived. Taran jolted them with lightning as they neared, but her strikes weren't as effective. The wolves yelped and twitched, yet continued to advance. Taran was almost out of juice. But she wasn't out of attitude.

She slumped a little when she saw me and shot the wolves a siren grin. "You're so screwed," she declared. "My sister is going to *kick your asses*!"

There were many moments throughout our lives when I wanted to slap the snot out of Taran. This was one of them.

The wolves' hackles collectively rose as they set their diabolic sights on me. They moved as a single unit away from Taran and toward their newest prey.

Thanks, Taran.

A black-and-tan wolf leaped on me. An avalanche of blasted bedrock wouldn't have rammed me as hard as he did. He aimed his bear-trap fangs at my jugular. My claws dug into his shoulders, keeping him from making confetti out of my throat.

In the wild, he wouldn't have stood a chance. A tigress could shred through the hide of a wolf like packing foam. But this wasn't the wild, and he was no mere wolf. Four hundred–plus pounds of abominable lupine threw me around like a dead squirrel. My claws and teeth appeared to have little effect. Unlike the students in the alley, this guy had seen his share of combat.

"Get 'em, Celia. Show these bitches what you're made of!"

Taran didn't get it. The most I could do was continue to dig my claws and fangs and use the wolf as a shield against his pack. He wasn't, however, a willing participant. His claws scratched and pressed into my chest with the bulk of his weight while the others continued to pound against him to get at me. Their frustrated growls and impatient hunger for battle terrified me, and my stomach lurched from the wolf's blood dripping down my throat. I needed to get him off me, but the floor wasn't thick enough to *shift* across. If I tried to *shift* down, I'd land in Misha's basement and damage my already battered ribs, allowing the wolf to easily finish me.

"What are you doing, Celia?" Taran screamed. "Beat them shitless and let's get the hell out of here!"

Taran missed her calling as a motivational speaker.

I tried to use the wolf's momentum to roll us into his buddies, but my bones ached brutally and my muscles begged to stop moving. We banged into a butcher block stacked with kitchenware. Plates, glasses, and a few pans *kerplunk*ed, banged, and shattered onto the floor as we shoved our way through it.

Taran must have finally reabsorbed enough magic and realized my struggle to the friggin' death. She detonated a clamoring jolt, sending the wolf airborne and into an industrial-size stove.

That would have been great had a brown wolf not ransacked me. I think my skull made a serious dent in the stainless-steel refrigerator—or at least it should have, considering the canaries circling my head insisting I not move and just die. My broken rib now had a friend. Or two. I couldn't tell, since my lungs had stopped working from the increasing strain of my attacker's weight. I briefly heard the beautiful howl of a wolf before the abundant mass lifted off my chest.

I didn't so much leap to my feet as creep. Even my eyelashes hurt. They fluttered, trying to help me focus. When the haze and pessimistic canaries vanished, I took in the remains of the ransacked kitchen. All the wolves had disappeared but two. An oil black wolf with a white spot on his front paw sniffed at my head. The other waited near my trash-mouthed sister. Taran was clearly all out of supernatural juice. Exhausted and terrified, she could barely hold on to the cabinet door.

Taran's wolf was the identical twin of mine, except the white spot was on his opposite paw. He watched her, but failed to move, whereas my wolf nudged me with his head, trying to encourage me to stand. It almost seemed strange for him not to try to eat me, but his touch remained gentle and reassuring.

Because my luck generally sucked big, hairy moose, Taran misinterpreted his actions as another attempt on my life. "Get the hell away from her!"

It appeared Taran had some juice left after all. She propelled her last bit of lightning at my wolf, hollering with the anger of a thousand Latinas.

The wolf easily leaped out of her path.

I didn't.

The force from the bolt knocked me back into the fridge. Sparks flew as the huge appliance short-circuited. Some might argue that it took the brunt of the shock. My scrambled insides argued not.

"Oh, *shit*," Taran muttered.

My wolf sped to the one at her side. I flopped onto my belly in time to see the pair curl their necks together as if embracing.

Before joining to form one enormous wolf.

The transformation happened so fast, I almost missed it. Two halves merged in unison, the perfect blend of yin and yang except beautiful, frightening, and mesmerizing all at once, like the death of two and the rebirth of one almighty.

Taran gawked as the wolf placed his paws, now both white, on the countertop. The scent of *were* magic tickled my whiskers as the wolf vanished and *changed* into Gemini.

Oh, hell. Never had another lived up to a nickname like this.

"Don't be afraid," he murmured to Taran. "I promise to protect you." He left Taran briefly to lift an overturned kitchen chair and place it next to the counter. With the elegance of a king, he took Taran's hand and led her down his makeshift staircase. "Are you hurt?"

Taran didn't answer. She went back to performing act two of *Romeo and Juliet* while I lay on my side sizzling and hoping my ribs weren't protruding through my fur. I don't even think she suffered a broken nail. *Seriously?*

I pushed up on my front paws, but my back claws told me to screw off and declared that any movement was an insanely stupid idea. My back legs knew what they were talking about. I collapsed, yet again, onto my ribs.

My grunts snapped Taran out of her Red Riding Hood fantasy. She rushed to my side, screaming for Emme. "Son of a bitch, Celia. What the hell happened to you? Your ribs are sticking through your goddamn skin."

I didn't want to be right about my ribs. The thought made my head spin. Or was it the multitude of blows to my head?

I tried to ignore my pain—and the rapid return of the damn canaries—and focused on Gemini's face. It had been years since I'd seen a man naked and, bless Danny's heart, nothing compared to these heart-stopping beasts.

Emme and Shayna gasped when they clambered in and caught sight of me . . . and Gemini in all his butt-nekked glory.

Taran blocked their view. "Don't just stand there," she snapped. "Heal your sister!"

Emme covered her eyes to avoid ogling Gemini, thereby landing on my tail when she slipped over what I hoped was someone else's blood. This was so not my night. But the bash to my tail paled in comparison to what it took for Emme to heal my injuries. Every part of me snapped, crackled, and popped back into place. The pain throbbed so unbearably, I lost focus and *changed* back.

Shayna left quickly and returned with a soft throw blanket. I wasn't *were*. I didn't want to be naked and vulnerable around anyone. I gripped the throw against my body as my ribs began their torturous return home, burying all the whimpers and tears hammering against my soul to escape.

I'd only just sat up with Emme and Taran's help when three wolves shot into the kitchen roaring in challenge. Gemini didn't bother to turn around. He didn't have to. One twin wolf tore out of his back like Velcro and faced the wolves.

The human half of Gemini gripped Shayna's wrists as she yanked out two daggers from her ankle holsters. His dark almond eyes seethed with anger as he addressed the other wolves. "Your orders are to leave these girls alone and escort Aric out."

Oh, God. Aric.

I ran out of the house to where the fight between Aric and Misha continued by the lake. The wolves from the kitchen sprinted past me and joined the other *weres* attempting to haul Aric away. I covered my mouth, horrified. Aric's T-shirt had been ripped off, chunks from both his shoulders were missing, and blood soaked his face, hair, and jeans.

The female vampires doted on their master, sealing his cuts with flicks of their eager tongues. Misha ignored them, remaining eerily still as he watched Aric with deep, unapologetic loathing.

Shock kept me from joining my sisters vomiting behind me. Misha stood in only his half-shredded pants. Blood colored his long blond hair red and darkened his once golden skin to brown. His left hand had been severed at the wrist, and his midsection bore one immense hole. Bile from his massacred liver dribbled down his right side like a sponge being rhythmically squeezed.

Aric and Misha hadn't fought. They'd mutilated each other.

Good Lord.

Aric's animalistic growls snapped me out of my horror. "You goddamn leech. This isn't over—you hear me? *This isn't over!*"

The urge to calm and care for Aric overtook me. I clutched the blanket against my breasts and darted toward him. His head jerked in my direction when he caught my scent. I was mere feet from him when a wolf in human form backhanded me hard enough to force me back several yards.

"Don't fucking touch her!" Aric roared.

Misha charged my attacker with a spine-tingling hiss. He was too late. Aric's blow catapulted the wolf into a wide support beam. The beam splintered in half, sloping Misha's grand terrace with a loud boom.

My claws protruded; I expected the wolf to retaliate. But the attack never came. His limp form slid down the beam, painting a thick red streak until he face-planted onto the patio like a wet fish. *Splat.*

I gasped. Aric's wrath appeared beyond reason. So did his need to protect me. He tore away from his pack and rushed to my side, his pace slowing as he neared. Soothing streams of warmth cascaded across my skin as he cupped my face and took in my injuries. "Jesus," he whispered.

My hands found his wrists. "It's okay, Aric. I'm all right." Despite the danger, his presence immediately soothed my beast. He felt so right.

Aric's blazing eyes locked onto mine as a swarm of *weres* surrounded him and yanked him from my grasp. A dull ache pounded my chest like stone meeting stone. I didn't want him to leave me. We stared at each other in silence until his pack wrestled him from my sight and toward the front of the house. Car doors slammed and engines roared to life. The pack was leaving, and taking Aric with them.

Taran gasped next to me. "Holy Mother. Who the *hell* was that?"

I wiped my bloody lip with the edge of the blanket. "My boyfriend," I answered quietly.

CHAPTER 11

"Misha. What the hell are you doing?"

Misha tore off his pants in a way that would shame *Magic Mike*. He tossed them aside, and—*good Lord*—the rest of his Adonis form was enough to distract me from his gruesome injuries.

He grinned at my crimson face. "I am going for a swim. Care to join me?"

I gaped at his outstretched hand, but it was still better than the alternative. Master vampires, it seemed, weren't fans of underwear.

When I failed to do more than snap my jaw shut, Misha strolled his smooth derriere to the end of the wooden dock and jumped. My skin reeked with about four different types of body fluid. Mud caked my feet and toenails. And God only knew what Shayna was trying to peel off my back. Still, skinny-dipping with a vampire should have counted as one of the seven deadly sins.

Shayna gagged. "It's a piece of flesh."

I reached around my shoulder, trying to stay covered. "It can't be."

Emme's green color matched her dress. She'd discovered the thing on my skin when she healed me. "A-a-are you sure?"

"I *think* I'd remember skinning someone." I found the edge of something leathery, slimy, and warm. I froze, suddenly not so sure.

Taran groaned, relieved. "It's a slice of ham." She pulled it off and waved it in my face. "You must have rolled on it while fighting the wolf in the kitchen."

The mere mention of the *weres* made me sick. Aric, Gemini, Koda, and Liam remained the few who didn't try to harm us. I couldn't comprehend what we'd done to infuriate those who supposedly protected the earth. But I did recognize the need to avoid all of them . . . except for Aric.

Shayna shook her head, verbalizing my thoughts. "Why did they come after us, anyway? And why did Misha jump Aric? Isn't there a treaty between their kind?"

One of the naughty Catholic schoolgirls glided to our side, a rare feat in the stilt-high boots she wore over her fishnets. "The mongrel challenged the master in his home, thereby temporarily violating the treaty. Our master was within his rights to defend his property." She circled us slowly. "The others recognized you as our allies; thus you became their target as well."

I fixed the blanket around me to keep me covered. "Aric didn't challenge Misha."

"Yes, he did." The vamp peered over her shoulder at me as she sashayed away. "He tried to take what belongs to the master."

She assumed I was Misha's property. She assumed wrong. My cool skin heated with resentment . . . until I realized most of the bimbos Misha encountered would likely sacrifice their pricey bosoms for the chance of becoming his. He had wealth, power, ethereal beauty.

But he sure as hell didn't have me.

I brushed the bitchy vamp's comments aside. There were more pressing matters. Bloodlust continued to run rampant, and Misha's death would likely spiral the plague out of control. And perhaps it was naive, but like Petro, I believed in his innocence. I also believed whoever caused the infestation would rise to inconceivable power in Misha's absence.

I peered out to where Misha had dove into the peaceful water. The extent of his injuries worried me. Masters healed fast, but only because they drew power and strength from their keep. The more vampires a master controlled, the more formidable he was. Except Misha was down to a mere handful.

I walked to the end of the dock, praying I wouldn't see chunks of Misha's liver floating above the waves. Fortunately, my eyes failed to spot any dismembered body parts. Unfortunately, they also failed to spot Misha.

"Dude, where did Count Hotness go?"

I knelt over the edge. "I don't know—"

Emme screamed from the other side of the pier. "Oh, my God. He's dead!"

We rushed over. Misha floated as if standing beneath the clear water, the bright dock lighting bleaching his skin white. His long blond hair fanned above him, swaying in time with the waves. My breath caught at his outstretched arms reaching as if pleading for salvation.

Emme crossed herself, her voice trembling. "May he rest in peace."

Taran swallowed hard. "Shit, Ceel. That settles that."

"He's not dead," I stammered.

Shayna placed her hand on my shoulder. "Celia, I know you wanted to help him—"

I shook my head. "No. What I mean is he *can't* be dead. There's no ash or anything." Despite what I said, my stomach lurched into my throat.

Taran gripped my arm. "Girl, I don't know. He sure as hell looks dead to me."

I ignored Taran *and* Misha. God, it creeped me out just looking at him. "Emme," I urged, "pull him out with your *force.*"

Emme once told me she could feel everything she moved with her mind, as if it brushed against her hands. The way she swooned at my request told me she had no desire to touch a potentially redeceased body with gaping organs. Still, she gave it the old college try.

I wiped my sweaty palms against my blanket and reviewed the steps for mouth-to-mouth in my head. *Sweet Jesus, please let him be okay.*

Emme gathered her courage, ambled to the end, took a deep breath, and . . . nothing. For thirty long seconds, nothing happened. Misha's head didn't so much as bob out of the water.

"Damn it, Emme," Taran urged. "Hurry up before we have a damn vegetable with fangs on our hands!"

Emme whimpered, her face turning purple from the strain. "I'm trying, but something heavy is pulling him down."

A strange feeling of dread numbed me down to my toes. "Get help," I said to Shayna.

She sprinted, screaming for Misha's vampires while my eyes searched the dock for something to haul Misha out. Diving in remained out of the question. My sisters couldn't swim, and I could manage a pathetic doggy paddle at best.

My rising anxiety threatened to unleash my tigress when I spotted one of those pole thingies used to maneuver boats into the dock. I used the metal hook at the end and tangled it around Misha's hair with as much finesse as a frat boy on ice skates after a wild Saturday night. "Go, Emme. Go!"

With a collective grunt, Emme and I yanked with everything we had . . . only to land on our butts, sweating, panting, and Misha-less.

My eyes crossed as I stared at the huge knot of Misha's hair at the end of my stick.

Shit.

I scrambled to the edge, completely out of ideas. A single bubble formed from Misha's mouth. And that's when I panicked. I flipped the pole and poked him hard in the head, between his shoulder blades, on his stomach, anywhere I could reach, desperate to move him.

"Why are you poking the master?" one of Misha's bodyguards asked. The lot of them scowled like I'd rammed the damn stick up his nose.

I pointed wildly into the water. "He's stuck. We need to get him out!"

Misha's other guard, Tim, narrowed his eyes like he wanted nothing more than to bowl with my decapitated head. "Haven't any of you learned to harness the power of the lake?" Our blank expressions answered for us. He rolled his eyes. "Just leave the master to his business and try not to get in the way." He left and followed the others back to the house, not bothering to glance back.

I wanted to pounce on him and slap him upside the

head—for not helping Misha *and* for being a monstrous prick. But then the water around Misha stirred and another bubble appeared, this time by his foot. A third bubble formed, followed by another, and another. To my horrendous shock, the water beneath Misha's feet rapidly simmered until a full boil concealed his entire body.

What the hell?

"Son of a bitch!" Taran screamed. "We're outta here."

Soft thuds fell upon the grass as my sisters hauled ass across the lawn. Their *Scooby-Doo*-ish steps dwindled to a halt when Shayna hollered, "Celia's not coming!"

My sisters bounded back in a frenzy and tried to lug me away. But I refused to move, hypnotized by the rippling magic cocooning Misha. The severity of the moment should have made me heed my sisters' shouts of warning, and yet even my tigress remained glued there with curiosity. Tahoe wouldn't just cook Misha like a lobster. Some deeply hidden secret was being unlocked within the lake. And this master vampire possessed the key.

I basked in the surging glory of the lake's magic, ignoring Emme's plea to run. My sisters' tugging became more urgent, but what happened next halted their frantic efforts. A beautiful golden glow spawned in the center of the whirlpool of bubbles, igniting fireworks *inside* the lake. Thousands of light blue sparkles shimmered across the surface before erupting in a spray of light against our skin. I jumped, expecting to be scorched. Except the bizarre magic didn't harm. Instead it fell upon me like warm water from a soothing shower, refreshing my skin and hair and eliminating my fatigue.

My sisters giggled uncontrollably as if tickled. I didn't share their reaction. Mostly I just relished the soft caress against my muscles, massaging my remaining weariness away.

A loud creaking snapped me out of my mellow haze, just as gentle fingertips swept along my jawline. I jerked away from the touch in time to see Misha surface, the water slicking his long hair behind his head like a drape.

I glanced around. My sisters appeared relaxed, as if they'd woken from a good, long sleep. Yet their physical appearances couldn't mask the smell of their apprehension. "What did you do to us, Misha?" I demanded.

Misha swam to the ledge and rested his muscular arms against the dock, beads of water cascading down his masculine face. All he needed was a bottle of Gucci cologne at his side and the photo shoot was good to go.

"Are you angry, my love?" he asked.

"Just tell us what you did, damn it!" Taran yelled.

Misha leaped onto the dock in one smooth motion. And suddenly, Taran didn't seem so irate anymore. Droplets of water glistened and streaked down his freshly regenerated physique as he stalked toward me, a perfect replica of man and Greek god.

Taran, dear, unapologetic Taran, fixed her eyes on Misha's backside, mesmerized by the tightening and relaxing of muscle as he walked. I don't even think girlfriend blinked.

Emme and Shayna stumbled backward, knocked off balance by the might of Misha's corporeal hotness. Yet if my sisters' actions made them prudes, they should have hailed me as their queen. At least *they* kept their eyes open. *I* buried my face in my hand like a displaced virgin at a nudist colony. Shrinkage, for sure, was not an issue for Misha.

He chuckled. Not that I could blame him. When it

came to the male species, there was no cure for my supreme dorkiness. Even sweet little Emme had more experience than I did.

Misha placed his hands on my shoulders and spoke softly—mostly, I suspected, to hold in his amusement. "You were attacked without cause. My desire was merely to invigorate your spirits. Please forgive me, ladies, if I offended."

"Oh, no. No. Not at all," my smooth-as-sandpaper sisters insisted all at once.

The mounting number of naked studs I'd seen tonight had reached exorbitant heights . . . not that I was complaining or anything, but my lack of sexual encounters hindered my ability to respond with confidence. I'd been dropped into unfamiliar territory, without food or a compass, and with a bare-ass lothario for a tour guide. Hell, most women would have flipped.

My tigress flicked her tail with excitement, wondering what was next. Between the bare bodies and the brawls, this was her idea of a fun night. Me, I'd rather have spent the evening consuming large quantities of buffalo wings.

Despite my beast's growing anticipation, she allowed me to draw from her courage. I dropped my hand and shrugged Misha off, focusing on his face like life, death, and a shipload of preschoolers depended on it. "Misha, I—"

"Oh, my goodness," Emme whispered. "Look at the house."

What I saw made me step back. Tahoe's light blue sparks slowly dissipated over where Misha's house had suffered the most damage. The terrace stood tall, grand, and whole above the fully restored beam. The loud creaking sound I'd heard must have been the wooden planks repositioning. I blinked. Even the cracked floor-to-ceiling windows had been repaired.

A vampire appeared in front of the dining window with a bucket, a towel, and a bottle of Windex. She plucked something that resembled an ear from the glass, pausing to squint at it before tossing it into her pail. In the library, two vampires pointed to the bloodstains on the cappuccino-colored walls. They seemed to be arguing about what kind of blood it was. The taller of the two sampled it with his tongue. *Werecat*, he mouthed. The other went for a taste until she noticed Misha watching. They noticeably paled before grabbing their mops and resuming their cleaning.

I faced Misha. "You combined Tahoe's magic with your own."

He nodded. "The energy I gathered will last me a few days at best, but it comes with a price. When Tahoe demands its return, I will be left weakened and possibly comatose for a period of time."

"Is that wise, dude?" Shayna asked. "I mean, what if another master challenges you while you're vulnerable?"

Misha glanced in Shayna's direction. "Considering my fate will be decided at the rise of the next moon, young miss, it's unlikely an issue I will have to deal with."

Taran scoffed. "Then why not conserve your energy instead of wasting it on home improvements?"

Misha regarded her slowly. "I own many houses throughout the world, dear Taran. Yet this is my home." He looked back at me. "Should I survive, I would like something beautiful to return to."

My eyes widened; I hoped he didn't mean me. "Um. We need to go," I said quickly. "I'll call you in a few hours."

Misha kissed the back of my hand before backing away and gracefully slipping into the water. My sisters exchanged glances, but failed to comment. They hustled up the small incline toward the front of the house, hurrying to get the hell out of vamp turf.

"Come *on*, Ceel," Taran insisted.

I didn't follow right away, choosing to trek to the edge of the pier where Misha effortlessly treaded water. He smiled. I didn't return his grin.

I straightened my shoulders. "Just so you know, I don't belong to you."

Misha's gray eyes reflected silver in the moonlit water. "I never claimed you to be mine, my darling," he answered patiently.

The nerve I'd built up to confront him disappeared, its empty space replaced by a sudden wave of foolishness. *Me thinks I presume too much.* I cleared my throat. "Good. So long as we're clear."

I hurried away, but not before I heard Misha whisper, "Unless, of course, you desire to be."

CHAPTER 12

Taran rolled our Subaru into Emerald Bay, a former state park situated on the southern end of Tahoe, and the place Zhahara called home, sweet home. Before she moved in, I didn't think anyone could buy a state park. But when you had the amount of moola master vampires possessed, laws, politicians, and the constitution were just minor inconveniences.

"This shit's fucked up."

"I know, Taran. You've mentioned it once or twice." I rubbed my eyes. It was close to two in the morning. We should have been in bed with visions of half-naked were-wolves dancing in our heads. But none of us could sleep following a steaming cup of Misha java. "Reenergized" was an understatement. My legs itched to run a few marathons while I read *War and Peace* and created origami birds with my free hand. We'd gone home, showered, and Googled directions to Zhahara's estate—much to Taran's audible hems, haws, and "*F* this"es.

"Maybe we should contact the wolves," Emme said quietly. "I mean, they are the experts in these matters."

Shayna turned around to face Emme. "Dude. Are you nuts? After what happened at Misha's do you really think they'll do anything to help him?"

"Maybe not him . . ." Emme glanced my way.

I knew Emme meant "wolf," not "wolves." I also knew which wolf in particular she thought might rush to help me. But Aric had proved . . . distracting. My fierceness tapered in his presence, not a good thing in the dawn of a bloodlust epidemic. I needed my tigress to protect me and keep me focused, not some starry-eyed tabby who developed a bad case of *nipplus erectus* at the sight of Aric shirtless.

I shook my head, trying to clear my thoughts from the intensity with which he regarded me . . . before his pack hauled him away. "I'm not involving Aric in this. He and Misha obviously hate each other." I shrugged. "Besides, he told me to skip town."

"Smart wolf," Taran muttered from the front.

My shoulders slumped; I was tired of arguing. "Taran, people are being gnawed on like trail mix. They'll continue to die if I don't do something." I stared out the car window into the pitch-black night. "Still, I can't help Misha unless I know for sure Zhahara is involved. Let me snoop around and see what I can find. If she's running a soup kitchen or nursing orphaned monkeys, I promise to never mention Misha, bloodlust, or withered corpses again."

Taran's narrowed eyes cut to the rearview mirror. "Don't think I won't hold you to that."

Zhahara's compound wasn't hard to find, seeing as a twenty-foot stone wall encompassed the fifteen-plus acres of her land. Taran drove until she found a small road leading to a probable service entrance.

I opened the door the moment she parked. "Wait here. I'll look around for anything suspicious."

Taran fixed her scowl on me. "Ten minutes. That's all you get."

I pushed my hair aside. "Trust me when I say I don't really want to be here."

"Be careful, dude," Shayna whispered.

"*Shift* out of there if you see anything creepy," Emme added.

I nodded and disappeared into the woods that ran opposite the wall. My predator side moved swiftly and almost silently through the cold night. Pine needles crunched softly beneath my feet. The temperature had dropped considerably, but my thick sweater, jeans, and UGGs kept me warm, especially at the speed I stalked.

The night fell silent except for my movements, which didn't make sense. My sensitive ears should have picked up the scurry of field mice, the flutter of bat wings, or even the hoot of a few owls. Yet nothing, just me. I continued along the thick pines until I reached the rear entrance and *shifted* across the narrow road for a better look.

I didn't get far.

Remnants of a shredded UPS uniform lay a few yards from the metal gates. Teeth sparkled in the moonlight against the black tar road like scattered pearls. A foot shoved into a big brown boot teetered near the edge of the road where thick ferns had begun to overgrow. Most of the skin had been torn from the bone except near the ankle, where dirt and bodily fluid flattened the short curly hairs against bits of leftover flesh.

I forced my legs to move past the foot and tattered pieces of cloth to where the nauseating odor of death grew more rancid. The road leading up to the back of the house glistened with what I only wished had been rain. The stench of rot and the hungry bugs crawling over the festering mess told me otherwise. A spinal column with protruding capillaries lay on the grass, the ends shriveling like drying leaves on a long-stemmed rose. Blood soaked the path, pooling at the bottom, where a brunette with matted hair lapped voraciously with her tongue, despite the flies swarming around her. She paused and sniffed, her stomach growling. She'd caught my scent.

I *shifted* before her head could snap up.

"Yup. Misha's got the right gal."

I slammed the car door shut and locked it. It took me a few tries, as my hands shook like I gripped a jackhammer. It was asinine to think the lock to our SUV would keep the bloodlust vamp slurping rancid blood from breaking in. But when your own blood turned to ice, and you were eight shades paler than you were when you woke up in the morning, you started wishing for crazy shit.

"Dude, are you sure?"

"I saw teeth, a spinal cord, and someone's shoe with a foot still attached."

Taran stomped on the accelerator.

The rows of thick firs spun into a blurring mess as we sped away. I scanned the trees, searching for any bloodguzzling monsters huddled in the branches, or a brunette munching on a kneecap giving chase behind us. Taran's Mach 1 speed made me dizzy, and so did the lingering scent of decomposing flesh. But no way in hell would I ask her to pull over. If I hurled it would be in the car and far—very far away—from any creatures capable of feasting on human flesh like rotisserie chicken.

"Oh, my God. We have to do something."

Taran glared at Emme while taking a particularly sharp curve. The wheels screeched and we coasted a few feet on two wheels. "What we have to do is get the hell out of Tahoe. We're packing our shit and leaving tonight before we're next!"

Emme shook her head feverishly. "No. We can't. We have to help Misha."

Taran's screams at Emme blasted my eardrums. "Didn't you hear Celia? Teeth and a goddamn spinal cord!"

She swerved around another corner. I gripped the "oh, shit" bar, cursing myself for not letting Shayna drive. Although Shayna's speed would have been faster, and more hair-raising as a result, her reflexes were lightning quick and she always managed to stay in control. Taran's driving currently mirrored her volatile personality.

Taran barely avoided crashing into a guardrail as she jetted down a steep incline. "We'll call Bren and Danny from the road. They need to haul ass, too. Celia, you snag our birth certificates and passports—they're in the safe. Shayna, grab our laptops and cell phones—don't forget the chargers. I'll write our resignations and call our managers. We'll put the house on the market online." She huffed. "Though who the hell is going to want to live in Tahoe now?"

Taran tore into our neighborhood minutes later. She screeched to a halt in front of our house and bolted inside without glancing back. The rest of us ambled out slowly, with Emme on the verge of tears. I didn't know what to say. My tigress paced restlessly. It was wrong to die like that. Wrong, and horrid, and terribly heartbreaking. Those poor women and the UPS guy hadn't stood a chance. They could have been armed and it wouldn't have mattered. Guns would do jack against preternatural creatures whose thirst would never be quenched.

Until their deaths.

"He probably had a family."

Shayna's head whipped in my direction. "What?"

My fists clenched against my sides. "The guy. Missing the foot. He probably had a family."

Tears glistened in Emme's eyes. "I'm sure he did. And I'm sure those women did, too."

Taran stormed out of the house with an armful of clothes, tripping over the long sleeve of one of her sweaters. She toppled onto her knees, dropping her things when she attempted to break her fall. "Son of a *bitch*." She caught us idling by the car as she struggled to round up her belongings. "What the hell are you doing? We have to get out of here now!"

I shook my head. "I'm not going, Taran. I'm staying to fight with Misha."

Taran threw the clothes she'd bunched onto the lawn. "You are out of your goddamn mind if you think we're leaving you by yourself!"

Emme placed her small hands over my fist. "I'm staying with her, Taran."

Taran's blue eyes widened. "No. No freaking way. Goddamn it, what is wrong with you?"

Shayna approached her, palms out. "Taran. Innocent people are dead. And they're going to keep dying. We have the opportunity to help. Can't you see that?"

Taran's face darkened with rage and something else I couldn't recognize. "We already help people every day *as nurses*. That's more than enough. We don't owe the goddamn world our fucking lives. For shit's sake, how much more can we go through?"

And there it was. Taran was afraid. And rightfully so. Our past was mired with sorrow and wickedness no one should ever experience. She wanted to end the nightmares. Not to create new ones. Here I was telling her that not only would I willingly subject myself to torment, but that our little sisters might come along for the ride.

Emme surprised me by smiling softly. "Don't be bitter, Taran," she said gently.

I just stared at Emme. As the smallest and most sensitive, she had been the most wounded by our past. And yet she had been the first to say we should help. She was the first to step in, ready to fight, despite her escalating dread and fear of pain.

Taran didn't say anything, stunned into fuming silence.

Shayna slung an arm around her. "Look at it this way: Maybe we've been given our abilities for a greater purpose. Maybe this is what we've always been meant to do."

Taran shrugged Shayna off. "March into impending doom? I don't think so. Quit fooling yourself into thinking we're something special. We're not. We're just a bunch of freaks."

Shayna smiled patiently. "Taran, you know that's not what I'm saying."

Emme squeezed my hand again. "What are you thinking, Celia?"

I sighed. "I think we were better off when no one knew about us. That said, we can't pretend to be blind." My face met Taran's. "Nor can we run away." Shayna started to say something, but I cut her off. "I'm going to do this. I'm going to help Misha. But I don't . . . I *can't* let you come with me."

Taran threw her hands in the air. "What the hell? Do you really think we'll let you do this on your own? It's all of us or none of us."

I cursed under my breath, certain we were signing our death warrants, but knowing we wouldn't be able to live with ourselves if we ran.

Taran fixed her glare on Emme and Shayna. "You two better know damn well what you're signing up for. Celia and I know what we're capable of. The blood from our first kills still stains our hands." She closed her eyes tight and shuddered. "That shit stays with you forever—no matter if the kill was righteous or not. If you can't deal with it—*don't*. We'll leave now and drag Celia's ass with us."

Shayna exchanged glances with Emme before stepping forward. "These aren't people we're going after. They're monsters." She shrugged. "Monsters have no place in a world I want to belong to."

Emme nodded despite the tears moistening her soft and trusting green eyes. "I never wanted to know what it's like to take a life. But if it's between our lives and theirs, I'll do what it takes to make sure we live through it."

The breeze from the lake brushed against my back like a gentle encouraging nudge forward from a friend. I clenched and unclenched my fists, terrified and yet raring for a fight. "Fine. I'll call Misha."

CHAPTER 13

The vampires greeted us on the steps of the mansion, standing at parade rest. Black cargo pants covered their muscular legs. Fine-gauge sweaters of black silk tightened over their powerful biceps, triceps, and abdominals. Combat boots sheathed their feet. These vicious creatures of the night looked dressed to maim, maul, murder.

We looked ready to crash at the nearest homeless shelter.

My sisters and I had decided on old jeans, sweatshirts, and sneakers after Taran said, "I'm not getting that nasty bloodlust shit on my nice clothes."

I zipped the front of my sweatshirt to conceal the spaghetti stain on my tank. Nothing like feeling like a complete jackass before charging into battle.

The vamps parted smoothly to allow their master through. Misha bowed his head. "Ladies, you have my deepest gratitude. If you will, please join me for an early breakfast. We shall leave within the hour."

"Early" seemed the appropriate term. Sunrise still remained hours away.

I shoved my hands into the pockets of my old sweat-shirt as the breeze from the lake intensified, turning the air dense and crisp. A dangerous storm brewed in the distance, threatening to fall upon us like the mighty fist of Thor. I glanced over my shoulder before following Misha inside. I'd hoped the break of dawn would bring strong light to aid my sisters in battle. Without the night vision the vampires and I possessed, the tremendous drawbacks they faced continued to escalate.

And so did my trepidation for their safety.

The vampires' steps echoed through the vast foyer, distinguishable from ours as they marched as one solid entity. "We will invade by boat and land on the eastern shore," Misha said as he walked. "As bloodlust worsens, the muscles of infected vampires grow too dense, imped-ing their ability to swim."

Shayna hurried to Misha's right side. "So if we have to, say, um, run for our lives, the water is the best place to be?"

Misha nodded slowly at Shayna. "Provided the depth of the water and our speed are sufficient. The thirst of bloodlust further amplifies a vampire's strength and ve-locity."

Oh. Goody.

Taran swore behind me. Bloodlust just kept sounding better and better.

"The boats are almost ready. We will divide into three separate teams."

"Excuse me, Misha," Emme said quietly. "But shouldn't we use two boats, or one big boat? With only seventeen of us, it might be better to stay in larger groups."

Emme's blush deepened as Misha regarded her. "Once we are on land, it will be to our advantage to stay as a group. However, smaller boats will dock closer to shore and will be faster should we need to flee."

My fingertips swept over Emme's tense muscles as I caressed her back. "And the more boats, the more options we have for escape, honey."

Emme nodded. I supposed I should have reassured her, but the reality of the situation offered very little in the inspiration department. As everyone veered into the dining room, I grasped Misha's arm. He stopped, as I'd intended, but he wouldn't allow me to pull him into the office across the way. His resistance didn't surprise me. Master vampires didn't take kindly to being led anywhere.

His spine straightened and those hard gray eyes skimmed along my arm until they fixed upon my face. "I need to see you privately, Misha."

A brief wind swept across my cheek from the speed with which he whisked us into his study. I'd only just felt his grip against my waist when the door slammed shut behind us. My eyes widened as he slowly lowered me to the floor. He said nothing, allowing his body to speak for him. The smell of lust surfaced immediately. He was aroused. And crap, somehow I'd caused it.

Lust remained unfamiliar, at least on a personal level. And while I'd scented it in clubs where dancers ground, at restaurants where couples stumbled out clutching each other in anticipation, and on Bren when he'd spotted his conquest for the evening, never had it been directed at me. Yes, Danny and I had sex as teens. But what Danny and I'd shared lingered as a distant memory of innocence, attraction, and a wish to please.

Misha's scent of bare skin and implied promises of bliss left no hint of innocence. What did I expect? After all, he'd had more than a century to learn the art of sex, and his growing aroma and need assured me he'd mastered his craft.

I swallowed hard. I hadn't expected such a response. Nor did I want it. My eyes wandered down. Misha obviously possessed the defibrillator to resuscitate my sleeping girl parts. But beyond my fear of intimacy at his hands lay the realization that Misha wasn't the male who haunted my dreams and beckoned my beast.

Misha leaned into me, his soft, perfect lips parting to reach mine. I shrank away. "I'm sorry, but this isn't what I want from you, Misha."

Judging by the blatant confusion hardening his features, I may very well have been the first woman in history to refuse Sir Misha Aleksandr. Several long seconds passed before he released his hold. His tight black sweater hugged every muscle on his two-hundred-pound-plus form. His mane had been swept back into a tail, revealing that angelic face with the devilish twinkle. I chuckled. Misha was without question the hottest thing with sharp incisors—the poster child for ethereal vampiric beauty. Yet whenever I closed my eyes, images of Aric inundated my thoughts: the way he held me, the way his gaze met mine . . . the way he smiled.

Misha crossed his arms, his Russian accent thick over his words: "Tell me then what it is you desire."

My eyes lowered to the bluestone floor—beautiful, despite all the cracks and imperfections. "I want you to watch over Emme. Out of all of us, she deserves to live the most." I forced the words out. "If it comes down to it, Misha, and the rest of us don't make it, I need you to get her to safety."

Misha raised my chin with a single finger, perhaps because he knew I couldn't move just then. "If you consider her weak, why do you anticipate you and the others will perish before her?"

My tigress rose to the surface. "Because Taran, Shayna, and I will die before anything happens to her. Emme is . . . different. She still believes in the good of others, despite the darkness that surrounds us." I shrugged. "The world needs more Emmes."

Misha's finger slipped from my jaw. He circled me slowly. "Is the world not as deserving of you?"

Sins have a funny way of resurfacing at inappropriate times. I smiled without humor. "Emme has enough heart for both of us. If her heart continues to beat, in a way, mine will, too." I stopped smiling then. "Make me this promise, Misha."

He waited briefly before whirling me around and exposing my palm. I gasped when his warm tongue slid against my skin. He licked it once before placing my hand over his heart. "I do not agree with your request, but I give you my word as a master."

Misha didn't release me; he kept his hand on mine as he led me into the Delaware-size dining room and to the marble table. My sisters lifted their heads from their plates. Most of their eggs Benedict and hash browns remained untouched. They didn't want to eat, yet they knew survival depended on more than just adrenaline.

I sat next to Taran. She pretended to fuss with the strap of my tank. "Did he say yes?" she whispered. I nodded, both to her and to Shayna, who looked up. Shayna smiled with sadness and relief before returning to her meal.

CHAPTER 14

Small drops of rain hit my face as we walked along the beach toward the boathouse, gathering twigs for Shayna along the way. I added the small stick to the pile I cradled and yanked up my hood. By the time we reached the lengthy dock, the droplets had temporarily ceased. It was just as well; the skimpy hood was no match for my long waves, even in the ponytail I'd wrangled them into. And besides, the thunder in the distance promised a thorough drenching with or without proper rain gear.

Four white boats, flashy and built for speed, bobbed next to a small yacht. Three vampires waited in the ones at the end of the pier—our captains, I presumed. But just as I stepped onto the first wide plank the scurry of tiny feet alerted my senses.

"Celia, look out!"

I was already looking over the edge of the yacht before Shayna could finish shouting her warning, watching the little brown field mouse disappear into the adjacent wooded area. I stood to leap back onto the dock, but the scowls from Misha's vampires halted me in place.

"A cat that's afraid of a mouse. *Nice*," one of Misha's bodyguards muttered.

My jaw clenched tight. "I'm not afraid. I'm just sort of . . . allergic."

"You're allergic to mice," one of the good Catholics repeated, disgust dripping from each word.

"Well, all animals, actually," Emme said, frowning at them as much as her angelic features allowed. "But that doesn't make her weak."

The Catholic schoolgirl jerked her head in Emme's direction. Her fair complexion and long red hair bequeathed her with a striking beauty. I might have envied her—if she also hadn't been bequeathed with royal bitchiness. "Yes. It does!" she snapped. "It also makes her a problem. *Our* problem."

"Colleen," Misha warned.

She dipped her head low enough so that the vee of her tight shirt showcased the crease between her enormous bosoms. "A thousand apologies, Master. But what are we to do if she develops a reaction?" She scoffed in my direction. "I'm fresh out of Benadryl."

I cracked my knuckles and landed in front of her, kicking aside the pile of sticks I'd dropped. "No Benadryl necessary. Beating your ass will fix me right up."

She hissed, her incisors protruding out, only to land with a hard thump on the dock. Her fair skin discolored and a small gurgle escaped her throat. I exchanged glances with my sisters.

Taran withdrew the fire from her fingertips. "Damn, Celia. I didn't even see you strike."

I slowly lowered my balled fists. "I didn't touch her. . . ."

With the exception of Colleen, who continued to lie

like a dying slug, and Misha, all the vamps resumed their parade-rest position with their gazes firmly dropped. Misha stared out over the water, his arms crossed in front of him, his expression blank. Yet his deadly tone left nothing to the imagination. "I find it grating to remind my family that guests—especially those who are attempting to save our very lives—*need to be respected*. Colleen. Is there something you wish to say to Celia?"

"Ir-kie," Colleen croaked.

Misha turned to me, smiling. "Colleen extends her deepest apologies, my darling."

"Apology accepted," I mumbled, stupefied by Colleen's clay-colored lips.

Tahoe's magic must have been potent enough to camouflage Misha's own. I hadn't caught even the slightest whiff of his power. Yet there it was, squashing Colleen to the pier like a woolly mammoth on a grape.

Slowly Colleen's natural color returned. The minute her lips tinged pink, she scrambled to her feet and joined the others, careful to give Misha ample space.

"Shall we, ladies?"

The vamps rushed to pick up the twigs my sisters and I had dropped when Colleen challenged me. They placed the neat piles at Shayna's feet once she sat in the nearest boat.

"I don't suppose I can convince you and Emme to ride with me?" Misha asked.

I leaped into the boat with my sisters and two other vampires. "No. I stay with them."

Misha watched me closely from the dock while six vampires piled into the boat farthest away. "Master," a vampire in the center boat pleaded. "You'll be safest with your own."

Misha joined the vampire and three others after a brief pause. "Stay no farther than six yards apart."

"Yes, Master," the captains echoed before the engines caught and the motors roared in unison.

Shayna adjusted the bow back onto her shoulder once she finished fastening her life vest. The vamps had eyed her suspiciously when she hauled the giant weapon out of the car, likely questioning her lack of arrows. Yet they failed to ask her directly. Perhaps they didn't want to risk pissing Misha off. His response to Colleen's behavior left little doubt that punishment in the House of Aleksandr was swift, severe, and potentially lethal.

No one spoke most of the way. Emme wriggled in her seat nervously and Taran kept lighting balls of fire between her palms. Shayna remained unusually still, focusing ahead, ready to attack. Her reflexes were as sharp as mine. And while she didn't have much physical strength, the sharpness of her blades compensated for her lack of muscle.

I moved next to her and nudged her with my elbow. "You okay?"

She grinned, surprising me with her typical sparkle. "Yeah. I'm ready, you know, dude? I mean, I'm scared senseless, but it almost seems like I've been preparing for a fight for a long time." Her brows quirked. "I never knew why I could pick up sword play and weapons training just by watching movies and stuff. It seemed like such a waste of a gift—with all the guns out there and all, who cares if I'm good with a knife?" She reached into her back pocket to check her toothpicks for the fifth time. "Maybe this is the kind of thing I've been working for." She shoved the little box away before returning her focus ahead. "I just hope I get more than one opportunity to show what I can do."

I tapped her thigh with my hand. "Yeah. Me, too, honey."

Thunder and lightning struck in the distant mountains. "Goddamn witches," our captain said. "They're probably the ones bringing the storm."

"What the hell are you rambling on about?" Taran asked.

The vamp rolled his eyes. "Witches often practice their spellwork in the mountains to avoid accidently killing anyone when they cast. The stronger spells charge the air with magic, stimulating nature to produce storms."

I watched the gathering clouds and the escalating bolts of lightning. Witches smelled of magic and the dried crushed herbs they used in their spells. Ambrosial scents of spearmint, sage, rosemary, and basil thickened the air.

Taran shuddered. "Damn. Their magic is strong."

The vamp smiled. "Yes. It makes their blood pretty damn tasty."

Emme winced. I shook my head. *Why did we always end up with the freaks?*

My tigress paced restlessly inside me. Neither of us liked the boat—not enough room to move, to roam. And the whole fear-of-drowning thing didn't help either. I stood and stretched my legs just as Fannette, Tahoe's only island, came into view. We'd arrived. It was time.

The vampires hustled to get their gun holsters on, cringing as the clips of gold bullets brushed against their bodies. The gold would soon make them sick, but nausea was a small price to pay in exchange for the firepower we'd need.

The motors cut as we approached the bay. We glided

across the fog-covered water, stopping a few yards from shore. Silence sliced like Shayna's blade. No birds flew, and the breeze ceased to a trickle. The only sound was Tahoe's gentle splashing against the smooth rocks bordering the beach. Yet its normally gentle lullaby failed to reassure me. An odd eagerness seeped into my pores, taunting me to draw closer.

"Come into my parlor," said the spider to the fly.

Misha and the vampires stood as a single entity, their eyes sharp, their claws protruding. The taunting sensation grew nearer, stronger. My inner beast growled, loud enough to rattle my heart.

"Wha-what . . ." Emme began.

"Something's here," I whispered to Emme.

My tigress eyes replaced my own, but her vision couldn't pierce through the thickness of the fog. I froze. Watching. Waiting. The urge to attack growing.

Water exploded like the start of a fountain to our left. I'd caught a glimpse of something wide, green, and thick before its arms encased the closest vampire. He vanished in a burst of water and a holler of agony. Shayna and I rushed to the edge, only to get flooded with an eruption of blood and ash.

Bullets shot wildly into the water, and the roars of my angered beast escaped. My sisters screamed—except for Shayna. Her eyes narrowed at the water as she reached for her stack of kindling. She placed the stick against her bow. As she pulled, gold light flickered from her necklace to her fingertips, transforming the wood into a thick gold arrow, the tip wide and deadly. She closed her eyes and pointed to where the vamp had dematerialized— only to aim four feet away at the last second and propel the arrow at an unimaginable velocity.

A two-hundred-pound infected female broke through the water, tipping the side of our boat forward. Green fluid bulged her thickened muscles; a maw full of sharp teeth snapped with hunger. She screamed, revealing the arrow protruding from the top of her skull down into her throat. Shayna failed to hit the heart.

But I didn't.

My claws struck hard through the vampire's chest, crushing her sternum until my fingertips gathered around the hot, pumping muscle. I yanked it out in an upsurge of putrid-smelling fluid and ash. The force knocked me back, but I jumped to my feet, landing on the starboard bow.

"Stay down until I say," I hissed at Taran and Emme.

Taran's mouth tightened as she clutched Emme against her. "I thought these assholes couldn't swim."

"We're in shallow water," Shayna answered tightly. She pointed another transformed arrow down into the lake, one foot on the floor of the boat, the other bent at the knee against the gunwale. Her hands stayed perfectly still as she waited for the next attack. Across from us, the vamps inched around the perimeter of the boats, the barrels of the gun pointing down. Misha stood in the middle, fury and hatred pushing back the mist around him.

Something bumped the floor beneath Taran and Emme. Emme's head shot up. I shook my head. *Don't move*, I mouthed.

The vamps in the boat next to Misha's didn't heed me. They scrambled away from the thud against the starboard, announcing breakfast time to the bloodlusters prowling beneath. They surfaced, hungry jaws snapping as they dragged two vampires into the murky depths—including Colleen.

A cluster of Shayna's arrows flew by my ear in high-pitched whistles over the rapid fire of guns. Colleen reached her arms up to the boat's edge, her screeches garbled by the blood pooling in her mouth. Half her scalp was missing and deep gashes carved most of her face. Beneath her, the water bubbled as if piranha feasted.

The bloodlusters continued to claw at the boat, splintering the edges. Misha's vampires emptied their clips, puncturing them full of holes. Their putrid green blood stained the sides of the boats. And still they wouldn't die.

One of Misha's vampires gripped Colleen's arms, while the remaining reloaded and fired at their invisible targets, stopping the onslaught as quickly as it began.

A bloodluster bobbed to the surface, his matted blond hair stuck between the serrated teeth of his slack jaw. A hole the size of a quarter had been drilled into his chest, and his breath heaved as if he were choking on vomit. Shayna pointed her arrow, but Misha stopped her with a raise of his hand.

"Ma-master," Colleen choked.

Emme covered her mouth, gagging. One of the other Catholic schoolgirls held Colleen against her chest, sobbing softly. Colleen's organs hung in nauseating clumps from the remnants of her demolished torso, droplets of blood turning to ash before they disappeared into the mist.

Misha's eyes bored into Colleen's as he communicated his thoughts through the blood bond all masters shared with their keep.

"Y-yes, Master," she answered. "I . . . I do, Master. Thank you, Master." She swallowed more blood, her voice shaking. "I'll always love you, Master."

With a deep sigh, Misha nodded at the vamp holding Colleen.

I blocked Emme's view when the vamp reached beneath Colleen's open chest cavity to yank out her heart. Tears slid down Emme's cheeks as a burst of ash signaled Colleen's demise. I would have given anything for the opportunity to lie to my little sister and convince her Colleen hadn't suffered and would be okay. But she had. And she wouldn't.

Misha heaved the floating bloodluster onto the boat by the throat and tore into him until ash caked his face.

As he straightened to his full height, his vehemence slowly simmered down to the demeanor of a quiet serpent waiting beneath a rock.

A small bubble popped before the horrible sense of being hunted returned. Five more bloodlusters broke through the water. Two pairs tried to take down the other boats, while the fifth landed *inside* our boat. I tackled Emme as Shayna's sword whirled over our heads, severing the vamp's neck at almost the same time her gold dagger found his heart.

"Get to shore!" I hefted Emme in my arms and leaped onto the rocky beach. No one followed. Misha and his vampires were engaged in hand-to-hand combat with the bloodlusters.

I bounced back into the boat and hoisted Taran over my head. "Emme, catch!"

Taran swore and kicked her limbs wildly as she became one with the air. Emme caught her easily with her force, then Shayna, when I tossed her after Taran. I screamed for Misha, but the bloodlusters gripped the vamps by their waists, ignoring the pummels, clawing, and biting of their enraged victims.

Good thing Emme had a beach full of weapons at her disposal. Mounds and mounds of rock hurtled, skipping and splashing along the water, pounding into the bloodlusters and forcing them to drop Misha's vampires.

Misha and his keep sprang onto land while Emme continued her onslaught. The bloodlusters swatted crudely and uselessly at the rocks, but Emme's telekinetic strength wouldn't be enough to kill them. And they *so* needed to die.

"Taran, blow up the vampires!" Taran sat on the beach, shaking her head, unable to focus. I grabbed her shoulders and shook her hard. "Taran, you have to kill them. You have to kill them *now*!"

Taran gritted her teeth. A sparkle of blue glimmered from her hands, then nothing. I released her abruptly and looked to Misha. "Emme can't hold them much longer; get ready to fight."

Emme slumped onto the ground moments later, exhausted. The bloodlusters shook their heads briefly and then dove into the water with the dauntlessness of great whites on a herd of sea lions.

Shayna formed another arrow and aimed toward the lake. My skin crawled as I sensed the bloodlusters' rapid approach. My knees bent into a crouch. My claws shot out like switchblades. Someone was going to die. But it sure as hell wasn't going to be me.

In a tsunami-high wave, all four infected vampires pounced out of the water, their green eyes gleaming through the mist, their fangs dripping with drool and thirst. I aimed for the one at the end, only to be cloaked in a stream of nasty ash and blinded by a shaft of light.

Taran's power ignited, surrounding her like a supernova of heat and flame, incinerating our attackers and the boats. I winced from the searing pain in my eyes until Taran slowly released her magic.

We all turned to her, momentarily stunned by the fight to the death that never came. I blinked the sting away as the white and blue flares enveloping Taran rescinded and unraveled her shaking form.

Taran always used her anger to incite her magic. This time it was triggered by fear. I took her gently by the hand, hating myself for dragging her into this abyss of unholy terror. She followed me without protest as I led her away from the slimy leftovers sticking to the rocks. As soon as our feet touched upon the grassy knoll, Taran wiped the ash from her eyes. "This is horseshit. I want to go home," she whispered.

I looked into the dark section of woods leading to Zhahara's compound. "Me, too," I answered her truthfully.

CHAPTER 15

"Sit down, Taran," I said when we reached the top of the small cliff. She sat, hugging her knees. I knelt by her side, disturbed by the major post-traumatic stress sliding across her aura. "Emme, I need you to heal her."

Emme frowned when she failed to see any obvious wounds. "Celia, I don't understand."

I stroked Taran's hair away from her shattered expression. "I need you to tend to her emotions, Emme. All the death, the blood—the fear of the unknown. It's causing Taran to remember the night Mom and Dad died." My voice grew hoarse. "And everything that came after that."

"H-how do you know?"

"Because I'm reliving it, too." Taran jerked her head in my direction. I positioned myself so I could view the forest bordering the compound, not wanting her to see my own pain. "Mom and Dad's death was just the start of something horrible." I kept my eyes averted. "So is this. So please, help Taran now so we can survive. Just like we did then."

Emme rushed to Taran's side. Her gift to heal often helped mend emotional wounds. "Oh, my goodness," she whispered when she reached Taran's inner turmoil. "It's okay, Taran. I'll make it better, sweetie."

Taran rose when Emme's pale yellow light rescinded. She seemed better, a lot better. I could almost see her kick-starting her inner bee-atch. "Thanks, Emme." Her eyes cut to mine. "You get me. Don't you?"

I nodded.

She let out a shaky breath. "Then I won't let you down." Taran marched toward the vamps. "I'm ready. Let's go."

"Wait. I have to help Celia, too." Emme reached her hands toward me, but I stepped away. "Celia—"

I shook my head. "I need the aggression."

Shayna drummed the hilt of her sword with her fingertips, her pixie face pained. "Are you sure it's necessary?"

I considered the bloodlust welcoming committee. "Trust me. It is."

The mist thickened as we returned to the vampires, cloaking the shore and edging its way across the grassy knoll like a giant tarp. Shayna sheathed her sword and adjusted the bow against her back while I caught up to Taran. Taran stormed through the dense forest, stepping on every broken tree branch she encountered. Johnny Wilderness she wasn't. "Taran, if you're going to lead, try being a little quieter."

Taran huffed. "Who gives a shit, Celia? After all the gunfire and screaming, these bastards know we're here."

Oh, yeah. She was back.

"Not if they are occupied feeding," Misha said. He walked directly behind me, flanked by Tim and Hank, his guards, who held two high-powered rifles they'd managed to salvage. "Quenching their thirst is often enough of a distraction," Misha continued. "As long as we don't invade their immediate vicinity."

I glanced over my shoulder. "Like we're doing now?"

The corner of Misha's pouty lips curved into a smile. "Precisely."

"But whom are they feeding on?" Emme asked quietly.

"Four buses filled with tourists disappeared en route to Tahoe a few days past," Misha said. "I suspect they emptied them with as much prey as they could manage, and disposed of the vehicles over a ravine."

Taran groaned. "That sounds like a lot of strategizing for bloodthirsty creatures."

Misha moved with pantherlike grace. "In the early phases of bloodlust, those infected maintain some ability to reason. They often hunt in packs to achieve greater abundances of food. As the infection progresses, their greed takes over and their thought processes diminish."

Emme hurried to catch up to me, her voice trembling. "And they grow strong enough . . . to lift *buses*?"

Misha paused. "Much time has passed, my dear. It's likely they can now raise a vehicle of that weight."

Emme's eyes widened. "But they're not very bright, right? At least that's something."

Emme always strove to think positively. Taran . . . not so much.

"No, Emme. They're just big, dumb-ass idiots with supernatural speed and the ability to beat us to death with a damn Greyhound Express so they can suck on our organs like Tootsie Pops."

"Zip it, Taran," I muttered when Emme blanched.

A sudden feeling of dread hit me like a rush of wind. The vampires hissed, low and furious, spinning to locate the threat. My beast beat against my chest, demanding to be released. I soothed her: *Easy, girl.* In her haste to protect me, she could get careless, and we both needed our wits about us.

Our group circled out instinctively, keeping our backs to the center. The problem was, not every danger slithered along the earth.

A sound mimicking the rattle of a snake and a plague of locusts resonated from above, first from one side, then the other, building and growing more fierce. Something—or some *things*—hid in the tall trees. Shayna whirled her transformed arrow point up. Tim and Hank cocked guns. I spun, wildly scanning above, except the denseness of the trees made it impossible to see.

Screw this. I threw my sweatshirt on the ground. My spaghetti stain was barely noticeable now that swamplike ash caked most of my skimpy tank. "Misha, does Zahara's compound have an open area? One with enough coverage for you to hide?"

Misha raised his chin, likely knowing what I planned. "There is a large field close to the stables encircled by trees and brush." He pointed between a section of trees. "That way."

"Okay. Good." I protruded my claws and sliced a gash into my arm. Damn, my nails were sharp. I pressed on my open wound until blood oozed out, then wiped the warm fluid over every inch of my bare skin. Misha hissed, giving me the impression I resembled the vampire equivalent of fudge brownies. He blinked his feral gray eyes at me. With ice cream. He stepped forward. And sprinkles.

My eyes narrowed. "Don't get any funny ideas."

Only Misha could smile with nasty green slop smearing his strong jaw. "I would never dream of it, my darling."

"Uh-huh."

"*Celia.*" Taran's voice told me she wasn't in her happy place. She glanced at my arm, Misha, and the trees. "What the hell are you doing?"

My voice hardened. "We need bait."

I ignored my sisters' gasps and Taran's gangsta-like tirade. Did I like being the proverbial virgin to the bloodlust volcano? Hell. No. But a strong offense beat a cowering defense.

Misha's BFFs stayed close at my heels, smacking their lips as I hurried through the trees. My blood worked on vampires like Doritos did on me. I'd traveled only a few yards when a bloodluster leaped on top of me. Misha ripped off his head before I could react. He helped me to my feet, flashing enough fang to prod me forward.

More yards. More vampires. Six kills before we finally reached the clearing.

"Wait here," I said quietly.

Shayna scrambled to my side. "Dude, please don't do this," she urged.

I avoided Taran's glare and placed my hand on Shayna's back. "We need to lure them out. Just . . . well . . . when you see anything, get 'em."

Shayna widened her large blue eyes. Perhaps we could have come up with a better alternative, but the monsters were picking us off one by one. I shoved my debilitating fear behind my inner hysterical female and crept forward.

The field expanded to about an eighth of a mile. Overgrown grass poked through the wide boards of the collapsed white fence. Festering horses lay against the borders. The poor things had probably attempted to flee the infected vampires. They'd been gutted and left for the bugs to devour.

My insides lurched; I was nauseated by the smell of rot. I inched to the center, fighting the urge to run away screaming. No cape waved behind me. No *S* covered my chest. And it wouldn't take funky green rocks to bring me down. But I wasn't helpless and I had to try.

I reached the middle of the clearing and forced more blood from my wound. I'd once read that deer hunters often waited hours for the perfect buck to appear. Well. Goody for them. In mere seconds, I had more company than my tigress, nerves, and bladder could handle.

Infected vampires popped up from behind bushes, trees, the barn, and its rooftop, barely covered by the torn, blood-smeared rags they wore. Sickly glowing green eyes sparkled with gluttony as they fixed on me. Tongues flickered with growing anticipation. Twisted smiles spread across eager, jagged mouths. And Celia Wird just about peed.

My new admirers were, hands down, the most infected I'd seen. Their skin was a mere film, barely keeping in the bulging green fluid pulsating beneath. Their stomachs had bloated to the size of watermelons. They'd fed well. Yet their insatiable appetites were far from satisfied. And now they hungered for me.

Rattled hisses thundered in my pounding ears as they charged. I searched the thick brush, unable to spot my allies as the bloodlusters closed in.

Oh . . . crap.

I *shifted* until my lungs begged for oxygen and surfaced right in front of a bloodluster. Shots fired, detonating the bloodluster's head, spraying chunks of skull and ash. His torso collapsed on top of me, spilling the nasty infection from his severed neck as rifles boomed and Taran's fire roared. I couldn't catch enough breath to *shift*, but a charging voracious female motivated me to shove the dying bloodsucker off me.

I rolled—*fast*—over a broken fence post and onto my knees, hauling the jagged timber into the soaring vampire's chest.

The female's leftovers spurted as javelins of broken tree branches rocketed through the misting rain at the herd of bloodlusters sweeping the field. Emme nailed every infected vampire, popping through their bulging muscles like algae-filled water balloons and impaling them to the ground.

We hacked through hearts and tore off heads until everything fell silent, except for the panting from our exhausted group.

I collapsed to my knees, landing on a pile of disgusting ash. Taran bounded to my side, shaking my weary shoulders violently with each word she shrieked. "Son of a bitch! Don't you ever fucking pull another goddamn stunt like that again. Do you hear me? I'll kill you; I *swear to God* I'll kill you if you *ever* try that crazy-ass bait shit again!"

"O-kay," I moaned.

My uncharacteristic compliance only freaked her out more. She shook me harder, screaming and cursing.

"Taran, *Taran*!" Shayna yelled, trying uselessly to pry her off me.

"What!"

"It's not over, dude."

"The hell it's not. We killed the bloodlusters. Time to take our toys and go home."

I wiped the blood from my eyes as Emme healed me. "Shayna means we still have to deal with Zhahara. She's still out there."

CHAPTER 16

Taran dropped me like a severed limb. Colorful curses, in a wide range of languages, tumbled out of her in one jumbled mess. Most of her vivid expressions didn't make sense, but I wasn't stupid enough to call her on it.

Misha knelt beside me, out of breath from battle. "How do you feel?"

"I'll get my second wind in a moment," I answered truthfully, stumbling to my feet.

Misha grasped my elbow. "Is your family fit to continue?"

Emme and Shayna nodded, shaken yet still determined. Taran made a rude gesture. I took that as a yes. "We're fine."

Misha led the way, his family close to his side. Shayna and Emme flanked me while Taran took the rear, bitching about needing a shower. *Yeah. Well. No kidding.* I thanked heaven Aric wasn't around to see me. My eyes widened when I realized where my mind had wandered. I blamed the rush of adrenaline for my girlie thoughts, not wanting to admit how I couldn't stop thinking about that wolf.

I sighed, longing to see him. Physical intimacy was something I hadn't engaged in in years. It frightened me . . . but it frightened me less and tempted me more in Aric's presence. Would he be gentle? I wondered. I remembered the softness of his touch against my body, despite all his preternatural strength. I smiled. *Yeah. He would be.*

"Taran's very angry with you," Emme whispered, interrupting my thoughts.

I glanced over my shoulder and met Taran's scowl and another windstorm of swear words. "What gave you that idea?"

Emme stumbled over a rock when she looked back at Taran. She blushed, though no one seemed to notice. "Celia," she whispered. "What you did—back there—was so very . . ."

"Ridiculously suicidal?" I offered.

"No. It was brave." She rubbed her hands together, trying to stay warm. "I wish I had an inner tigress."

I slipped a nasty, bloodlust-coated arm around her. "Every woman has an inner tigress—that part of her that gives her strength and helps her to survive." I smiled softly. "I'm just able to bring mine to the surface."

I helped Emme up a steep incline. She seemed so weak. I was going to ask for a rest period when the vamps fell into a crouch. I crawled up the hill, Taran right behind me.

"If the goddamn theme from *Halloween* starts playing, I will seriously wig the hell out."

Taran wasn't exaggerating. We crouched in the woods, gawking at a three-story Gothic castle. Thunder boomed in the darkening sky and lightning crashed, illuminating the mammoth structure. 'Cause God forbid we didn't get the *full* house-of-horrors effect.

Misha tensed next to me as the two vampires standing guard at the back entrance adjusted their positions. I touched his arm. "What is it, Misha?"

The sharp scent of his anger twisted up into my nose. "The guards are not infected."

Shayna's soaking-wet ponytail whipped behind her. "Dude, are you sure?"

I groaned. "He's right. Their eyes haven't glimmered."

Misha's head angled toward mine. "And they are not Zhahara's vampires."

My heart stopped. "Are you sure?"

He nodded. "Neither bears her mark."

I bit my bottom lip. So not a good idea. "You can tell from here?"

Misha's eyes filled with enough menace to start a fire. "My deepest worries have been confirmed. More than one master seeks to destroy me."

A wave of fierce and angry mutterings spread among Misha's family. Taran swore. "So then who do these idiots belong to? And why haven't the bloodlusters attacked them?"

Misha stood, his fury growing with every word he spoke. "I have no answers. They could belong to a foreign master."

Emme coughed as if she were choking before her eyes rolled into the back of her head. I caught her and turned her on her side. "Easy, honey," I cooed as she dry-heaved. "You're okay." My eyes narrowed at Misha. "What's happening?"

Misha frowned. "She must have exhausted a great

deal of the lake's power during battle. She may not be able to go on."

Emme struggled to sit, jumping as the thunder pounded the skies. "I'm okay. I just need a minute."

"No, Emme. You're done." It hurt just to say the words. I couldn't face her, and turned to Misha. "Remember your promise?"

Misha locked eyes with Tim. Tim stumbled back, fear and anger distorting his features. "No, Master. I die with you and only you."

"Obeying your master supersedes all, including my destruction," Misha commanded. "Now. Do as I ask."

Tim scowled—at me, of course—before placing the barrel of his rifle over his shoulder and tucking Emme against him with his free arm. Emme shot me all her hurt and betrayal in one last glance while her legs kicked in vain. I averted my gaze and so did my remaining sisters.

Misha's family hissed my way. Vampires were all about the warm-and-fuzzies. I ignored them to take in the mammoth dwelling. "Let's circle around and get close to the castle."

Everyone stood except for Hank. As Misha's bodyguard, he didn't appreciate my taking charge. Taran slapped his arm. "We all want to go home alive—well, you dead freaks know what I mean—so back off and quit acting like a little bitch."

Misha's hard stare motivated Hank to his feet. We moved swiftly and silently, circling the perimeter of the forest. The rain and thunder the only sounds. We stopped when Hank crouched and held up his fist. I moved to his side and peeked around the trees. A third guard had arrived in the short time it had taken us to reach the side of the building.

I turned to Shayna. "Do you still have your tooth-picks?" She reached into her pocket and brandished the box. "Okay, time to take out the bad guys."

Shayna snatched a few toothpicks up in her hand, then skipped toward the guards with her dark ponytail bouncing merrily behind her.

The guards eyed Shayna, dumbfounded. One guy wiped his eyes. "The *fuck*?"

Hank looked incredulous. "Why the hell is she skipping?"

"It is a tactic to distract the guards," Misha whispered. "I am sure of it."

Taran huffed. "Actually, the little goof always skips when she's excited."

Just as the vampires let out a collective groan, Shayna proved just how bad a good girl could be. Their eyes widened when she transformed three toothpicks in her hands into long needles and she launched them into the guards. One. Two. Three. Shayna didn't miss. Three explosions of ash. Three redeceased vampires.

We slipped in through the back door, moving cautiously. Candles dimly lit a large kitchen right out of the Dark Ages. Hank motioned us forward, down a long stone corridor. I listened for any signs of movement, breathing—anything, but all was quiet.

We reached the end of the passageway and spread out along a vast foyer. Tapestries covered the walls, and a huge gas chandelier shone light against the carefully polished and heavy Elizabethan-period furniture. Nothing big and green attacked, and no dead bodies littered the floor. There was only quiet. And in a way that scared me more.

Taran threw her hands in the air. "Son of a bitch," she muttered. "Where the hell is that psycho Zhahara?"

And that's when the "psycho" decided to show.

A roar, deep and throaty at first, then high-pitched and squealing, shattered the stained-glass windows, forcing me to *change* and emerge as my beast.

I lifted my head toward the escalating pounding and amplified cries, and moved to stand in front of my sisters. One of the vamps yanked a battle-ax off the wall and shoved it into Shayna's free hand. If Shayna hadn't thought she needed it, another toe-curling bellow reassured her the more weapons, the merrier.

The pounding grew louder.

Thump. Thump. Thump. Slurp.

Slurp?

Taran's hands fired bright with blue and white flames. "Oh, shit."

Thump. Thump. Gurgle.

A growl rumbled my chest, the urge to attack growing.

Misha's eyes turned into that tumultuous gunmetal gray right before the first funnel of a tornado takes shape. "You belong to the House of Aleksandr," he hissed in a voice I no longer recognized. "You will show no fear, feel no pain, know only triumph."

"Know only triumph," his family repeated.

Thump.

Then silence. Only silence.

Before the dungeon door aviated off its hinges.

A leg extended out, long and thick as a log yet as elegant as a homecoming queen's. Zhahara's new and scary ten-foot frame stepped out smoothly, sucking a man's neck like a mango while three other limp and very dead humans hung tucked beneath her arm. Zhahara's smooth mocha skin and beautiful features had vanished, replaced by a contorted bat face and pig ears. Green blood coursed beneath her densely muscled skin as she stood naked before us. In her defense, not even a set of curtains could have enshrouded her massive form. But Lord, I'd wished her thirst had allowed her time to throw *something* on. Every section of hair on her body lay in thick, matted clumps. *Every* section.

Taran gasped. "Girlfriend needs a wax."

Zhahara blinked her black, beady eyes my way, tilting her head in curiosity. She tossed the mummified form she'd been working on over her shoulder and drew another to her mouth. We jerked at the sickening crunch her fangs made when they bit through her victim's neck. She suckled patiently while she pondered her "there's a tigress in my living room" dilemma.

She paused, mid–human drainage, and her nostrils flared. She'd noticed Misha. And that's when her royal pissed-off-ness returned. She dropped her pile of people. They fell in a cluster, their heads lolling against their backs as Zhahara narrowed her soulless eyes at him. She screamed.

And we attacked.

Thunder hammered, rattling the castle as Taran's fire sent Zhahara soaring down the hall. Taran's power held strong—too strong; her body shook, and she screamed from the conduit of heat she pummeled into Zhahara. And still it wasn't enough.

Zhahara's limbs parachuted out like an *X*; she dug the nails of her hands and feet into the stone walls until they halted her descent. The vampires rushed her, giving Shayna mere moments to drag Taran's failing body away from the fight.

Zhahara squashed a vamp's head between her hands

and swatted the others off like insects. They fell in a heap with a hard smash. The vampire who landed at her feet screamed when Zhahara's foot crunched through her chest and into her heart.

My sisters muffled their cries. The fall of Misha's family took seconds—so did my reaction time. My fangs found her neck; my claws dug into her back, a mere breath behind Misha's vicious onslaught.

We rolled on the floor, crashing and demolishing furniture, overturning statues lining the wall, striving to get the upper hand, but managing only to keep from dying. Zhahara beat her boulder-size fists into my back until my muscles screamed in agony and my bones snapped.

I drew in an agonizing breath and *shifted* Zhahara down to her waist, her form too large for my declining strength. My claws scratched the stone in my attempt to scramble away. Zhahara's thick fingers clasped my ankle, shattering it with a single squeeze, while her other hand drummed Misha against the floor.

Shayna appeared, wielding her battle-ax and driving it into the wrist that held me. In a furious holler, Zhahara hit Shayna with Misha's body, sending her screaming into Taran.

Misha's eyes shot open. He whipped around while Zhahara continued her vise grip to his thigh and attacked—peeling her burned, distorted face off in chunks. My back claws pushed into her neck, twisting and cutting through the putrid flesh, while my front claws dug into the floor as I tried to break away. Misha stripped her face down to bone, spilling the green blood like foaming sewer water. But it took more than that to kill a creature sick with hunger.

Zhahara twisted my leg, separating my femur from the socket, and hurled me toward the sweeping staircase.

A rush of warm fluid filled my mouth. I spit out the bright red mess and wheezed. A long piece of railing protruded through my chest. Below me, Misha staggered to his feet, barely keeping his balance. His head flopped against his back and blood spilled from his mutilated leg. Taran and Shayna lay near the doorway to the hall. Their breath rose and fell slowly in sync as frustrated tears streaked their bloodied faces.

Clumps of gray ash scattered from the relentless wind sweeping in through the destroyed windows while the rolling thunder continued to hammer. Out of Misha's family, only four remained. They struggled like babies, using the walls and furniture to help them stand, frantic to help their master.

Zhahara's fists busted the pavers, despite her missing face, despite her dangling wrist, despite my gashes to her neck sputtering her blood. She was almost free. I knew it and so did Misha.

Misha stumbled as he rose and snapped his own neck back into place. He met my eyes. "Forgive me," he whispered, then marched forward to meet his fate.

I wanted to help Misha. I wanted to help all of us. And yet I couldn't even help myself. My body screamed at the unfairness. But then I heard it: the rumbling sound of a runaway train, hurtling toward the castle as it gathered momentum.

I smiled on the inside.

Shit happened.

But so did magic.

Giant headlights illuminated the foyer as a deep horn blasted and the earth shook. The vampires launched themselves to shield my sisters. Misha leaped on top of me, covering my head with his body as the blaring force sideswiped the entry and jolted the entire castle. Chunks of granite and stone battered my hide. Metal twisted, glass shattered, and a little voice screamed with growing strain. Above us, the gas chandelier erupted into a fireball and the walls and ceiling cracked and crumbled.

It wasn't until the last shudder ceased that Misha slid off my stunned form.

A Greyhound bus rested in a tilt over what used to be the foyer. Part of the castle's second story hovered over its roof like an awning, spilling bricks in loud clangs against the warped metal. The castle's entire front facade had been demolished into nothing more than a pile of rubble, powder, and broken glass.

Zhahara's legs stayed fixed to the floor. Part of her spine remained attached, spinning in circles, searching for her other half, while her torso lay sprawled behind the bus.

Soft footsteps crunched over the chunks of gravel. Emme ambled in, blinking and coughing through the cloud of dust. Tim remained close to her side, his rifle aimed at Zhahara.

Emme fell onto what I prayed wasn't Zhahara's disintegrating stomach. "I found the bus," she mumbled.

The vampires moved off my sisters, slowly at first, until Zhahara pushed up onto her arms.

She. Still. Hadn't. Died.

Tim fired his last round into her head. Only a portion of her skull broke off. She spun on her hands, baring her fangs and hissing through her skinned face. Emme screamed. The vamps attacked. Shayna sprinted after them, a sword in each hand.

Taran scrambled to me, her eyes bulging wildly as they swept across my injuries.

The vampires piled on top of Zhahara while Misha bashed her skull with the butt of the rifle. In the middle of the pile, Shayna lifted her swords and plunged them into Zhahara's heart. The mound of bodies shuddered fiercely for a moment. Then, one by one, everyone climbed off the giant pile of green ash.

Shayna, Emme, and Misha ran to us. Misha grabbed the piece of railing jutting out of my chest and pulled. I growled and instinctively bit him. He jerked back in shock, staring at his bleeding arm and glowing in a strange white haze . . . just like his vampires.

"*Dantem animam*," his vampires all said at once. They hurried to Misha, kneeling at his feet and kissing his hands as their collective light receded.

The hellish agony shooting through my chest and leg forced me to turn away. Emme touched my furry face. The pain gradually receded as her gentle yellow light surrounded me. I *changed* back, lacking the strength to keep my second form.

Misha knelt beside me, regarding me with awe. "Salvation granted by a golden tigress." He covered my naked body and carried me to where a fleet of limos waited near a set of open garage doors. "It is time to make our departure," he murmured.

Misha placed his hand over the hood of the largest vehicle while continuing to hold me with ease. The engine started with a hum and the locks disengaged.

Misha Aleksandr, key fob. *Must be nice to harness Tahoe's magic.*

Tim slipped into the driver's seat while my sisters piled into the back. Misha gently laid me across Emme's lap. Our bodies were caked with blood, ash, and monster juice, but I couldn't help the soft sigh that parted my lips. Once again, we'd survived.

"I will not forget what you did for me," Misha said before he shut the door.

I couldn't tell for sure whether it was a good thing or bad, but resolved to think it couldn't be that bad.

Tim nodded at Misha before rolling out of Zhahara's compound.

Shayna wrinkled her nose. "Hey, Tim. Why did you guys all start glowing when Celia bit Misha?"

Tim glanced over his shoulder, fangs sparkling. "Simple. Celia just stimulated the return of the master's soul."

CHAPTER 17

"What?" I sat up, clutching Misha's sweater against my bare skin. Funny how certain things, like passing a test you thought you'd fail, finding a twenty-dollar bill in your pocket, or learning you were capable of returning a vampire's soul, could give a girl her second wind.

Tim drove along like I was Miss Daisy. "I said you stimulated the return of the master's soul."

Taran's glare sparked her eyes with danger. "We heard you, dipshit. But what the hell does it mean?"

Tim's voice turned hollow and distant, as if he were speaking from the end of a long, dark tunnel. "It means Celia and the master are forever linked—in spirit, in heart, in marriage—from this day forth until eternity."

Audible clicks signaled our jaws dropping in unison. "Oh. No. *Hell. No.*" Taran faced me, fury angling her brows like an *American Idol* reject. She pointed a nasty finger at me. "You better get that shit back. I'm not having the Prince of Darkness for a brother-in-law—no matter how hot he is."

I threw my hand out. "How can I get something back if I'm not sure how I gave it in the first place?"

Shayna gripped the edges of her seat. "Tim, Celia can't marry Misha! She doesn't love him or anything. And . . . and . . . and . . . stuff."

Who needed a defense attorney with Shayna around? Emme blanched worse than when she'd sat on Zhahara's insides. "There must be something we can do. Celia has a huge crush on Aric. And I'm sure he wouldn't want—"

I cut her off with a "please don't drag Aric into this crap storm" stare. I tried to keep my voice calm, but it cracked the minute I spoke. "I refuse to be Misha's vampire soul mate. Now tell me what I have to do to stop, reverse, or terminate the process."

Tim's voice resonated in that same eerie tone. "There is no end. There is only eternity. A love for eternity."

Taran swore when Emme fell against her. The events of the day hit me all at once. We hadn't slept in more than twenty-four hours, and we'd just helped bring down a close-to-indestructible vampire chock-full of nastiness. Karma alone should have allowed me to swing by the nearest drugstore and buy the winning lottery ticket—as in the Powerball, not a master vampire for a lifelong snuggle bunny.

I buried my face in my hands. "This isn't happening to me."

"You're right. It's not." Taran squirmed her irate butt across the length of the limo to the open chauffeur's window. "Damn it, Tim. Unless you want to receive the deepest tan of your life via my sunshine borne of magic, you better tell us how Celia can get a quickie divorce."

Divorce. The word echoed in my head. I'd only ever

slept with one guy. How had I ended up married to a master vampire?

Tim's demeanor turned deadly calm. "Do you realize what this means to the master? A chance to redeem his past sins and join his beloved family in heaven should he die. Until then, his beauty and youth remain. He has an opportunity none of us have. You cannot refuse him!"

Taran thought I could. "The hell she can't. Let me spell this out for you. Celia is not birthin' no babies with fangs." She snapped her fingers to stimulate her fire. "I suggest you start talking, and start talking now."

Tim pulled off to the side of the road as I hurried to yank Misha's sweater over me. Loathing tightened his jaws when he faced me. "The only way to break the bond that *you* started is through death."

Shayna jumped in her seat next to me. I couldn't jump. I needed a pulse to jump, and my heart had stopped functioning. "Death? Did you say death? You mean one of us has to *die*? There's no other way to reverse this?"

Tim turned away, took a breath, and faced me once more. "Perhaps . . . No, never mind, it is too dangerous."

I hurried to move closer to him. "How can it be more dangerous than dying? Tell me how to fix this!"

Tim's face set like a frozen tundra. "There is only one way, but it involves the darkest of magic. Demonic possession and loss of limbs may occur."

My tongue and throat dried and I lost the ability to blink. "Demonic po-possession?"

He frowned. "Do you want to end this or not?"

"Um, yes. Yes, I do. Tell me."

"There are many steps, and it's rather complicated."

Emme took out her phone and hit the "Notes" icon. "Go ahead. I'm ready."

Tim's slow, drawn-out breath made me believe he was sharing something he shouldn't—and in doing so would release a chain of events no one could stop. I listened like my future depended on it. Because, God knew, it did.

"The spell must be performed on a high peak at the rise of the next full moon."

Which meant I'd be married to Misha for a freaking month. Still, it beat eternity.

Shayna gripped my arm. "That means either Mount Whitney or Mount Williamson. They're the tallest around."

Emme typed feverishly. Tim ignored Shayna and continued. "You will need to gather herbs: wolfsbane, belladonna, nightshade . . ."

Taran tapped her ruined nails on the leather seat. "There's an organic vitamin shop in South Tahoe that sells herbs. I bet we can find that garbage there."

Tim's scowl deepened. "There's more. You need a piece of alabaster, the whitest you can find."

Alabaster? I gave my sisters a blank stare.

Shayna pointed an excited finger at me. "Ooh—eBay. You can get anything on eBay!"

Shayna's logic kick-started my heart. "Right, eBay. Of course. Okay, what else, Tim?"

"Last—and most important—you will need two virgins and a goat."

My head slowly turned to meet Tim. He burst out laughing. His whole body shook with hysteria, and tears streaked down his face. I crossed my arms and glared. "You *asshole!*"

Emme stopped typing and exchanged confused glances with Shayna. Taran launched herself onto Tim, smacking the back of his shaved head like a set of bongo drums. Tim cackled, failing to notice. "You girls are so gullible. I was ready to sell you swampland in Jersey."

Shayna wrinkled her brow. "So Celia's not engaged?"

Tim continued to laugh. "Of course not, the master wants a bang, not a bride."

I debated whether I should feel deeply disturbed that a master vampire wanted to sleep with me or deeply relieved that I didn't have to decide on a ring bearer. Knowing Misha and I weren't going to be picking out china made me lean toward deeply relieved. Though that didn't stop me from punching Tim in the back of the head.

"Ouch!"

"Quit whining and drive," I snapped.

Tim pulled back onto the road, muttering how I couldn't take a joke.

"Excuse me, Tim—"

"Emme, tell me you're not being polite to this prick!" Taran shook out her hands, which were bright red from beating on Tim.

Emme blushed. "Um . . . I just want to know what the glowing was all about."

Tim rolled his eyes in the mirror, but then caught the aroma of Taran's anger and rising magic and decided against further pissing her off. "All master vampires are soul takers—*susceptor animae*. They possess the power to take one's soul in order to *turn* them vampire. Celia is the rare *dantem animam*—a soul giver. We felt the master's aura return when she bit him; that's when we recognized her power."

Shayna thought about it. "But that seems like some pretty powerful magic. How does it not link them?"

Tim spoke like it was obvious. "Because Celia is not

giving him a piece of her soul, just returning his own back to him."

Shock spread across Taran's lovely yet bloodlust-caked features. "Damn, Ceel. You sent a lot of vamps to hell today."

I shuddered. Vampires were notoriously egocentric, but that shouldn't have given them an all-access pass to hell—especially when their actions were a result of an infection beyond their control.

Tim groaned when he caught a whiff of my sadness. "For a tigress, you're a real puss—" My growl cut him off. He cleared his throat. "The return of a soul is something only a master is capable of receiving."

Shayna leaned toward Tim's window. "So then she did return Zhahara's?" She smiled weakly in my direction. "I'm not trying to upset you, Celia. But you did bite her."

Tim shook his head. "No. Bloodlust is too powerful and foul for the soul to penetrate. Which goes to show the master has no trace of it—even after the level of exposure he had today."

I thought about what Tim said. "So if direct contact with those infected doesn't cause the bloodlust, then what does?"

Tim shrugged. "Who cares? The master is safe and it's no longer our problem."

"Way to be selfless, Tim." My mind mulled over my strange newfound power until unease twisted my small intestine into a Christmas bow. I pictured master vampires from all over the world lining up in front of some whacked-out, supernatural kissing booth advertising soul returns for a buck . . . and me chained on the other side. "Tim, I want Misha's word that no one else will find out about my *dantem animam* thingy."

Tim chuckled. "Relax, Celia. Trust me when I say most masters would prefer not to account for their sins." He turned onto the main road. "Besides, I suspect the master would prefer to keep the return of his essence to himself. A vampire with a soul juggles both life and death at once. Constant touch with such powerful forces grants him greater strength." Tim fell into a more serious demeanor. "Thereby making him a greater threat to those who oppose him."

Silence fell among us, yet the events of the day prevented it from lasting. Shayna flashed Emme a grin. "You were quite the hero, Miss Watch Me Lift a Bus. Thanks for coming back to save the day."

"My power seemed to refresh the closer we got to the lake. Tim was scared to go back—"

"I wasn't scared!" Tim insisted.

Yes, he was, Emme mouthed. "But I convinced him it's what Misha would want. The bus was parked along the front driveway. Tim scaled the wall and looked inside. When he told me you'd trapped Zhahara in the floor, hitting her with something big was the only thing I could think of."

I laughed. "Well, it worked. I'm so proud of you, Emme."

Taran smirked. "You did good, baby girl."

I hugged Emme close just as the phone inside the limo rang. Tim picked it up without hesitation. "Hey, Ana Clara. You still at Z's?" She whispered something too low for me to hear. "What? Oh, hell, hold on." He talked over his shoulder. "They found another cluster of infected vampires in the dungeon. They killed most of them, but two escaped." He ignored our groans and returned to his conversation with Ana Clara. "Look, urge the master out before anything else happens. Tahoe's magic will leave him soon. I'll be back as soon as I drop them off. Later— Oh, yeah. I'll take a brunette and a redhead. Make sure the master eats well before he falls into the sleep. Yeah, yeah, I know they're pains in the ass, but the master will be pissed if I leave them on the side of the road."

Taran narrowed her eyes. "And we shouldn't kill this prick why . . . ?"

Emme placed her hand over Taran's. "I'm sure he doesn't mean it. It's probably just a front."

Tim flashed more fang Emme's way. It told me two things: No, it wasn't a front. And, yes, he was a prick.

CHAPTER 18

I smiled at the sign announcing only three miles remained until we reached Dollar Point. A shower. All I longed for was a nice long, hot shower. It was so close, I could almost smell the olive-oil-and-juniper shampoo.

I made the mistake of examining my hands. There had been times in my life when I'd felt disgusting—after one of my more grueling runs in the sun or a particularly nasty delivery involving body fluids from every human orifice. Those moments paled in comparison to the putrid carnal waste dump my skin and hair had become. An irate woman beating me with her placenta would have been more welcome than the copious amount of Zhahara snot gluing my fingers together.

Taran grimaced when I tried to pry them apart. "Celia, you're flaking that shit all over the place. Just stop already."

I ceased my efforts and sighed softly. Nitpicking over grime that would eventually scrub off seemed like a waste of energy. We'd survived, after all—thank God we'd survived. But the danger threatening Tahoe remained.

"There's still so much we don't know," I said aloud.

Tim shrugged. "Yeah. But like I said, what's important is that the master is safe."

"I don't get how he's safe. We didn't exactly figure out how the bloodlust spread." Shayna fished around in her bra. She paused when she gripped something in one of the cups, and paled to the color of chalk when she pulled out some poor sap's finger. She rolled down the window, tossed the digit, tossed some cookies, and slumped back into her seat. A flock of crows wasted no time fighting over their incredible find.

I rubbed her shoulder and set my frown on Tim. "What's the next step?"

Tim smiled in the rearview mirror. "One of the family will notify the master's superiors. Ash from an infected vampire coats the surrounding air with an aroma of boiled anise. With the high levels of bloodlust infection and the number of kills we made, the scent should linger for the next month. That alone will trace the start of the infestation back to Zhahara. And once the human remains are discovered, my master will be perceived as not only a hero, but as the one who avenged their deaths and saw that justice was served."

Taran scowled. "You, Misha, whoever the hell can take all the credit, for all we care. Just don't bother calling us again. Your favors have been used up for the next goddamn century."

Tim regarded us through the mirror, running a hand over his shaved head. "The master is in your debt. You know this." His eyes met mine. "Don't expect him to vanish from your lives. Especially now."

"Home!" Emme tugged Shayna's sleeve excitedly as

we pulled into our neighborhood. "Shayna, look! We're home."

The sparkle returned to Shayna's eyes when she smiled. Except her smile didn't last. "Oh . . . no."

I jumped out of my skin. Four shiny hybrids—a Highlander, an Escape, a Yukon, and an Escalade—hugged the curb in front of our house. There on the front steps sat Liam, Koda, Gemini, six other *weres* I didn't know . . . and Aric.

Good thing I didn't look like hell or anything.

Taran desperately yanked at Tim's destroyed sweater. "Drive. Now. Just keep going. Whatever you do, don't stop!"

"Where—"

"I don't give a shit where! Just get the hell out of here. Now!"

Tim started to turn the cruise ship he called a car around, but I stopped him. "Tim, just . . . don't go anywhere."

He stopped in the middle of the cul-de-sac, pissing Taran off further. "Celia! I—"

"Taran, we have to get out. The *weres* need to know what's happening. And . . . we need to . . . shower." Like I mentioned, I'd never cheered a team on to victory, and I sure as hell didn't belong arguing before the Supreme Court. Emme and Shayna blinked back at me like I'd suggested a sleepover at Zhahara's and reminded them not to forget the marshmallows and Ouija board. "We're getting out." I meant to sound firm, but my voice trailed off when I noticed Aric had leaped off the steps and now stood next to the door.

My door.

Tim coughed into his hand, trying not so hard to hold in his laughter. "May I get the door for you, ladies?"

"I got it. Thanks, moron." I opened the door and slowly ambled out, yanking at Misha's sweater to keep my bare backside covered. Those steamy brown eyes I hadn't been able to erase from my thoughts widened before locking onto mine with all the power of a bulldozer. I tried to convince myself I had nothing to be ashamed of. So what if I smelled like sewage and dead, festering things and donned nothing but the clothes of his mortal enemy? These things happened. "Hey," I mumbled.

Aric's knitted brows told me nothing I could say would piss him off any more than he was. I angled around to allow my sisters out. Funny thing, none of them seemed excited about leaping out of the car and doing the runway walk for the wolves.

"*Damn*," Koda muttered when he got a good look at me.

"What. *Happened?*"

Aric's deep voice mimicked the same tone he used when he'd asked what I was doing at Misha's pad. Gee, I wondered why. Could it be that beneath all the grime, blood, and lingering aroma of gruesome death, he still managed to draw in Misha's scent?

I sighed. "Misha's innocent. Zhahara's compound was loaded with vampires in various stages of bloodlust. They'd been hunting humans for weeks and bringing them back for her to eat. We wiped out most of them, but at least two got away."

Aric spoke to the werebear next to him while his eyes stayed locked on mine. "Take two teams and check it out. If you pick up the trail of any vampires, find them. If they're infected—kill them. Anything else needs to be brought to The Den for questioning."

The werebear whipped out a phone as he and the other nonwolves jumped into the Highlander and Escape. "I need my clan and Aric's assembled in South Tahoe now. Zhahara's compound. Don't act alone. We're on our way."

"Shayna!" Koda ran to her when she scuttled out, but stopped short, dropping his head as if embarrassed by his actions.

"Hey . . . dude." She punched him affectionately on the arm, but drew back when she realized she'd left a brownish stain on his shirt. "Um. Sorry . . ."

I walked toward the house as Koda asked her about being hurt. Liam yelled, "Oh, shit!" when he caught a gander at Emme.

Gemini stepped in front of me. "Where's Taran?"

"Um. She'll be out in a minute." *Maybe.*

His dark almond eyes shadowed with worry. "Is she harmed?"

No, just covered in slop and possibly vomit. I sidestepped him and hurried toward our slanted driveway. "Ah, no, she's just, um—"

I never knew Taran could move so fast. She raced past us, covering her face as flaps of tangled and infection-smeared hair bounced behind her. She struggled to unlock the dead bolt, swearing in a way that made Emme blush, until she finally pushed open the door. Within seconds I heard the shower turn on in her room.

"Would you boys like to come in for a bite? It will only take a minute for us to freshen up."

Emme took positive thinking to a whole new level. I

didn't think anything but a bleach bath and an Ajax scrub would get the crud off my body. And of course, things just continued to get better and better.

A 1971 blue Ford Mustang roared into our neighborhood like a pride of angry lions. Strips of rubber burned into the asphalt as the car slid to an abrupt halt.

Lo and behold, a rabid werewolf stormed out. "Are you crazy?" Bren growled. He stormed toward me, more pissed than I'd ever seen him. Danny leaped out of the passenger seat, tripping in his haste to chase after Bren.

Aric stepped in front of me, blocking my body with his. "Stay away from her."

Bren snarled. "Fuck. Off."

I forced my way between them when Aric growled in challenge, locking onto Bren's wrists and shoving him away with my back. "Aric. Don't. These are our friends." The other wolves spread out, circling the three of us plus Danny, who twitched like a cornered squirrel. Shayna and Emme ran to his side, pleading with the wolves not to hurt him.

Aric wouldn't peel his eyes off Bren. "You're friends with a *lone*."

My spine straightened. "He's not a *lone*. He has us. We're his pack." I faced Bren when Aric relaxed his attack stance. "What are you doing here?"

Bren's glare softened slightly when he regarded me. "I've been trying to find you since getting Shayna's e-mail."

I groaned and whipped my head toward my blabbermouth sister. She scraped her nasty sneaker against the asphalt. "I didn't give him the deets. I just told him we were helping Misha . . . and warned him that if we didn't come back he and Danny needed to flee Tahoe."

I threw my hands up in the air. "Oh. Is that all?"

"You should have texted me, Shayna. You know I rarely check my e-mail."

Shayna continued to play with the pebble at her feet. "That's sort of why I e-mailed you, dude. I knew you'd come after us if you knew right away—"

"And you still did it anyway." Bren shook his head, his frustration practically burning a hole into the asphalt.

"And we'd do it again," Shayna countered.

She and Emme rushed ahead of us, their wolves trailing them. Bren watched them disappear into the house before meeting my stare like I knew he would. "I told you to stay out of this vampire shit, Celia. Not only did you not listen to me; you dragged your sisters into it."

"I didn't drag them." I rammed my finger into his chest. "You know I wouldn't do that."

Bren gnawed on his teeth. "They'd follow you to hell and back, and you damn well know it."

If he intended to make me feel guilty, it worked. I hugged my body and turned away, walking toward the house. Aric followed, keeping his eyes on Bren. Bren caught up and reached for my hand. "Don't hurt her," Aric warned.

The deep creases of Bren's frown softened as he watched Aric. Whatever he saw in Aric's expression lightened Bren's eyes with mischief. "I don't hurt those I love," he answered with a smirk.

Aric leaned back on his heels, crossing his arms. I glanced at both of them. "How did you know we were home?" I asked when I couldn't determine what had transpired between them.

Bren put his arm around me and pulled me close. "Cut it out, Bren," Danny muttered behind me.

Bren's grin widened. "We went down to that bitch Zhahara's. The place reeks of infection, and there's a goddamn bus in her living room. When we couldn't find you, we headed back to that asshole Misha's place for some answers. On the way there, I got the call you were back."

Okay, that didn't make sense. None of us had contacted Bren. "Who called you?"

Bren motioned toward Mrs. Mancuso's house. He'd given the old biddy his number in an effort to watch over us. I hadn't liked the idea then and I absolutely resented it now. The old bat stood behind her floral window drapes, watching the drama. Good Lord, if her hair curlers were any tighter her scalp would bleed. She raised her window, giving Aric, Bren, and Danny the once-over before scowling at me like she could will my death. "Celia Wird, have you no shame? Standing out there half-naked, flashing those young boys like some kind of streetwalker!"

Aric's dark brows shot up to his crown. "What the fu—"

"Mind your own business, you goddamn raisin with legs!" Taran screamed from inside the house.

Mrs. Mancuso flipped me off, of course. Bren flashed her a panty-dropping grin. "It's okay, Mrs. M. I'll be sure to take Celia to confession later so Father O'Callaghan can slap the sin out of her."

"Be sure that you do." Mrs. Mancuso gave Bren an approving nod, and me another stiff one. Aric remained fixed to my front walkway. He may have been a guardian of the earth, but I doubted he'd ever encountered evil the likes of Mrs. Mancuso.

Emme called from the upstairs bathroom. I didn't need to see her to know her cheeks shone like ripe strawberries. "May-maybe everyone should just head in. I'll be down in a minute to fix dinner."

Before I could follow Emme's lead, Bren turned me around so my back was to him. "Ceel . . . are you going commando?"

Aric growled, low and deep. I smacked Bren's hands and shoved him up the front steps. "Just get inside!"

The sound of his laughter told me his temper had begun to cool—at my expense, like always. I tried to follow, but stopped when I realized Aric continued to watch Danny.

"Why are you armed?" Aric asked him.

I inhaled deeply. Aric was right: Danny was packing heat, full of gold bullets. Not a comforting thought, considering he couldn't shoot a wereelephant at close range.

Danny adjusted his Coke-bottle glasses nervously, smashing his mop of black curls between his forehead and the thick, dark frames. Aric's daunting presence rattled Danny's lanky frame and made his voice tremble. "We weren't sure what we'd find. My buddy Bren didn't want me unarmed."

"Danny's human," I explained to Aric.

"I could tell by his scent," Aric said. "So how does he know about us?"

I idled toward Aric. "We've known each other since we were teens." I couldn't stop my smile when I looked over my shoulder at Danny. "I trust him with all of my secrets." Danny grinned, but then stopped short and stepped back at Aric's scowl. "Be nice, Aric. He's my friend, and you're scaring him."

Aric pinched the bridge of his nose with his thumb before extending his hand to Danny. "I apologize. Aric Connor."

Danny shook his hand. "Dan Matagrano. Nice to meet you . . . sir."

I couldn't blame Danny for greeting Aric formally. He gave off a certain aura of stature. Aric, however, didn't appear comfortable with the title. "Just call me Aric, Dan."

"Okay." Danny headed toward the door, but Aric stopped him.

"Look, Dan, I know this isn't my home, but I need to ensure my safety and that of my wolves at all costs. Could you leave the gun in the car?"

"Oh, yeah. Sure, sure. I didn't mean to insult anyone." Danny jogged to Bren's car, popped the trunk, and deposited the gun, then raced just as swiftly into the house.

It was just me and Aric, him in a dark red sweatshirt that complemented those sizzling baby browns and faded jeans that hugged his strong legs, and me . . . in all my nasty glory.

"You should've called me, Celia." Aric's voice dropped lower. "I would have handled the situation. There was no need for you to get involved."

"I didn't have your phone number," I answered like a dumb ass.

Aric walked ahead of me. He picked up and handed me a simple blue gift bag tucked behind the wooden railing. "Look inside," he urged when I just stared at it.

I pulled out the latest and greatest iPhone, complete with some Bluetooth thingamajiggy, a high-tech earpiece, and a sleek lavender case with little white birds on it.

Aric cleared his throat as I examined the case. "I had a female sales associate pick it out. If you don't like it, you can exchange it for something else."

"I like it. It's sweet." I smiled. "You went overboard, though. This stuff is nicer than what I had."

Aric didn't blink. "I told you my students would replace your things." He held his hand out. "May I?"

I handed him the phone, thankful the smooth surface would help me wipe the putrid prints off easily. He punched in a few numbers and handed it back to me. "That's my number. You ever need me, you call. If the vampires give you any shit, you call. If there's a mansion full of infected vampires, you call. You don't go looking for trouble." He let out a long breath. "You can't heal, Celia. The right strike by the wrong foe could kill you. I don't want that to happen."

Aric Connor cared what happened to me. *Whoa.* He'd given him his digits . . . and a whole lot of attitude. "So did you come to my house just to give me the phone or is the reprimand an added bonus?"

Like Misha, Mr. King of Wolves probably wasn't used to getting any lip. His voice dropped another octave. *"Celia."*

I held up my hand, trying to squelch my grin. Knowing he'd come to see me made me giddy. "We'll talk as soon as I get a shower. I promise," I insisted when he tried to argue.

"We'd better," he answered.

I held the edges of Misha's sweater down as I climbed the steps . . . and then took the fastest shower in history.

CHAPTER 19

Everyone sat at the kitchen table except for Emme and Shayna, who busied themselves heating the food. The wolves leaned back in our chairs, arms crossed, eyes fixed on me. Aric wasn't a happy wolf. His ungodly pissed-off expression worsened as we spilled more details about our seventy-five near-death experiences.

Bren sat next to me, draping an arm around my shoulders. "And you didn't take me along because . . . ?"

Aric leaned forward, taking in Bren's close proximity to me. Normally Bren's affections didn't bother me, but they made me uncomfortable in Aric's presence. I kept my voice casual as I inched away from his hold. "Because you wouldn't have stopped with just the infected vampires, and I couldn't risk your going after Misha's family."

Gemini rubbed his goatee and regarded me carefully. It was the first time he'd pried his eyes off Taran, who sat in a slinky black dress on the other side of Danny. "Tell me more about the vampires you encountered. It seems odd they would remain at the compound. Their hunger should have compelled them to constantly hunt for food."

I shuddered, thinking back to the brawl at the field. But Gem was right: Why would they hang out somewhere as isolated as Zhahara's property? "Is it possible something prevented them from leaving the premises?"

"A binding spell might be able to," Danny offered.

The scowls from the other wolves made him shrink back into his seat. Aric watched him carefully. "A spell like that wouldn't be strong enough against a bloodluster's thirst."

Koda knitted his brows—not typically a scary expression for most. For Koda it bordered on a mug shot for *America's Most Wanted.* "For a human, you seem to know too much about things that go bump in the night."

Taran rolled her eyes. "What do you expect? He's a research hound who lives with a werewolf." She patted Danny's back until she caught Gemini's disapproving glance.

Danny coughed into his fist. "I'm actually fascinated by anything supernatural. I've studied magic dating back to—"

Liam growled. "No one cares, squirt."

Bren growled. Danny was his best friend. The only one who could mess with him was Bren. I placed my hand over Bren's chest. "We care," I told Liam flatly.

Emme dropped what she was doing and rushed to Danny's side. "Don't be mean, Liam."

Danny stood. "I don't want to cause any problems."

I kept my hand on Bren, but spoke over my shoulder. "You're not, Danny. Please don't go."

"Liam. You owe Dan an apology."

My head jerked in Aric's direction. His tone, while casual, meant business.

Liam gawked at him in disbelief. "What? Why?"

Aric smiled in my direction. "Dan is a friend of theirs. And you've insulted him in their home."

"Sorry, human," Liam muttered, but then caught Emme's attempt at a scowl. "I mean, sorry, Dan."

Dan sat slowly. "Ah, sure. No problem."

I released Bren when his muscles relaxed beneath my hold. He'd still *change* in a blink and tear out throats if he interpreted a threat against us or Danny. But for the moment, he seemed satisfied with the apology.

Aric met my appreciative smile with a wink and a grin that transformed me into the goofy vulture from the Bugs Bunny cartoon. My face reddened, and it became harder to continue staring at him.

Bren pulled me close and chuckled in my ear. "Damn, kid. Are you in trouble." That was bad enough. His next comment was worse. "Don't worry, Aric. Celia and I don't have sex as much as we used to."

My elbow to his ribs had him doubling over. Aric raised his chin in the way most males did before brawls involving bashed heads and bail money. "You two are together?"

Bren coughed out a yes, at the same time I said no. Shayna, of course, just had to come to my rescue. "No way, dude. Celia is totally single. She hasn't had a date in what, two years?"

I buried my molten-lava face in my hands. *Oh . . . God.*

"Do you kill all the infected vampires you find?" Dan asked quietly.

Aric tore his attention away from me for the first time since I'd come downstairs. I welcomed the distraction like an all-you-can-eat buffet. "What else would we do with them?" he asked Danny. "They're too dangerous to keep."

Danny rubbed his thighs hard, careful not to make direct eye contact with Aric. I could see the wheels turning in that brilliant mind of his, but his insecurities and shyness held him back. "What are you thinking, Danny?"

Danny rubbed his thighs again. And that's when I knew for sure he was onto something. "Danny?"

Danny tried to smooth back his hair, but as usual his fingers tangled into his thick, messy curls. He shuffled his seat closer and whispered, knowing the wolves could hear, yet feeling more confident if he pretended I alone listened. "I'd like to examine the infected blood—you know, test it to see if I can find anything."

Aric and Gemini exchanged glances. "Examine it for what exactly?" Gemini asked.

"Danny's a biochemist. He's done a lot of research with blood-borne infections," Emme explained from near the stove.

Aric rested his arms against the table. "What good will that do? Are you trying to find a cure?"

"Oh, no. A cure, if possible, would take decades to develop—especially if magic is the underlying component. I'm thinking if I could get a sample of infected blood and compare it to the blood of a healthy vampire, I may be able to find a link, or at the very least something that can help."

Aric thought about it. "Based on what Celia has said, I don't expect the plague to end until we find the cause. All *were* clans have been ordered to hunt and kill all infected vampires. But . . . if we catch one, do you have a way to preserve the blood? I won't keep a bloodluster alive just to use as a lab rat."

Danny tapped his fingers on the table. "I have several blood tubes with varying preservatives. One of them should be enough to keep the blood from turning to ash—at least for a little while. Do any of you know how to draw blood from a vein?"

Koda shook his head. "No. But it's not necessary. We could probably bite off a wrist and just pour the blood-lust into the vials."

Liam shrugged one shoulder. "Yeah. No problem. Or sever part of his neck if the fucker gives us any problems." He smiled at Emme's blanched face. "Sorry, Emme. I didn't mean to swear."

Gemini acted like we were playing a round of Monopoly, not discussing ways to drain a vampire of his or her nastiness. "Where will you get healthy vampire blood?"

I didn't appreciate the attention my sisters and Bren slammed me with. "Don't look at me that way," I grumbled.

Taran smirked. "Ceel, you know perfectly well that rich bastard would give you his blood if you asked. God knows he'd do anything to get in your pants. . . ." Her voice trailed off as she caught Aric's not-so-thrilled expression.

I wished we were outdoors, so I could dig a hole and bury my burning face. Some days it didn't pay to have chatty sisters. "I'll see what I can do." I shoved away from the table to get a drink, careful to hide my mortified expression from Aric.

He followed me to the refrigerator, leaning against the opposite door. "You and the vampire . . ."

"There is no me and Misha. There is no me and Bren. There is no one in my life, I assure you." My eyes pleaded with him to believe me. The gleam in his irises and that irresistible grin told me that he had. Damn, that smile should have been illegal. "W-would you like something to drink?" The heat from his body stroked my skin like a physical caress. It was all I could do not to unravel.

Aric shrugged. "Sure. I'll have what you're having."

I reached in the fridge for a root beer and then grabbed one for myself before sitting on a barstool next to the raised counter. Aric sat next to me. "Will you sit with me at dinner, Celia?"

"Yeah. I'd like that."

Shayna and Koda stood across the counter facing each other. Shayna had taken a large piece of salami and placed it on the cutting board in front of her. She snagged a wooden spoon out of the drawer and held it by the ladle. At once she transformed it into a long, sharp silver knife. Koda and Aric tensed watching the chopping machine with the long ponytail get to work. She flipped a slice into the air and caught it in her mouth, totally showing off. I couldn't blame her. It was a relief not to hide what we could do.

Shayna tried to catch another piece, but Koda caught it first. While he chewed, he slipped Shayna an arrogant and kind of scary smirk. Shayna laughed. Although Koda looked like he ate toddlers for breakfast, I knew he didn't stand a chance against my sister.

"I don't scare you?" he asked her in a bewildered tone, making me wonder whether he'd heard my thoughts.

Shayna batted her eyelashes. "A sweet little puppy like you? No, of course not."

"Excuse me," Emme said quietly. A cabinet door opened and a row of plates and glasses flew out and set themselves on the table. Utensils followed. The wolves stiffened, falling back into a relaxed state at Emme's blush.

Aric nudged me playfully with his elbow. "What can Taran do?"

I motioned in her direction. "You're looking at it," I whispered.

Blue and white sparks ignited over her head as she and Gemini fell into Barbie-loves-Ken mode. Liam sniffed at the pot of meatballs and sauce Emme stirred. "Whoa, this smells awesome."

Emme smiled. "Thank you, but I can't take the credit. Celia prepared them and made the sauce two nights ago. I just heated everything up."

Aric quirked an eyebrow at me. "You can cook?"

Shayna swung an arm around me before I could answer. "That's right, dude. One day, this little lady is going to make some lucky guy a heck of a wife."

Never in my life had I wanted to kill Shayna more.

Aric threw back his head as he laughed. I was grateful when his phone announced a text, giving my cheeks a moment to cool. He read through the message and then put his phone down. "How many vampires did you say escaped Zhahara's?"

"Tim told us two."

Aric smiled as he read the text again. "Dan. We might not be able to get you the blood. My pack just found and killed the infected vampires."

CHAPTER 20

"Are you cold?"

I should have been. The temperature dropped quickly as the sun set across the lake, and my hair remained damp from my shower. But with Aric sitting so close to me on the porch swing, all I felt was his warmth. His pack continued to prowl the area for more infected vampires. Tomorrow, he and a fresh set of *weres* would relieve them. For the moment, I had him to myself.

I leaned back against the arm he'd draped across the length of the swing. "I'm fine, wolf."

Aric pushed his thick hair out of his eyes, although I'd have given anything to do the honors. It reminded me of dark chocolate, while his eyes were more like melted caramel, so intense, so—

"Why did you help the vampire, Celia? Does he have something on you?"

I freed a bare foot tucked beneath me and pushed against the light blue floorboards, rocking us gently before I hid my foot again beneath my long sweater. "Misha didn't force me into anything." I glanced out into the midnight blue sky. The clouds had begun to clear. Stars sparkled like crushed diamonds, and a hint of the full moon reflected along the lake. "You may think me naive, but I felt bad for him."

Aric drew out a long sigh, his voice deepening once more. "He's a manipulator and a bastard. Don't be fooled into believing he meant to save anyone but himself."

I thought about how Misha kept close to Emme during battle, how he'd carried me in his arms . . . and how his family shielded my sisters when the frigging Greyhound took out the entire front hall. Yet I kept those details to myself. Aric hated Misha. Nothing I said could change that. And arguing the point meant arguing with him . . . and the last thing I wanted then was to fight with Aric. I adjusted the thick sweater around me. From inside I could hear my sisters bustling around in the kitchen. I'd offered to help clean, but Shayna had practically shoved Aric and me outside together.

I lowered my lids briefly. "I understand what it's like to feel the world is against you. My sisters and I have always been ostracized for being different . . . even as children." My fingers played with the big round buttons of my sweater. "The kids at school knew we weren't like them, but they didn't know why. Since our last name is Wird, our classmates nicknamed us the 'Weird Girls.' No matter what school we went to, the nickname followed."

"That must have been hard." Aric's voice lost that edge and grew quieter.

"It was." I kept my tone casual, like the cruelty we'd experienced no longer bothered me. Some things, though, hurt forever. I nibbled on my bottom lip, wishing I hadn't brought my past to Aric's attention, and thought it best to move on. "But my sympathy alone is not what compelled me to help Misha. In the end, saving Tahoe seemed like the right thing to do—the only thing to do."

"You sound like a *were*. Our kind is always trying to save the world from something evil."

I smiled, feeling humbled. "I think you're giving me too much credit. I don't always do the right things." I examined my palms. From time to time it surprised me that the blood from my first kills hadn't left permanent stains. I'd been so vicious, brutal . . . and they'd been only human. "I've made a lot of mistakes."

"Like what?"

My head angled toward him. I hadn't expected him to be so direct. I wiped my hands against my sweater. The soft cashmere remained gentle against my palms in spite of how hard I rubbed. "Nothing I'm willing to discuss, at least . . . not tonight."

Aric nodded, remaining preoccupied with my face. My pulse raced; I was unsure his focus was a good thing. My sisters had strutted out of their rooms like they were going club hopping. I'd slipped on a pair of jeans and a short-sleeved gray tunic, and hadn't bothered with shoes or socks. No, I wasn't the odd sister out or anything.

A soft breeze blew my curls into my face. Aric took a long strand and tucked it behind my ear. The trickling heat as his fingertip slid along my neck made my toes wiggle beneath me. "Another day then?" he whispered.

I didn't answer, caught up in the strong angles of his heart-stopping face. Aric leaned closer and smiled. He had such a nice smile, one I found easy to return. And his eyes—they were business and bedroom all at the same time.

Aric's clean, enticing aroma mixed with the fragrance of male spice. I wanted to taste his lips, to run my hands against the hard muscles of his body, to feel him pressing against me—

Liam threw open the front door. I jerked back like we'd been caught naked. He shoved a beer in Aric's hand, then mine. Aric stared at the beer and back at Liam like he'd handed him an irate scorpion. "Hey, Aric. One of your babes keeps calling my phone wondering where you are. I think her name is Selene. She said you had a date tonight."

Aric glared at him while my jaw fell to the floorboards. He had a date. With someone else. Not the chick who preferred bare feet, comfy clothes, and lip balm instead of lipstick. I stood abruptly, unable to keep the bite out of my voice. "Maybe you should give her a call."

I stormed inside, more pissed at myself for getting my hopes up than at Liam. Damn, what was I thinking? Aric probably needed Shayna to beat females off with a battle-ax. "Do you need help with dessert?" I asked Shayna a little too loudly.

Shayna paused in the middle of placing strawberries around the chocolate fondue pot. "Ah . . . you could set the table if you want."

I threw the silverware on the table and grabbed an armful of plates. Shayna abandoned her fruit and rushed to yank the plates from my grasp. "Ceel, let's do paper instead."

She probably worried I'd break our ceramic ones. She was probably right. Liam trailed in, taking a swig from his beer. Koda frowned. "Where's Aric?"

"He's calling one of the girls who're after him."

Koda glanced my way. *"Now?"*

"Yeah, apparently they had a hot date scheduled for tonight." Liam popped a strawberry in his mouth. "She's texted me four times telling me everything she wants to do to Aric." He laughed. "She sounds wilder than the last three."

I could have smashed the fondue pot over his damn head, especially upon feeling the weight of everyone's gaping stare. Outside, Aric paced along the length of our porch, talking low into his phone. His voice amplified, sounding angry before he finally disconnected. He hesitated at the doorway before walking slowly toward me.

"Sorry about that," he said quietly. He motioned to the paper plates Shayna placed in my hands. "Can I help you with that?"

I shook my head and set the table, trying my best to ignore Aric. He gave me space, but the moment I finished, he stepped in front of me. "I'm sorry we were interrupted. I was enjoying our time together. Do you want to skip dessert and take a walk?"

"Don't you have other plans?" I meant to sound harsh and cold, because then I could hide my disappointment and pain. Except the harsh and the cold flipped me off, leaving the hurt to fend for itself.

Guilt mixed with sadness along the planes of Aric's face. "I only want to spend my night with you."

My lips parted with surprise. I jerked away, knowing this ... situation with Aric would eventually leave me devastated. And yet my tigress insisted we should take a chance. I fiddled with the plates in my hands, tracing the floral pattern before finally answering. "Okay, Aric ... Let me get my shoes."

Aric handed Danny a card. "Bring the blood vials to this address, in case we find more infected vampires."

Danny stared at the card. "You're staying at the Granlibakken Lodge?"

Aric nodded. "Just until we find a place to buy. We're relatively new to the area. And while we can stay at The Den, we don't want to live with our students full-time."

"I'll swing by the lab and get them to you tonight."

Aric shook his head. "Don't trouble yourself. It can wait."

"It's no trouble. Besides, I want to help."

Bren yawned and tossed Danny his keys. We followed them into the crisp night. Mrs. Mancuso dragged out her garbage cans just as Bren and Danny piled into the car.

Bren rolled down the window and motioned me over. "Come here, Celia. I forgot to tell you something."

Like an idiot, I went over. "Celia!" he yelled at the top of his lungs. "For the last time, I will *not* have sex with you!"

Danny peeled away before it cost him a roommate. I looked for Mrs. Mancuso, and she did not disappoint. From the base of her porch steps she flashed me the stiffest, meanest finger *ever*.

Aric couldn't hold back a chuckle. "What a horrible woman."

"Yes, she is."

We meandered toward Tahoe. While most of the neighborhood remained well lit by street lamps or lighting installed to show off elaborate landscaping, only the stars blinking through the branches illuminated the path to the lake. Like Aric, I could see in the dark, and I was tough. But darkness usually made me edgy, especially after playtime at Zhahara's. With Aric by my side, though, the instinct to be overly alert seemed unnecessary.

We crossed the main road and headed toward the beach. The clouds spread apart, and a full moon broke through as our feet hit the sand. "You seem in charge of the wolves, but at the same time, I can tell you're close with them."

Aric focused ahead, though nothing approached. "Gem, Koda, and Liam are more like brothers than friends. At the same time, they are my Warriors. As I am their Leader, it's their job to protect me with their lives if necessary."

I jumped over a sand castle that had begun to crumble and thought about what he said. "So, one day, they could possibly die for you?"

"Yes, one day I could lose them."

Aric's comment bothered me. I'd never allow my sisters to die for me. "Then why did you choose them?"

Aric slowed to a stop. "I didn't, Celia. They volunteered. It's an honor to be named a Warrior. Only our best fighters are granted that title." He pushed the hair from his eyes. "What those knuckleheads don't realize is that they honor me by standing at my side." He sighed. "Nor do they realize that I would also die for them."

"There's nothing like family, huh? Even one you've made for yourself."

"No. Nothing at all." He flicked the silver Native American earrings I wore. When I laughed, he did it again.

His teasing made me want to throw my arms around him. "You're lucky they aren't gold."

Aric curled his upper lip in disgust. "Yeah, just another way the vampires screwed us."

"What do you mean? Gold is their kryptonite, too."

"You don't know the legend?"

"There's a lot I still don't know about the supernatural world." I smiled softly. "Will you teach me?"

Aric's eyes zeroed in on my lips. "Ah . . . yeah. Sure."

He paused. At first I didn't think he was going to say anything. But then he cleared his throat. "When the world was still new and magic was at its strongest, a witch fell in love with a vampire. The vamp didn't love her in return. He loved his gold and the power it granted him. So the witch cursed the gold, believing if she couldn't have her love, he couldn't have his."

Aric was so tall I had to wrench my neck in order to see his face. That face of his, though, was worth the effort.

"The curse, fueled by the witch's anger and bitterness, was powerful enough to extend to all preternaturals. None of us can hold gold without it making us sick. If we're shot in the heart with a gold-tipped bullet, it's like an atom bomb going off in our chests."

I winced. "Have you ever been shot with gold bullets?"

"Yeah, it burns like a mother." He regarded me once more. "Does gold affect you?"

"No. But bullets in general do." I kicked at the sand. "I wouldn't need one dipped in gold to kill me."

Aric's tone grew hard. "Well, then, let's make sure that never happens."

I smiled a little. "Yes. To either one of us."

As we veered away from the water's edge, Aric spoke again. "Is most of your family out here?"

Aric asked a simple question—had I lived an average life. "The family I know and love is here." I elaborated when he frowned. "It's just been my sisters and me for a long time. We're estranged from our family."

Aric tensed. "Even your parents?"

I concentrated on how little my human feet disturbed

the sand. It was easier than the emotions the deaths of my parents riled. Aric didn't push me to speak. Perhaps that's why I chose to. "My parents were murdered during a home invasion. We went into foster care when both sides of the family refused to take us."

Aric's body blocked my path. "My God, Celia. Were you . . . safe?"

I averted my gaze from his, unable to keep the shame from invading my voice as it shook. "No. Not at first. But eventually we found a foster mother who loved and cared for us. Ana Lisa . . . made everything okay . . . for a while."

Aric's compassion permeated his aura, warm enough to heat my skin through my sweater. "I want to help you. Tell me who hurt you."

"You don't have to worry about that . . . they're all gone now."

The absoluteness of my tone made it clear I'd played a strong part in their departure. That in itself should have sent him bolting. It didn't. His compassion continued to sizzle against me. So did something else. . . .

"Good," he murmured.

We walked in silence for a long while. He, like me, didn't seem the type to fill the quiet with worthless ramblings. I liked that. I liked him. And the soft smiles he flashed me made me think that perhaps he liked me, too.

When we reached the rockier part of the beach something stirred behind a large boulder. I prowled along the sand to investigate, but Aric stepped in front of me. When he snarled, a guy jumped out. I could tell by his scent he was a wereweasel. He smelled . . . sleazy. I didn't know what he was doing until he took a picture of us and ran.

Aric watched him disappear into the night. "What the hell was that about?"

Resentment burned deep in my stomach. "Since vamp court, every kind of supernatural beastie has shown up to get a look at us."

"Tell me you're joking."

I shook my head. "It's really annoying. That was the first photo, though. I'll kick his ass if I ever see him again."

"No. If you see him again, you tell me. I don't want anyone bothering you or your family."

I hid my shock and continued walking. I couldn't understand why Aric had taken on the role as my savior, especially after I survived the predator showdown at Zhahara's without him. "Don't you know by now I can take care of myself?"

Aric's face hardened. "I don't deny you're tough or that you can fight. You have to be to endure the shit you have. But stop feeling like you have to rely on yourself all the time. I'm around now, Celia. You're no longer alone."

Despite how his words made me swoon, I refused to fall at his feet. At least, for the moment. "Why do you feel the need to protect me?" I asked softly.

His expression remained serious, yet he nudged me playfully and made me lose my balance. "I told you. You're an innocent."

Aric's confidence, chivalry, and pure sexiness drew me to him like magnet. My tigress should have questioned or resisted his gallantry, but his wolf also attracted my beast. I coughed to hide a come-hither purr and scaled a large boulder. I breathed in Tahoe's soothing aroma, trying my best to stay calm and not pounce on him like a werepoodle in heat. *Must not tackle big, hunky werewolf.*

Thunder cracked in the far, far distance, and the air filled with the sweet fragrance of witches' magic. Aric joined me on the boulder, crouching when I did. He adjusted his position so he could sit, all the while keeping his eyes on me. "Tell me more about you."

I sat next to him and hugged my knees against me, mostly to keep from squirming. "What do you want to know?"

"The same thing I've wanted to know since I met you. What are you, Celia? You're a mortal of magic, but I've never met anyone like you."

Being the center of attention had never appealed to me. That was Taran's job. Yet Aric's deep, gentle, voice made it all right to speak, and so did the way his knuckles grazed along my arm. "To be honest, Aric, I don't know what I am." I watched his hand as it continued to stroke along the length of my limb. "You come from a family of *weres*—a *were* mother, a *were* father." He nodded, despite his obvious uncertainty where my train of thought headed. "My sisters and I come from human parents with no trace of magic. I guess you can say we're the products of a backfired curse."

Aric stopped rubbing my arm. A strong breeze swept some strands of hair across my face. I didn't bother pushing them aside, preferring to hide my face. My uniqueness bothered me then more than ever. But since I'd already begun to explain, I thought I owed it to Aric to finish. "My mother was born in El Salvador. She moved to the U.S. when she was four years old. Most of her family didn't like her. She had lighter skin and eyes, and I think they resented her for fitting in so well with the American culture. When she married my dad, a Caucasian American, they disowned her."

"For marrying outside her race." It wasn't a question. Aric understood based on his pureblood heritage.

"Yes. When Mom became pregnant with me, one of her crazy aunts showed up at the door and cursed her unborn children. But instead of harming us, the curse gave us our special gifts." I twisted my hair until it rested against my shoulder in one long curl, waiting for Aric to say something, and petrified my "weirdness" would affect his opinion of me. When the worry became too much I stole a glance at his face. "Does it bother you not knowing what I am?"

Aric's intensity spread into the warmth of his soft smile. His hand swept around my neck, separating the strands of my long waves. He played with them until they fell wildly against my back and shoulders. "I don't care what you are," he muttered. "I like what I see. You're beautiful, Celia. . . ."

My mouth went dry.

But not in a good way.

I felt myself falling backward. Aric caught me on the way down. "Celia. *Celia!*"

My vision blurred and I couldn't stay awake. My last memory was of Aric as he raced us along the sand.

CHAPTER 21

I stumbled down the stairs and into the kitchen. The sun was shining, my head was pounding, and I needed to consume every last morsel of food in the house. Damn, my stomach growled like a cave full of pissed-off cheetahs ready to claw the nearest— *Ooh, doughnuts!*

I tore into the box like a woman possessed, pausing between swallows to pour milk into a glass. I rubbed my belly after the third powdered doughnut. *Feel better, sweetheart? No? Let's get you some nachos!*

Nachos, a carton of bacon, and a few breakfast burritos later, I checked my phone. There were several texts from Aric, wondering how I was, asking me to call him . . . and one from the vampires.

Celia,

   The master fell into a deep coma. That means you and your sisters will, too, since he gave you freaks some of his energy to help him fight Zhahara. Do not operate any heavy machinery, drive, or jug-

gle knives or anything because you could like crash or die or something.

Hugs and kisses,
Ana Clara

Friggin' vampires. The time on the text told me they sent the message around the time Aric and I had left for our walk . . . two days ago.

My body went numb. This meant my sisters and I had been asleep for two days. I called Aric as soon as I checked on my sisters.

"Hey."

There was a pause. "Are you okay?"

"I'm fine." Beneath Aric's growl I heard his concern, and because of it, I continued to speak reasonably. "I'm sorry I haven't called. I just woke up."

Another pause. "Why didn't you tell me you'd borrowed that idiot's power?"

"I didn't borrow it. He gave it to us following the fight at his house."

"So you'd have the energy to risk your life to help him battle his enemies."

Aric's tone told me he thought Misha had manipulated and used me again. And that I'd lain down like a sap and let him. "He was only trying to help, Aric. See, getting the tar kicked out of us by your pack left us a little drained."

Silence. Followed by a low growl. I paced around the island in our kitchen. "I didn't call to fight with you, Aric." *I called to hear your voice . . . because I miss you, damn it.*

His growls stopped. "I don't want to fight with you either, Celia. And I'm not mad at you."

I leaned against the counter. "You could have fooled me."

Aric sighed. "I just don't want anyone taking advantage of you, sweetness."

Sweetness . . . ? My heart flew out of my chest on the wings of a dove, soaring around the kitchen until it crash-landed against my sternum. "Thank you. Ah, thank you." I repeated my words in haste, trying to find something worthwhile to say. When nothing came to mind I reached into my inner tigress for courage. "Would you like to come over for dinner again tonight? You and the wolves, I mean." I supposed I could have asked him over by himself, but even my tigress remained a little shy.

There was a brief pause that felt more like a lifetime. Rejection pounded my heart with every passing second. "I'd like that very much. But this time let us bring the meal. We don't cook, but we can barbecue. Do you have a grill? If not we can bring one."

I smiled into the phone. "We have one built into our back deck, but we've never used it."

"If it doesn't work, we'll build a fire out back."

"Oh, you're manly men, I see."

He laughed. "Yes. For werewolves, that is. Does six work for you?"

No. I want you here now. "Sure. I'll see you then. Bye, wolf."

"Good-bye, sweetness."

I stared at my phone as my thumb grazed over the screen. Bren was right. I was in trouble.

The doorbell rang at exactly six. I hurried downstairs. Koda and Liam sauntered in carrying several bags of food. It struck me as odd to see Emme with someone like Liam. He personified the typical bad boy, in his faded jeans, tight T-shirt, and spiky hair. But looks were apparently deceiving. Liam killed malicious creatures on a weekly basis, yet treated Emme with all the kindness she deserved. He bent to kiss her lips gently, only to laugh when she blushed. "You're such a doll," he told her.

Koda lowered his head when Shayna skipped toward him. "Hi, baby," he whispered when she hugged him and kissed his cheek.

Gem came in next, awkwardly carrying a bouquet of purple roses. He smiled shyly and handed them to Taran. "I wanted to bring blue ones to match your eyes. I'm sorry I couldn't find any."

Taran approached like the shy virgin she so wasn't. "They're beautiful. Thank you for thinking of me."

Aric stepped in last, carrying a large box and greeting me with a warm smile. "Hi, Celia."

My natural impulse was to welcome him with an embrace and a kiss—a ridiculous thought, considering we'd only recently met. And yet his warmth drew me hypnotically to him. Liam stepped in my path to whisper in my ear, "Aric's been thinking of you, too, Celia. He brought you a special treat."

My bashful smile vanished when Liam hurried out of the way. Every part of me was stunned stupid by the smell of fur, moist forest soil, and whiskers—lots of whiskers—wafting from the box Aric held. His grin faded the moment he caught a gander at my face.

Emme glanced over her shoulder at me while my mind raced with what to say. "Um, Celia. Don't you want to see what Aric brought you?"

I shook my head slowly and backed away, my mind

stuttering with fear of what might happen and terror that I'd scare Aric away. Emme widened her eyes as I stood there like a jackass. She stepped forward. "Um, here, I'll get it for you, Celia."

My hand reached out to stop her. "Emme, *don't—*"

She screamed upon lifting the flap. Eight wild rabbits scampered around inside. Koda picked up one by the ears like a prize bass. "We thought we'd skin them and roast them over a fire."

Like that was the greatest idea ever. My sisters joined me in my petrified state. "Oh, *shit,*" Taran muttered.

Oh, shit was right. One of the fuzz balls poked his head out of the box and narrowed his little evil eyes at me. I tried to prepare myself and block his spirit, but the bastard bunny didn't give me a chance. He leaped out of the box and nailed me in the chest. I fell backward as if tackled by a high school varsity team. A violent seizure rocked my body as my skull bounced off the hardwood floor.

Aric reached me before my sisters could, dropping the box of bunnies. I was vaguely aware of an army of scampering little paws and him yelling. "Oh, God, Celia!"

My sisters surrounded me. "Damn it, don't touch her!" Taran yelled at him.

Aric ignored her and swept me into his arms. "I'm taking her to the hospital. Koda—get the truck!"

My skin peeled excruciatingly away where Aric held me. Emme inhaled sharply as my back bowed, and I clenched my jaw tight to keep from shrieking in agony. "Aric, *no.* You're hurting Celia!"

Aric pulled me tighter, probably thinking his body heat could soothe me. I beat my screams back down, but couldn't muffle my whimpers. "Sweet Jesus," Aric whispered as tears streamed from my eyes.

Fortunately, Shayna kept her voice calm and managed to reason with him. "Aric, you have to let her go. Her skin is more sensitive during the seizure. Please, Aric. I promise she'll be fine in a moment."

Aric released me slowly. I knew he meant to be gentle, but the glide of his hands over my skin was like metal barbs scraping the span of my body.

"Breathe, Celia, just breathe. That's right, honey," Emme cooed at me.

The convulsions worsened until slowly my body shrank and my ears lengthened. I lay on my side as my body curled into a ball. Instead of panting, I felt my nose twitch in rapid succession, and my whiskers tickled as they brushed against the dark-stained floor. When the spasms subsided, I scampered out of my clothes. I sat back on my haunches and gazed up at everyone.

My sisters sighed with relief. "Damn, that was a bad one," Taran said.

The wolves stepped in front of Aric, guarding him protectively. Gemini's dark almond eyes watched me, waiting, it seemed, for the killer rabbit to attack. "She's a shape-shifter."

Aric shook his head. The doubt shadowing his features dissipated like a storm cloud in the face of the noon sun. "She can't be. She's not evil. . . . I can sense her heart." He took a step in my direction, but Koda pushed a firm hand into his chest.

"No, Aric. It could be dangerous."

My little body trembled with shame. Koda referred to me as "it" and not "she." Sweet God in heaven, what did they think I planned to do to him?

"Careful, Liam," Koda said when Liam circled around to my other side.

"What the hell are you doing?" Taran seethed with boiling rage. "Nothing's changed. She's still Celia."

Emme walked to Liam and took his hand, trying pointlessly to lead him away. "Liam, stop it. You're scaring Celia."

Liam scratched his head before glancing up at the others. "What if Emme's right? I'd hate to have to kill her."

My sisters went ballistic at the same time Aric rammed his way through the wolves. *"Don't even think about it!"*

The hall table overturned, shattering the pot housing our fern as Koda and Gemini tried to haul Aric out of the house and away from me. The screams, growls, and chaos overloaded my sensitive nerves. My newfound instincts told me to run. So I did, up the stairs and under my bed. Seven pairs of feet paused briefly before scrambling after me.

I was probably five times the size of an average rabbit. It was a tight squeeze under the box spring. But my growing terror and mounting humiliation propelled me forward. *The wolves think I'm a danger to Aric . . . and that he should stay away from me.* My bunny eyes burned from impending tears. I covered my face with my little paw until part two of my dilemma sank in. *Holy Mother. They also think they have to kill me!*

A high-pitched sizzle followed a yelp and a snarl from Liam. Taran's voice sounded muffled from beneath the bed. "You do anything to hurt my sister and I swear to God, I'll fry your freaking snout off!"

"I don't want to kill her," Liam insisted. "I'm just worried she'll attack Aric."

"Celia would never hurt Aric." Shayna may as well have told them I wanted to mount him with how hard the silence fell around the room. Heat rose from my twitchy nose to my bushy tail. Had I been human, I would have resembled a tomato with green eyes and big hair.

Gemini's voice grew calm, like the discussion of how evil I was or whether I should be allowed to live never took place. "No one will hurt Celia. I promise. We just never met a shape-shifter with any trace of humanity left. I'm sorry to be the one to tell you, but the sister you know will soon leave you and fall into a pit of darkness so great, only a coldhearted killer with a thirst for power will remain."

"Jesus," Koda muttered from somewhere in the hall. "How many kills do you think she's made?"

Taran's voice stiffened. "She's never killed anyone who hasn't deserved it. And Celia is anything but cold-hearted." The back of my sisters' feet appeared beneath the dust ruffle. I could almost picture them crossing their arms and scowling at them. "Maybe you should leave. Celia's been humiliated enough."

No one moved for the longest time. Finally, Aric's big hiking boots stepped forward. "I apologize if we've offended you. Her . . . situation caught us off guard. Will you allow me through?" His voice rumbled with concern. "I just want to make sure she's safe."

Emme's small feet parted, followed by Shayna's and Taran's. Aric peered beneath the bed skirt at my shaking form huddled in the corner. "She's scared senseless." His eyes softened. "She's no shifter. I'm sure of it. She's just . . . Celia." He reached for me, but I scuttled farther into the corner. "It's okay, sweetness. There's nothing to worry about."

"I've got an idea." Liam hurried downstairs to the

kitchen. When he came back, he stuck his head under the bed and poked me in the nose with a carrot.

Take that carrot and ram it up your ass, Liam.

Aric frowned. "Liam, get the damn carrot out of her face."

Liam ignored him. "It's okay, Aric. I got this one. Come on, little bunny. No one's going to eat— *Ouch!*" He dropped the carrot when I bit him.

"She may look like a rabbit, but she's still Celia. Don't freaking patronize her," Taran snapped at him.

Shayna spoke up. "Why doesn't everyone head downstairs? Aric and I will look after Celia." She stuck her thin arms under the bed. "Come on, dude." I allowed Shayna to pull me out. She held me close and kissed the top of my head before placing me on the bed.

The wolves wouldn't budge. Aric growled low and deep. "If she wanted to kill me, she would have tried long before now. Leave us. I don't want her frightened."

Gemini nodded once and led the others out. Taran and Emme followed, but not before Emme shot me a nervous glance.

Aric backed away and leaned against the dresser. I hoped it was just to give me space and not because I finally creeped him out. Shayna smiled at him. "When Celia was about nine years old, she got really sick. We thought she had the flu. We found out later she was undergoing some kind of magical growth spurt." She took a seat next to me on the bed. "When she started feeling better, our parents took us to the zoo to pick up her mood. They had new tiger cubs, and we won an opportunity to pet them. When Celia touched the golden cub, she fell into a violent seizure, similar to the one downstairs.

"Our parents rushed her to the hospital. The doctors

thought it had been related to her illness and released her after they did some neurological testing. That night she turned into a golden tigress more than three times her size."

I still remembered that night vividly. My mother prayed and doused me with holy water. I was beyond terrified and sought comfort in my father's arms. My large paws wrapped around him. Taran and Shayna kept yelling, "Don't eat Daddy. Don't eat Daddy!" I tried to talk, but all that came out were growls and roars. Despite the fear I sensed in my father, he helped calm me. "It's okay, sweetheart. Daddy's here." My father had been my rock and my strength. His soothing words helped me to relax. As I calmed, I returned to my human form.

"She eventually learned to control her *change*," Shayna continued. "But if an animal brushes against her and she isn't prepared, she'll turn into that animal." She giggled. "That's why we don't own any pets. Although . . . if Celia could just walk around as a tigress all day long we could adopt a kitten. For some reason, another animal doesn't force her *change* if she's in her tigress form."

"It's probably because her beast is so strong."

Shayna nodded. "Yeah. I guess that makes sense."

Aric fixed his gaze on my small, furry form . . . and smiled with understanding no sane wolf should have gathered so quickly. "What about the other animals she's come in contact with? Can she return to those forms?"

"No, dude." Shayna rubbed my ears. "This is just temporary. Her tigress form is the only one she's ever been able to control. We figured it's because it was the first animal she touched after her magic-like illness."

Aric's smile faded. "So why isn't she *changing* back now?"

Shayna pulled the small throw blanket from the edge of my bed so it covered me up to my neck. "When she's scared or stressed, she can't relax enough to *change* back. I think since you're a wolf, her rabbit instincts are telling her to be afraid of you."

"She has nothing to fear from me."

My nose twitched. *Except for heartbreak and further humiliation.*

Shayna rubbed the area between my ears and spoke softly. "Then why did Liam think he may have to kill her? And why did the others try to protect you?"

Aric kept his eyes on me. "They mistook her for a shape-shifter. Shape-shifters are born witches and spend years making blood sacrifices to command any form of their choosing."

Shayna stopped rubbing my back. "Dude, Celia's so not a witch. And I assure you she's never sacrificed anyone." She paused, her voice trickling hints of sadness. "Except herself . . . to keep the three of us safe."

Aric smiled at her gently. "It's obvious she would do anything for you."

Shayna squeezed me tight. "And she has . . . but she's so lonely because of it."

I nudged her with my paw. The last thing I needed Aric to hear was more, "Golly gee, you wouldn't believe how pathetically friendless and love-starved Celia is" testimony.

She laughed and whispered low into my bunny ears, "Don't worry, Ceel. I won't mention how long it's been since you've had . . . *relations.*"

It was times like this I wished my powers included manifesting rocks to stone Shayna with. She might as well have screamed it out loud with how well Aric could hear.

She continued as Aric coughed nervously into his elbow. "Aric, I don't mean to insult you, but trust me when I say Celia doesn't want the rabbits—live, roasted, or otherwise. I know you meant well, but rabbits aren't her thing."

Aric's face reddened before he averted his gaze. "Of course. I didn't mean to upset her." He adjusted his weight, causing one of my picture frames to fall over. He glanced at it before placing it back on its stand. It was a photo of me wearing overalls and two big ponytails. Something about it made him smile. "She still looks the same in a lot of ways."

Shayna laughed. "Oh, I'm sure a couple of things have developed since then."

I thumped my hind leg with annoyance, causing Shayna to laugh harder. She smoothed down my ears and rose. "Aric? Would you mind taking over soothing-Celia duty? I think she's in better spirits." She nibbled on her lip. "Not to mention I'd like to spend time with that cute little buddy of yours."

Aric chuckled as he sat on the bed. "I'm sure Koda would like that. Thanks, Shayna."

Aric lay across the bed next to me as soon as Shayna left. He stroked my fur from my head all the way across my back. "In case you're wondering . . . I still don't care what you are." He smiled. "And you make a damn sweet bunny."

Said the big, bad beast to the little wabbit. I backed into his chest and rested my fuzzy face against the crook of his bent arm. For a bunny, I was pretty brave. Had I been human, I wouldn't have dared to lie so close to him.

Aric stayed quiet for a long time, hypnotizing me with his strokes and the warmth of his body. The others moved around downstairs, and I could smell the coals burning when the barbecue was lit. Shayna laughed out loud at something Koda mumbled to her, and Liam fumbled with the playlist until he found a hard-thumping classic rock song. But in my room just then, things felt strangely peaceful. I wished I had the ability to freeze time, or at least slow it down. This moment between Aric and me was more perfect than the sun setting across Tahoe on a warm summer night.

And yet as much as I wanted to hold on to my time with Aric, I was no match for his gentle touch and the sound of the soft rain splattering against the window. My ears flopped against my head and I felt myself begin to *change* back.

Aric adjusted the blanket over my shoulders. He stood with his back to me, allowing me some privacy, but not appearing anxious to leave. "I like your room," he said quietly.

Weres frequently walked naked around one another. *Changing* as they did didn't allow much room for modesty. I wasn't a *were*, and, despite my toned body, I remained extremely modest. I adjusted the sheet around my breasts. "Thank you. Shayna helped me decorate it."

Aric studied the room while keeping his back to me. "It's not girlie."

I agreed. My walls were a deep cream with white trim. A few pictures of my sisters, and places we had visited, hung around the room. On either side of my king-size bed stood two dark wood end tables that matched the bed frame. Emme had placed bamboo plants on each. She had a green thumb. I didn't. I managed to keep them alive by leaving the two silver table lamps on during the day.

My comforter was chocolate brown with a crocodile pattern. I'd splurged and bought eight-hundred-thread-count white sheets. If it were up to me, that would've been the extent of my color scheme. Shayna believed otherwise. She folded a copper blanket between the bed-sheet and comforter, and added copper and tiger-print accent pillows to brighten the darker shades. My dresser stood on one side of the double doors leading to the bathroom, and my brown leather chair and matching ot-toman were on the other. During the day, I often sat on the chair to read, using the natural light from the large picture window to help me make out the words on the page. It was a simple room, and it fit me perfectly.

"I'm not really the girlie type," I told him.

He turned around to grin at me. "Good."

Aric's smile could melt the Arctic in the middle of the coldest night. So could his eyes. I swallowed hard and tugged the edge of the sheet closer to my chin. Aric quickly spun around. "Sorry," he said. "I'll wait for you downstairs."

I slipped on a tank top and jeans and hurried into the kitchen.

While I was convinced the bunny fiasco would live in infamy, Aric didn't seem the least bit shaken. He draped an arm around me several times during dinner and took me on a romantic walk following dessert.

"It's supposed to be nice tomorrow. Would you like to go for a hike? I know a spot with a great view of the lake where we could picnic."

The night had drawn to a close too soon. It saddened me to know he was leaving. But when he wanted to see me again, I jumped at the opportunity. "I'd love to." His grin held me in place. God, I wanted him to kiss me. "Would you like to come in?" *So we can make out on the sofa and I can finally touch you?*

Something about the way I looked at him then made those steamy brown eyes shadow over with desire. He answered by closing the distance between us and wrenching the door open. "After you," he murmured.

As soon as we stepped over the threshold, the vapors from the petting festival on the couch practically knocked me on my butt. Shayna and Koda jumped when they saw us. If we'd arrived a few minutes later I was positive their clothes would've been scattered all over the floor. Shayna's cheeks were red and flushed with sweat, and her ponytail sat completely askew.

Koda panted like he'd just run down a herd of deer. He strategically placed one of our throw pillows across his lap. "Hey. What's up?"

Like we didn't know in more ways than one.

I fell into Aric and shoved him back onto the porch, shutting the door on my way out. I turned around, laughing. "So now what do you want to do?"

Aric's eyes widened slightly as he glanced back at the shut door. "Ah . . . I thought you wanted to go inside."

I stopped laughing. Had he thought I was inviting him to my . . . *bed*? The way his face reddened told me yes. I didn't do one-night stands . . . but I'd also never shared a connection like I did with Aric. His gaze searched mine while my mind struggled with what to do. My inner beast stirred, warming me to my core. She wanted Aric's wolf, and she rather insistently reminded me I wanted Aric.

My tigress nudged us forward. Aric's hands slid onto my hips while mine slipped behind his head to stroke his thick hair. Our bodies shuddered as my breasts grazed against the muscles of his powerful chest. He leaned down, brushing his soft lips against mine. He paused to assess my reaction before meeting my lips once more.

Oh, my God.

A barrage of heat pounded every delicate part of me. Our mouths parted.

And his phone rang.

He swore and jerked it out of his back pocket, keeping an arm fastened around my waist. "What do you need?"

"We have a situation. We just killed two more infected vampires and we're tracking a third."

"Where?"

"Just North of Kings Beach. This one is old, real old, Aric. She'll be hard to kill." The *were* growled on the other end. "Crazy leech already has a bitch of a scar from the last bastard who tried."

I gripped Aric's arm as my lungs clenched. "Where's the scar?"

"What?"

My grip tightened. "Aric, ask him where the scar is."

"Who the hell is that?" the *were* snarled on the other end.

Aric watched me carefully. "Just answer her."

The *were* paused. "It runs from her jaw across the length of her throat. But what . . . ?"

My hand fell against my side. *No. Not again.*

"Celia. What is it?"

I swallowed hard. "It's Antoinette Malika. Your wolves are tracking another judge."

CHAPTER 22

"You're to stay behind me at all times. No leaping into danger. No taking unnecessary chances. No attacking. No *changing*. Unless we're all incapacitated or dead, you are *not* to engage any vampires. Even then you are to flee to safety. Do you understand?"

"I understood you the first five times you told me, Aric." He growled something under his breath, but stopped when I placed my hand on his thigh. It wasn't like me to be so forward, but touching him felt as natural as breathing, despite the flush it sent to my cheeks. "I'll be careful. I promise." I sighed dramatically. "I know I'm just a poor, helpless little feline and I should leave any dismemberment to you big, ass-kicking lupines."

Aric focused straight ahead, except he couldn't stop his grin. "Damn straight."

Koda chuckled behind me. His good cheer surprised me. But then again he'd spent quality time with Shayna, and now his beast was going to have fun mutilating a vampire.

Aric's Escalade bounced along the pitch-black wooded

path hard enough to make my teeth rattle. I knew then why the wolves drove SUVs. Evil knew no boundaries. All-terrain vehicles were a must.

Aric hit the Bluetooth thingy when his phone rang. "It's Aric."

"We snagged the leech. You want us to kill her now?"

"Not unless she starts to break from your hold. I'm bringing a witness to identify her. If she's who we think she is, we have bigger problems on our hands."

"Got it. You have our location?"

"Koda's tracking you through your cell phone. Koda, what's our ETA?"

Koda hit a few buttons on his cell. "Park here. If we cut north up the hill, we'll be there in less than five."

Aric veered off to the side and hit the brakes. "Stay close to me, Celia."

We hit the ground running. Aric and Koda barely made a sound. When they saw how easily I kept up, their steps pounded faster, pushing until they reached their full human speed. My feet sped lightly over the moist soil, barely kicking so much as pebble. The brisk night whipped my hair behind me. Aric glanced over his shoulder just to wink. I smiled, but the agonized roaring ahead easily erased my grin. My tigress growled along with the wolves. Aric didn't like that one bit. "Remember what I told you," he said in a low voice.

We stopped in a small clearing where the wolf pack stood as humans . . . naked humans. Buff, strong, strapping, very naked humans.

Holy crap.

I dropped my gaze. Except for some guy holding a cell phone and a bazooka-looking thing draped over his shoulder, we were the only ones dressed. Aric frowned. "Why aren't you watching her?"

And why the hell are you naked?

The guy with the phone held out his hand. "Relax. The rest of the pack is with her. It took all the senior wolves to corner her and take her down. Some vamp showed, too, insisting he see her." He rolled his eyes. "Wait till you see this idiot. He's as sturdy as a kangaroo with a busted leg, but he claims to be a master."

I winced, knowing who'd made an appearance.

Aric followed the other wolf. Koda placed his hand on my shoulder blades and nudged me forward when I hesitated. My tigress didn't like the idea of walking through a wall of wolves. And they didn't exactly welcome me with open arms. Deep amber eyes watched me as I passed, scrutinizing my every step. My tigress perceived each small gesture—like the narrowing of eyes or the subtle raise of a hand—as a challenge.

"Don't worry, Celia. They know better than to touch you."

Koda's tone told me his words were more a warning to them than words of comfort for me. He had my back. Between him and Aric, I didn't feel alone. But that didn't mean the situation bothered me any less.

We walked through another cluster of trees until it opened into a larger field. A fire had ravaged the area at some point, but the forest was reclaiming the land. Thick ferns grew beneath our feet, and saplings sprouted through the dense forest floor. And skipping across the field toward Aric was none other than Blondie, his date from the other night.

Her Victoria Beckham bob swayed picturesquely

against her. And so did her damn boobs. She threw her arms around Aric's neck. The same neck I'd had my arms around less than an hour ago. "Hey, baby. I knew you'd come."

My jaw fell hard enough to splinter the twigs at my feet. My tigress wanted to rip her throat out with my human teeth. And yet my human side wanted to *change* and dart away. It hurt to see him with anyone.

Aric jerked his jaw to the side when she tried to kiss his lips and forcibly unclasped her hands from his neck. He stepped away. "I told you. It's over." He glanced over his shoulder. His hard scowl softened when he caught me watching. He held out his hand. "Come on, Celia. I want you with me."

I walked to Aric's side, neither too fast nor too slow, keeping my sights on the she-wolf. I tried not to react to her threatening glare—an easy task once Aric's hand encompassed mine. He stiffened at the same time his soft warmth spread through my body. I studied our interlinked fingers. This connection between us seemed more tangible than mere body heat.

Aric squeezed my hand, pulling me closer. Koda took up my left, stopping only to glower at the she-wolf.

Petro waited at the top of a small incline, carefully wiping his brow with the handkerchief while he stared hard at what hissed below.

"Stay close to me," Aric reminded me again. He approached Petro. Petro didn't seem surprised to see me and barely glanced in my direction. "What are you doing here?"

Petro handed the handkerchief to his driver, his voice shaking as he spoke. "My brother has fallen from our grand master's favor." He rose to his full height, trying to demonstrate bravery his trembling form professed he lacked. "I thought perhaps in coming here, I might see or do something that could help."

Aric frowned. "Like what?"

Petro shook his head, his demeanor growing so sad I could practically taste his tears. "I don't know . . . I just want things to go well."

Aric ignored him to address the other *were*. "As soon as Celia identifies the vamp, the leech dies."

Petro's eyebrows shot up. "I assure you I've already made a positive identification."

Aric growled. "Yeah. Like I'd trust a vamp."

I glanced apologetically at Petro as Aric escorted me down the incline. The horrible roars intensified, as did the aroma of bloodlust. The circling wolves licked their chops and snapped their powerful jaws, eager to get the evil-killing started. They parted upon seeing Aric, allowing us through to view their prey.

The bloodluster faced away from me, held down by thick black cord strong enough to dig into her green skin and tattered clothes. She forced her head around as I neared, scraping her face against the netting. Her breathing deepened; her cries grew hungrier; her fangs elongated. "*Celia*," she hissed.

Okay. That didn't sound too psycho or anything.

Aric yanked me back. "I take it we have the right vamp?"

Her infection had advanced enough that her muscles bulged against the fabric of her clothes, but not enough to alter her face. Judge Malika still kept her beauty despite the sickly green of her skin and eyes. It was almost sad to see the once regal vampire reduced to nothing more than a dangerous animal.

I nodded. "Yes. That's Antoinette Malika."

Aric draped his arm around my shoulders and led me away. "Kill her," he ordered without bothering to turn around.

Aric rushed me up the incline and back through the field. Snarling and hisses echoed behind us. There was a scream, but not from Malika. Yelps replaced growls. Whimpers replaced snarls. And shrieks ripped through my eardrums. We whipped around. Malika was free and bounding toward us at full speed, arms pumping, eyes fixed on me. "Celia. *Celia. Celiaaa!*"

Aric and Koda exploded into wolf form, *changing* as they leaped. Aric went for Malika's throat while Koda gutted her stomach. A snow white wolf tackled me when I bolted toward them. I'd been tackled a lot lately, but the grace and gentleness she used threw me for a loop. Her obvious concern and lack of aggression kept me from *shifting* her or worse. She held me in place and shook her head, making it clear to stay put.

More wolves joined Aric and Koda, piling on the judge like she had the damn football until the popping sound of a balloon signaled the end of Malika. Aric raced back to the other wolves, but when he disappeared beneath the incline it was his human voice that roared, *"What the hell happened?"*

"That female you brought worsened her hunger," another voice yelled back. "She broke through the net and charged after her. You shouldn't have brought her, Aric."

Growls replaced voices. Aric *changed* back to communicate with his pack . . . so I wouldn't understand the argument that ensued. An argument I likely triggered.

The white wolf climbed off me and sat beside me when I stood. Petro appeared in the arms of his driver, bleeding from a head wound. He must have stepped into Malika's path. I moved toward them, but the driver held out his hand. "No. Let him keep what pride he has."

I nodded, but I couldn't stop the pity I felt for him. Petro reminded me a lot of Danny. But Danny had all of us. Petro had only Misha watching out for him. If Uri took out Misha . . . I shuddered, not wanting to think about what could happen to either Misha or Petro.

The white wolf waited with me until Koda approached . . . naked. "Thanks, Heidi," he said to the other wolf. "Come with me, Celia. Aric will meet us back at the car."

"How do you know what Aric wants?" I kept my eyes straight ahead. Shayna was patient and friendly. But she'd likely ram a toothpick in my eye for gawking at Koda. "In part because I've known him forever. But as his Warrior, my wolf is tuned to his emotions. He'll want you where it's safe."

"I'm sorry . . . if I caused any trouble."

Koda's thick brows furrowed. "You did nothing wrong, Celia. The others should have done a better job of guarding the bloodluster rather than counting on that damn net."

We walked in silence until reaching Aric's SUV. *Weres* must have kept the local sports equipment place in business. The back of Aric's Escalade was packed with sweats in every size, which, fortunately, Koda slipped on immediately. "Are you coming back to the house?"

Koda's ears seemed trained on the dark wooded area around us, but he still answered. "I don't want to overwhelm Shayna." He shrugged like he didn't care, except it was obvious that he did. "I told her I'd call her in the morning."

He perked up at the soft movement of feet behind us.

Aric appeared, wearing only sweatpants and a pissed-off face. Koda growled.

I hurried toward him. "What happened?"

Aric stroked my face, his voice deepening. "Tell Dan we'll be getting him that blood. Another pack called. They just killed eight more infected vampires."

CHAPTER 23

Taran drove us home after work. Both Shayna's and Emme's wolves were given the night off from hunting. They met our sisters at the hospital, anxious to see them again.

Goody for them.

I'd received only a few texts from Aric. All stated he'd call soon. But he didn't, hadn't, and likely wouldn't. Naked females with perky body parts literally threw themselves at him. We barely shared a kiss—fully clothed! My lack of confidence threatened to eat me alive. I knew he had a job to do. I realized infected vamps ran amok. I knew this. But it didn't make a difference. Part of me wished I had invited him to my bed. My more practical, nonobsessed, less scary part didn't want him needing me only for sex. And, if memory served, I wasn't the ideal tigress in bed. I resembled more an awkward lamb or a George Costanza.

Taran blared her horn at the car in front of us. The light had turned green, but the driver was preoccupied making out with his passenger.

Bastard.

"Sorry, Celia."

The misery in Taran's voice snapped me out of my "woe to me" moment. "Huh?"

Taran focused ahead. "All those times when you sat at home by yourself while the rest of us were out must have been hell." Tears glistened in her eyes. "How did you do it? Weren't you lonely?"

I still am. I shrugged. "Gemini hasn't called?"

"No! For shit's sake, usually I can't get rid of men." She held up a finger. "He's texted me once—*once*—just to say they're still hunting. No, 'I can't wait to see you. I miss you. Let's go out.' Nothing. No-*thing*. Can you believe the goddamn nerve?"

No. I couldn't. Just like I couldn't believe how badly it affected her. Taran went through men. It wasn't in her nature to tie herself down to anyone. I knew her beauty and spirit would eventually land her "the one," but I also thought for sure the sap would salivate at her feet. I wanted to ask her more about it, but her rising temper needed a distraction.

"Have they found anything?"

She huffed. "Nothing but a shitload of infected vampires. They're averaging eight kills a night. That's thirty-six vampires since we left Zhahara's. Where the hell are all these vampires coming from?"

"I don't know. But the *weres* can't continue to keep the human population safe until they find the source of the outbreak."

"No. They can't. And if that nastiness spreads outside of Tahoe . . ." She shuddered. "At least with the wolves out, I haven't heard of anyone belonging to the area missing."

I glanced outside the window at the darkening sky. "No, but another tour bus disappeared last night. This time on the Nevada side."

"Aw, hell, Celia. I *so* didn't need to hear that." Taran abruptly turned off the radio like the sappy song bothered her, and lost herself in her thoughts. "Do you want to go out tonight? Just me and you? I'm tired of sitting at home."

It had been a long three days of wallowing in self-pity, but that's all it seemed I had the energy to do. "No. Sorry. Maybe dinner tomorrow?"

"I meant . . . to hunt for bloodlusters ourselves."

My head shot up toward her. I almost jumped at the idea. The thrill of a hunt enticed my tigress, pulling me out of my sadness. But then realization hit me like a freight truck. "Are you prowling for monsters or are you gaming for wolves?"

Taran grew silent.

"Taran?"

"Damn, Celia. I'm turning into one of those desperate, pathetic girls I used to make fun of."

Yeah. Join the friggin' club, order the comfort food, and bring on the chick flicks. I dug my claws into my thighs, willing myself to support Taran. "You need to give Gemini time. He has a genuine and honorable responsibility to the earth. I don't think he's purposely avoiding you."

"Will you show Aric the same courtesy?"

My chest hurt at the mention of his name. "That's different. And you know it."

Taran easily pulled into our neighborhood—no simple task during one of her more annoyed eye rolls. "Aw, hell, Celia. We've all seen the way that wolf looks at you—Oh, *shit*!"

I jumped up out of my seat as our house came into view. The front had been converted into an elegant restaurant. Three chefs busied themselves cooking in the outside kitchen situated along our sidewalk, while a fourth drizzled a three-tiered cake with chocolate. That seemed extravagant enough. The orchestra—complete with a pianist, a cellist, two violinists, and an entire woodwinds section perched on our lawn—much, much worse.

"Is that a boar on a goddamn spit?"

I nodded at the boar on the goddamn spit. "Yup."

A stark white canopy was draped along the entire overhang, tied with scarlet satin ribbons at each pillar. Elegant china, stemware, and linens covered the table positioned alongside the porch swing. Yet it was the master vampire standing at the top of the steps who drew my attention.

I stumbled out, eyes wide, mouth open, only to be greeted by one of the good Catholics in a naughty French maid uniform. Lord, I couldn't imagine shopping with them. "Good evening. The master wishes you to join him for dinner."

Misha winked back at me, his long, luscious hair loose over the shoulders of his charcoal tux.

"Ah. Yeah. I can see that." I glanced desperately at Taran.

"You're on your own, Ceel." She sashayed toward the house. "I'll be inside knitting or whatever the hell old maids do. Hey, Misha," she said with a wave.

"If you wish to go inside and change first, the master prefers thongs or crotchless panties," the vampire whispered.

"Ah, thanks, Ana Clara. But I'm not changing."

Ana Clara wrinkled her face like she'd stepped in

something nasty. Or perhaps she just didn't like me. I went with the latter. I still wore my plain blue scrubs and my hair pulled back in a twist. But damn it, I hadn't been expecting . . . *this*.

Misha walked down the steps and held out his arm. "It would be my pleasure if you joined me."

"Last chance," Ana Clara whispered. "If you want, I'll lend you my panties."

I gave her a hard stare. "I can honestly say the answer will always be no to that one."

Ana Clara scowled like I was the unreasonable one. I took Misha's arm and followed him up the steps. I had nothing better to do. My plans included the same old Saturday-night ritual—takeout, a *Laverne and Shirley* marathon, and shoving ice cream down my throat.

My porch was long enough to fit the table, but the porch swing made it so we could sit only across from each other. A very good thing, considering how Misha's aroma of sex and chocolate thickened as he regarded me. A waiter bustled over to drape the cloth napkin across my lap and fill my glass with wine. "Would the lady care for an additional beverage?"

"Just water, please." I chuckled despite myself, and leaned my arms against the table. "Misha, what are you doing here?"

"You've denied my gifts of gratitude."

A "gift," in my opinion, was something tied in a pretty package—a nice sweater, perhaps, or a four-pack of movie tickets. Master vampires took gift giving to astronomical proportions. "Nothing personal, Misha, but a vacation home in Bermuda and the four Aston Martins were a little too extreme." Although Taran had insisted otherwise. "And we're still paying you back for the house."

Misha hadn't absorbed Zhahara's power. While he'd cast the fatal blow to end Zhahara's existence, bloodlust had technically led to her redeath. Her power had likely transferred to the vamp responsible for her infection. Misha had, however, inherited her fortune and doubled his billions.

He leaned back in his seat, watching me as I sipped the water the waiter brought. "I wish only to thank you."

I smiled. "You just did."

Misha quirked an elegant brow. "Mere words are not sufficient for all you and your sisters have done."

"They are for us." I shrugged. "We have everything we need." *Almost everything* . . . My mind wandered back to the bloodlust. "Why won't you help the *weres* hunt the infected vampires?"

A steaming bowl of seafood bisque was placed in front of us. It smelled scrumptious, but Misha didn't bother to glance at it. "My darling, the cause of the infection remains unknown. I refuse to continue to risk the well-being of my family by exposing them to the infection."

I couldn't blame Misha. Hank, Tim, and the three naughty schoolgirls were all that remained of his once large family. Except there was a way he could help. "I need a favor."

Misha's smooth smile lengthened across his beautifully masculine face. "A mountain of diamonds, a sultan's fortune, and the last beat of my heart would not be enough to express my gratitude. Tell me what you desire and it shall be yours."

All righty then. "Um . . . Will you let me take your blood?"

Misha paused, his gray eyes widening before they

lightened with a sinful shimmer. He tugged off his tie, popped off a few buttons of his shirt, and exposed his jugular ... along with a few other body parts. I held up a hand. "I mean for research purposes—not for consumption." I tried not to think about how easily Misha would let me feed from him.

"There are many ways to examine me, my darling."

I'm sure there are. I stole a glance at the bulging muscles of his pecs. *And that many have tried.* I cleared my throat. "My friend Danny wants to compare the blood of an infected vampire to that of a healthy one. To see if he can establish a connection to the bloodlust."

Misha's vampires scaled the porch and surrounded him, hissing with menace directed at me. "Our master's essence is not something for you to toy with," Tim snapped.

I stood growling. "This isn't a game. Your family may be safe for the moment, but the rest of Tahoe isn't!"

Misha held up a hand. In an instant, the vampires vanished from sight, yet my tigress could sense their presence nearby. Along with the scent of their fury.

Misha's frown appeared more troubled than angry. Enough for me to think he would deny my request. "As you wish."

"Huh?"

He fixed his shirt and tie, the smile returning to his face. "I said you may take me."

Vampires lived—in an undead sort of way—to come up with more sexual innuendos than humanly possible. I excused myself and returned with the phlebotomy supplies Danny had dropped off. I purposely didn't glance at Misha while I drew his blood. When a vampire drank from another, the experience was both emotionally intimate and orgasmic. The thought alone made me nervous. Although I'd grown to like Misha, it wasn't in the way he wished. I returned to my seat once I secured the sample in the house and washed my hands.

Misha reached for my hand the moment we finished our first course. "May I?"

"May you what?"

He chuckled. "Allow me this moment to thank you."

I stared at his palm. "Does this involve teeth?"

"No."

"Blood?"

"No."

"Tongue?"

Misha considered me quite the comedian. He laughed. Hard. "Only if you wish it so, my darling."

I held out my arm. His hands slipped down from my elbow until they both covered mine. A brief sizzle sparked against my nail beds before what felt like a bevy of feathers traced up my arm. He released me as I squirmed from the touch.

"What was that?"

Misha smiled. "I believe the saying is 'my digits.'"

"Excuse me?"

Misha leaned close. "My dearest Celia, you are the most unique of beings. You risked your life for mine, you returned my essence, and yet you seek neither wealth nor power nor recognition in exchange. I am forever in your debt. Should you ever need me, call my name and I shall thunder through hell itself to reach you."

I turned my hand back and forth, half expecting to see, "For a good time call," inked across my skin. "So, what, you're like my guardian angel master vampire now?"

Misha thought about it. "Yes. Your guardian angel master vampire who wants to bed you until you scream in ecstasy."

I blinked back at him. "Um . . ."

The sound of a familiar car engine had me turning toward the street. I did a double take and jumped out of my chair, toppling it over. Aric's black Escalade veered into our neighborhood. At first he traveled the speed limit. Suddenly he slammed on the brakes, likely when he spotted the Tavern on the Green the front of my house had become. Several long, sweat-soaked seconds passed before the Escalade gradually pulled forward again and slowed to a stop . . . right across from the damn spit.

That's when I knew for sure I was on Saint Peter's shit list.

I bustled down the steps and stopped short when Aric ambled out. "Hi," I squeaked, sounding like a prepubescent boy undergoing a major voice change.

Aric's walk was slow, purposeful, bordering on deadly. It was likely due to Misha's coming to my side and slipping an arm around my shoulders. *God, please kill me.*

Aric fixed on Misha's arm like he planned to rip it off with his jowls and eat it. His fists clenched tight, cracking his knuckles before he turned to face me. "I caught an infected vampire today. I came by to drop off his blood so you can get it to Dan. But I see you're busy."

I believe my spleen fell down to my toes. Aric could have brought the sample to Danny directly. Why would he have come to my house . . . unless he had wanted to see me? I ducked away from Misha as Aric stormed to his SUV. "Wait! W-would you like to join us?"

I really needed to work on that open-fangs-insert-paw thing. Aric froze with his back to me. The angry scowl and the "hell, no" refusal I'd expected never came. He peered over his shoulder, surprising me with an impish grin before jogging away from his Escalade and positioning himself between me and Misha. He looked right at my guardian angel master vampire when he spoke. "Sure. I'd love to."

Misha inclined his stone-cold face, acknowledging Aric with his own devilish grin and motioning with a grand wave. "After you."

The corner of Aric's mouth curved. "No. After you."

I stepped between them. "How about we walk together?" Because that wasn't masochistic or anything.

I kept my focus ahead, but that didn't mean I couldn't feel the heat between the ultimate preternatural staredown taking place on either side of me. "Ah, just as a reminder, my house is neutral territory, so neither of you can, like, dismember each other and . . . stuff." At least, that's what I hoped the friggin' treaty said. Up until the last week I hadn't been curious enough to ask to read it. Now it seemed I should have requested a notarized copy and taken notes.

Good gravy, my words did nothing to ease the tension. If Misha could have *changed*, I imagined he'd take on the form of a king cobra, mostly because of the hypnotic cadence of his voice. "Only an ignorant mongrel would dare insult you in your home, my sweet kitten."

Aric's widening smile made me whimper. "Or a bloodsucking leech who's too much of a pansy to fight his own battles." His smile dropped. "And don't call Celia your damn kitten."

My hands clasped their arms as I encouraged them—rather forcibly—to separate further. "Let's sit, okay?" I said, unable to suppress the growing hysteria in my voice.

Aric picked up the overturned chair for me, but Misha yanked it from his loose grasp and held it out so I could sit. Aric nudged his way through to push it in for me, giving Misha ample time to grab the other chair. "I fear you'll have to stand for the remaining feast. Then again, perhaps you'd prefer to eat from the floor on all fours?"

Aric didn't blink. Instead he leaped onto the porch swing, landing so his long legs stretched out toward Misha and his back lay against the armrest . . . side by side with me. "No worries, Meesh." His hand rubbed my back affectionately, sending warm tingles ricocheting along my spine. "I have all I need right here."

I adjusted my napkin over my lap as Taran stuck her head out. "Celia, did you . . ." Her head whipped to Aric, then Misha, before one of her siren grins crept out. "Aw, hell. It's either feast or famine, huh, Ceel?" Taran didn't wait for me to answer. She went inside, slamming the door shut behind her. Except it did little to muffle her uproarious laughter.

I'd like to say the salad portion of the meal was filled with quiet, polite conversation. But pissing contests seldom are, even to the beat of "Canon in D" played via orchestra.

"What troubles you, mutt? Flea prevention not up to par?"

"Don't get testy, bat boy. It's not my fault you've run out of prom queens to devirginize."

"Wit is not your forte, dog. Stick to what you know—drooling, scratching, and licking body parts typically unreachable."

"Damn, you are pissed. Did one of the angry villagers leave a pitchfork rammed up your ass, Drac?"

Okay, this is fun. The breeze from the lake pushed a loose curl against my chin. I unclipped my hair to straighten it. My long tresses fell around me in a big, tangled mess. I used my fingers to comb through the strands. As I twisted it back into place, I noticed silence had fallen along the porch.

Aric and Misha watched me with deep fascination. I turned around, expecting Ana Clara to be pole dancing against one of the pillars behind me. She wasn't. She stood near the steps, adjusting the straps on her four-inch shoes and appearing bored. I turned back slowly. After years of having men ignore me or step away in fear, how the hell had I caught the interest of two very sexy males . . . with fangs and sharp claws?

I adjusted my position in the chair nervously, grateful when the waiter and Ana Clara appeared with plates of roasted boar piled high over garlic potatoes and vegetables.

Aric sniffed his food. "Hmm. Smells great." He yanked Misha's plate away and replaced it with his.

Misha quirked a brow. Ana Clara appeared and stole the plate away before Misha could take a bite. "Excuse me, Master, but I'd seasoned it more for the mongrel's taste." She handed it to Hank over the railing; he quickly dumped the plate and the entire contents in the trash. *Arsenic,* she mouthed before disappearing to get Misha more food.

I stopped with a forkful of food inches from my mouth. Aric winked. "It's okay, Celia. Yours is fine."

I pushed my plate away, just to be cautious. Misha scowled, blaming my sudden lack of appetite on Aric, of course. 'Cause heaven forbid he'd point his finger at "Fifi," his arsenic-toting Catholic schoolgirl. "Celia wouldn't have hesitated had you not interrupted our lovely dinner."

Aric peered through the family room window. "Huh. It would have been lovelier in the house. Oh . . . but then I guess that's not possible, since she didn't invite your unholy carcass in." He took a bite of his food. "Good. Very good. Still, not as delicious as your meatballs and sauce, Celia."

I knew what Aric was trying to pull. And yet my tigress went into "aw, shucks" mode.

Misha seethed before relaxing into his chair. His composed demeanor worried me more than his anger. "Ah, the mutt knows how to charm the ladies." He chuckled as he regarded me. "Yet I am not surprised. Surely after the multitude of females he's bedded in his young life, he's learned many a way to entice those he wishes to conquer."

Multitude?

Misha's frostbite stare shifted to Aric. "And they all have been of your race—purebloods, in fact. What a pity your Elders forbid you from courting a non-*were*."

"At least none of them have been young enough to be my great-great-great-great-granddaughter, you creepy bastard."

All humor dissolved from Aric's face as he took in the hurt causing me to recoil like a wilted rose. A frigid cold swept throughout my body, freezing my muscles against my bones. Misha had accused Aric of "bedding" a lot of females. And Aric hadn't denied it. Knowing the mass of naked flesh he'd touched caused my insecurities to dig a hole into my sternum until my heart threatened to pull apart like boiled meat. Worse yet, the females he'd slept with all shared common traits. They had all been of his kind. They had all been of pure blood. And none had been anything like me.

Had that been the true reason he'd failed to call me?

Aric dropped his fork with a loud clang against the table. He swung his legs onto the floor, preparing, I believed, to pounce on Misha. So his soft voice and the gentle touch of his hands on mine threw me for a loop. "Listen to me, Celia. My kind is in the best position it's been in for centuries. The purebloods are plentiful and continue to have large families. I shouldn't be held under the same constraint." He narrowed his eyes at Misha. "Despite what my Elders say."

The corners of Misha's mouth angled into a malicious smile. "To anger your Elders is to risk tremendous repercussions, mutt."

"My problem. Not yours, parasite."

A white limo sped into our development, screeching to a halt behind Aric's Escalade. Petro's driver rushed to open the door for him. Good Lord, Petro trembled so badly he needed help rising from the car.

My gaze cut to Misha. "He's getting worse," he mumbled to me. Petro tried to hurry up the steps, but his shaking made his movements awkward. Still, he smiled pleasantly upon seeing me. "Good evening, Celia. Forgive me for interrupting." His smile faltered when he addressed Misha. "My brother, our grand master is . . . displeased. He demands a conference call at your residence and requests that all in our family be present."

I rose slowly. "Why your residence?"

Misha tossed his napkin onto the table and stood. "Uri will likely use the large video screen in my home to assess the condition of our keep. I fear he believes bloodlust remains present within our family." After all Misha had endured, his master should have demonstrated a little more kindness—especially for how devoted Misha appeared to be to him. Then again, should I have expected more from a grand master? "Misha, if you need me to speak on your behalf—"

"No." Misha's voice deepened over Aric's growling protests. "I would prefer my master to know as little about you and your sisters as possible."

"Okay, Misha." I gave him plenty of room to pass, hoping he wouldn't try to kiss my hand, or any other body part. He smiled, but his haste to meet with his master made him behave. Well, sort of.

"Good night, my sweet kitten." He nodded to Aric. "May mange leave you bald and infertile, mongrel."

"Run along, blood licker; the master calls," Aric growled.

"A word of caution, canine." He winked my way. "She bites."

My face burned under Aric's scrutiny. Of course, Misha wouldn't be Misha without one more dig. He motioned as if lifting a phone receiver. *Call me*, he mouthed before stepping into his limo.

I watched the limos speed away, knowing my guardian angel's problems were far from over.

CHAPTER 24

Aric pulled into the parking lot of the research facility where Danny waited for our arrival. I pointed to the right corner. "Park on that side. It's closest to the lab where Danny works."

The tension between us remained. Though Aric continued to appear interested in me, knowing most of his pack didn't approve of our interaction made me wonder if anything between us was possible. I didn't want a mere one-night stand. Whenever I saw him, I desired so much more.

I opened my door when he parked, but he pulled it the rest of the way before I stepped out, reminding me just how fast he could move "Chivalry's not dead, you know," he said with a wink.

"I've noticed." I slid out, working hard to appear tigress smooth, not dorky-teen awkward. "Thank you for looking out for me when Malika broke free."

"About that . . . I want you to stay away from this situation. You've been lucky so far, but your lack of knowledge about the supernatural world could lead to your downfall."

"Financial or social?"

"I'm serious, *Celia*."

"I know, *Aric*." I imitated his gruff voice. He scowled at first, but then glanced away to hide his grin.

Our hands swung close enough to touch as we swept through the parking lot. This time Aric didn't link us together. Maybe finding Misha on my doorstep upset him more than he'd allowed me to see. I wanted to show him he meant more to me than Misha and thought about reaching out to him. I angled a little closer, gathering my nerve to try.

Aric opened the wide glass door for me. We stepped inside, wincing from the obnoxious fluorescent lights bleaching the industrial white tile floor.

I instinctively clasped his hand as my eyes burned. "I'm sorry, Aric. These lights are designed to kill any bacteria brought into the building. They're brutal on our vision, but the sting will pass soon."

Aric opened his eyes and fixed them on our hands. The warmth between our palms assembled into a solid force, just like the other night, only more intense. "You make me crazy—you know that?" he murmured.

I released his hand, unsure whether the heat electrifying my body was something special . . . or if Aric had this effect on every female.

He paused before following me into the elevator and watched me as I hit the button to the fifth floor. "What's going on between you and the vampires?"

Aric's change of subject made me think his strong sex appeal naturally sizzled every gal's core. *Damn it.* I shrugged. "Nothing."

Aric crossed his arms and slumped against the wall of the elevator. "Then why were you having dinner with that idiot?"

My fingers tapped against the metal railing. "Misha just showed up, Aric. I was as shocked to see him as you were."

"Somehow I doubt that."

For a wolf, Aric really knew how to work the Catholic guilt.

The elevator doors opened. Aric grasped my arm and planted his foot to keep the doors ajar. "I don't trust him, Celia. And neither should you. If he tries to pull you back into this mess, you let me know right away."

His hand held me with gentle firmness, telling me he meant business, but with a promise that he'd never hurt me. I focused on his hard knuckles, wondering whether he'd ever allow himself to really touch me. And although my tigress argued against it, I considered the objection of his Elders. "Your pack might not approve," I said softly.

Aric rubbed my arm with his thumb. "I don't want you to worry about them."

"Ah. Hey, guys." Danny stood holding empty buckets in each hand, sporting a polo shirt and jeans beneath his stain-smeared lab coat. He glanced away from where Aric and I remained in the elevator. "I'll take the samples if you have them. You don't have to stick around if you have other plans."

Aric released his hold. "It's all right, Dan. I want to know what you find." His eyes cut to me. "So long as it won't take long."

"The basic steps will take only a few minutes." Dan hurried away.

I waited for Aric to step out before following Danny . . . and was rewarded by his hand slipping against the small of my back and rubbing gently. A purr rumbled softly in my throat before I could stop it.

Aric's voice fell to a deep bedroom gruffness. "Have I mentioned you're driving me crazy?"

My lids fluttered. *Good . . . Lord.* I concentrated hard on taking one step at a time, forcing my body straight into Danny's lab and not into one of the dark offices.

Danny's workspace was about the size of a high school science classroom, with counters and cabinets to match. Aric kept his arm around me while he dug into the back pocket of his jeans for the two vials. He tossed them to Danny . . . who dropped them on the floor. Good thing they were plastic.

Danny scrambled to pick them up. "Sorry, Dan," Aric said. "I forgot your reflexes aren't to the level of ours."

Danny tried to hide his humiliation with a chuckle. "It's all right. My reflexes don't meet most human standards either."

I smiled softly at my friend. What he lacked in coordination he made up tenfold in heart and brains. "Do you need help with anything, Danny?"

"No, Celia. I set everything up when you called." He took Misha's blood and smeared it on a glass slide with a swab and then placed it under a high-powered microscope. "Holy . . . Wow! Celia, come here."

He moved so I could view the slide. Science was never my forte. Had Danny not tutored me through physiology, I never would have graduated nursing school. Yet I remembered what cells looked like. Misha's cells, while similar to humans', were significantly smaller, pink tinged around their perimeters . . . and still alive. They also held three nuclei at their center and moved in a swirling pattern as if searching for their host. "That's so cool. Aric, would you like to see?"

Based on his scowl, I would have guessed for sure he

would have said no. Yet curiosity grabbed stubbornness by the throat and pimp-slapped it a few times. Aric stood at least a foot taller than me. He had to bend practically in half to view the cells. "They're trying to regenerate, since the idiot is still alive. They'll die soon enough," Aric muttered. "Ours are similar, but have a blue tone to the edges instead of that pansy-ass pink color."

Danny shook the vial and held it up to the light. "How have humans not discovered your idiosyncrasies before?"

Aric stepped away from the scope. "Our preternatural magic helps camouflage our differences. The cells revert to a more human appearance when exposed to air. What preservative did you use to keep their form?"

Danny frowned when he read the top of the stopper. "One I didn't think would work . . . a highly potent saline."

Aric smirked. "It's the salt. Salt has a strong use in our world. It's used to capture and hold evil."

I couldn't hide my chuckle. Aric's view on vamps was very black-and-white. Dan busied himself preparing the infected blood for examination. Aric used the opportunity to hook a finger into my belt loop and pull me against him. I glanced up at Aric as my back rested against his chest, hoping Danny wouldn't be too much longer.

"Oh, crap," Danny whispered. His fingertips quickly played with the knobs of the scope. "It . . . can't be."

"Danny, what's wrong?"

Danny ignored me and hauled out another microscope from beneath the table. He wiped his finger with alcohol and pricked it with the edge of a lancet. His hands shook as he smeared his blood along the slide and examined it under the scope. He raced back and forth between his blood and the infected vampires until the preservatives holding the bloodlust together broke apart and the cells disintegrated to ash.

Sweat moistened Danny's brow, and the whites of his eyes bulged like ostrich eggs. My tigress stirred with growing angst. So did Aric's wolf. He fixed his alpha stare on Danny. "Dan. What did you see?" .

Danny's troubled expression bounced from the ash-coated slide to Aric. His voice trembled as he spoke. "The vampires are infected . . . with *human* blood."

CHAPTER 25

Aric's rage filled the small room. "That's impossible. All preternaturals are immune to human infection."

Danny backed away from Aric's wrath. "I know, but those are human cells."

I blocked Aric's path as he moved toward Danny. He wouldn't hurt Danny, but his formidable presence intimidated the hell out of him. "Danny, I saw the green blood coursing beneath the skin of those severely infected. No human disease does that."

"Celia, the fluid surrounding the cells is green—the bloodlust, I presume. But the cells are human. There's no doubt in my mind." Danny scratched his thick curls. "They have the same shape, size, and single nucleus as mine. If they were vampiric or *were*, they would have been smaller and held three nuclei—like the ones you saw."

Aric shoved his hands to his hips and swore. "How the hell are humans becoming infected?"

Danny didn't answer. His eyes darted back and forth on the floor, and he appeared lost in his thoughts. "So much of this doesn't make sense." He turned to me. "Celia, if you were to eat a burger, your digestive system would break down the food—not send cow cells into your circulatory system. When a vampire feeds, the process should be the same."

Aric stepped around me. "So then why were there human cells in this infected vamp's system?"

"I don't know."

"What do you know?"

"Nothing yet."

Danny backed away at Aric's growl. I placed my hands on Aric's chest. "Aric, please. You're scaring him again."

Aric covered my hands and took a breath. "I apologize, Dan. My anger is not directed at you. Nor will it be taken out on you. I'm worried about what's to become of the innocents."

Danny's shoulders slumped with relief. I could have told him Aric wouldn't harm him, but it meant more coming out of the big, scary werewolf's mouth. He returned to examine Misha's blood. He sighed. "Misha's blood holds no trace of human cells. Which supports my theory that their digestive process mimics ours. Something else is happening. . . ." He rose and rubbed his chin, springing up when his mind latched onto a theory. "Celia, have any of the human populace come to your hospital with any unusual symptoms or strange infections?"

My eyes widened; I knew the direction his mind had wandered. "No . . . if they had, the Centers for Disease Control would have been contacted and we would have been notified across the board."

Aric frowned at Dan. "Why do you ask? Bloodlust doesn't affect humans."

I twisted my hands to grip his. "I think Danny is suggesting they might be carriers."

Aric's jaw tensed so tight, I feared the bone would snap. "Carriers of a virus. A goddamn bloodlust virus."

I nodded. I wanted to tell him no; the possibility too frightening to admit. But living in denial solved nothing.

The air surrounding Aric heated, but not in a good way. Fury cloaked us like an invisible sheet. "So you're telling me there are humans infecting the vampires—but we can't tell which ones, since they likely aren't developing symptoms?"

Danny glanced at me nervously. "Ah. Yeah. That's what it seems like."

I released his hands. "But until we know for sure, it's not safe for the vampires to feed."

"Shit." Aric rubbed at the stubble on his chin. "But if they don't eat, they'll develop the other kind of bloodlust." He whipped out his phone and hit a number on his speed dial. "I have to call my Elder— Martin, it's Aric. We have a situation."

I called Misha while Aric growled into the phone. Misha had just finished his conference call with Uri. And while he didn't say how the conversation went, his icy tone told me it hadn't been a pleasant chat. But when I shared Danny's findings, he flipped out.

"Humans! Humans are infecting my keep!"

I glanced at Danny. He gripped the counter with white knuckles. Misha scared him stupid. And he wasn't even in the damn room. "That's what we're thinking, but we don't know which ones or how many. Misha . . . is there anyone you trust whom you and your family can feed from? A priest perhaps, or a friendly neighbor . . . possibly a nice librarian?"

"I'll fly in my mistresses from Chicago, Montreal, London, and Paris."

I gawked at my iPhone. "Okay, I guess that can work. What happens when you run out?"

He paused. "I have enough mistresses to last us . . . awhile."

"Oh. Okay. Don't eat until they get there." I hung up when I saw Aric disconnect.

Aric placed his hands on my shoulders. "I'm needed back at The Den. I'm sorry, but I have to go now. Dan, could you drive Celia home?"

"Yeah, yeah. We can leave right now." Danny grabbed the vial of Misha's blood and dumped it in the sink, instantly destroying any evidence that might linger. He then grabbed his keys and we followed him out.

Aric opened the passenger door to Danny's Prius for me. "I'm sorry about this. I'll call you soon. Okay?"

"Okay."

Danny pretended to fumble with an old road map while Aric brushed his lips against my forehead. "Good night, sweetness."

"Good night, wolf."

I was watching Aric speed away when Danny touched my shoulder. "Celia, we have to figure out who's behind this. If the bloodlust is a virus, that means it can mutate. If that happens, even the *weres* won't be enough to save us."

I froze upon seeing the blond she-wolf on my porch as Danny drove off. She ambled down the steps, her pompousness lost despite the perfect hair and the black designer suit she wore.

She crossed her arms. "Are you and Aric together?"

I fell into a crouch, ready to pounce if she attacked. I

didn't know what Aric and I were. But I wasn't about to tell her that. "You need to take that up with him."

She played with the edges of her angled bob. "I prefer to take it up with you. Especially since he refuses to see me."

I narrowed my eyes. "That's not my problem. Get off my property and stop trying to drag me into your drama."

"I'm pregnant. It's his."

Her words hit me like darts shot out of a cannon. My heart screamed. "You're lying."

She tightened her hold around herself protectively. "Am I?" I watched her as she circled me. "Our pack hates you, Celia. They don't want you tainting Aric's sacred bloodline." She scoffed, meeting my gaze full force as tears trickled down her cheeks. "But I don't care about that. What I do care about is the child we conceived together." She clasped her hands over her mouth and jerked away. "I beg you. Please don't come between us and our baby."

CHAPTER 26

Dawn remained an hour away. I lay in my bed, reviewing the texts Aric had left on my phone over the past week.

Sorry. I've been busy. I'll call you soon.

Still hunting. Will call soon. Miss you.

Yeah. Right.

When he finally did call he left several messages.

"Hi, Celia. I'm sorry it's taken so long. My responsibilities as a pureblood are more extensive than the average *were*'s. Call me. I'd like to see you."

Extensive responsibilities? *Wait till the baby comes.*

"Celia. It's Aric. Call me. I want to talk."

His final message was the kicker. "I haven't heard from you. If you're mad, call me and we'll talk things through."

I rolled over, exhausted from lack of sleep, but unable to relax knowing wolves lay in my sisters' beds. Not that I believed they'd hurt them, but more out of longing to have my own wolf in my arms. Despite my feeling a hotter-than-hell connection to Aric, my wish to get to know him had been pulverized to dust. The she-wolf's pregnancy disclosure rocked my world and ruined my chances with Aric. My temper ran deep and fierce, yet my morals stayed tried and true. I didn't interfere with relationships, and I sure as hell wouldn't come between a male and his child.

I flipped onto my side, hugging my pillow tight to suppress the guilt gnawing at my chest. I had punched the she-wolf in the stomach at the fight at Misha's. *Were* or not, I could have killed her baby. The moment she'd left, I erased Aric's number from my phone and made my sisters promise to stop mentioning him. They didn't understand until I shared the couple's happy news. And, God, they fell so silent, I knew I wouldn't have to insist any further.

Around six, I gave up on snoozing and dressed in my running clothes, hoping a few miles after breakfast would ease my frustrations. I headed into the kitchen and turned on the lights over the stovetop. Soft illumination from the drop-down ceiling lamps shone against the polished black-and-tan granite counter and our dark-stained cabinets. The previous owners had wrecked the place. In a way, it was good thing. We were able to buy it for a steal—well, for Tahoe prices, anyway. But it took a lot of TLC to bring the thirty-eight-hundred-square-foot house back to its original splendor.

I'd just placed the waffle iron on our center island and reached for a spoon when the softest of steps trotted down the front stairwell. I stuck my head around the corner. Koda was leaving in a rush, his behemoth shit-kickers in his hand. He reached for the doorknob, not realizing I stood mere feet away.

I growled. "Are you sneaking out on my sister?"

Koda froze. "Ah, no. I just have somewhere to be."

I crossed my arms, still holding the damn spoon in my hand. "At six o'clock in the morning? On a Saturday. You *asshole*."

Koda's dark brows knitted tight. "Don't yell. I don't want to upset her."

I marched across our dark wood floors and poked him in the shoulder with my spoon. "I think she would be more upset knowing you used her!"

The pungent scent of Koda's fury practically burned off my nose hairs. *"I haven't used her!"*

I waved my arm out dramatically. "Then what do you call this?"

Koda bowed his head. "I only have one-night stands with females."

I nodded. "I see."

Then I broke his nose.

Koda staggered back covering his nose, the whites of his eyes blazing with shock and anger. "Wha da heln?" he said as his bones slowly crunched back into place. "Dat's not wha I mean."

"Really. 'Cause that's what you just said."

Koda squeezed his eyes shut and let out a breath. His sinuses must have been on fire. Poor man-whore bastard.

"It's not by choice, Celia. Women want very little to do with me after we . . . are intimate." His head dropped again. "I'm told I'm too . . . intense."

I swallowed back bile. "Did you *hurt* her?"

Koda's head snapped up. The scary beast I'd first met rushed back with a vengeance. My beast fought against my hold, sensing my fear and desperate to protect me. Still, I refused to show it and hissed low and deep.

Koda straightened, his voice a soft rumble in the dimly lit foyer. "I would *never* hurt her!" He trembled. "And God help anything that does."

If the world were ending, and the only thing that could save it was my ability to sniff out lies, we were all screwed and might as well dig our graves. But despite my lack of sniffing talent, I believed him. Something was up. Koda obviously adored Shayna. Hell, he practically wagged his tail every time Shayna skipped into a room. And God knew he'd stepped up to protect her.

"If you leave like this, I promise you *will* hurt her." I picked up my spoon off the floor, hoping to stall his departure if nothing else. "Come on. I'll make you some breakfast."

I returned to the kitchen. Koda paused momentarily before following, dropping his canoe-size shoes on the floor near the door. I handed him a wet towel to wipe the blood off his face before grabbing eggs and sausage out of the refrigerator. But it wasn't until I poured the batter into the waffle maker that either of us spoke.

"I've had a lot of sex, Celia."

I cringed and set a plate in front of him. "I know. I'm just down the hall."

Koda chuckled. "I mean in general. But . . . that's about all I've had."

I filled his plate with eggs, sausage, and a waffle, but waited before handing him the syrup and sitting across from him. Everything told me it was wrong to discuss Shayna's private life in her absence, but part of me felt Koda should know more about my little sister. "Shayna dates fairly frequently."

Koda stopped eating.

"A lot of men find her attractive."

Koda bent the fork with his teeth.

I held up my hand. "But she doesn't usually engage in deep levels of physical intimacy—like she did with you." I sighed. "If you care about her—"

"There is no 'if.' I do care about her." Koda's brow softened at his words.

I shook my head. "Then don't presume she's another one of your trampy one-nighters."

Koda swallowed with great effort. He probably ingested a few prongs. I glanced at his fork. Yup. He did. "What if you're wrong? What if—"

Shayna's footsteps silenced him instantly. By the way her soles scraped against the thick white carpet, I knew she hadn't bothered with shoes or socks. She walked down the back stairs with her arms circled around her body, seemingly heartbroken. It wasn't until she caught sight of Koda that the usual skip to her step returned. Her ponytail flicked behind her as she wrapped her pencil-thin arms around Koda's gigantic shoulders.

She kissed his cheek. "I was worried you'd left, puppy."

A deep shade of red erupted from Koda's neck to his face. But I didn't think it was because she'd called him "puppy." I gave him my best "I told you so" expression, but decided to spare the big guy from further humiliation. After all, I did belt him in the schnoz.

I pointed to his plate. "Koda was hungry."

Shayna swept a section of his long black mane over his shoulder. "Why didn't you wake me? I would have made you something."

I could almost see Koda's inner wolf panting back excitedly. He pulled her onto his lap and cupped her face. "I didn't want to bother you, baby."

I left the table to pile food on my plate the moment their lips met . . . and nearly jumped out of my skin when Liam appeared. Naked.

"Can I have some sausage?"

I shoved my plate in his hands. "Here. Take mine." I turned my back on him and concentrated hard on mixing more batter.

"Why is your face all red, Celia? You hot or something?"

"*Liam*," Koda growled. "Go put on some clothes."

Liam spoke between chews. "Why? It's warm in here."

"Because the girls weren't raised among beings that are frequently naked."

Understanding spread across Liam's boyish features. He shook his head. "Celia, you have to get over your modesty. The body is a gift. Here, take off your clothes so you can see how freeing—"

I threw my spatula in the sink. "Go upstairs, Liam. And don't come back down until you put on some damn pants!"

Liam frowned. "But what about Emme? She's probably hungry, too. We've been making love all night and—"

I threw more food on a plate and pointed up the stairs.

Liam kissed the top of my head. "Thanks, Celia. You're a good egg." He stopped at the base of the stairs. "Still, do yourself a favor and take off your clothes sometime. It's quite refreshing."

I pinched the bridge of my nose. "I'll take your word for it, Liam."

Shayna buried her face in Koda's chest, laughing. When she finally calmed down I placed a plate in front of her. She and Koda ate together, feeding each other from time to time. Koda had seconds, then thirds in the time it took Shayna to finish her first meal. He frowned at her. "Aren't you going to eat more, baby?"

She grinned. "I don't have Celia's metabolism. Trust me, this is more than enough." That's when she noticed I didn't have a plate in front of me. "You're not eating, dude?"

I sipped on my tea. "I'm not really hungry." It wasn't a lie. Preparing the food had been more therapeutic than a desire to eat.

"But you made all this food."

"I'll have something after my run."

They rose together and started to pick up their plates. I took the dishes out of their hands. "I got it."

Shayna watched me. She knew I was upset and probably needed the distraction. "Okay, Celia. If that's what you want."

Koda leaned into her, placing his arm around her and pulling her close. I nibbled on my bottom lip. "Yeah. It's what I want."

Shayna wrapped her arms around Koda's waist and grinned. "Do you want to go back upstairs?"

Koda kissed the top of her head. "I'll be right behind you." He watched her walk up the back stairs until she disappeared. "I'm not good at saying thank-you, Celia, but . . . thank you."

I smiled weakly. "You're welcome." I stopped him when he headed toward the steps. "Koda . . . just be good to her. Okay?"

Koda nodded, his tumultuous dark eyes probably seeing a lot more of my sadness than I wished. "I owe you. Big-time."

I gathered the dishes quickly. Another few moments passed before I heard his large feet amble up the stairs.

The doorbell rang a few minutes later just as the shower went on in Emme and Shayna's bathroom. I tossed the dish cloth I was using to wipe down the table into the sink. It was only seven in the morning. I hurried to the door before the bell woke Taran, and just about died when those brown eyes I adored blinked back at me through the glass pane. My hands shook as I unlocked the bolt and turned the knob, sadness dissolving my resentment. God, it hurt to see him, knowing he couldn't be mine.

Aric's grin faded when he caught my expression. "Hey, Celia," he said quietly.

"Hi." I sighed. "What are you doing here, Aric?"

Aric leaned back on his heels, crossing his arms over his thick gray sweatshirt. "Koda called. He said you needed a running partner."

CHAPTER 27

"I'm sorry, but you're mistaken. I'm not going for a run."

His eyes skimmed down my tight white T-shirt, sweat-pants, and running shoes. "Did you just come back from a run?"

"No."

He rested his back against the doorjamb. "You're not going for a run or you're not running with me?"

My averted gaze answered for me.

Aric pushed his hand through his hair. "Celia, what the hell is going on? You refuse to talk to me and now you've blocked my calls."

Knowing my actions hurt him bothered me more than it should. I was doing the right thing, damn it. It shouldn't have been so hard. "I can't have anything to do with you."

Aric leaned toward me, his jaw tightening. "Why?"

Was he kidding? "You know why."

Aric frowned until understanding brightened his irises. "I see. I just didn't realize it would matter to you."

If he had slapped me then, it wouldn't have offended

me as much as his words. What did he take me for? The very slut Mrs. Mancuso believed me to be? "Well. It does. Forgive me for having morals."

The expression on Aric's face reminded me of those talk show guests who just found out their wives had been sleeping with their fathers. So not right. How was I the bad guy?

Aric's voice cut through me. "If I can ignore this whole damn thing, why can't you?"

Aric gawked at my slack jaw as if a leprechaun danced a jig across my tongue. "Oh, my God. How can you be so callous? This is a child we're talking about."

"A *what*?"

Emme's screams halted my "get the hell off my porch" tirade. I bolted up the steps and crashed through her door, racing into the bathroom separating her room and Shayna's. Liam's blood ran in a red river along the green marble tile. Deep claw marks cut into his arms and back, revealing the shiny white of his bones. He stood in the corner, far from the window, protecting Emme's naked body with his own and snarling over his shoulder.

The scent of decomposing, burning flesh made me gag as it scorched a path through my nose. Koda stood glaring toward the window dressed only his jeans, and holding a hand out to keep Shayna back. He growled with enough menace to stand my neck hairs on end. "You're not allowed in, *bitch*."

That's when I saw her: a savage, naked, infected vampire perched on the window. Her bulging arms didn't match the green of her face. Instead they blistered and sizzled, charred from the sacred aura protecting our home. She'd tried to get in uninvited. And while she managed to hurt Liam, her efforts had cost her.

Aric's body heat warmed my back. "Koda, keep her in your sights." His voice sounded more wolf than man. "I'll go around back."

Most severely infected vampires lost their reasoning, but this vampire wasn't too far gone. She understood Aric loud and clear, and bolted with a hiss.

Oh, no, you don't.

"Celia!"

I ignored Aric's roars and dove through the window, *changing* before the strong paws of my beast hit the cold grass. A blur of green streaked into the woods behind the house. I charged after her, pushing my legs into the dry pine needles and up the incline of the small mountain. The large paws of two wolves thundered against the earth behind me.

I focused ahead, inhaling deeply to track the scent. Her long, lean legs propelled her like a jet and I quickly lost sight of her. But I wouldn't lose her aroma. My God, beneath the scent of crispy flesh smoked the sickness of the bloodlust. It reminded me of the ailing surgical patients I cared for when I first graduated. The illness permeated through their skin, masking their natural—

Oh . . . no. My eyes widened. The bloodlust did cloak her natural aroma, but it didn't extinguish it completely. I knew who she was, and the recognition fueled my anger. The cool breezed whipped back my whiskers as I pushed myself faster. I couldn't lose her. I had to find her.

I skidded to a stop at the subtle scratch of tree bark and the sudden disappearance of her scent. The bloodthirsty psychopath had scurried up a tree.

But which one?

I panted while my eyes searched the cluster of trees she'd led me to. The sun beamed through the thick branches, casting moving shadows as the firs swayed chaotically in the increasing breeze. Oh, yeah, this predator hadn't lost her ability to strategize.

A single pine needle dropped to the dense forest floor, alerting my tigress to haul ass. I jerked out of the way, narrowly missing getting body-slammed by a clawed and hungry sadist. She landed in a crouch, thick, sharp nails out, and torn rags for clothing.

We circled each other, my growls challenging her hisses. My suspicions were verified. The bulging green fluid beneath her skin distorted her formerly slender features. Except traces of the once beautiful vampire still remained. Run a brush through the matted and blood-stained chestnut hair, throw on a powdered wig, slap on a long velvet robe, and voilà, all stand for Judge Sofia.

I *shifted*, hoping to surface behind her, but her heightened senses must have felt the gentle stir of the soil when my head broke through. She pounced on me. I allowed the momentum of the tackle to spin me so I ended up on top. We clawed and swatted each other, both of us vicious and screaming for blood. My beast matched her power almost equally. She would have been hard to take down, but then, I was no longer alone.

Koda, the red wolf, appeared, just behind a powerhouse gray wolf a good two hundred pounds bigger than my tigress. Aric made a gruff sound before he and Koda bit into Sofia's upper arms and yanked hard. An oil spill of green fluid sprayed in their direction, yet their efforts seemed worth it. Bloodlust vampires were a hell of a lot easier to kill when they lacked limbs. I broke through Sofia's chest at almost the same moment Aric severed her neck in a single bite.

The three of us shook off the ash that blinded us in a

windstorm of decay. Aric approached me, nudging my nose with his.

I smiled as much as a tigress could. *I'm all right, wolf.*

The thought formed in my brain before I realized he wouldn't be able to understand. Without thinking, I rubbed my face against his neck and purred, comforted by his strong presence. His warm fur slid like silk across mine. My God, I didn't want to leave him.

Aric wagged his tail, melding his body against mine. His throat vibrated long and deep, releasing soft wolfish sounds that filled me with peace . . . until he licked a scratch on my face.

Holy . . .

The tingling warmth from his taste spread down my spine in a flash of searing heat, pounding my girl parts like the beat of native drums. My lids peeled back and so did his. Koda backed away into a white fir sapling in his haste to escape whatever the hell had ignited between Aric and me. Six hundred pounds of red beast scurried over the plantlet. It bent from his weight and rebounded back with a *whoosh*. He took off toward the house. I blinked at Aric's stunned beast before chasing after Koda and passing him like my tail smoked with fire.

Oh, crap. Oh, crap. Oh . . . crap! Someone else's baby daddy should not have had this effect on me. My muscles burned as they stretched the claw marks Sofia had dug into my skin. Aric's . . . lick . . . caress . . . *kiss*—whatever it was pushed my beast to race faster than I had when I chased the judge.

I was less than a quarter mile from the house when I caught the scent of the wereraccoon who had rifled through our garbage a few weeks back. What the hell was he doing here? I roared. He jumped before *changing* and leaped through the trees like a flying squirrel.

Yeah. That's right. Don't piss off the angry tigress who wants to mount a wolf who knocked up someone else.

I slowed when I reached our back lawn. My sisters waited on the rear porch. Taran paced, rubbing blue and white flames between her palms. Shayna stood on one of the patio chairs with her new bow out and an arrow ready to fire. Emme remained tucked beneath the crook of Liam's big shoulder. His amber eyes narrowed when he saw me. "Did you get her?" I nodded and leaped onto our wooden deck. "Are Koda and Aric behind you?"

I didn't have to answer; Aric and Koda jetted across the lawn. Taran extinguished her fire and opened the back door for me. Emme followed behind me as I barreled up the stairs. As soon as she finished healing me, I rinsed the ash from my skin and rushed us downstairs. "Come on, Emme. I need to talk to Aric."

All the wolves donned sweatpants. Aric and Koda stood at separate sinks wiping off the bloodlust goop with old towels.

"It was Judge Sofia."

Aric stopped midwipe. "Are you sure?"

I nodded. "I recognized her scent first, then her face."

Koda swore.

Taran moved over to Emme. "I can see that." She drummed her nails nervously against the granite counter. "She wanted Emme back in vamp court; of course her hunger would make her want her even more now."

Liam pulled Emme closer and growled. "They can't have her."

"That doesn't make sense." Aric folded his arms. "Bloodlusters seek large clusters of humans to feed their hunger. She could have targeted any of the bigger communities in the area instead. Why come here specifically for Emme?"

"Magical beings emit a stronger, more attractive aroma—infected vampires prefer mystical blood." Liam's hand swept around the kitchen. "There are seven us gathered here. She could have fixed on our collective scent and just spotted Emme first."

Aric shook his head. "Her condition was advanced enough to leave a death trail on her way here. Any attacks would have been reported to me by now." He double-checked his cell phone before focusing back on Liam. "What happened upstairs?"

Liam rubbed Emme's arm. "We were about to take a shower. I scented the vamp just as Emme passed the window. She dug her nails into me when I hauled Emme out of the way."

Koda's fury filled the room. "Aric, you came from the outside. She should have sensed you and gone after you first. Why wait to eat? Patience is a foreign concept to a famished bloodluster. I think she specifically targeted our girls." The thick muscles of his forearm wrapped around Shayna's slender waist. She trailed her fingertips along his wrist until her small hand covered his at her hip.

I hopped up on the counter. "Someone has to be controlling the vampires. It's the only possible explanation."

Aric moved next to me. Unlike my sisters, who welcomed the closeness of their wolves, I squirmed away from mine. Aric dropped his head and sighed. Guilt stabbed my chest like one of Shayna's daggers. The dagger twisted deeper as I took in the disapproving faces of the other wolves.

Aric ignored them. "No one has ever been able to control an infected vampire."

My fingers knitted together. "I know that's the theory. But none of this has followed the normal path of bloodlust—even the method of infection."

"I'm not saying it's not possible," Aric snarled.

The tension between Aric and me exploded in the kitchen like a barrage of firecrackers. My tigress snapped to attention and so did his wolf. We locked gazes, but the anger that riled our beasts slowly disappeared as those brown eyes softened beneath my stare.

Koda cleared his throat. "I want to stay here, Aric. Just in case something else shows."

"Fine." Aric didn't look away. "You and Liam can both stay. I'll call Gem and the rest of the pack. We'll search the surrounding area and see what we can find."

Taran tapped an irate foot. "You need to go after the other judge." She glanced in my direction. "And Misha's master."

Koda scoffed. "We can't. The treaty between our kind and those leeches prevents us from interrogating the masters unless we witness a direct violation. Our Elders will have to speak with their grand masters. It will take some time before we can seek them out."

Time we don't have. I twisted around and disconnected my phone from the charger plugged into the wall, finally breaking my eye contact with Aric. "I'd better call Misha and tell him what's happening."

"Why are you calling *him*?"

Aric's growl kept me from dialing. I jumped off the counter. "He has a right to know. This is the third judge. It affects him, too." Aric's eyes narrowed further, like I'd somehow betrayed him. "God, why does everything

have to be a fight with you? I know you hate him, but . . ."
I stopped. His piercing gaze went right into my core, stirring more emotions I couldn't bear to hold on to and
keeping me from gathering a single breath. I stomped up
the stairs to my room, taking my phone with me.

Liam's words slowed my steps as I reached the landing. "Damn, Aric. What is up with you and Celia?"

I hurried into the solace of my room and fell against
my closed door. I hated fighting with Aric. And I had
the feeling he hated it, too. Worse yet were the final
words he spoke before leaving our house: "Keep Celia
safe."

The touch screen on my phone locked out twice before I finally dialed.

"Hey, Misha," I said when I heard his voice.

There was a brief pause. "What troubles you? Are you
hurt?"

It bothered me that my voice shook so hard, but
Aric—*God*—Aric had taken my feelings for him on an
emotional loop-the-loop. I tried to relax as I explained
to Misha what happened.

At first I believed Misha would erupt like an earth-
quake and the floor beneath me would tremble. I could
almost smell his seething anger on the other end. A very
long and very tense minute passed as I paced around my
bedroom, waiting for him to respond. But the outburst I
expected never came. "You have to investigate the remaining judge, Misha."

"I. Can't."

"Why?"

"My master, Uri, fears I am too invested and my anger will cloud my judgment. He has ordered me to stay
on my premises. His plan is to return to the Americas in

three days' time. At that point he will decide how best to proceed."

"Three days? A lot can happen in three days." I wanted to flop onto my bed, but decided against smearing it with the bloodlust. "Do you think . . . do you think he's behind this?"

He paused. "It remains a possibility I cannot ignore."

The pain in Misha's heart resonated through the harshness of his voice. Someone he loved likely wanted him dead. "If it is Uri, is there any way you can stop him?"

"No. He gathers his strength from all in his keep. My power fuels his."

I groaned. "And now you have more because I gave you back your soul."

Misha's tone softened. "Do not ever apologize for granting me such a gift."

"Yeah, but I bet you're wishing I'd kept the receipt." I welcomed his laughter, but it also saddened me. "Misha, what can I do? I want to help."

"Nothing, my love. Continue to keep me informed at all costs, but do nothing. I will not have you risk your life for me again."

I stared at my phone when he disconnected. *Crap. Now what?*

CHAPTER 28

"My wife wants to have a natural birth. No medications. No IV. We are refusing any and all interventions. Western medicine is destroying our nation."

I nodded at the first-time father-to-be as I finished my internal exam of his wife. I smiled at the woman as best I could. "You're one centimeter dilated and your cervix is about seventy percent effaced."

Her eyes widened as she looked to her beloved for support. "What does that mean, exactly?" he asked for her.

I removed my gloves and washed my hands. "Well, it means it's not quite time for the baby to be born." I smiled at the wife. "Your bag of water is still intact, the baby is moving well, the heart tones look fantastic, and you're not showing signs of infection. I'll call the doctor and let her know the facts. Most likely she'll be sending you home. You can take Tylenol for pain and a warm bath for any further discomfort. Call us for strong, pain-ful contractions occurring every five minutes, or if your water breaks, you develop a fever or bleeding, or your baby stops moving regularly."

The father blinked back at me like I'd informed him he was having gremlins and that he shouldn't feed them after midnight. "But ... but ... she's *contracting*."

I skimmed the fetal heart rate tracing on the computer. "Yes. About every twenty-two minutes now."

"But they hurt her ... a lot when they come."

I sat on a rolling stool and scurried over to where the father sat in a chair next to his wife's bed. "Let's talk." I smiled once more. "Labor—*true labor*—occurs when contractions come at strong, regular intervals and the pain is such that you can't walk or talk through them." I looked at the wife. "You updated your Facebook status during the last contraction. During labor your cervix will also open up and thin out." I shook my head. "I'm afraid that hasn't happened yet."

The woman tilted her head. I was pretty sure she understood, especially when she started texting all three thousand of her closest friends. Her beloved remained unconvinced. "So she'll continue to experience the same amount of pain, but the contractions will occur more frequently—every three to five minutes?"

"No, the pain will continue to increase and become more severe." *Until it feels like Godzilla is reaching up inside her and tearing out her intestines.*

"You don't understand," he said, like I was the stupid one. "She's in pain when they come. More pain than I've ever seen her in." He frowned and pointed a stern finger at me. "What you mean is, the pain will stay the same and the contractions will just come more frequently."

It was getting harder to keep smiling. He was lucky I didn't bite off his damn finger. "Sir, there is a human being trying to come out of your wife's body. Trust me when I say the pain will get much worse."

Panic spread across his features. "Oh . . ."

I stepped from behind the triage curtain to where Shayna was doubled over trying to suppress her giggles. The doctor sitting at the desk next to her smirked.

"Hi, Dr. Summers. I was just about to call you."

"No need. Heard the whole thing." She handed me a slip of paper. "Here's your discharge order." She rose and walked around the desk to the patient's triage bed. "I'll just say hi."

I leaned over the counter. "What are you doing?"

"Just finished a nonstress test. Everything is fine; she's going home, too."

Amy, our charge nurse, poked her head into the triage room. "Celia, can you go down to the emergency department? A woman was brought in. She's about twenty weeks pregnant and they need to make sure the baby's okay before they treat her."

"Sure. Can Shayna come, too? Both our patients are going home."

Amy thought about it. "Yeah. That might be a good idea. The ED called in a panic. They always freak when someone shows up pregnant." She rolled her eyes. "Remember the last pregnant woman who came in? Two IVs running in her arms, covered in EKG leads, and no one bothered to check her vagina."

Shayna and I left as soon as we discharged our patients. Our hospital, like most of the area hotels and restaurants, resembled a beautiful mountain resort, complete with Native American tapestries and wood carvings of totem poles and animals. Every visitors' lounge had beautiful mosaic tile patterns depicting various forest animals. My favorite, of course, was the one near the main entrance portraying a wolf baying at the moon.

"Thinking about Aric?"

We had only just stepped into the elevator. "Why do you ask?"

Shayna shrugged as she adjusted her long ponytail. "You've been so sad. Especially after Aric left yesterday."

My foot traced a circle on the floor as images of his anger flashed through my mind. "I didn't like how we ended things; you know, he seemed so angry." I shoved my stethoscope deeper into my pocket. "I can't stand having him hate me, but in a way I guess it's better. Maybe he'll stop coming around."

The doors opened. We stepped into the large foyer and walked across the beautiful wolf made of brown, black, and rust-colored tiles. The gloss to the wolf shone bright against the sunlight peeking through the tall windows of the front entrance.

Shayna draped her arm around me. "Aric doesn't hate you, Celia. And I don't think he was mad. If anything he's jealous."

"What could he possibly be jealous of? He's the one with a pack of gorgeous, half-naked *weres* chasing him, ready to rip his clothes off at the first howl from his lips."

Shayna laughed. "Oh, I don't know. That hot hunk of fangs who vonts to drink your blad . . . among other things."

"There's nothing between me and Misha. Besides, even if those other girls weren't around he has a baby to think about." I scoffed. "If he's any kind of man, that is." I told her about our conversation.

Shayna smiled weakly. "Aric doesn't strike me as deadbeat-dad material."

I thought back to his sexy grin and how he'd fought to protect me. "I didn't think so either."

"Don't give up on him so easily, Celia. There's something special between you. I see it every time he looks at you ... and every time you see him." Shayna's eager hand tugged on my arm. "Will you let me ask Koda about it, please?"

I groaned. "No. I don't want—"

An agonized howl from the ED pierced right through my sensitive ears, sending every one of my senses into "oh, shit" mode.

"Celia, what's wrong?"

"We've got trouble. Call Emme and Taran to the ED." I took off at a dead run. The howls turned threatening, deadlier. "Get the wolves!"

Preternaturals stayed away from hospitals. They relied on their families, packs, and clans when injured. The fact that one was here meant trouble.

I shoved through the automatic doors. A doctor in a bloody white coat flew through one of the glass partitions that made up the ED. A panicked tech punched numbers into the phone, but he continued to misdial. The snarls turned into roars.

"What's happening?"

The tech jumped when he saw me. He shook horribly. "A-a-a couple were attacked by b-b-bears in the woods. The husband just died." His trembling worsened when he gawked at the demolished doorway. "I think she knows."

A second doctor soared through the window, along with a nurse and two security guards. They fell limp near unconscious doctor number one. I raced inside and gasped at what I saw. A she-wolf thrashed on the bed;

blood—her blood—saturated her shredded T-shirt and jeans. Both her legs and an arm were bound in leather restraints. She'd chewed through the restraints on one hand and she was working on the other. Syringes filled with the pungent odor of sedatives remained lodged in her thighs, while the one piercing her jugular flapped against her neck as she thrashed. The meds likely kept her from *changing*, but despite the extent of her injuries her metabolism would soon burn through them.

I threw my body on top of hers, trying to keep her still, knowing her thrashing would worsen her injuries. Her carotid artery had already been severed and both femoral veins damaged. Her clammy gray skin told me her blood loss exceeded the amount that would allow her to heal completely. *Sweet Jesus.* The couple hadn't been attacked by bears; they'd been mauled by infected vampires. I shuddered at the extent of her injuries, confused as to how she'd survived.

The wolf buckled beneath me, growling and trying to wrench her arm away. When she realized she couldn't toss me like the others, she growled and snapped at my shoulder.

"Listen to me; I'm trying to help you—"

"Give me my mate!"

"What?"

"I'm going with my mate. I'm going with him now!"

She yanked my nursing scissors out of my chest pocket and tried to stab herself through the heart.

Shayna muffled a scream. "Oh, my God."

I twisted the she-wolf's wrist and forced her to drop them.

The wolf broke through the other restraint, punching me hard in the head and knocking me into a metal table full of instruments. I rebounded and grabbed her in a full nelson. "Shackle her arms!"

Shayna manipulated the metal bars of the stretcher and snaked them along the wolf's arms. The wolf lashed out violently, vengeance and heartbreak fueling her strength, twisting the metal. Taran flew into the room as a slew of reinforcements pounded into the ED. "Son of a bitch!"

"Taran, knock everyone out; wipe their memories. Do it now!"

Taran paused briefly before the scent of her magic filled the room. A storm cloud of blue and white shot from her core, expanding as it seeped out into the hall, engulfing the entire ED. Screams faded into yawns until only silence remained.

Silence except for the increasing snarls from the she-wolf and Taran's cursing. "For shit's sake, I knocked out Emme!"

The wolf kicked her legs out, freeing her feet and further damaging the bleeding veins at her hips. "Get Emme up. We're losing the wolf!"

Tires screeched near the front entrance. My heart pounded. I left Shayna to continue to strengthen the shackles she'd fashioned around the wolf's arms as I dove on her legs. She kneed me hard in the stomach. I couldn't control her flailing limbs.

But then I was no longer alone.

Aric and Gemini grabbed onto her legs while Koda and Liam locked onto her arms. Aric growled. *What happened?*

I fell back to search the cabinets for packing and tape while Shayna retracted the metal bars away from the she-wolf's arms like slithering serpents. I grabbed another metal tray and poured my supplies on top of it. "She and her partner were brought in. The staff thought they'd been attacked by bears." I paused to look at Aric. "Her husband didn't make it."

The collective fury of the wolves filled the room like a heat wave. The she-wolf thrashed harder, snarling through clenched teeth. "They took my Paul! They took my Paul from me!"

Aric's head snapped up. "Liam, go find him."

Gemini and Koda took over flailing-limb duty as Aric and Liam released their hold. Aric stroked back the she-wolf's blood- and sweat-soaked hair. "Leya, calm," he whispered before murmuring sounds that resonated more animal than human. Aric took slow, deliberate breaths. Within moments, Leya began to mimic his breathing. "That's it. Breathe with me, Leya."

Liam returned. "Paul's dead. His neck was in pieces and his heart was torn out."

Leya stopped breathing. A wet sob tore out of her as she wept like a small, hurt child.

"Shhh . . . we're going to take care of you, Leya." Aric's voice stayed soft and reassuring. "I need you to trust me."

Leya's eyes rolled back into her head with Aric's very next stroke. Her arched back relaxed until she lay flat on the gurney. "Don't let go of her," Aric instructed the wolves. "Her grief is such that she could easily break my hold." The wolves nodded, relaxing their grips enough so her limbs weren't twisted against theirs. He motioned for me to get started. Emme stumbled in behind Taran, frazzled like she'd been startled awake by an obnoxious alarm.

"Seal her wounds," I whispered. "She's bleeding out."

Emme staggered toward her, dazed by all the blood saturating Leya's body. She touched Leya's ankle. As her soft yellow light encased her, Leya's eyes shot open and she bucked her off.

Aric's voice grew more stern. "Leya, *stop*. These are friends of the pack. Let them help you."

Leya stopped struggling, but this time wouldn't fall back into a relaxed state; her breathing bordered on the verge of hysteria. I grabbed her wrist and felt her pulse.

Taran leaned in. "How is it, Celia?"

"Weak and thready. She's lost a lot of blood. We need to transfuse her or she'll code soon."

I could sense Aric's worry, yet his voice remained smooth as silk. "Tell me what happened, Leya."

"We were out with the pack, hunting the infected vampires. Paul didn't want me out because . . . because of our baby." Her choked sobs barely kept her words audible. "He was walking me back to the car when a cluster of them attacked. They took me down. Paul tried to protect me but . . . there were too many, Aric." A whine broke through her core, thick and heavy with misery. "I watched them feast on my m-m-mate, Aric. I watched them eat him alive."

My sisters covered their mouths as tears slid down their faces. The wolves growled, demand for vengeance squelching Leya's cries of hysteria. Emme released Leya. Her wounds were sealed, but she still needed care.

I shoved away my sadness and examined Leya closely. With all the volume she'd lost, her veins had collapsed. "She needs blood. And she needs it fast." I glanced at Taran, who'd turned away, not wanting anyone to see her cry. "Taran, can you start an IV in her femoral vein? I think that's the only option we have to transfuse her."

Taran wiped her eyes and nodded. "Shayna, go to the blood bank and get some platelets. We'll need a few units."

Gemini shook his head. "Human blood is not compatible. It will cause an allergic and potentially fatal reaction. Take ours instead."

"Mine first," Aric insisted. "As a pureblood and her Leader, my blood will stabilize her faster."

Shayna's panicked face met mine. "But how will we transfer it?" Her eyes danced to Koda's. "Your blood clots quicker, doesn't it?"

Taran grabbed a set of scissors and cut through the side of Leya's jeans. "I'll get the catheter into her vein. You draw her blood in a syringe and pass it to me right away."

Shayna gripped the side of the stretcher. "But if the blood clots too fast, we can send an embolus into her heart."

Koda placed his arm on Shayna's shoulder. "It's okay, baby. Blood clots don't kill us." He skimmed Leya's graying tone. "Usually."

Shayna and I set up the catheters Taran needed. Taran shrugged off her jacket and directed the wolves on how to hold Leya's legs. Emme wiped the blood from Leya's face with a warm washcloth.

Aric spoke to Leya as we rushed to get things started. "How did you get away?"

Leya's glassy eyes blinked back at Aric. "They let us go. In the middle of feeding on us, they turned toward the mountains like something had called them. And just like that, they were gone." Her pale lips pursed together. "I picked up Paul and carried him to the road. Some humans stopped and brought us here. They kept trying

to take Paul from me . . . but I didn't want to let him go."
Leya's voice trailed into an echo before her lids closed.

Aric and his wolves exchanged glances. I groaned.
Someone is controlling the infected vamps.

"We need to hurry," Taran muttered.

Aric sat in a chair Emme placed in front of him. He
rolled up the sleeve of his thick navy sweater. I brought
the tray with me and stared at his muscular arm. *Were*
veins didn't rise to the surface like human veins. They
were embedded deep beneath the muscle, where other
preternaturals couldn't easily reach them. I showed him
the tourniquet. "I'm going to have to make this tight."
They were the first words I'd spoken to him since our
fight. And while I recognized the need, I wished I'd said
more.

Aric's eyes met mine, his voice gruff. "Don't worry
about me. Do what you have to."

I screwed the eighteen-gauge needle onto a fifty-
milliliter syringe. "Taran's in the vein," Emme whispered
behind me.

"Okay." I applied the tourniquet on Aric's upper arm.
And although Aric's *were* blood prevented infection, I
wiped the bend in his arm with alcohol.

"It's not necess—"

I cut Aric off, clenching my jaw tight enough to grind
my fangs. "Give me a break. I'm a creature of habit." My
voice shook as I spoke. I'd started IVs and drawn blood
more times than I could count. Yet I was scared senseless
to pierce Aric's vein, knowing it would cause him pain. I
would have turned him over to Emme and Shayna . . .
but I didn't want them touching him. My fingers swept
over the crook in his arm, trying to find that thick, juicy
vein all humans had. The warmth of Aric's skin sizzled

beneath my touch. He turned his head, groaning softly. Our skin hadn't connected as much as I would have wanted. And although I'd longed to touch him, I'd never imagined the next time would involve a needle the size of a dart. I cleared my throat. "Your veins are buried in deep. I'm going to have to dig around to find one."

Aric kept his head turned. "Go ahead."

I stuck the needle far in, guessing where his vein might be hiding. I drew back on the plunger slowly, not wanting to collapse his vein. When I didn't get a return, I swore and pushed further in, only to jerk the needle almost immediately back out.

Emme hurried next to me. "What's wrong, Celia?" She muffled a scream.

"Damn it, Celia, hurry . . ."

Taran's voice trailed off as she caught a gander at the bent needle. I bumped Emme blindly with my elbow. "I'm going to need a sixteen-gauge or bigger."

Emme tottered backward before I heard her little feet racing down the hall.

Liam held out his arm to me. "Try mine. I'm not of pure blood, but I can still help Leya."

I switched syringes and started working on Liam. His vein was hard to find, but I managed with the same-size needle I'd tried on Aric. My hands also didn't shake with Liam, and I couldn't help but notice the lack of heat between us. I tried to reason that *weres*—pureblood *weres*—ran naturally hotter. And all that rising heat Aric and I shared was nothing more than a physiological response between two extremely warm-bodied creatures with superhigh metabolisms who had gotten too close to each other.

Yeah. Right.

I passed the filled syringe to Taran as Shayna handed me another. Taran flushed the catheter in Leya's vein, fast. We paused, each of us likely expecting her to go into cardiac arrest. When she didn't, Taran stretched out her hand. "I think she's okay; give me another."

I made ten more passes with Liam, then stopped. "It's okay," he said. "You can take more."

I was about to, but then Emme returned with something that resembled a meat thermometer. My eyes widened as I looked back at Aric.

His expression of calm drank me in. "Celia, I'm next. Liam's blood will help stabilize her. Mine will stimulate her body to begin to repair itself." I didn't move. "Leya needs me, Celia. And I need you to do this for me."

I nodded and absentmindedly took the clip out of my hair, looking to release some of the throbbing in my head. My waves fell against my shoulders, granting me some tension relief, yet not enough. I bent in front of Aric, tied the tourniquet again, and took the interrogation device Emme handed me. Aric flinched when I stabbed him through the arm. Every part of me wanted to scream for him—to take some of his pain. "God, I'm so sorry."

Aric's opposite hand massaged my left shoulder before smoothing over the nape of my neck. "Don't be. I'm fine. Keep going."

My breath came out in a shudder. *Keep going. Keep going. Keep . . .*

I didn't know about Aric, but I would have given up a secret formula. Nausea dribbled my stomach like a basketball as I continued my torture session. My God, it killed me to hurt him. Finally, I found the vein and began to hand off Aric's blood like it scorched me.

He smiled as his thumb stroked my earlobe. "Good job, sweetness."

I almost dropped the syringe. Despite the direness of Leya's situation, Aric's touch, his soothing tone, and his term of endearment melted my soul. Except I couldn't allow him to. I needed to distance myself, and I needed to do it soon. My contact with him only made me hunger for more.

"Leya's coming around." Gem smiled softly. "It's working. Your blood is motivating her body to regenerate, Aric."

"We'll use the others' blood now." I unsnapped the tourniquet and yanked out the needle, slapping a large piece of gauze on Aric's arm like it had been naughty. "Here. Hold pressure."

I avoided Aric's gaze, but I could smell his shock at my rebuff. Emme moved toward him. "Um . . . here, Aric. Let me bandage that for you—"

"He's fine, Emme. Don't touch him." I leaned back against the wall and crossed my arms. Good thing I didn't appear schizo or anything.

"Ah . . . Okay, Celia. I promise not to touch him." Emme gathered the tourniquet and needles and smiled at Koda. "I'll draw your blood. Don't worry; I'll be really gentle."

Shayna swooped in like a falcon and yanked the supplies from Emme's hands. "I got it, Emme." Her ponytail flicked behind her as she marched to the big man-eating brute who couldn't hide his smile.

I rubbed my face, grateful I didn't stand as the sole Wird sister acting possessive . . . and crazy.

"Don't even think about it," Taran snapped when poor Emme approached Gemini.

Emme's bottom lip went down to her toes. "I'm only trying to help Leya."

Taran pointed a pissed-off finger toward the demolished door. "There is a shitload of staff who would be tickled pink to receive your lovely healing touch. Go to it, girl. Work that magic till it hurts."

Emme wrinkled her brow. "Fine," she said with all the menace of a Chihuahua.

Taran righted herself. "Celia, take over. Shayna and I will pass you Koda's and Gemini's blood." She clamped the catheter and I switched places with her. Aric took over holding Leya down while my sisters gave their wolves a good leeching.

I worked robotically, well aware Aric watched my every move. As I pushed in the last syringe of blood, Leya stirred. "Let me up, please, Aric," she asked.

The moment Aric eased up on her, Leya lunged at the scalpel resting across the opposite counter. Aric tackled her and clasped her wrist. She wrenched her arm in an arc, slicing across my chest before Aric twisted her wrist and forced her to drop the scalpel.

Aric pulled her back as Leya fought with everything she had. "Leya, *stop*."

Aric's words had no effect on her. She thrashed harder, strengthened by the wolves' blood, forcing the others to jump her.

"I want to go with my mate. I want to go to him now!"

The wolves tried to wrangle Leya without harming her, an almost impossible task once she *changed* into an immense black-and-gray wolf.

Liam rushed in at the sound of Aric's roars. Leya clamped down on his forearm, breaking through the bone. "Hold her," Aric growled to the others. "She's trying to get us to kill her."

My first instinct was to grant her wish for hurting Aric. I forced the thought from my mind, scanning the room for tape to bind her jaws shut.

Leya bucked the wolves off. Immediately they hunkered back down around her. Aric's growls turned ferocious. "Liam, get the girls out of here!"

Liam ushered my sisters out fast. When I ignored him, he encircled my waist and tried to haul me out. I broke out of his hold. "No. I'm not leaving him!" I meant to say "her," but in my heart I knew I meant Aric.

Then it hit me. Leya needed a reason to live. "Shayna!" I called, keeping Liam and Leya in my sights. "Did you bring the Doppler?"

Shayna jetted back in, tossing me the minidevice as the wolves crashed toward her. I tore through the cabinets until I found a bottle of lotion. I poured the lotion on the transmitter. "Hold her," I begged the wolves. "I need to reach her belly."

Leya continued to resist, lashing out until the faint whisper of a baby's heart rate wafted into her ears from the Doppler.

Whish-whish. Whish-whish. Whish-whish.

Leya's wolf form abruptly fell still. I spoke quietly, trying my best to stay calm. "That's your baby, Leya. That's your baby's heartbeat." My brain searched for more to say—some words of wisdom and kindness that would reach into the ocean of torment her heart had become.

When nothing seemed right, Aric took the lead. "Your baby lives because you do, Leya. Give your child and Paul's a chance at life."

Aric's gentle words didn't appear to reach her at first. But then Leya released a wretched howl that turned into the tortured cries of an inconsolable woman. She *changed* back, slower than I'd ever seen. Koda took the warm blanket Emme handed him and covered her naked body. She curled into a ball as Aric leaned over her, murmuring in her ear once more. "Sleep, Leya. Sleep. You're not alone. Your pack will care for you always. And in your child, Paul will continue to live."

Leya's eyes slowly shut as she fell into the sleep Aric's pack magic bespelled on her.

"Oh, God . . . Celia." Shayna's eyes focused on my chest. Taran swore, but it wasn't as loud as Aric.

A line of red traced the length of my upper chest. Leya's slash had cut through my scrubs, inches from my throat.

Aric abandoned Leya and surged toward me. I shriveled away from him. "I'm fine. Don't touch me." I covered my bleeding chest with my hands and shot out of the room. My sisters chased me. It wasn't until I reached the linen room that I slowed down, allowing Emme to heal me. I tore off my scrubs the moment she finished and used a towel to wipe off my blood. My hands shook as I yanked on fresh scrubs, pausing briefly to acknowledge the worried faces of my sisters.

Taran's harsh tone hit me hard. "What's wrong with you?"

My voice came out in a shaky rasp. "It's Aric. His presence compels me to be with him. I have to stay away."

CHAPTER 29

The way Aric carried Leya demonstrated the closeness he shared with his species, affirmation that he didn't belong with me. He belonged with those of his kind. And that knowledge made my tigress weep on the inside—only on the inside. The tears that fell for Aric would not be ones I would permit him to witness. No matter how much the release banged against me like an avalanche.

As Aric placed Leya's sleeping form in the backseat of Gemini's car, I was certain this would be our last encounter.

He turned back to me. I hoped it was to say a peaceful good-bye and not to scream at me for my erratic behavior—no matter how much I'd deserved it. "Thank you for taking care of her."

I nodded and stepped away. His kindness affected me more deeply than his harshness would have. Perhaps because it remained one of Aric's strongest qualities.

Crap. Why does it have to be so hard to walk away?

"Wait, Celia. We want to escort you and your sisters

back home. To make sure you're safe," he added when my stunned face blinked back at him.

"It's not necessary, Aric."

"I think it is," Taran answered for me. She watched Gemini drive away in his sleek black Infiniti. "Liam can ride in our car with Emme and me after I'm done altering a few memories. You and Shayna go with Koda and Aric." She turned on her heel and sashayed back into the entrance of the ED, where her crowd of swaying and hypnotized humans waited quietly in the corner.

"Come on, dude," Shayna said softly. "It's been a rough few hours."

We waited in silence until Koda pulled his silver Yukon up to the curb. Shayna quickly scrambled into the passenger seat, leaving Aric holding the door open for me. I slipped in and shimmied across the seat, huddling in the corner and away from Aric. It was as far as I could get from him, but not far enough to keep his warmth from reaching me. I didn't want to like it so much.

And I didn't want to need it. Especially then.

My head spun from the tragic events of the day. We were only two miles from our house when my restlessness got the better of me. I asked Koda to pull over.

"Are you going to be sick, Celia?" Shayna asked when I jumped out.

"No. My tigress is on edge. I need to walk off some tension."

Aric leaped out, too. "Fine. But I'm coming with you."

"No, I—"

Koda's menacing scowl was enough to take down the thick cluster of trees aligning the side of the road. "After all the shit that happened to Paul and Leya? Do you think this is wise?"

Aric's stare hit harder than Koda's, and his tone put any further arguments to rest. "I'm staying with Celia. You'll hear my *call* if anything happens."

Koda didn't appear any happier. Yet he nodded at his Leader and peeled away in an angry huff.

My intention was to put some distance between us, not generate alone time. I crossed my arms and hurried up the steep incline, wishing things could be better. Although my Dansko shoes weren't meant for climbing small hills, I managed to reach the top without slipping.

Aric rushed to catch up. "Where are you going?"

"This path runs parallel to the road. It's safer than walking along the highway."

"All right, but you're walking closest to the side of the road. If anything happens, you're not to go deeper into the woods."

My eyes narrowed. "Do you like ordering me around?"

Aric rubbed at his five-o'clock shadow. "Yes. Despite that it does nothing but piss you off."

My cheeks burned. Okay, he had a point. As the sun began its descent across Tahoe, and the long branches of the thick firs darkened the path, my tigress eyes replaced my own. As much as I knew being alone with Aric wasn't in either of our best interests, I relished this last moment between us. Half a mile passed with only silence. I hated the tension, and, against my better judgment, I spoke.

"Do you think Leya will make it?"

Aric shrugged. "Physically, she can. . . . Emotionally it may not be possible. She and Paul were mates."

I cocked my head toward him. "You mean married?"

Aric smiled softly. "No. I mean mated, the real deal."

Dried twigs cracked beneath my feet. "I'm not sure I know what you mean."

Aric focused ahead. "All *weres* have mates, the one he or she will love and share a soul with for eternity." He sighed. "If one mate loses the other, the mourning is so great the surviving half of the union typically dies at the rise of the next full moon."

My throat tightened. "So even after all we did for Leya, she may still join her mate at the next moon?"

Aric nodded, his expression growing grim. "I'm hoping she'll choose to live for the sake of their unborn child." He kicked a few stones from the path. "My presence is what kept my mother alive when my father was killed."

My body straightened. I hadn't expected such a bombshell. The sadness in Aric's voice at the mention of his father nailed me in the heart. My own father had been my hero. And he'd been brought down like a piece of meat.

I said nothing, allowing him to continue. "Our females tend to be stronger when it comes to their young. They fight more viciously for them. And, sometimes, their children are the only ones who can help them survive a mate's death . . . but not always."

I stroked Aric's back without thinking, wanting to comfort him. My hand slid along his spine and up to his shoulder blades. Warmth flooded my fingertips. His hard muscles tensed beneath my caress. A soft, wolfish sound similar to a growl escaped his lips. I dropped my hand and gave him space, certain I'd offended him and angry at myself for stroking him.

Aric groaned as my hand left his back. His face darkened to red and he seemed to be working to control his breathing. Except his expression wasn't one of a slighted wolf; it was one of desire. I stepped back. Good Lord, I shouldn't have touched him. He had fathered another woman's child, for heaven's sake. "So-sorry."

He shook his head, his steel gaze locking onto mine. "I wish you wouldn't be."

Aric closed the distance between us. I shrank back, away from the path and into the trunk of a dying tree. *Please don't look at me that way.*

He reached for me, but I jerked away, stumbling back onto the muddy trail. "Why are you here with me? You should be with your girlfriend." I hurried around the bend until Aric's throaty voice sliced through the air behind me.

"What girlfriend?"

I froze before slowly glancing over my shoulder. Aric stood on the muddy ground, confusion knitting his brows before they angled fiercely. He bounded to my side in what seemed like two strides. "Celia, what are you talking about?"

At that moment, I was no longer sure about anything. I glanced around, as if searching for answers along the shadows of the darkening forest. "That blond wolf I've seen you with. She showed up at my house a few days ago. She said . . ."

Aric's jaw tightened the longer it took me to form my words. "What did she say?"

"She told me she . . . was pregnant with your child."

Something crunched. It might have been a few of Aric's teeth. "She's not my girlfriend. And *if* she's pregnant, the child is not mine."

My muscles tightened and my blood pounded through my veins. "Are you sure?"

"I didn't sleep with her, Celia. That night you saw us together was the first and last time I went out with her."

Joy should have made me dance to the beat of something Gaga. Except all I felt was stupid. Stupidity made worse by Aric's next comment.

"Is this the reason you've been blowing me off?"

My lids shut tight; I was embarrassed by how I'd treated him. When I opened them, my eyes stung with tears. I wanted to apologize, but all I could do was nod like the fool I was. I should have confronted him sooner, but my lack of expertise with men made me run from a fight, not to it.

Aric huffed. "You can't sniff a lie, can you?"

"No. Bren's tried to teach me . . . but . . . no." I'd continued along before I realized my feet had taken the first few steps. "You didn't sleep with her," my voice repeated numbly.

"No."

"And that night . . . I saw you together was the only time you were with her?"

"Yes. She's pursued me. But I'm not interested."

It almost seemed impossible to believe. Blondie could have been my complete opposite. She had everything I didn't—gorgeous features, perfect makeup, eye-catching clothes. "Why?" I asked without thinking.

"Why what?"

I brushed my hair out of my face. "Why don't you want her?"

Aric blocked my path, his breath increasing its pace as his gaze bore into mine. "Because I want you. I haven't been able to think of anyone else."

I couldn't have heard right. Males like Aric didn't fall for weird girls like me. They went for the Blondies of the world. And when they tired of one, they sought another. Except then his hands enveloped mine.

As our skin touched, a wave of heat warmed my body. I thought for sure he'd step away, but then he released my hands and drew me to him, melding our bodies together. For the first time in my life, I felt completely safe, protected, and whole. Yet I fought against the solace, not believing it was possible . . . or deserved.

Aric inhaled deeply, taking in my scent as his lips swept along my crown. "I've been waiting for you, Celia. Please don't push me away."

The comfort of his voice and the security of his powerful arms collapsed my defense mechanisms like a wrecking ball. And just like that, the walls built from fear and strengthened by years of cruelty disappeared. My hands encircled his waist, tightening as they met. I shuddered, wanting to cry from the relief his strong presence granted me.

And just like that I realized my beast had met her match.

"I won't," I promised.

Aric's hand pressed against my lower back while the other stroked along my shoulder and neck until his wide palm cupped my face. He greeted me with that sexy grin and smoldering eyes that stopped my heart. "I've wanted you for so long," he whispered.

Something rustled behind the trees. I thought I caught a whiff of the wereraccoon before the furious howl of a wolf blared from high in the mountains.

Aric swore. He grabbed my hand and started tearing down the path away from the howl. "The pack found the vampires."

I tried to break from his hold. "Aric, wait. I can help!"

He ignored me, propelling us forward. "No. I'm taking you home. I won't risk your getting hurt."

At the speed our feet pounded we reached our house minutes later. Koda paced outside his Yukon. He jumped in the moment he caught sight of us.

"Don't leave the house!" Aric growled before leaping into Koda's moving car.

I watched him leave, worried he'd get hurt, and terrified he wouldn't come back to me.

CHAPTER 30

"That's it. You're doing it, Carrie. Good job." My words were reassuring. My voice calm. The delivery was going smoothly. But I was screaming on the inside. We hadn't heard from the wolves since they disappeared last night. No e-mail, no texts, no calls.

None of us had slept. My first instinct was to search for them in the direction I'd heard the howl. But after the attack on Leya and her mate, it would have been a stupid move to hunt for them alone. Worse yet, my sisters would have insisted on tagging along.

My focus returned to my patient. "Okay, Carrie, one more push and we'll see your baby."

Without fail, the beautiful sound of a baby's cry filled the room. Dr. Summers handed me the sweet infant to place on her mommy's chest. "Here's your little girl, Carrie."

"Congratulations," said Lori, the second nurse, who had come in for the delivery.

Above us, the overhead paging system clicked on, followed by some static. Lori frowned. "That's strange.

They're only supposed to turn that thing on during emergencies."

A few more clicks followed before Taran's voice rang loud and clear. "Celia Wird. Please report to the cardiac catheterization lab."

I stopped wiping the baby. A shiver traveled down to my toes. I threw a warm blanket on mom and baby and headed toward the door. "Take over, will you, Lori?"

She nodded, staring blankly at the overhead pager.

Tap. Tap. Tha-lump.

"Celia Wird. You are needed in the cardiac catheterization lab—immediately."

My quick steps turned into a sprint. Shayna rounded the corner, eyes wide. "Meet me down there!" I yelled to her.

I didn't bother with the elevator. When I saw the coast was clear in the foyer, I leaped down an entire story. I landed in a crouch in time to hear Taran's increasingly panicked voice. "Celia Wird! Get your ass to the cardiac lab—*now*!"

My nursing shoes beat against the tile, moving so fast I tumbled into a skid and kept going as I turned into the hall leading to the lab. I burst through the double doors in time to hear, "Son of a bitch! The lab. You're needed in the goddamn cardiac lab—"

My tigress eyes took in the scene at once. Bodies— lots of bodies—of nurses, doctors, and patients were scattered like crumpled trash around the tiled floor, over procedure tables, and along the steps leading up to the glass control room where the patient's vital signs were closely monitored.

Taran had barricaded herself in the control room by welding one of the metal file cabinets to the door. She looked up from the microphone she'd been screaming into, her face red with fear and fury. She pointed to the giant oxygen tanks against the opposite wall. Calling her fire would have ignited the lab . . . and most of the hospital.

A pity, considering four infected vampires stuck to the glass like bottom-feeders.

Crap.

They pounded against the thick crackling glass in expensive suits and dress shoes. These freaks weren't as sick. The tinge to their skins varied from fair to dark brown—but after fighting varying levels of bloodlust vampires over the last few days, my tigress had come to recognize the scent of their infection, no matter how subtle.

I crouched and ambled around one of the overturned tables. They hadn't noticed me in their haste to get to Taran. I fell into a crawl. If I could sneak up through the middle, I could *shift* two into the tile and possibly hold off the others until Shayna and Emme arrived.

It sounded like a great plan. It might have worked if I didn't hear a sniff followed by a stomp.

A set of loafers landed in front of me. My eyes skimmed up the legs to the voracious mouth, watching the vampire's incisors lengthen and snap. He pointed to me and whispered, "magic" with the same enthusiasm I would say "cookies."

Double crap.

He dove on me like a seasoned pro wrestler. I rolled out of the way, tearing through my scrubs and *changing*. The two vampires who decided to help their buddy paused at the sight of my three-hundred-and-fifty-pound beast. I hoped to intimidate them enough to think twice.

They didn't. They pounced on me, and the closest one bit hard into my neck, narrowly missing my jugular.

I swatted him off as Shayna appeared. She lifted an IV pole and transformed it into a long, sharp scythe. She spun with it, decapitating one vampire as I tore into the chest of another. Shayna and I scrambled to our feet. Two vampires left.

And one of them had Emme.

The vampire wrenched back Emme's hair, exposing the straining cords of her neck. His thick arm held her tiny frame close to his body. "*Mine*," he hissed.

No. She's. Not! The roar from my chest rattled the instruments lining the metal stand behind me. My massive paws stepped forward; I was ready to pounce. The fourth vampire flopped like a fish out of water beside us, jerking from Taran's bolts. He'd broken through the glass and reached in. His mistake.

My legs bent in a deep lunge; my tail flicked behind me. This bastard was hurting my sister, and I was going to make him bleed.

"Don't, Celia," Shayna whispered urgently. "He'll break her neck." Her hand disappeared behind her back, reaching for a metal clamp, shaping it into a dagger behind her.

A terrified whimper broke from Emme's throat as silent tears of pain leaked down her chin. But it was the vamp who screamed.

He released Emme and spun. About eighteen different surgical instruments stuck out of his back like quills on a porcupine. Emme used her *force* to skewer him like a shish kebab. She wiped her eyes, refusing to watch as she drilled the instruments into her attacker's back until he burst into ash. Shayna ran to her shaking form.

"He was too fast. I didn't see him coming," Emme cried.

"It's okay, Emme. You got him. You're safe now, dude."

I *changed* back and used one of the metal tables to finish breaking through the glass to free Taran while Emme scrambled to heal all the limp bodies.

Taran's blue-and-white mist surrounded the large cluster of victims as Emme slowly brought them back to consciousness. Taran paced in front of them as I commandeered a white lab coat from one of the docs and wrapped it around me. She kicked at a metal pan. "Shit, Ceel. How am I going to explain away this mess? If I tell them it was an exploding oxygen tank like I did last night, OSHA is going to shut our asses down."

Taran had a point. Thank God there were no surveillance cameras in the wing. "I don't care, just—" I froze as my eyes darted around the lab. "Where's the other vampire?"

Shayna jumped and pointed to an open area. "He was just flopping right there a second ago."

Shit.

My sisters and I scrambled out into the hall in time to see the doors leading out to the dock shut behind someone hauling ass.

No, no, no.

I bolted after him, only to see him disappear into the thinly wooded area behind the hospital. My sisters stumbled next to me, out of breath and jabbering away in a jumbled mess of anxious verbiage.

"Damn it, Celia. Where the hell did he go?"

I stared at the four-wheel-drive ambulance parked a few feet from where I stood. A cold sweat ran down the length of my bare back. I glanced at the woods, then back at the ambulance. We had to catch the vampire. And we had to do it now. But I didn't like our only option. And, sweet Lord, I didn't want to need it.

Taran tugged hard on my arm. "Celia. *Celia.* Damn it, are you listening?"

My voice echoed in my head. "We have to go after the vampire. . . ."

Taran threw her hands in the air. "Yeah, well, no shit—"

I swallowed hard and looked at Shayna. "You're going to have to drive."

I only remember Shayna ever looking like that once. I was seven. She was five. It was Christmas. And Daddy had bounced into our tiny apartment dressed as Santa.

"Woo-hoo!" she screamed.

A snowstorm of swear words flew out of Taran's mouth. Emme fell back against the cinder-block wall. "No, Celia, no," she begged me. "Please don't let her drive."

Shayna rushed into the driver's side without hesitation. Her head disappeared as she searched the cab. She jumped up, waving the keys at us. "Got 'em. Let's roll."

Taran swore again. I ignored her and jumped in the passenger side, dragging Emme with me.

Taran hopped in the back and pulled Emme between the seats with her. Taran was still swearing, but resolved to the fact that there was no other choice. We needed a vehicle that could cut through the thin section of woods *and* Shayna's hyper-oh-my-God-we're-going-to-die speed.

Shayna adjusted the seat and mirrors in record time, starting the engine with a powerful roar. Taran released a ball of blue-and-white mist. It swerved out the window and into the forest, fixing on the vampire like a magnet to a set of jacks. And while Taran couldn't track him by scent, the vampire's magic remained close enough to draw her own power to it. Especially at the velocity we traveled. "Follow the bouncing ball," she muttered.

Shayna rocketed around the trees well over eighty miles an hour. Bark and mud flew through the air, spraying the windows. My knuckles turned white from my grip on the "oh shit" bar, and my claws dug into the dash. Shayna's eyes cut to me. "What's wrong, dude? You seem upset."

My hands trembled as they gripped harder. "Oh, I don't know, *dude*. I'm half-naked in a stolen ambulance, chasing a lethal infected being back to his crib, where his entire family is probably waiting to eat us."

Taran spoke behind me. "The she-wolf's blood. It must have attracted the vampires, since the cardiac lab is next to the ED. I'm sure they fixed on my scent when they couldn't find her."

"Yeah!" I didn't mean to scream. And I wouldn't have had Shayna not careened over a small creek à la *The Dukes of Hazzard*. The entire ambulance landed in a skull-rattling thump. Shayna ignored the tires we blew to thunder into a field of ferns.

I glanced over my shoulder. Taran held tight to the bars welded into the sides of the ambulance. Her irises had turned white from the strength it took to work her magic as she banged to the beat of Shayna's car ride from hell. "I can't hold the track much longer, Ceel," she muttered through clenched teeth.

And then she didn't have to. My senses shot ahead of Taran's magic ball. The vampire was in sight. He was fast. Shayna was faster.

I shrugged out of the doctor's coat. "Get me close." Shayna yanked the ambulance to the right with a hard jerk as the vamp abandoned the field and tried to disappear into the woods. I leaped out as my beast and tackled him into the tree. I pinned him into the trunk, hoping to get some answers. But when his fangs elongated and he went for my throat, I sliced my claws across his neck. He exploded in a mound of ash.

The back of the ambulance doors banged open and Taran and Emme fell out. Shayna tried to help them, but Taran jerked away from her. "You are the devil's chauffeur! How the hell did you ever earn your goddamn license?"

Shayna frowned. "Why are you so mad? We got him, didn't we?"

"We're in the middle of nowhere with a busted stolen vehicle! Now what are we going to do? For shit's sake, does anyone have a phone?"

"I left mine in my locker," Emme mumbled, looking as green as Kermit's backside.

Shayna dug into her back pocket and showed them her little box of toothpicks. "With everything that happened yesterday, I swapped my phone out for weapons."

Taran slapped them out of her hands. "We need a phone. Or a working vehicle. Or a goddamn compass. Saving the world sucks donkey balls!"

Taran fell against the ambulance and took a deep breath. When she calmed, she retrieved Shayna's toothpicks. "Sorry. I needed a moment."

No kidding. I left them and sniffed around the area. My tigress silently moved among the thick trees, hoping to pick up anything that might suggest nearby civilization. A soft breeze swept toward me. My tigress's eyes widened when I caught not only more vampire aroma, but the smell of witch magic as well. The witch's fragrance mimicked the one I'd caught on our way to Zhahara's. Lightning and thunder struck as the spell gathered strength.

I hurried back to my sisters, *changing* when I approached. They'd paused, mesmerized by the darkening skies. "Oh, shit," Taran muttered. Her irises had turned white again. She'd sensed the rising power. "Celia . . ."

I nodded. "I know. I think we've hit bloodlust central." My sisters fell silent. I pointed to where I'd roamed. "There's bloodlust and witch magic that way, but my nose tells me the bloodlust concentration is too high for us to charge in alone." I huddled my arms around my body. Crap, it was cold, or maybe it was the knowledge that we'd found our golden ticket. "Still, it warrants an investigation. Start following the tire marks back to the hospital. You'll be able to go a few miles before the ambulance kicks it. I'll catch up as soon as I can."

A clang like two butcher knives meeting had me veering toward the back of the ambulance. Shayna hopped out with a brand-new sword she'd converted from one of the metal bars. "Why don't we just go together?"

Taran's narrowed eyes told me she agreed with Shayna. Emme hurried to grab the doctor's lab coat. "Something to wear when you *change* back from your beast."

I groaned, knowing there was no way to force them to head back to the hospital without me. "Fine."

I returned to my tigress form. Taran dug her nails into the nape of my neck as she climbed aboard. "I get the front. Emme, get on next. Shayna, you get Celia's rear." She chuckled. I didn't. Playing pony was downright insulting, but my sisters' feet would be too easy to hear. I waited until everyone was situated and hurried off into the woods.

My racing speed was more like a trot and yet faster than my sisters could have jogged. The aroma of magic drew me deeper into the thick vegetation of the forest. I thought for sure we'd trekked into one of the many state parks, until the trees cleared over an industrial commons.

I crouched too fast and too deep for Emme. She fell with a hard crash to the side, taking Shayna with her. None of us were "outdoorsy," but at least my tigress gave others the impression that I was formidable in the wild. My sisters' actions insinuated they'd be mauled by a pack of chipmunks if they ever wandered in the woods unattended. And yet they tried their best. Shayna and Emme crawled along their bellies in true Rambo-meets–Bridget Jones style until they planted their slender figures on either side of me. The good news? We had a great view of the industrial park. The bad news? I didn't like what I saw.

Two giant buildings with metal siding took up most of the area. A couple of old rusted trucks stood abandoned, surrounded by weeds that had broken through the cracked asphalt. Rust stains discolored their aluminum beds in long streaks similar to those on the sides of the buildings. Neither the trucks nor the buildings had been used in years. Yet one of the buildings didn't have the thick growth of moss the other had, despite its dilapidated condition. Clumps of dried moss lay over the sides, like someone had brushed it off with a broom. It didn't make sense, considering rust had punched the roof into Swiss cheese.

The scent of magic boiled and rumbled like a rising

geyser before an explosion of yellow-and-black smoke swept through the holes of the roof. The building shook hard enough to rattle the trucks and the opposite building, banging the metal like old tin garbage cans. Another stream of magic erupted, followed by a long, pained scream.

"Jesus, what's happening?" Taran whispered.

A U-Haul truck pulled in alongside the trucks and parked. Two vampires hopped out, not bothered at all by the screaming building into a crescendo. They waited with their arms crossed until the level of power faded and the smell of magic and smoke drifted into the clouds. The vampires stiffened and jerked away when a metal door swung open near the loading dock. A seven-foot-tall, severely infected male stomped out, dragging three women by their hair. My eyes fixed on the buxom brunette as her body scraped along the filthy and decrepit loading dock.

"Oh, my God," Emme whispered. "That's the prostitute from the other night."

Shayna's voice fell low. "They're all prostitutes, Emme. All of them."

They were right. I recognized them from the clubs. Two of them had been on Petro's arms the night I'd seen him stepping out of the five-star restaurant. . . . My heart stopped beating. Everything around me became eerily quiet as my sudden awareness shattered the bloodlust haze. *Oh . . . God. They've been the ones infecting the vampires.* The realization made my head pound. And if they'd been with Petro, that meant he was now infected, too.

The bloodluster dragged the women like sacks of waste. I wanted to act and save them from being eaten, but then he dropped them in front of the other vampires and stepped away. Drool dripped onto his chest as he eyed their wilted forms. And yet he wouldn't feed.

I nearly charged when I saw who exited next. Roberto Suarez, the last remaining judge. *Bingo.*

A witch with long ebony hair was draped from his arm, her dark eyes sparkling with the remnants of her spellwork. "Steady, Celia," Shayna whispered.

The driver of the U-Haul approached the judge cautiously, bowing before speaking. "We cannot wait for the others. It is time to take what is rightfully yours."

The judge seemed to be keeping his witch from stumbling. The skirt of her long velvet green dress flowed in the breeze as she fiddled with a talisman around her neck. She chanted words in a language I couldn't recognize. The two vampires who brought the truck hurried to open the back doors. And just like that, Mr. STD on two green legs ambled in like a remote-control robot.

The vampires quickly locked the doors, hesitating briefly before securing themselves in the cabin of the truck. "Do not fear," she told them. "I have him." Her wobbly form suggested otherwise. Her olive skin appeared peaked, likely drained from whatever magic she'd conjured. I watched them closely, trying to decide what to do. The bloodluster appeared more infected than Zhahara had been. He would be nearly impossible for the four of us to take down without backup and the lake's power behind us. Throw in a few vampires and a witch and we might as well pick out coffins.

Damn it.

A limo pulled in from alongside the opposite building and parked. The judge helped the witch inside before following and shutting the door behind him. The vampire driving the limo popped the trunk and ambled out of the car. He scoffed at the prostitutes lying on the ground before tossing them in the trunk like luggage. Two of them groaned as he slammed the lid shut over their twisted bodies. He rolled his eyes like they annoyed him before returning to the driver's seat and speeding away. The U-Haul followed moments later.

None of us said anything until the vehicles drove out of sight. "Son of a bitch," Taran muttered.

Yeah. Pretty much. A witch had somehow transferred bloodlust into human prostitutes. Evil genius at its finest, considering it had no effect on humans. She also controlled the infected vamps. Awesome, since she had an army of bloodthirsty critters at her disposal. Or, more accurately, at the judge's disposal. We had our bad guy. We had his accomplice. I *changed* back. "We have to get to the wolves. *Now*."

CHAPTER 31

"Don't look at me like that, Celia. This"—Taran waved an irritated hand over my feather-covered body—"chicken shit is not my fault."

I clucked as badass as a chicken could cluck. Despite what she said I blamed her. We'd followed the road leading out of the industrial park onto the main highway. Taran had one job. One. All she had to do was use her magic to hypnotize the driver of the first car that Emme and Shayna flagged down. Her haste to get the hell out of bloodlust central, however, prevented her from focusing. She allowed both a soccer mom toting her kids and an elderly couple on their way to church to pass. When she finally relaxed enough to work her enchantment, the next car was an old blue pickup truck driven by the hillbillies from *Deliverance*, schlepping two chickens and a sheep in the back.

I'd barely crawled half-naked into the truck bed when a bitchy little hen pecked me in the arm. A full-out seizure and some chicken drool later, I'd ended up tucked on Emme's lap. Emme stroked my feathers. "It's okay, Celia. We're almost home."

Billy Bob's truck sputtered into our development and pulled onto our driveway with a bump and a bang. Never had I been so thrilled to be home . . . until our front door opened and Aric and the wolves piled out.

I turned to Emme. *"Cluck?"*

"Um . . . Liam and Koda had planned to stay the night. I sort of gave Liam a key." She held tight to me as Liam lifted her from the back, not because she worried about dropping me, but more out of fear that I'd smack her with my wings.

Taran swore under her breath as she and Shayna jumped out and Billy Bob drove off, polluting the air with a cloud of exhaust. I had to give Taran credit: She smelled like a barn, and she had chicken plumage stuck to her hair, and sheep crap on her shoes. Yet she tossed back her hair and strutted into the house like she modeled for Dior. "I'll be with you in a minute," she told the flabbergasted Gemini with a wave.

Aric slowly stalked toward me, eyes widening until they narrowed on my latest and greatest form. "Is that Celia?" He didn't wait for anyone to answer and lifted me from Emme's grasp. I turned my head to the side so I could see him better. "Are you all right?"

I nodded my damn chicken head and prayed—prayed like the world and all the victims of war, famine, and disease counted on it. *God . . . please don't let me lay an egg. Not now.*

Aric's anger and worry heated his palms. His soothing presence and scent forced my body to *change*. Aric lowered me to the ground, growling at the wolves as he slipped his warm cream sweater over my head.

I rose . . . on chicken legs.

Shit. Aric had released me too soon. From the waist down I remained very much something Colonel Sanders would raise a flag over. I yanked his sweater over my fine feathered ass.

"Can we turn around now, Aric?" Liam asked. The wolves kept their backs to me while Emme gawked and Shayna jumped up and down, pointing at my legs.

"Depends." Aric peered over his shoulder. "Celia, are you decent?"

Talk about wanting to die. Aric growled something in wolf that equated to, "Lucy, you got some 'splainin' to do."

The other wolves circled me slowly. Gemini rubbed his goatee, his troubled expression zipping between me and Aric.

"Holy shit," Koda muttered.

I cleared my throat, gathering as much courage as a chicken possessed. "We found Roberto Suarez, the last remaining judge. His witch has been infecting prostitutes with bloodlust and, I assume, sending them out to contaminate the vamps. If you'll excuse me, Shayna and Emme will tell you the rest." I shoved down Aric's sweater further and strutted into the house on freaky legs that bent backward at the knees. Taran, I wasn't. The steps were a bitch to climb and I practically fell through the front door.

A hot shower relaxed my body enough so only my chicken feet remained from the ankles down. Downstairs the wolves spoke on their phones, organizing the packs in the area to search for the remaining judge.

I finished drying my hair. Aric's anxious growls echoed through the vent. "If anyone finds him, call me or the Elders. This shit ends tonight."

I slipped on a teal sundress with a built-in bra and spaghetti straps. The hem needed altering. It pooled past my feet—perfect for hiding what remained of my "condition." I tucked Aric's sweater beneath my arm and lifted the skirt just enough to allow me to descend the staircase. With my opposite hand I gripped the railing like a madwoman, determined not to topple down the stairs.

Aric's eyes trailed up my legs and to my face when I appeared. "Don't act alone," he said into the phone before disconnecting.

With all the grace I could manage in bird feet, I walked to the couch and sat. Liam approached me with deep fascination lighting his amber eyes. He bent and lifted the hem of my dress and peered underneath. I smacked his hand away at the same time Aric growled.

He apologized. To Aric. "Sorry, Aric. I forgot she's yours."

My lips parted in shock at Liam's words as Aric took a seat next to me. "Um. Here's your sweater. Thank you for lending it to me."

Aric tossed the sweater over his shoulder. "Why didn't you call me?"

I glanced at my sisters. "None of us had cell phones. And there wasn't time to use one of the hospital lines. The infected vampire would have escaped if we hadn't chased him."

Aric's eyes fired with anger. "You keep putting yourself in danger, despite my warnings. When are you going to learn it's not safe to hunt infected vampires? Shit, Celia, you could have been killed—*again*."

My anger met his with equal force. "When are you going to learn we're not helpless? The only reason you even know what's happened is because we did chase that vampire, we did find the bad guys, and we did get the answers."

Aric shook his head. "You don't get it, Celia. It's not that you're not capable; it's that you can't heal. Sure, you have Emme. But what happens if she gets hurt? Or if your injuries are so severe that she can't help you?" He focused hard on the fireplace behind me, concern softening the rage across the planes of his face.

My anger melted away. Aric's frustration brewed from fear. Fear that I'd get hurt, fear that I'd die. He didn't want to lose me.

I didn't understand males and I'd putzed my way through whatever sparked between us. Yet I knew then his feelings for me went beyond the physical connection soldering us together. My hand swept along the rough stubble of his sexy five-o'clock shadow to hold his face. He moaned softly and leaned into my touch. "I'm sorry for worrying you, Aric."

He turned to kiss my palm and tucked me against him. "You scare the hell out of me—you know that?"

I crossed a leg to be closer to him, exposing my chicken feet. His chest rumbled with laughter against my face. "Maybe I can help," he murmured. He slid his warm hand up my bare arm, igniting thousands of arousing fireworks. He shuddered at the same time a soft sigh broke through my lips. And just like that my bizarre feet went the way of the weredodo.

The door to the deck swung open. Gemini raced in, followed closely by Taran. Gemini cleared his throat upon approaching us. "Aric, our investigative team located three residences for the fourth judge. Two are on the Nevada side of Tahoe. The bear clans are headed there, since it falls within their territory. That leaves one more in Truckee. Six wolves are already there, waiting for you."

I stood with Aric. He gave a stiff nod. "Let's go, then."

Aric kissed the top of my head and stomped toward the door. The wolves' heavy boots marched across our hardwood floors like soldiers charging into battle. A battle to the death. Fear punched me hard in the gut. Anxiety twisted my intestines. Tears burned my eyes. Aric was strong, tough, brave. But Aric wasn't invincible.

Please don't leave me, too.

My passion for him compelled me to jet after him. Aric wrenched open his driver's-side door. His head jerked toward me as my bare feet reached the edge of the porch. "What's wrong?"

I lingered at the top of the steps. A strong breeze from the lake blew my hair back. I searched for the right words, not knowing what they were until they fell from my lips. "Do you think your wolf can match the strength of my beast?"

Aric frowned. "I don't want to fight with you anymore, Celia."

"That's not what I mean." My gaze connected to his, pleading with him to understand what I meant—what he meant to me.

Liam stepped out of the car and tugged on his arm. "Aric, we gotta go, man."

"I'm sorry. Never mind." I sighed, feeling like a fool for keeping him from his duties, and turned back toward the house.

My foot had taken the first step inside when Aric spoke. "Celia . . . just tell me what you need."

I froze. *Say it ... just say it.* "You," I whispered. "I need you, Aric. You're all I ever think about."

Aric's response wasn't one I expected. He bolted up the steps, dragging me to him, smashing his lips into mine. Nothing I imagined had prepared me for this. One arm wrapped around my waist possessively while his other hand tangled into my hair. The kiss was soft, yet demanding. I melted into him, kissing him back with every part of my being as my hands gripped his shoulders. He pulled me tighter, but it wasn't tight enough. I never wanted him to let me go. His taste was sweet, warm, and seductive.

His phone rang from the pocket of his jeans. Hesitant steps ambled onto the porch. Gem cleared his throat. "Ah, do you want me to get that, Aric?"

The phone continued to ring, but Aric didn't respond. Someone attempted to approach us, but Aric's deep warning growl made them back away. The vibration in his throat almost pushed me over the edge. It was so sexy I could have screamed.

The warmth we shared amplified into a deep, thriving heat as Aric's hand found my bare back. The skin-to-skin contact increased our fervor. His initial slow, soft massage turned insistent. I began to think I'd die without his touch.

Once again, his phone rang. This time, someone else was successful in approaching. I heard fumbling.

"There's a moon on the screen," Emme said quietly. She must have levitated it out of his pocket.

"Aric. The Elders are summoning us," Gemini told him.

"Come on, man. We have to get out of here," Koda urged.

Aric stopped our kiss, gently tugging my bottom lip with his teeth as he drew away. The fire had returned to his eyes, but this time it burned bright with passion.

We gasped, struggling to control our ragged breaths. "I don't want to leave, but I have to," Aric whispered. "I'll come back to you as soon as I can."

"Okay," I whispered back.

Aric rested his head against mine as we continued to pant. He cleared his throat. "One of you will have to drive. I'm going to need a moment."

He took a deep breath and inhaled my scent. Then he kissed my forehead and ran down the steps. I stumbled against the wall, trying to deal with what just happened. My sisters' eyes locked on me.

Taran went insane. "Hot *damn*. How the hell was that?"

The heat in my body continued to scorch my veins. My heart pounded against my chest, and my unmentionables zinged. I slumped to the floor. "All kisses should be that good."

CHAPTER 32

Shayna bounced around my room. "I knew you had it in you; I just knew it." She pointed an accusing finger. "And you thought he didn't like you! Omigod, you guys, like, practically swallowed each other."

Taran's siren grin flashed as she fanned herself. "Damn, Ceel, if he kisses you like that when we're around, what's he going do to you when you're all by your lonesome?"

I stopped midway into yanking my long-sleeved tee over my head. Slowly I slipped it through, sweeping my thick hair out from under the tight fabric. Taran had a point. What was I going to do? "I don't know."

My sisters' grins faded at the sight of my worried expression. Emme, who'd kept quiet, slipped off my bed and crept to my side to hold my hand. "Just do what feels right. Yes, Aric seems to really want you . . . physically." She blushed. "But I'm sure he'll be patient if you want to take things slow."

My face heated worse than Emme's. "I'm not sure if I want to take things slow." I thought back to that outrageous sizzle coursing through my body, and the taste of his tongue. How his body clung to mine. The pressure of his hard form against my soft parts. His scent, his eyes, his touch . . . "Misha."

Emme's eyes widened. "Um. Don't you mean Aric?"

A cloud of pain and torment darkened the marvelous emotions Aric's kiss had stirred. "No. I mean Misha." I went to the window and looked out, expecting to find Misha on our front lawn. I shoved my feet into my UGGs and barreled down the stairs.

"Dude, wait! What's wrong?"

I didn't bother with the porch steps and landed on our front walk in a crouch. My tigress stirred, pawing at the ground, growling. Her eyes replaced mine, and she took in our surroundings in one sweep.

"Celia . . . ? Honey, what's wrong?"

My head jerked back to the house. Emme clasped her hands against her mouth. Shayna and Taran exchanged glances, sensing my tigress rising to the surface.

I couldn't mask my increasing angst. "Get the car keys. Something's wrong."

Shayna rushed inside, but Taran yanked the keys out of her hands when she emerged. We piled into the car. "Where're we going?" Taran asked.

"South."

Taran scoffed. "South where?" She pulled out of our development onto the main road. I pointed. "I don't know. Just south, that way."

"Dude . . . we're not going back to Zhahara's . . . are we?"

I shook my head. "I don't know. But I think Misha—" A dull ache throbbed in my chest, similar to when you heard someone you knew died. "Oh, my God. Misha's in trouble."

Our Tribeca bounced along the dense gravel. The wind intensified, sweeping pine needles and leaves into our path. Taran swore. "This isn't a road; it's a goddamn work in progress."

Taran wasn't kidding. White rocks kicked up, dinging our windows and side worse than those friggin' bits of rock that flew out of construction trucks. Someone had begun to lay a foundation, but never completed the task. I dialed Aric, worried he hadn't returned my texts. "Aric. It's Celia. I hope you're okay. You know how you told me to call you before I march into danger?" The increasing worry threatened to suffocate me, making it hard to speak. "Well, I'm marching into danger, so I'm calling. Please call back."

I disconnected and ran my hand through my hair. Taran swore again when a rock chipped our front windshield. "Celia, are you sure about this?"

"I'm not sure about anything, but we're making too much noise. I think it's best to pull over and walk."

"Shit! Walk where? We're in the middle of the woods."

Shayna played with her phone. "Koda's not answering either." She leaned in from the back. "They must be in deep if they're not returning our calls. I've tried him four times, Liam twice, Gemini three times—"

Taran glared into the rearview mirror at her. "How do you have Gemini's number?"

Shayna shuffled in her seat. "Ah . . ."

Taran clenched her jaw tighter. "Shayna, how do you have his number? Even I don't have his damn number."

"He, uh, gave it to me a few nights ago in case I, ah, ever needed anything."

Behind me, Emme held the phone away from her, trying to keep Bren's growls from rupturing her eardrums. Because that's what was missing from my life: another pissed-off werewolf. "Why are you going after that asshole? You should have called me, goddamn it. How the hell am I supposed to track you now?"

Emme spoke reasonably. "I'm sorry we didn't call, Bren. But Celia felt an urgency to help—"

"An asshole! Just say it, Emme. Celia felt the urge to help some master vampire asshole! Son of a bitch, you couldn't have waited fifteen freaking minutes for me to get there?"

"We're off Highway Eighty-nine in South Tahoe. Take a right at the white fir sapling and the first left onto a gravel road."

"Take a right at the white fir sapling! Are you crazy? There's a million fu—"

Emme disconnected her call. "Bren says he's disappointed we didn't call him sooner. He'll try to track us now and will hopefully join us momentarily."

Emme missed her calling as a White House spokesperson.

"He hates me." Taran gripped the steering wheel tight.

I cut my eyes from the road. "Who?"

"Gemini."

I groaned. "Taran, he doesn't. I think he's just a little shy."

"Do you think it's all the swearing? Son of a bitch, is that it? I swear too goddamn much?"

"Well, dude, you could try toning it down a little."

Shayna jumped in her seat at the sight of Taran's

death glare. "Listen, Miss I Have Every Damn Wolf Eating from My Hand, I don't need—"

"Taran, stop the car!" I rushed out as the trees cleared and a house came into view . . . an empty, half-built house. Only the foundation and skeleton frame had been completed in the McMansion. There was no roof, and the second floor hadn't been laid. I ran around the house, sniffing the air for any hint of vampiric aroma. Nothing. *Nada.* No trace of magic at all . . . except for Tahoe. The house sat on top of the hill. I trekked to the back, where I had a view of another monstrous estate situated near the edge of the lake, a few acres from where I stood. The road we'd taken must have angled back around. This estate resembled a giant Tudor . . . or I should say about seven Tudors pushed together. A two-acre-wide maze of hedges ran from the side of the house to the bottom of the small cliff where I stood.

Taran wiped her muddy shoes on a flat rock. "So much for Misha's reverse speed dial. Can we go now?"

Shayna bounced to my side. "Koda just texted back. They've been searching the last judge's property in wolf form, so they haven't had their cell phones on them. He's worried and says to stay put. He'll locate us through my phone." Her ponytail swung happily as she shifted her weight from side to side. "He's so sweet. But I can just text him and tell him we don't need them."

My tigress eyes locked onto the back of the estate. A wood door banged open and out ran a vampire . . . dressed in a Catholic schoolgirl uniform.

"Shayna . . . ?"

"What, dude?"

My voice fell into a distressed whisper. "We need them . . . *now.*"

I barely heard the taps as Shayna's fingers swept over her keyboard. Emme muffled a scream. Ana Clara's long hair sailed behind her from the speed at which she ran. She tried to go through the hedge instead of around. Yellow-and-black magic sparked from the branches as she bounced off like she'd rammed a stone wall. Blood poured from her nose and from a thick gash on her head. She stumbled to her feet just as four severely infected vampires burst the hinges of the back door.

"Emme, grab her with your *force*!" I jumped up and down, waving my arms. "Here! Run here!"

Emme's magic stirred. "I can't. She's too far. My power can't reach her!"

We watched in horror as Ana Clara staggered into the wretched maze, the bloodlusters right behind her. "Left, goddamn it, go left!" Taran screamed. "Right. Now right!"

Ana Clara struggled even with Taran's instructions. The first bloodluster approached, tracking her by blood. She drew closer, closer, Ana Clara screaming as she closed in.

Swoosh. Swoosh.

Shayna's arrows found the bloodluster's head and chest. She exploded close enough to smear Ana Clara's back with putrid green ash. Another bloodluster neared. Shayna followed with two more arrows. One pierced an eye, the other a shoulder, but it didn't hinder him. He pushed on, his thirst propelling his legs faster.

He tackled Ana Clara and raised a claw in the air. Shayna nailed him with an arrow through his palm and a thicker one through his temple. The infection hadn't advanced too far. His blood spilled red, distracting the other vampires. Ana Clara crawled away, sobbing as the two vamps feasted on the other. She rushed to her feet and sprinted.

And so did I.

Emme screamed. *"Celia!"*

I couldn't watch any more. I leaped off the small cliff, landing in a *shift,* and surfaced as far as I could into the maze. "Ana Clara! Run to my voice!" I continued *shifting*. The magic prevented us from crashing through the wall of hedges, but it didn't penetrate beneath the earth. Every time I emerged, I called to her. And every time her sobs grew louder. I surfaced once more, out of breath from *shifting*. My heart thundered against my rib cage as I searched along the endless labyrinth of green until I finally caught sight of her.

Ana Clara tore around a bend, crying, grunting, her arms pumping wildly as her bare feet dug into the muddy ground.

"Hurry, Ana Clara. Hurry!"

The hedges twitched and crackled. Black-and-yellow mist rose into the sky. I no longer felt the sting of dark magic prick against my skin. *Oh, no.* The barrier had fallen.

One of the bloodlusters crashed through the thick branches between me and Ana Clara. I *shifted* him through the ground and kicked his head from his shoulders. Another bloodluster broke through, then another, and another.

Shit.

All the air was squeezed from my lungs as my feet left the ground. Ana Clara and I flew through the air on the wobbly wings of Emme's *force*. Four bloodlusters chased us below. My head jerked to find Emme. She and my sisters were only a quarter of the way in through the maze. We moved fast. But it wasn't fast enough. Six more infected vampires crashed through the thick field of green, heading toward my sisters.

"*Run*. There's more. *Run!*"

Ana Clara screamed as a Zhahara-size bloodluster leaped up and yanked her out of Emme's *force*. She crashed with him on top. He tore into her like a piñata, spilling her insides. I jerked my head away when two more piled on top of her. She screamed. She screamed the whole time. Until the silence announced her end.

My sisters ran, Emme dragging me behind her like a kite.

But they were too slow. Taran turned and launched a stream of lightning. The vamps leaped out of the way . . . and onto my sisters.

CHAPTER 33

"No!" My roars were cut off by a sharp tightening around my throat. Something yanked me free from Emme's *force.* I crashed hard on the ground, struggling to breathe.

My body twisted and buckled. Each time I fought my way to my feet, I was immediately brought back down, until I finally succumbed from lack of breath.

Silver satin ballet slippers stepped into my line of vision, splattering mud against my face. "Relax your hold," the dark-haired witch from the compound whispered quietly. "Your master doesn't want Celia to die. Yet."

The whip around my neck loosened enough so I could pass air, but not much. I protruded my claws and cut through the leather strap. I rolled back, only for a second whip to cut off my breathing again the moment I struggled to my knees.

My head spun from lack of oxygen, and tears blurred my vision. The whip loosened once more and my hands were roughly bound behind me. This time I was too breathless and weak to act.

So were my sisters. Mud soaked their clothes, and

they bled from their mouths and noses. They must have been squashed by the weight of their bloodlusters. Zhahara had been huge. Four males, all bigger, all hungrier, all deadlier, danced eagerly from side to side, smacking their lips and drooling as they held my sisters like dolls. They couldn't wait to eat.

Us.

Taran swore under her breath, cringing every time her vamp's tongue extended near her jaw. Shayna kicked futilely. Emme whimpered and shut her eyes tight. A large contusion swelled across her crown. She'd banged her head. It would take time for her body to heal her and her mind to act. Time we didn't have.

The witch's head angled as she regarded me, her coal-colored eyes filling with hatred. More hatred than should have been possible for someone who didn't know me. "Come, my children," she said, her voice oddly childlike considering the darkness surrounding her. "Your master is waiting."

Oh, great. Time to meet Daddy.

I was half dragged through the mud. The infected vamp holding me laughed each time I stumbled to my feet. Each time I rose, I grew stronger. Each time he yanked on his hold, I grew angrier. And each time he laughed, I knew he'd die.

And that I'd be the one to kill him.

Misha's gut-wrenching screams made my head snap up. So did the currents of power drifting from the threshold of the demolished door. The vamp holding me hissed. "Why isn't he dead yet?"

Yet?

The vamp tugged me harder through a large kitchen where entranced women bustled at tasks on countertops and busied themselves over simmering pots. Their eyes glazed over from hypnosis. Chunks of skin had knitted over their horribly mauled wrists and necks, perspiration giving their grotesque pallor a sickly glow. These women teetered on the edge of death. Yet the force driving their efforts compelled their frail bodies forward.

Vegetables steamed in pots, rolls baked in the oven, and lamb roasted in the rotisserie. The aroma of food would have sickened me, considering the state of the women who prepared it, yet the scent was barely noticeable over the escalating fragrance of vampiric power and Misha's tormented bellows.

A tremendous surge of the energy caused the vampires dragging us down the dark wood-paneled corridors to pause. God, it was so strong it pressed like a wall against my chest. I coughed and gagged, desperately trying to draw a full breath as we crossed into another room.

We entered a tremendous antechamber decorated à la Museum of Natural History meets ghetto bizzaro. A chandelier fashioned from dinosaur bones and lit with candles hung from the center of the wood-beamed ceiling, illuminating the virtual gallery of ancient relics. Gaudy furniture made from animal skins and accented with leopard-fur pillows had been pushed out to create space within the two-story-high room. Stuffed animal heads from elephants, bears, wolves, to freaking zebras were fastened to the walls between the tapestries and paintings in thick brass frames. Armored knights encased in giant glass boxes stood on either side of the marble fireplace. It seemed like a stressed-out museum curator had thrown up in here . . . a demented, cruel, and masochistic curator.

Misha's four remaining vampires were fastened to the

large wooden beams by chains. The hum of the metal told me they'd been reinforced with magic. The witch had too much power. She definitely topped my "needing to die" list.

Misha's family hissed with rage, fighting against the chains. Tears stained their blood-smeared cheeks. They barely noticed us enter for how badly they hurt for Misha, cringing with each roar from their master's pain. Their hatred could have singed the pillars. They wanted to spill blood, and, as the bloodlusters watching the show parted like a curtain, I very much wanted to give them the opportunity.

All I could see was the vampire's bare, muscular back as his arm sliced across Misha's chest with a cursed gold dagger. But his crew-cut blond hair gave him away.

Petro. Misha's so-called brother. The so-called weakling.

Good God. Never underestimate the underdog.

Petro carved into Misha's body with an arc of his hand, appearing more an artist painting a masterpiece than a monster cleaving into a being who breathed and hurt.

Petro glanced over his shoulder. The polite smile he usually demonstrated was gone, replaced by one so filled with malice, I wanted to cringe from it. Except the growing need to make hamburger out of his throat kept my gaze locked on his jugular. No, Petro wasn't weak. He was simply a master manipulator and one hell of an actor.

"Good evening, Celia." He stepped aside, giving me a full view of Misha. My heart clenched. I tried to look away, but my captor yanked my head back so I could take in the state of my guardian angel.

Misha's head drooped against his chest, draping his blood-soaked hair against his knees. Droplets of red fell like rain against the dark marble floor. He wheezed with every ragged breath. The hilts of two gold daggers protruded from his thighs, anchoring him into the large wooden throne and sending the cursed gold to poison his blood. Like the damn gold chains wrapped around his open, nonhealing wounds weren't enough.

Misha slowly raised his head—a miracle, considering Petro's efforts should have killed him by now. Petro had made mincemeat of Misha's once beautiful face. His strong gray eyes were fogged over from pain. But when he fixed them on me, they cleared like the sun breaking through an ugly storm, showing me his fury and the strength that remained. I couldn't hear his thoughts, but his unsaid words rang clear. He wasn't ready to die. And I wasn't ready to let him.

Petro drove his dagger into a side wooden table and removed the thick rubber gloves he wore. He extended his arms so his servants could circle him and lick Misha's splattered blood clean from his body. "What's the matter, Celia? You don't look well, my darling."

I always look this way before I kill someone. "Don't call me your darling. I felt sorry for you!"

Petro smiled, his familiar gentle demeanor returning, although this time I knew it was all a lie. "Everyone did, *darling.* That's what made my coup that much easier. All I needed was time, and a little patience." He glanced over at Misha in a strangely adoring manner. "Time I likely wouldn't have had if my brother hadn't spared me from our grand master's destruction."

I closed my eyes tight, trying to calm my raging beast. The whip would crush my larynx before I finished *changing.* But my increasing fury made it hard to focus. Petro had used Misha. Hell, he'd used all of us. *Prick.* "Tell me,

Petro. Was it you or your witch who discovered how to magic the bloodlust into viral form?"

I opened my eyes to catch Petro's frown. He didn't like my putting a damper on his big reveal. "The theory was mine. I just needed to find the right enchantress strong enough to work the spell." He approached the witch, who continued to regard my sisters and me with loathing, calming only slightly when Petro kissed her lips. He whispered against her mouth, "My love uses her blood and magic to create the virus. Thus a part of her lives inside the infected vampires, permitting her to control them."

Petro's witch refocused her dark, hateful stare on me, but otherwise said nothing. Petro stepped away from her and took a breath just to flex his supersize vamp mojo. Sheer waves of vampiric force rippled across the room, rattling the windows and shoving us back. I grimaced. I didn't like the feel of Petro, and neither did my inner beast. The power that pampered and played around him dug needles into my skin and pushed them out through my pores. *Damn it.* Petro had never been weak, but was rather freakishly strong. Strong enough to hide the true extent of his power. No wonder he shook and resembled an ad for Right Guard; concealing that much power must have been like trying to brace back a crumbling dam. Now he held nothing back. Not that he could have. After all, he'd absorbed the power of three ancient vampires after we'd killed them for him.

"Where's the fourth judge?"

Petro scowled. He didn't like my interrupting his show of force either. "Upstairs, waiting like a good little puppet for slaughter."

"The judge isn't with them?" Shayna asked. Her voice

trembled and stayed low; she didn't want to attract attention to herself, but still wanted answers.

I shook my head. Big mistake, seeing how the whip had rubbed my skin raw. "No. Just Zhahara . . . until they no longer needed her."

The corners of Petro's smile lifted. "You have it all figured out, don't you?"

"I'm smarter than I look."

Taunting a master vampire of his caliber probably fell under the same danger category as swimming in a pool filled with anglerfish, or wearing red at a werebull convention. But if Petro targeted me, it would distract him from hurting my sisters . . . at least for the moment.

"I take it you heard of Zhahara and Misha's breakup and used her anger to get her to do what you wanted."

"Every great conqueror must take advantage of opportunity when it arises." Petro spun like a top and kicked Misha in the face. Bones broke with a sickening crunch. The vampires hissed, except for Misha.

"You are courageous when your victim is tied down. Free me, and attempt to strike me again," he snarled through shattered fangs.

Petro drew back his foot.

"What's with the stuffed zebra heads, Pete? Did you kill them to impress slutty spell wielders?" My eyes danced to the witch. "I see that it worked."

"Celia, please be quiet."

Emme preferred I remain silent. I preferred to distract them from Misha, and from the spark of magic Taran had slyly called forth. Taran cut her eyes to mine, her irises already blanching from the gamut of power she'd quietly gathered. She would release it soon in one giant phoenix of energy—incapacitating her completely, but hopefully giving us time to escape. She dropped her head at the sight of my subtle nod, allowing her dark waves to hide her face.

Without a word, Petro's family released Misha's vampires and shoved them through the wide French doors leading out to a stone terrace. They attempted to thrust their way back to Misha, but the sheer number of Petro's family easily held them back. Petro smiled. "I suggest you run."

Something like the sound of locks snapping rang the length of the upstairs hall before bare and heavy feet thundered above us. Twelve severely infected vampires leaped over the railing. The closest one grabbed one of Petro's keep and tore into his neck like corn on the cob before the witch regained control over her.

Misha spit blood from his mouth. "Run!" he ordered his vampires. They paused briefly before racing across the terrace and leaping over the railing. The witch brought her hand down like an Indy 500 flag and the bloodlusters barreled after them, graceful in their movements despite their hulking forms.

Petro motioned six of the vampires holding assault rifles forward, including his driver. "Keep them in your sights." They bowed to Petro and quickly followed.

If I could have, I would have gone after Petro's throat then. Misha's vampires were far from kind, but they loved Misha, and he cared for them as much as any master could. And with his final breath he'd know his family was hunted down and mutilated.

The infected vampire holding me twisted my arm, making me grunt. "I'm going to enjoy watching you scream," he whispered in my ear.

My temper took over and put me in touch with my

inner Taran. "Is that what you tell Petro when you play with his boys?"

The vampire hissed. But it was the witch who spoke. "You need to learn respect," she said in that odd little-girl voice. Her coal-colored eyes simmered as she smiled. *So not a good sign.* She yanked one of Shayna's daggers from her holster and sashayed toward me, her long, sheer yellow gown flaring like a trickling stream behind her.

Oh, great. It was one of Shayna's pointier numbers, too.

The bloodluster holding me tugged back my long hair, exposing the flesh of my neck the whip didn't cover. She pressed the pointy tip into my jugular. It hurt, but I wasn't the one who screamed.

The dagger launched into the wooden beam where Petro's head had leaned seconds before. Emme had attempted to take out Petro on her own. Except he now harnessed the power of three ancient vampires, and their speed as well. Even if Emme had managed to stab him, it wouldn't have been enough to end his life.

Petro's tramp resented the attempt. She glared, shaking out her wrist. Emme had wrenched it hard to steal the knife. She stomped toward Emme, losing her swagger. My fangs shot out like bullets the moment her hand connected hard against Emme's face.

She slapped her over and over again. Emme's choked sobs pounded my eardrums with every strike. Finally she stepped away when Petro grabbed her wrist and kissed it. "My love, please calm. There are more ways we can play." He flashed Emme a predator's grin. He bent, his hand disappearing beneath the hem of Emme's long skirt. Emme's face paled and her eyes glassed over with terror, but Petro's hand didn't get far. I kicked out my leg and brought it down hard, cleaving Petro's hand off with my back claws.

I growled over his screams. *"Keep your goddamn hands off her!"*

My claws had connected with an artery. Petro's blood spilled out with the force of a busted fire hydrant. The severely infected vampires went insane upon seeing the hot spring of red. They tackled him at full speed, breaking through the witch's hold, feasting on him like piranha. Petro's family attacked in an attempt to defend their howling master. The witch shrieked her incantations, sending her power out through her hands. But that only garnered the attention of a very thirsty bloodluster.

My nails sliced through my binds and tore out my captor's heart before I yanked free of the whip. I cut Shayna and Emme free, careful to avoid Taran's building power. Blue and white flames encased her form as her magic synthesized into a small inferno. The entirety of her eyes went white as she surrendered to a deep trance. I dove on Misha, yanking the daggers from his thighs so fast he doubled over in agony. "Hang in there, fairy godfather. I'm gonna need you real soon."

He hissed low and deep. "That's guardian angel, my dear."

My fingers ached from how hard I yanked off the first chain fastening him to the chair. I threw it to Shayna. She willed the chains to separate and transformed them into two deadly gold swords, slicing into the first bloodluster who approached her.

Shayna cut off the infected vampire's arm as he reached for her, but despite her skill and speed, she couldn't fight him by herself.

Emme made sure she wasn't alone.

Glass shattered as Emme sent the two knights charging after the infected vampire. The "WTF" brain pause distracted the vampire enough for Shayna to launch Petro's cursed gold dagger into the vamp's chest, erupting his heart like a volcano.

The knights and Shayna forged after another loose vamp. Emme didn't know how to fight. But her metal soldiers felt no pain and held sharp and deadly weapons within their grasps.

The witch screamed with rage, regaining control of the infected vampires and ordering them to attack—us. Emme launched three into the wall. Except she didn't stop there. With her ears covered tight to muffle the vampires' agonized bellows, she yanked their lolling heads away from their bodies. Flesh strained and tore like fabric as Emme ripped their skulls from their torsos. She collapsed with tears of angst and fury leaking from her eyes, but then quickly crawled to my side to help me unravel Misha's binds with her *force*.

Two more chains left. Taran's surging magic made my hair stand on end. Blood and ash rained as Shayna sliced and diced through anyone attempting to reach us. "Hurry, Celia. There's too many!"

One chain left.

Taran released her power with a guttural roar.

"Cover your eyes!" I screamed over the chaos.

Even with my eyes closed, the explosion of light was blinding. I blinked the spots away as the light receded like a slow-dimming bulb. Clumps of ash spread like sand around the foyer amid the destroyed antechamber. The witch held Petro's still, bleeding body against hers as she sobbed. Though more vampires spread throughout the grounds, Taran's magic-borne sunlight had obliterated the majority of Petro's vampires.

Shots fired outside followed by the familiar sounds of the naughty Catholic schoolgirls wailing in triumph. *Yes!* They'd taken the guns out of their enemies' hands and now they planned on using them.

Emme raced to Taran, who collapsed to her knees, all magicked out.

The black irises of Petro's witch expanded, encasing the scleras. She released Petro and pounded toward us, generating a giant yellow-and-black fireball in her hands. She aimed the blaze at me. I abandoned Misha, diving behind a wooden pillar. Chunks of wood pelted me like hail as the pillar exploded. Shayna launched one of her swords. The shimmering gold blade disintegrated into powder from the heat of the witch's protective shields, inches from her chest.

I swore, not knowing how to fight magic without magic.

Misha screamed, his body straining beneath the sickening effect of the cursed gold chains. I thought the poison rushing through his body had burned him, until the force of Tahoe's magic shattered the windows and jetted inside in a ray of blue sparkles. Through his pain, Misha had called upon the power of the lake. Except instead of accepting it into his failing body, he shot it right into Taran's core.

Taran's body arched from the crash of energy. She rose in a single motion, her irises clear and focused on her target.

The witch's fury beat against my body like a drum. "No!" she screamed.

"Oh, *yes*," Taran hissed back.

CHAPTER 34

Blue and white fire clashed with yellow and black as both women went for the kill.

From somewhere in the distance a wolf howled. "Koda!" Shayna screamed.

I shoved her and Emme through one of the demolished windows. "Get to the wolves!" I urged. Shayna nodded once and took off into the darkness. I grabbed Emme's arm before she could follow. "And find Aric."

Emme's eyes widened. I caught a glimpse of her smile before she ran off as fast as her little feet could carry her, trailed closely by the two clanging and sword-wielding knights. More shots fired in the distance, followed by the sounds of Misha's vampires hissing with vengeance.

I rushed back to Misha. He slumped against the chains, his breaths shallow. He could have used Tahoe to save himself. But instead he gave Taran the power to protect us. Not bad for a master vamp.

The last chain was thinner, but knotted as if welded together, making it impossible to break through. My claws bled beneath the skin as I yanked and tugged.

Petro's witch hollered as she vented her displeasure on Taran. Taran threw herself to the floor to avoid a deadly strike. She scrambled to her knees, sending a funnel of fire barreling into the witch's torso with a mighty shriek. The dark magic ate the light. The witch mixed it with hers, striking Taran with a burst of flame that blasted her through the wall.

I roared in horror, thinking Taran was dead . . . until I caught her alarmingly "crispy" scent drawing nearer. She scrambled through what remained of the wall, resembling a giant piece of charcoal, her head bald, and her clothes in tatters. She rubbed her face, revealing perfectly healthy skin. As she ran her hands over her scorched head, her beautiful, wavy dark hair reappeared. She flicked her arms clean with a little magical brush of her fingertips.

I almost fell over with shock. Tahoe's magic amplified her shields, saving her once more.

Taran locked her crystal eyes on her astonished foe. "*My* turn."

Taran gathered her magic and launched a meteor-size blue-and-white fireball. Petro's witch screamed once. And detonated like a car bomb. Something, maybe her kidney, hit me in the face. The explosion ignited the drapes and paintings in a wash of fire. Flames shot toward the ceiling, lighting the wood beams and pillars like rice paper. Taran's power combined with Tahoe's turned the mansion into an instant inferno.

Taran gawked at the flames eating away at the wood paneling. "Son of a *bitch*!"

"Taran, get out!" I yanked harder on Misha's chains. "I'll be right behind you!"

Taran took a few hesitant steps back, unsure whether

to leave me. But the flaming piece of plaster that landed by her feet motivated her to listen. She reared back, clambering through the shattered windows and swearing as the broken glass sliced her legs.

Falling embers burned my back, and the growing flames heated Misha's chains. *Screw this.* I gave up on freeing Misha and began to drag him across the room.

I'd just crossed the foyer when I caught a jerky movement out of the corner of my eye. *Uh ... oh.*

Petro staggered to his mutilated feet, resembling a skinned, bloody corpse more than an evil, omnipotent master vampire. His eyes scanned the area like a stoned meth addict, disbelief twisting his raw face. He clenched his remaining fist and screamed, bulging his exposed muscles until they popped and expanded, adding bulk and lengthening his small stature. His incisors shot out past his jaw as his body morphed like a giant inflatable doll.

Terror had me yanking the last chain off in one pull. "Okay, Misha. Time to show me what you got."

Misha collapsed on the floor like a pile of wet laundry.

Petro charged.

I cursed.

Petro leaped in the air, gunning for me. His sole hand extruded nails the length of my forearm. Drool dripped down his deadly fangs. His muscles rippled as he roared. Freaking roared like a goddamn lion.

I did what any tigress would have done in the face of such a predator.

I hauled ass and dove behind the smoking zebra couch.

The whole room shook as Petro took out the wall next to me. His new form may have been powerful, but it also made him clumsy. Flames sizzled his skin as he rose. He charged yet again. I sprinted toward the window, but he was suddenly in front of me. Then behind me. Then in front of me once more. He laughed. He may have been clumsy, but his speed trumped mine.

I jerked to my left, then quickly veered to my right, narrowly avoiding the slash of his claws. "Do you feel pity for me now?" he asked, his long fangs distorting his words. Petro continued to laugh, his mirth growing stronger with every sweep of his arms.

He stopped laughing when I rolled and kicked my heel into his mutated man parts.

Petro backhanded me with the stump of his severed hand. I slammed into one of the pillars, struggling to rise, too stunned to *change*. Petro lurched toward me, batting the flaming furniture from his path, his dark eyes promising more pain. I backed away, sliding across the floor of sharp debris as my hands searched blindly for weapons.

My back hit something hard. I'd reached the stone fireplace.

I was out of space. Out of time. Out of options.

But not out of hope.

Glass exploded in a screech as a large gray wolf soared through a side window, tackling Petro across the length of the room.

Aric.

His presence beckoned me to my feet. I stumbled forward, crashing onto my knees as he and Petro tore into each other like monstrous pit bulls.

I crawled to Misha while fragments of ceiling fell like flaming coals. Snarls and hisses rose over the deafening sound of crackling fire.

"Misha. Misha, wake up!" Misha didn't respond to my

hard shakes. He remained limp and barely breathing. I reached beneath his arms to drag him out, but Aric's pained howl jerked me away.

Petro had slashed his claws across Aric's face. Aric reeled back. Petro had only grazed him, but his nails were sharp enough to slice through Aric's fur. Blood ran into Aric's eyes, blinding and enraging his beast. Aric's jaws snapped Petro's remaining hand like rotting bark and spit it at his feet. He aimed for Petro's throat, but Petro's fangs found Aric first.

Petro's long incisors pierced Aric's chest. Aric refused to let him feast. His mammoth paws dug into Petro's over-cooked flesh, sending chunks of Petro's muscles to sizzle on the hot floor. Petro released Aric with a powerful shove. Aric rebounded back, launching himself at Petro.

The only thing that saved Petro was his speed. He caught Aric in midair and threw him. Aric rocketed past me and into a pillar. Half the ceiling tumbled down, creating a flaming barrier between me and him.

And trapping me with Petro.

Aric's snarls penetrated the booms of the collapsing house. I could hear the thundering of his powerful legs racing back and forth as he tried to find a way to me, but I didn't dare shift my gaze from the grilled psycho vamp coming at me.

I grabbed the discarded gold chain as Petro rushed me, flinging it against his shins with all my might. The cursed gold seared his raw skin, sending the poison into his bones. His haunting cries amplified as he tugged them with his mutilated arms, thrashing in agony.

I scrambled away from him, taking Misha with me. Through the thick black smoke, Aric's human voice called to me: *"Celia! Get to the front of the house!"*

My eyes darted around frantically. The room resembled a virtual hell storm, the walls seconds from caving in. I didn't know where the front was, but I knew I needed to move, *fast*. I lugged Misha into a fireman's carry and bolted to where Aric's voice beckoned me.

We swept through a narrow, flame-ridden hall and into the grand foyer, where I caught a glimpse of the front doors through the haze. There was our way out. But the loud crunch of wood halted my steps. Beams crackling with fire fell across our only exit.

Shit.

I backed away from the flames, momentarily stunned. Except the sound of Petro's roars and chains being tossed motivated me to race up the steps.

Fire boiled the sweat on my skin. Tears ran hot down my face. My heart pumped with fear. Death by fire was not how I wanted to go.

And neither was death by a second-rate asshole master vampire.

The pounding steps behind me urged me down the hall. I kicked open the last door, dropping Misha as Petro dove on top of us. I fell with a hard thud against the blistering floor before Petro kicked me across the room and into an antique bureau.

The mirror shattered, slicing at my breasts. Blood soaked my shirt, but I barely felt the pain. Funny how hatred could run so deep it numbed. In the cracked glass I watched Petro trudge toward me.

I also watched my guardian angel rise behind him.

Petro advanced slowly, his dismembered face contorting with hatred. "You're going to hell, Celia. You just don't know it yet."

This unholy bastard had used me to fuel this nightmare. But you know what? I was done being nice. "You *first*."

I grasped his arm when he tried to strike and dug my fangs into the seared muscle, using my unique ability to return his soul. The glow from his body burned as bright as a star. Petro's crazed, horrified eyes stared at his illuminating form. "No. *Noooooo!*"

I kicked Petro into Misha, using his shock to our advantage. Misha wasted no time. He dragged Petro against him and dug his claws into Petro's heart while his serrated fangs ate through his neck like acid.

Flames chewed on the room. Misha fell to his side, covered in Petro's remains, his words mere pants. "We need . . . to get out."

"Yup."

I hauled Misha up by the shoulders and threw him out the window. Loud grunts and angry swearing in Russian accompanied his landing. Good thing master vamps were immune to fire. Bad thing? The walls collapsed after him and the ceiling came down, blocking my exit with a barricade of flames. I stumbled back and fell, my lungs burning, my head spinning. From somewhere outside, my sisters screamed my name.

It was the last sound I heard before everything went black.

CHAPTER 35

Petro had it all wrong. I didn't go to hell.

Only heaven could fill my lungs with such a sweet, wondrous aroma. Aric's scent surrounded me. I opened my eyes to find him sleeping next to me in my bed, my body tucked protectively against his. I thought I'd dreamed my fight to the death, until fragmented bits of memories flooded my mind. The sound of the walls crashing. The feel of strong arms wrenching me from the burning floor. The cold night breeze slapping against my hot skin. And Emme's healing light.

I raised my fingertips slowly and pushed the singed hair away from Aric's brow.

His steamy brown eyes blinked open. "Hi, sweetness," he whispered.

"Hi, wolf." My smile faded. "You saved me, didn't you?"

Aric stroked my tears away with his thumbs and gathered me to him. "I didn't think I'd reach you in time."

"But you did."

"Yeah. I did."

Worry made my insides churn. "What about my sisters?"

Aric stroked my back with his large hand. "Safe. In their rooms. With my wolves. Except for Taran. Gemini left after he brought her home. He patted her head good-bye." Aric chuckled. "I don't think Taran liked that very much."

"Probably not." Aric wore only sweatpants. I smiled against his bare chest, wondering what I looked like . . . and who had dressed me in my tank and shorts.

"Your sisters cleaned you up," Aric answered, likely scenting my sudden nervousness. "I stayed to make sure you were safe. It was a hell of a fight, but we ended the bloodlust." His hand stopped against my lower back. "Do you mind that I stayed?"

My husky voice fell lower. "No. I like you with me."

A gentle purr rumbled against my breasts. Aric growled—soft and sexy—beckoning me closer to him.

But something didn't seem right.

I lifted my head and peered over his broad shoulder. He frowned. "What are you looking at?"

I slumped back down and nestled my body closer to his. "It almost seems strange not to find a fire-breathing ax murderer with a forked tail and six eyeballs lurking next to the bed."

"There aren't any mutant vamps with chain saws in the closet either. I already checked."

We stopped laughing when Aric fixed his gaze on my lips. "I had to give you mouth-to-mouth," he murmured.

I swallowed hard, trembling as the surging warmth between us amplified into a tantalizing heat. "Sorry I missed it."

No vampires. No bloodlust. No psychotic preternaturals waiting to eat me. Just me and Aric.

In bed.

He leaned in, drawing me to him, his lips meeting mine hard.

Aric was a force of nature. And for once my beast was no match for the elements. . . .

Please read on for a sneak peek at the next exciting installment in Celia's story,

A Curse Embraced

Available from Signet Eclipse in July 2013

We reached the end of the alleyway and stepped onto the worn frozen path. The snow had melted, but it seemed the grass hadn't quite recovered from the winter's bashing. The rain and warming sunshine of April would soon resuscitate it. Come summer, the shop owners would struggle to maintain the large section of lawn. For now it lay asleep. Parts of it yellow, other parts balding. Only a few shoots of green daring to make an appearance.

The path widened as we traveled up a small incline leading into the forest. "Would you like to have dinner with me?" Taran asked Gemini. She tried to sound casual, but I recognized the underlying hope. He hadn't, after all, responded to her suggestion.

Gemini gave a stiff nod, but didn't speak. And it wasn't due to his shyness. His entire demeanor changed as the thick pined forest swallowed us whole. His dark watchful eyes took everything in. Except he wasn't the only predator reacting to unknown territory. Aric's touch turned from affectionate to protective once the trees shadowed the path and blocked out the faint afternoon sun. My tigress stepped forward, sharpening our sense of smell, sight, and hearing. Even Taran knew better than to speak. Chitchat didn't allow the full use of our senses.

My ears focused on the sounds of the forest, ignoring the way Taran's boots passed along the hard ground. Ravens cawed in the distance and a few chipmunks and rabbits scampered along the crisp pine needles. As we drew farther in, the sounds of the forest reduced to the brush of branches in the wind. Nothing moved. Nothing breathed. Just us.

The world of the living vanished in one gradual space of time. "Do you feel that?" I whispered to Aric.

Aric nodded. "Yeah. Stay close to me."

Funny. That was usually my line to my sisters when evil was afoot.

The path curved to follow along the Truckee River. The melting snow from the mountains had caused the river to rise to the edge. Chunks of ice slid over the roaring rapids. I shuddered, dreading an accidental soak. Swimming remained a skill I'd never mastered. And by the looks of the raging stream, it wasn't an optimal place to learn. *Note to self: Avoid having some scary evil thing take you for a dip.*

The firs along the river dwindled. Benches fashioned from tree trunks rested between the more open spots. A beautiful place to enjoy I supposed, minus the intensifying creepiness digging a hole into my chest.

The growing heaviness forced Gemini to escort Taran next to me so he and Aric could flank our sides. But then something stirred in the wind, like the heavy sweep of an invisible sail. Pained howls blasted my ears and the gallop of massive paws shook the ground beneath our feet, sending pebbles rolling like marbles along the trail.

Taran instinctively reached for me. The wolves didn't possess her ingrained response. Then again they never had my unique ability to rely on. I grasped their wrists and *shifted* the four of us far beneath the ground. My rare gift broke down our bodies into tiny molecules minute enough to pass across the packed earth. We surfaced in the thickness of the woods just as a herd of black bears raced past us along the path.

We probably could have sprinted out of the way, but I would have risked contacting one of the bears. Animals and my "weirdness" didn't play nice. With my protective shields down, I'd fall to the ground in a massive seizure and emerge as Celia the Bear. Considering I'd have no way to *change* back to Celia the sort-of-human or Celia the formidable tigress, *shifting* us from harm seemed like the ideal way to go.

Aric and Gemini's mouths parted as they examined their forms. I'd never *shifted* them before and they were likely surprised all their important parts remained intact. "Sorry. I didn't have time to warn you." My face heated, but my unease kept me from experiencing the full range of my humiliation.

"It's all right," Aric said. We stepped back onto the path cautiously, unsure what lay ahead. Aric didn't finish watching the bears disappear around the bend. Instead his preternatural side searched where I searched, in the direction they'd run from. "Gem," he said, his voice bordering close to a growl.

Gemini slipped his sweater over his head, revealing the muscular T-build common of all wolves. Taran's jaw fell opened and I think she might have drooled. "Will you hold this?" he asked.

She nodded. This time it was her turn to fall speechless. Gemini cracked his neck from side to side. A large black wolf punched his head through Gemini's back, sniffing the air. Like solidifying ink, he slid his powerful form onto the hard soil and sped off in a blur of black. The human half of Gemini that remained blinked his dark eyes. "Come. I'll let you know if I find anything."

Gemini's ability to split into two remained, hands down, the coolest supernatural feat I'd ever seen. Taran squeaked when he whisked her in his arms and raced after Aric and me.

My tigress made us fast, faster than wolves. Common sense, and the realization that "danger lurked, Will Robinson," kept me from bolting ahead. Aric still felt I moved too quick despite being a breath behind me. "Don't get ahead of me, Celia."

"I found it," Gemini's low voice said behind us. "This way."

The path veered in two separate directions. One led deeper into the woods. Gemini kept us on the one paralleling the river.

The sour stench of death stung my nose just as Gemini's other half appeared before us, baring his teeth. We followed behind him. Our pace slowed as we ambled down a small, steep hill where an abandoned mill hugged the edge of the river. The large broken wheel sat in the water, moving just enough to squeal. The rest of the large structure dented inward where the moss-covered roof had partially collapsed. A deathtrap in the making, and one long forgotten. Someone should have demolished it decades ago, but the small town didn't strike me as possessing funds to see its destruction through.

The closer we neared the mill, the more the foul odor increased, its acidic scent sharp enough to make my eyes water. "Son of a bitch," Taran muttered. Her blue eyes blanched to clear. Something skulked inside. And it didn't want us there.

Aric whispered into his phone. "We found something. Track us."

"On our way," Koda said on the other end.

Gem eased Taran onto the ground as we crept onto the rickety porch steps. A few good tigress strikes and the moldy and graffiti-lined brown building would collapse inward. Too bad we had to investigate before sending it, and the malevolence lurking inside, to hell's trash heap.

A padlock the size of my palm lay discarded on the mud-splattered floor, its hook twisted as if broken off. Slowly, Aric opened the creaky door.

Footmarks cut into the thick layer of dust. Drops of dried blood were splattered like raindrops alongside of each step. My growl rumbled in sync with the wolves. My tigress didn't like it here. But she hated what waited even more.

Pockets of light trickled through the holes in the wall, illuminating sections here and there in the otherwise pitch-black room. The increasing aroma of death forced my claws and fangs to shoot out. I barely kept my tigress from emerging.

A set of stairs led up to the second floor. A small office with a door opening to another room sat to our far left. The vast room on our right housed bent and broken pieces of metal office furniture. This must have been the area where the administrative staff worked back when the mill had still struggled to stay open.

We abandoned the small sectioned-off area without so much as a sniff. After all, the revolting fragrance of sulfur permeated stronger to our right. A few folding chairs leaned against the dirty 1960s wood-paneled walls and a tattered armchair lay tucked in the corner. The calendar push-pinned into one of the panels remained opened to February of many years past.

We followed Aric through the large room, trailing the footsteps, and of course, the blood. I bit back a gag, the smell of decay threatening to bring up my lunch. Taran swore beneath her breath. She didn't have to possess an inner beast to sense the death. Death slapped at our faces and demanded respect.

The roar of the river echoed from the back. Likely a section of wall had caved in based on how loud the sound of rushing water carried through the mill. We passed through a small room where the branches of firs poked through the busted sections of moss-eaten walls. Despite the growing Grim Reaper aroma, I thought we'd have to cover more of the building until we found our quarry.

I thought wrong.

The mill opened to one enormous area strewn with burlap sacks, broken rakes, and oh, yeah, a stack of corpses. Most girls got flowers, or maybe chocolates on their dates. I got dead bodies. Lots of them. Lucky me.

Taran stumbled away, choking back her sickness and burying her face into Gem's chest. Aric gripped my arm, offering me comfort. He didn't need it. He witnessed death as often as I witnessed life as a labor nurse. And yet as much as I wanted to mirror Taran's actions, my tigress kept us in place and took in the horror.

Four males lay slumped like a deck of cards toward our right, their bodies rigid, but no obvious signs suggesting cause of death. The lack of decomposing flesh and the few flies circling their forms suggested they'd met their demise fairly recently.

And yet as gruesome as I found them, they didn't compare to the naked woman left abandoned in the center of the room. My hands trembled. Perspiration slid like ice against my chilled skin. Her clouded eyes stared blankly at the ceiling while an expression of sheer terror and agony froze the features of her young face. Her entire abdomen appeared chewed open from the inside out and her half-eaten bowels lay over her hips like wet ropes. Flies swarmed her and took their fill. Small water bugs crawled along her bloody nails. She'd clawed at the splintered floor. God only knew the pain she'd endured before her heart had mercifully stopped beating.

Part of me wanted to run screaming. The other part struggled not to release my tears. Humans generally feared me. Their fear often manifested into dislike and more than often hate. I'd been mistreated to the point of cruelty throughout my life. But as horrid as others had often behaved, no one deserved to die like this. No one.

Aric pulled me into him, his voice harsh yet gentle all at once. "You don't have to look, Celia. And you don't have to be brave. If you prefer, Gemini can escort you and Taran outside."

I shook my head, unable to rip my gaze from the poor soul in the center of the room. "No. I'll stay."

Aric gave me one last hug before releasing me and stepping forward. He said I didn't have to be brave. So I wasn't. I stayed put as he and Gemini's wolf examined the bodies. They inspected the males first, circling their forms and drawing in their scent. I stopped trying to work so hard to smell. It remained my last ditch effort to keep from hurling. All the dead men had their mouths opened. They likely screamed until their last breath. A cricket crawled out of one whose tongue hung out. That's when I stopped looking as well.

I heard Aric and Gem's wolf tread toward the woman. They paused. "Do you see what I see?" Aric asked, rage clipping his words.

"Yes," Gemini's human side answered. He clutched Taran close against him with his head lowered. I supposed he could see with his other half. "Two burrowed out in separate directions."

I forced my mouth opened. "Two what?"

Gemini raised his dark almond eyes. "Demon children," he answered.